BRANDON

BRANDON

Lee J Morrison

authorHOUSE®

AuthorHouse™ UK
1663 Liberty Drive
Bloomington, IN 47403 USA
www.authorhouse.co.uk
Phone: 0800.197.4150

Published by AuthorHouse 03/08/2016

ISBN: 978-1-5246-2921-2 (sc)
ISBN: 978-1-5246-2923-6 (hc)
ISBN: 978-1-5246-2922-9 (e)

Print information available on the last page.

CONTENTS

DEDICATION

Sometimes the value of one's own immediate family is overlooked because of closeness or distance or familiarity; and so I would like to show my appreciation and dedicate this book to Ann, Hebe, and Dyon. You are always in my thoughts. I would also like to dedicate it in memory of my Father Lawrence and my Mother Dorothy.

PREFACE

Does anyone read a preface? Is not a preface just a distraction from launching straight into the first chapter? A preface can be an entertaining part of the book, or a vehicle for the Author to expound his or her theories and his, or her, intentions, which a reader may not be really concerned about, so long as the story is good. Good from a reader's point of view is according to whether they get from it what they expect or desire. The author I suspect hopes that even if the reader is not satisfied, they may appreciate his or her efforts. Rather like a meal prepared by someone else when one might say that it is beautifully cooked and presented, but not really to my taste.

I often like to read a preface and I have read those which appear to be a lengthy self-analysis, which can be very interesting. However, in this preamble I would like to state that this book as with my previous one is written in the first person, rather than as a third person narrator. There is a danger in doing this as the narrative may be taken as autobiographical to myself, which is not the case. Obviously there is a little bit of myself in the character but it is not an unfolding autobiography. Neither is it in that case entirely a fantasy, as the narrative is firmly grounded in reality and the characters may be influenced by people I have known and still know. I ought to stress of course that as in most fictional work, the characters are not intended to directly represent any persons alive or deceased, and all locations are approximate, and many trade names are fictional. In a sense, I find a contradiction in the fact that sometimes fiction is considered good, because it reflects reality. I am also aware that a fictional reality allows the reader, and this includes myself, to view reality in a detached manner in order to advance one's knowledge and understanding of it.

If anyone has read any of the prefaces in my recent books, such as 'Xerses Franklin: The Saga of Gabriel & Melona' published in 2015, they will know that I always wish that anyone reading the story will not be tempted to read the ending first. The temptation to do this is greater, I think, when there are illustrations. Because I almost invariably look at all the illustrations in a book before I read it. The illustrations by Dr Derek Vernon-Morris tell the story, but do not always relate directly to every principal character or to all of the action. So, would it not be fun to read each chapter avidly as the story develops and arrive at the ending with a degree of surprise as though it was a TV series or Film that one was viewing for the first time? Or to congratulate oneself with an – 'I knew that was going to be the case, I know the way that this Author thinks.' Of course an alternative view is that a reader can enjoy discovering how the Author arrives at the ending even if they are fully aware of it. I do know that there are readers who must know the ending as a necessity, before they allow the Author to take them on a literary journey and buy the book.

As I mentioned just now, the illustrations are all original hand drawn illustrations. Some of them are esoteric and surrealist when dealing with abstract emotions such as heartbreak, or a recurring nightmare induced by trauma. Others are more specific and depict a particular scene or character in the story. I hope that these varied approaches will not appear incongruous, but add an interesting diversity. The illustrations are unified somewhat by certain stylistic methods of representation. For the Artist it is quite an interesting challenge to try to give Black & White illustrations some of the same impact and interest that ones in full colour might have. Hopefully this is achieved by the use of tones and textures and sometimes dramatic contrast of white and black, and etching techniques. For me, the illustrations are an integral part of the whole, and not just decorative additions, so that the artistry of the illustrations and that of the text are a complete experience.

Would one call reading a book an experience? I think so, even if it is an unsatisfactory one. Hopefully Brandon will be a good experience and a satisfactorily entertaining one. But I am depressed. This is because as I write, story lines which I have thought of as original often appear in reality in a newspaper article or on line or on TV. It seems like the quest for originality is a futile one in any genre. It is maybe how a writer deals with their characters which makes one familiar story line different from another. Sometimes I think why do I write? Just reading a daily Newspaper from just one area provides the crimes, the characters and events which appear in truth far more outrageous and unbelievable than anything which I could imagine in order to be controversial. I want to be controversial. I want my writing to have a substance beyond titillation and fantasy. Ideally I want to be thought-provoking and ambivalent in addition to providing a diverting narrative. I try to create my characters a little larger than life and provoke in my readers a sense of outrage maybe, or sorrow at an injustice, or an empathy with them. And yet, I want it all to appear believable. I write so the subject matter and the result of the interaction between characters is on my terms, with my ending, my beginning and my middle. How often do you say – 'no, I did not want it to end like that, or, if I were that character, then I would have acted differently' - when watching a movie, TV series or reading an absorbing story? I say it to myself all the time, so it is with great alacrity that I command the action, the moral considerations, and the Fate of my protagonists. I hope at the same time that you are with me and maybe want to shake the hand of Brandon or give him a hug in appreciation for a job well done.

In this book although I always tell myself that I do not have a formula, Brandon Edwin Martin-Schally finds that his happy and routine life is changed suddenly when he is inadvertently caught up in traumatic events. I find that my character of 'Theo: A Nephew of Chrystabell' published in 2012, suffers the same fate, and so does Xerses Franklin, but the story lines are definitely not the same. In a sense Xerses Franklin finds himself running from the law, but Brandon finds himself working hand in hand with the law as represented by his friend Gordon Daniel McArthur, and his son Nigel, albeit subversively.

This book does not fall within the Romantic Passion category, but Brandon is passionate about his beautiful wife Naomi, about his Graphic Art and Painting, and his Fitness Regime. It is not really a Romance although there is a considerable amount of Romance. The story touches upon the Supernatural, and I am not a sceptic, but I think I would call it on the whole, a Detective story. My interest in writing this kind of novel began with 'The Many Faces of April Jade' which I published in 2014. Brandon feels compelled to discover the covert murderers of his best friend

Hanwell Nnagobi, a Poet, who like himself is a Tutor at the University in New York. Brandon feels also that his own safety is at risk and that of his family because of his association with Hanwell. Hanwell with his lovely English wife Clarisse who is in fact a titled Lady is a talented Poet, and Brandon is a successful Painter and Graphic Artist.

In this book there is less featured Poetry than in my previous books, because Brandon is a visual Artist and not Literary. I have mixed my genres in previous books, as I like to switch between Poetry and Prose for dramatic effect, and I feature work supposedly written by one or more characters in the book. Lovers of Opera like myself might be aware that Russian Author Alexander Pushkin wrote a novel entirely in verse, which Tchaikovsky adapted for his three Act Opera 'Eugene Onegin' with the help of Konstantin Shilovsky. This beautiful work was recently realised exquisitely in a Metropolitan Opera production in conjunction with the English National Opera in 2013. I am not claiming equality with Pushkin, and this novel is not about youthful or unrequited love, but I like to try and impart a sense of poetry and lyricism within my stories. I might add that all the Poems are written by myself and are not transcriptions or copies. Sometimes I think that I try also to write a symphony in prose, with a stated theme, variations and deliberate repetitions, an adagio and an allegro, as I hopefully change the pace of the action from chapter to chapter with a return to the stated theme at the ending. As I mentioned already I am a great lover of Music, and the Theatre, and I do play and read music, so writing is not a substitute, but an extension of my own interests. Maybe it is a cliché, but I write because I love the written word.

I would like to mention some of the symbolism in the narrative and the illustrations. The image of a gigantic and merciless Bird of Prey is often a symbol of a tragedy, an emotion or a Fate which is inescapable. The symbol of a bird can mean many other things, but in this story the bird looms ominously, or overtakes Brandon in his post traumatic dreams symbolising circumstances which call for all of his inner strength and tenacity to emerge victorious.

I hope that this short preface has done what I think it is supposed to do, and say a little about the thought processes behind the storyline and to introduce some of the characters to enhance the reader's enjoyment of the action, without divulging the whole story.

Dr Lee J Morrison
2016.

CHAPTER 1

South River

Christmas and New Year are now behind us, but as ever the joy runs concurrent with the news of deaths, the memories of deaths, and the celebrations are respectful of the departed and are also for them in their absence maybe. How often do I hear – 'if Mom were here she would have enjoyed this, or remember Berkie, let us have a drink for him?'- And one hopes that there is joy in the rest of the world as there is in one's own group of friends and family.

It sometimes it seems that there is no joy in the world, just a small percentage enjoying all that the Earthly life may yield, whilst the rest raise their arms out of squalor and deprivation in an attempt to reach for the Heavens. What fun it would it be to think of a Heaven above like the naïve concept depicted with consummate mastery in 14th Century paintings. Duccio in Siena, and Giotto in Padua. Rich gold leafed representations of a blissful hierarchy of human likenesses to which everyone could aspire. Materialistic wealth of course led to a Renaissance of Earthly yet Mythological splendour depicted in paintings, and what finer blend of spiritual and secular bliss is there than depicted by Botticelli in the 15th Century AD.

Hey! I am not about to write a travel guide or a thesis on the influence of Florentine Art upon the world, but everyone should visit the Uffizi Gallery in Italy and spend time in the awe-inspiring Botticelli Room. His Venus is truly exquisite and his youthful Madonna's are wistfully beautiful, and to the naked eye hardly a brush stroke is visible. What more impressive way is there to depict spiritual values, than through visual means. The human brain is predisposed to a respond to visual stimulus, but it is both exciting and daunting to know that there is a hidden Universe beyond my range of vision. It is exciting and daunting and strangely comforting to know that the fabric of the Universe binds the not yet discovered to that which is visible, and that to which is unseen.

I am sitting on a pier beside the South River Park, and New York is cold but beautiful. The river is calm and glistening towards sunset and the Statue of Liberty is in the distance becoming engulfed in blue shadows. The small orange and yellow water taxis are still buzzing backwards and forwards creating a slow wash which reaches the river wall and quickly subsides. Lights are beginning to glow more brightly and there is a great sense of peace in the air. Several joggers pass me and on my left just across the cycle lanes a youth practises netball in a small enclosure. Other spectators of the majestic sweep of River sit on nearby seats and I seem to forget the continual rush of the lanes of vehicles on the nearby carriageways. The abundance of cyclists almost matches that of the cars, busses and yellow cabs.

As I walk along the quayside, the shimmering facades of the waterfront front buildings become dark monoliths dotted with warm and homely lights against a deep blue sky. I always think of the song written in 1925 and later immortalised by Ella Fitzgerald in 1960 – Manhattan – It certainly is an Island of great variety with many more attractions than when the song was written. The Empire State Building was not completed, the Chrysler Building was not a landmark and Top of the Rock was only a dream when New York was described as a wondrous toy for a girl and boy. As I walk I think also of the Universe hidden by the Earth's atmosphere and maybe the big bang theory which caused the solar systems and dark energy to exist. Yes, I ask myself the inevitable question what caused the big bang in the first place, and how was the incredibly large mass and the energy in existence in the first place? No! Do not try and answer me, it is more of a rhetorical question.

I think I am more concerned with the Universe in my head. I may be a walking microcosm in the macrocosm, or even a microcosm of a microcosm as it were, but in my animal existence I am thinking of relationships at the moment. I have just indulged in quick sexual activities. Well, not exactly now, but in a lingering memory of this morning before I left to instruct my laser-age students in some of the traditional techniques of Fine Art Printmaking. I was running late, but my wife wanted a little more than a quick kiss, which was – nice. An actual wife. Is that a surprise? You may have thought that I was leading up to one of those stories about a guy hanging about the waterfront in search of lost love or on the off chance of finding a brief encounter. No. Tonight I am looking forward to a full Karma Sutra session. Yes! We have books to aid our imagination and our only regret is that we are not quite flexibly jointed enough to enact some of the ancient positions as also depicted and translated in matter of fact modern illustrations. We have not yet discovered the secret of how to stand on one leg with the other leg wrapped around the partner's waist and copulate simultaneously. If we copulate in unison we begin to fall over, and if we stand successfully, copulation does not come easily. Well, it is still great fun anyway, and obviously stimulating. I wonder what it will feel like when I am old and maybe not quite so physically hot. Will I miss this, or will the memory of more youthful activities be sufficient? I expect that when I can hardly sometimes stand on my own two feet to execute simple chores, and find it painful to raise a foot to step off the sidewalk, I will not feel regretful but accept the passage of time and be thankful for what I was able to do. I hope so.

Now, away with the momentary lapse into pensive speculation and let me continue with the narrative. But first I would like to include a poem written by a good friend of mine Hanwell Nnagobi. He named this, Joy To The World.

I am going to sing Joy to the world,
Although it may seem that there is not any,
I am going to sing Joy to the world –
Why refuse a season to be merry?
I am going to sing Joy to the world,
Because the Spirit moves me.
I am going to sing Joy to the world –
East or West or North or South, all around me,
I am going to sing Joy to the world,
Everyone may look inside to find it.
I am going to sing Joy to the world,

Everyone everywhere can share it,
I am going to sing Joy to the world –
There is enough to light the Planet,
I am going to sing Joy to the world –
Sorrow, illness and death are intrinsically intertwined,
But Joy will leave all my troubles far behind.

Yes he was a very optimistic guy, and liked to laugh a lot. He was a very good Poet and Songwriter and produced his own recordings. He taught Literature and we had been friends since University days, which are not that far away. He was married to a lovely woman, who however was not as lovely as she appeared to be. She had graduated at the same time in Literature, but she resented his success. She had left her career to look after their two children, and she often felt personally neglected.

Hanwell loved to entertain and was very hospitable, often taking three or four of his students home to continue an informal tutorial, or to show them what musical project he was working on. Clarisse received us very coolly on one of the few occasions I accompanied him with some other friends and informed him that if he wanted a cup of tea or coffee, he knew where the kitchen and the kettle was.

"Have you seen your Children today?" She asked curtly whilst still gazing out of the window. I could not take my eyes away from her as she stood framed slightly silhouetted against the afternoon light. What a perfect picture. What a well-toned figure with stepped thick dark hair just below ear length. Her simple fine white blouse and smooth petrol blue denim skirt accentuated every curve. She was British and still retained her perfect accent. She could have stepped from a pre-Raphaelite painting by Burne-Jones in spite of her more modern stylishness. Clarisse was not expecting guests but she wore black medium high heels and was perfectly groomed. She eventually turned slowly to grace him with a cool impartial gaze whilst ignoring the rest of us.

"Yes, are they alright?" Hanwell replied.

"Of course they are, but no thanks to you." Clarisse retorted with just enough bitter resentment in her refined tones to make me almost want to shiver.

"Oh well that is good, I have just brought a few friends – we will go to my studio." Hanwell replied gravely, as he indicated us to follow him.

"So I see." Clarisse replied with as much disdainful dismissiveness that she could deliver with three curt syllables, as she turned back to the window.

It was a Saturday afternoon that I recall, and apart from his studio the apartment gave the impression of being cold and bare. Somehow light grey and blue and bare, where not even the sparse furnishings allowed even the faintest glimmer of warmth or love.

It was like entering an avant-garde minimal stage set in which a morbid and terrible tragedy was about to be enacted. And a tragedy there certainly was. It was not the fact that one day he returned home to find his computer and some of his musical equipment smashed, so that he lost his current project. No. On no, Hanwell and Clarisse had still lived together through scenes like that. Somewhere buried beneath the ice, there must have been the love and passion which first brought them together.

Hanwell occasionally sat with me by the South River Park, and I had sketched and taken photographs for my Printmaking and paintings, and he had found similar peaceful and resplendent inspiration there for his songs and poetry. There are some weather worn protrusions from a former structure that give the appearance of breakwaters. To some people these might be an eyesore, but to us of an artistic nature, they made an interesting contrast to the polished and glinting steel railings and smooth concrete of the quayside.

I often jog along there and sometimes follow the decking path through the shrubs, and I often ride a bicycle too, I am not a sedentary person and I like to keep myself well-toned and fit for my Karma Sutra, as well as meditating on my artistic work. One very early Sunday summer morning whilst I was jogging and thinking about the home made 'New Yorker' breakfast I was going to return to with eggs over easy, and maybe fresh grapefruit instead of orange, I saw an unfamiliar dark shape spiked on one of the points of the worn posts. It crossed my mind that it might be a Sea Lion that had somehow drifted with the melting arctic waters. After all, stranger things had happened. The Hudson lapped around it, to and fro, backwards and forwards but it did not move. As I drew close and leaned on the railing I could see it was a man wrapped in black polythene, and then suddenly a small wave pulled the polythene from his face and I knew that face.

As cold shivers ran up and down my spine with shock realisation that I tried to suppress, I saw the face of my friend Hanwell Nnagobi. It was bruised around the mouth and forehead, and his eyes were fixed open in an expression of fear. The spike of the post protruded from his body just below his rib cage and the apparent stiffness indicated that he had been dead for some time. It was too far for his body to have been thrown from the quayside, so he must have been planted there by someone in a small boat.

Why? What or whom was he involved with? Had he been left there as an example, as a warning to whomever it might apply?

He certainly was not the victim of a casual mugging, and it certainly was not suicide as he could not have wrapped himself and spiked himself so neatly. Without thinking of the consequences of my own involvement I called 911 on my cell phone and sat down in mild shock on a nearby seat to await the Police.

The South River.

CHAPTER 2

McArthur calls

"Just call me Brandon, I am an artist and I always sign my work that way and I am a Tutor at the faculty of Art and Design." I instructed the tall thin Police Officer who seemed to be in charge of the investigations.

"We have to have your full name sir." The Policeman answered patiently.

"Brandon Edwin Martin-Schally. Now you know why I keep it short." I replied "It takes me half an hour to fill out a form and that is just for my name."

"Thank you sir, I have actually seen your work in a gallery near the Media Centre. My son is a student of yours. I am pleased to make your acquaintance, but can I ascertain again what your relationship to the victim is, but we will have to have him identified formally by a next of kin." Officer McArthur replied.

"Oh, really, good, well I was not expecting that, it is a small world as they say. I have been a friend for quite a long time. Hanwell is – er – was a Tutor of Literature, and we sometimes worked together. He on his Poetry, and me on my Illustrations and Photography. He has two children Benjamin and Amelia and a very, er very lovely but, em-er – a lovely wife!" I replied beginning to somehow feel flustered and wishing that I was back home with my eggs over easy.

"Why do you say it that way? Is there some problem which might give a clue as to how the victim met his death? We assume that Mr Nnagobi has been the victim of foul play, but it will still need to be proved in the lab." McArthur picked upon my faltering and I could have kicked myself for not answering more simply and vaguely.

"No. No not at all. I have not a clue as to what happened, but it is just that he and his wife Clarisse do not always seem very happy together. The last time I visited their apartment with some other friends, she virtually accused him of neglecting her and the children. Not in a material way of course, but emotionally and mentally." I replied as I recalled her bewitching blue eyes and fine sculptured cheekbones and that perfect English diction issuing from the subtle pale ruby rose lips.

"I see sir." McArthur said contemplatively with a twinkle of knowing complicity in his eye. "Well, we will have to notify her formally, and I hope that you will be available to assist in our enquiries later, and just for the record again – could you state your whereabouts say, between 22.00 hours on Saturday, and 4.00 this morning, Sunday."

"I was at home with my wife Naomi and our two small children." I replied, recalling two, - no, three successful sexual positions.

"Good. Well thank you Mr – thank you Brandon. This looks like a possible cult killing off the record, and may be linked to other investigations, so I would appreciate your confidentiality. Oh I know this case will make the news and we will be asking any witnesses to come forward, but could I ask you not to contact Clarisse Nnagobi until we have had time to visit her?" McArthur concluded with a friendly but troubled countenance.

By now a small Police launch with a forensic team and photographers and a diver had moored carefully by the breakwater, and a larger one moored a short distance away to deter inquisitive spectators travelling on the Hudson. Part of the Quayside was cordoned off with tape and attendant officers. I could see that it would have taken quite a lot of force to spike the body the way it was and I could imagine the shattered vertebrae and torn intestines and diaphragm. A wave of sorrow hit me now that the excitement and shock had subsided and I wanted to shed tears of both pain and anger. I managed to fight them back and placidly accept a lift to my apartment. The Police probably wanted to check the authenticity of my address any way.

"Oh Brandon honey, I was so worried when you called to say that you would be delayed, are you okay? You are not injured are you?" Naomi rushed to meet me at the door and stopped with her mouth open when she saw an accompanying Policeman.

"Everything is ok Mrs Martin-Schally, Brandon fortunately notified us of an incident at the South River Park, but he is all safe and sound. I apologise for any inconvenience Ma' me, have a nice day." The Police Officer departed with a quick official nod.

"I could sure use that coffee now." I said as I hugged Naomi. I gripped her warm body as though I was a drowning man clutching a life belt, and I wanted to cry on her shoulder as the vision of the pitiful state of my friend refused to leave mind, but I decided to remain strong and not alarm her any more than she was already.

"You are shaking and cold." Naomi observed with concern. "What really happened?"

"Oh, I was the first on the scene of an awful accident that is all, and I had to stay and answer a few questions. This jogging suit is fine, but standing around in the cold wind has chilled me a little, I think I will head for the shower after my coffee, and then I may have that breakfast, or rather late lunch by now." I managed a little nonchalance, and to my relief Naomi accepted my explanation for the moment. I know I can trust her confidentiality but for the moment I could not bring myself to tell her of the fate of Hanwell.

After a shower and my long awaited breakfast, now dinner, I felt more restored to normality, but little did I realise that my life would be changed. I was sitting with little Andrea on my lap in front of the TV when a news programme began. There were pictures of the South River and the Quayside and a number of Policemen moving spectators on. There was a quick shot of me entering a Police Car, but thankfully the hood of my track suit hid most of my face. Naomi was in the kitchen preparing another meal in advance and I think that she had switched to a food channel. Kurt eighteen months older than Andrea was attempting construction with Lego Bricks. The relief I felt at not having to explain myself was short lived. I even somehow felt like a suspect although I was completely innocent. I wished that I had not ventured out at first light as usual, and then some other unsuspecting chump would have been the 'Good Samaritan' so to speak.

A knock and the bell ringing on the apartment door made me jump and I stood up sharply almost dropping Andrea who began to protest. I could see Inspector McArthur through the spy lens and so I opened the door reluctantly.

"Ah, Brandon, sorry to inconvenience you sir, but I would like to ask a few more questions. May I come in?" McArthur gave a faint smile, but I see that this was not really a social call.

"Of course, come this way and take a seat. Can I offer you a drink, or tea or coffee? I showed him into the reception room which we reserved for entertaining, free from toys and clutter.

"No thank you, this is a duty call, is your wife at home?" McArthur was abrupt but polite.

"Yes, but is it really necessary to involve her? I have not really informed her of the terrible scene down by the river." I had almost forgotten I was holding Andrea, who now began to squirm now that her interest in McArthur had faded.

"Pretty little daughter – What is your name?" McArthur asked kindly, whereupon she stuck her thumb in her mouth and buried her face in my chest. "I need to speak with her to authenticate your alibi. It is a formality so that you are not a prime suspect."

"A suspect? I would hardly arrange my friend's death, and then call the Police and wait at the scene, would I?" I felt a sudden surge of anger as I spoke.

"Probably not sir, but some killers are devilishly clever psychopaths, who might revel in the situation. As I said, it is a necessary formality. McArthur answered firmly but impartially.

"Naomi honey could you spare a moment?" I shouted as I left the room and seated Andrea back in front of the TV.

"What is it? Naomi exited the kitchen looking worried. She was wiping her hands on a small green towel and looking lovey in spite of her alarm, in a fitted dress with black, white, yellow and red irregular shapes, and a matching ribbon tied towards the back of her head holding her wiry black hair smoothly in the front, and allowing it to bunch into curly waves at the back. Her usually calm brown eyes were wide and troubled.

"Don't worry, I am sorry I did not explain properly earlier, but Inspector McArthur would like a word with you." I did not have time to say more as she headed for the spacious reception room. Kurt began to follow, but I ordered him to look after his sister for a moment.

"Forgive the intrusion Mrs Martin-Scally ma' me, but I need to verify a few points. It is just part of the elimination process in connection with this unpleasant affair your husband has become involved with. I am Detective Inspector Gordon Daniel McArthur." McArthur rose and held out his right hand to her.

Naomi took his hand graciously. "Good evening Inspector, how may I be of assistance?"

"Well, first of all can you verify the whereabouts of your husband, Brandon, between say 20.00 Saturday night, and 4.00 on Sunday morning - this morning?" The Inspector asked as someone began a report faintly on his intercom. "Yes, okay, got that, thank you." He replied, and then apologised for the distraction.

Naomi looked at me with a slight smile on her lips, and then back at the inspector. "We put the children to bed, and turned in early ourselves, and then Brandon went out jogging about 5.00am."

"I see, and does he often go out jogging so early?

"Oh yes, very regularly on Sundays, and then he usually comes back about 6 to 6.30, takes a quick shower and then we have breakfast. Sometimes if Andrea has been restless, Brandon makes the breakfast, it gives me a break." Naomi answered very charmingly and truthfully.

"Fine, and can you tell me of his whereabouts before 20.00.

"We had dinner about 7, and he watched a bit of TV with the children and played some games with Kurt, very much like this evening. In the morning he went out to netball practise with one or two friends, and one or two of their wives called in for coffee here, and then he was working on a new painting in the studio during the afternoon. He likes the South River area very much, and sometimes a fellow Tutor, Hanwell, accompanies him, He is a Poet." Naomi continued affably, but I knew she was calculating the effect of her words, our information matched exactly.

"Good, I may need to ask you to name all of those friends to help with our enquiries. Would it surprise you to know that Hanwell Nnagobi met a rather horrific death, and that Brandon was public spirited enough to report it, being apparently the first to notice his body in the river about 5.20 hours this morning." McArthur narrowed his eyes slightly and inquisitively as he spoke.

"Oh my God. Oh my God. Poor Clarisse. I mean poor Hanwell, I just cannot believe it – who would want to kill him? He was a lovely guy, but just so preoccupied with Poetry and Music and whatever was going on in his head, to ever interfere with anyone else." Naomi looked at me in disbelief and the realisation now, of why I appeared to be so upset.

"Well, that is exactly what I want to discover Mrs Martin-Schally. Who killed him, and why, and who was able to plant his body in such a brutal way."

"Inspector, he and Brandon have been friends since University days, it must have been a terrible shock for my husband to discover him and you surely do not suspect him do you?" Naomi asked slightly indignantly.

"Honestly Ma' me, in my business I never rule out any possibility. Sometimes the most ingenuous are the guiltiest, but I have heard a lot about Brandon from my son Nigel who is presently one of his students and I have seen his beautiful modern paintings based on the river, and he behaved as every good citizen should, so I will say he is not a murder suspect, but I have to begin the process of elimination. We have found no weapon as yet as it seems Mr Nnagobi was stabbed, mutilated and beaten to death before he was wrapped in black polythene and impaled on a post in the river, a place that he also drew inspiration from." McArthur spoke quietly and almost like a friend, as Naomi screwed up her face in distaste at the description of Hanwell's demise.

"Well thank goodness for that, apart from recognising one of my best friends, I just performed my duty without thinking of what my involvement might entail." I interjected.

"Thank you very much for cooperating but if you would not mind I would like to take samples of your finger prints for elimination purposes, if you could call at this station tomorrow, and show them this form. There are some bloody ones on the inside of the polythene, and all over his ID and credit cards. It was all there as though his killers wanted to make sure that his body was identified." McArthur handed me a form with a case number as he concluded.

"What have I got mixed up in here? Of course I will oblige, about lunch time will that be okay? I have to start things off on Monday morning and then my students can carry on with their own projects. How did Mrs Nnagobi react to the news of her husband's death, if I might ask?" I would have liked to refuse, but that would have been childish.

"In view of what you said, I sent a Policewoman round and I think there is someone with her at the moment, I am afraid that is all I can say." McArthur remained very implacable.

"Poor Clarisse." Naomi repeated again.

"Yes, and I see that you are a creature of habit Brandon, so might I suggest that you change your routine a little. Maybe not frequent the South River so often whilst this case is unsolved." McArthur spoke in earnest.

"I do frequent other places, and I like to visit Tryon Park, but that is a bit too far. Sometimes I jog as far as Brooklyn Bridge, and sometimes over it and back again. I was born in Brooklyn. Let me tell you Inspector, the only criminal act I would vaguely consider is stealing the Lady and the Unicorn Tapestries from Tryon Cloisters Museum. They are so exquisite, I would like to have them on my own walls. Oops I should not have said that. If they disappear one day it is not me, you know where I live." I did not mean to become light hearted but the pressure was beginning to get to me and I still had not got used to the idea that I would never share the beauty of sunsets with my friend again.

"Seriously - be careful. Do you see where I am going here at the moment? We do not know who might be involved in this incident and supposing someone has been watching you both, and they hoped that you would be the one to find him to somehow involve you in whatever he was mixed up in. Supposing it is some kind of underground movement, they may think that he shared his secrets with you." McArthur gave me a momentary steely look as he paused.

"Of course I understand, and I assure you that I know nothing more of him than his Poetry and Music. Come to think of it, I do not know his parents. I think he mentioned a brother and sister but I have never met them. He only occasionally accompanied me, but we often had lunch together with other members of staff on weekdays. His Poetry is somewhere between the beat poets of the 1960's and Rap." I was now beginning to understand where McArthur was leading. He was hoping that I could fill in some background with informal questioning rather than being interrogated at the Station.

"How long have you lived near the Village?" McArthur suddenly asked very abruptly.

"Oh since I left University and started teaching at the faculty – Oh since we left University--." Naomi began to answer in unison with me.

"I was at University at the same time as Clarisse, she was brilliant, a literary genius." Naomi continued.

"I did not know that you knew Clarisse before we met her on that rare occasion when she accompanied Hanwell to a faculty Christmas dinner." I inadvertently replied with genuine surprise.

"Oh yes, but we did not keep in touch or anything like that, we were not close friends." Naomi continued and I knew that she regretted her burst of spontaneity.

"How about your family Brandon, are they still in Brooklyn?" McArthur was obviously pleased with the progress of the questioning.

"My Father is British and an Art Historian. He returned to teach in London whilst I was at University. His Mother was Irish, and his Father was originally from Germany. My Mother was originally from New Orleans of African descent and she stayed in Brooklyn – er – they are in effect amicably separated but not actually divorced. My sister lives near Coney, and one of my brothers lives in Manchester England, the other one lives in Chicago, it sounds like a cliché, but he is quite a well-known figure in the Jazz scene." I thought that I might as well tell him, after all I had nothing to hide.

"Both my parents were born in Montreal, Canada, and I speak French as a second language. One set of Grandparents migrated from the French Caribbean Islands and the others from Paris. I studied French and American literature, and I do some part time translating from home." Naomi answered brightly looking very alluring in the slim line dress as she sat slightly sideways in the arm chair and my thoughts temporarily returned to the Karma Sutra.

"Quite diverse families, as many families are. I do not think that we need to involve any of them at the moment. I know this is all upsetting for you and quite a shock, but I would be grateful if you both could think of anything that might throw some light upon this case, you can email me or call the Station any time. Thank you again for your cooperation, it is a pleasure to meet you Ma 'me, and Brandon, do not forget about those finger prints." He rose and shook hands briefly before exiting with a pleasant nod that was somehow full of suspicions, and he left us both deeply troubled.

Retrieving the Body of Hanwell.

CHAPTER 3

The Ice Maiden Melts

I was still amazed that Naomi had never mentioned that she already knew Clarisse. Somehow I could not get her out of my mind, and I wondered what kind of horrors she must be going through in HER mind. McArthur's words sank into my brain very slowly, and on the following Tuesday I found myself sitting in my favourite position watching the changing light of the river and the dying swell of a calm evening as the water Taxis passed less frequently. The dark spikes protruding from the water held a new menace for me now whereas I had found them interesting previously. Some were capped by green moss, but others appeared like the black teeth of some gigantic animal waiting to devour me. I even imagined that they beckoned me to greet my fate, and that it was only a matter of time before I too was found stiff and impaled.

I did not wait until complete darkness fell, and began to walk towards Ground Zero, but I hurried back and along Canal Street, to change my routine slightly. I felt more angry than afraid, that someone had not only taken a good friend and notable Poet away from me, but also had taken part of the pleasure from my own life. I could not shake off the feeling however, that I was being watched. Was it just that I felt this way because McArthur had suggested it, or was I being watched by the Police who maybe thought I would lead them to subversive contacts?

"Oh CURSES!" I shouted looking up to the darkening sky with my fists clenched. "Two days ago I felt like a free man, and now I am a suspect and a possible victim".

I knew that Hanwell must have done something to someone to end up the way he did, and I resolved to visit Clarisse and question her. It also occurred to me that she may be grateful and needy for a little extra comforting during her period of mourning. I decided the next afternoon would be appropriate. There would be no quick burial for Hanwell, as the Police were still conducting forensic tests. A murder if this nature required very serious consideration indeed.

This incident had certainly cast a cloud over our happy life, there is obviously a price to pay for being a good citizen. I tried to be my usual self, as did Naomi, but the children were beginning to be fretful as they noticed the change from our usual carefree attitudes. I wondered if their safety was threatened in any way. It may be true that people born with an artistic nature might be more susceptible to mood changes and hyper active imaginations than those born with other gifts. I was beginning to think that my own little Universe was ready to implode as I looked at the starlight drifting from entities which had already died. How like Hanwell I thought. His light as a Poet and Musician would still shine, even though his present body had died, and the faculty had already asked me to be involved in a tribute to him.

I made my way on a sunny lunchtime to the 'Palace of Ice'. Somehow in my mind I remembered Clarisse and Hanwell's apartment that way. I may have called it an Igloo, but it was larger, and Igloos were often transformed into very homely dwellings glowing with warmth. I actually did expect to see the Police still carrying out investigations there or preventing anyone from visiting, but from the outside everything appeared as normal. I was aware that I would be observed on CCT, as I buzzed the intercom. There was a pause and I feared that she may not be there, but then I heard Clarisse's perfect intonation.

"Good morning, how may I help you?" Apart from a slight distortion by the system she sounded as cool as ever.

"Hi, do you remember me? I am Brandon and it was I who discovered and reported your husband's body to the Police. He was a good friend, but it is quite a long time since I visited your apartment." I tried to exude my most charming demeanour but I felt that I was not convincing.

"Yes. I know that you paint and are a Tutor of traditional Printmaking." Clarisse spoke in a non-committal way.

"So – is it possible to speak with you, I apologise for not beginning by offering my condolences in your time of bereavement."

"Yes, you may enter, but only for a short time, I expect investigating Police Officers to return later."

Clarisse looked as beautiful and classically composed as ever, wearing a very appropriate black dress with a modest V neck, and the splayed hemline swung attractively around her knees as she walked in front of me and offered me a seat on the pale blue leatherette couch in the room where I had last seen her standing by the window. Her medium high heels were stylish and expensive. I knew they were because I sometimes accompany, or should I say, restrain, Naomi on shopping trips. She did not sit but continued a little way towards the window and then turned abruptly.

"I know what you must think of me Mr Martin-Schally – sir – that I am some kind of proverbial Ice Maiden. That is the case is it not? Clarisse spoke with the formal imperiousness of a Queen.

"Er no, well-maybe more of a Queen from a very cold country." I did not really intend to make that remark, but it kind of escaped.

"I see, well I am not. I have an excellently educated brain, but I am also a woman with emotions and passions, and – and needs." As she spoke I saw the hint of a faint smile spread briefly from the edge of her lips and irradiate her fine cheekbones very briefly. It was magical.

"I apologise, I know, and I know what a traumatic time this is for you, but I need to know some more about Hanwell if it is possible." It was hard to keep my mind on the reason for my visit. "By the way, my wife Naomi was at University with you..."

"I know, I read the literary magazine which she translates for, better than a computer, and she no doubt told you that I was brilliant or a genius." Clarisse interrupted impartially. "Well, I refused the offer of the best position of my life in order to be a perfect Mother, and sometimes we so called Genius's lose our way and our intellectual sacrifices are not appreciated, and time is our enemy."

"I am very sorry about that, but could you now accept something less than yours and everyone else's expectations, and find your way back?" I answered and tried to maintain a comforting tone without being patronising, because I understand this familiar problem.

"I do not know what Hanwell told you, and I could never regret caring for our two lovely children, but he was never at home, and when he was he was embedded in his studio, and more often than not he would not eat the dinner that I prepared, saying that he would grab something later whilst he was out, and hardly ever paid attention to Benjamin or Amelia." Clarisse continued.

"I really – when we reach the bottom line Hanwell was still a mystery to me apart from our occasional artistic connection, that is why I have come, as I may be a possible victim of those that killed him, and I need to know more." I must say I was a little surprised at Clarisse's frankness.

"May I be very frank with you Mr Marin-Schally?" Clarisse gave me an uncustomary wide eyed look, and turned back towards the window covering her face with her hands.

"Call me Brandon, - please." I answered, as I rose and spontaneously put a comforting arm around her. "Please do not cry, but you can tell me anything? Let it all out."

"In recent years he has not even slept with me. I keep myself in excellent shape, I have taken culinary courses and he practically ignores me. I mean literally he does not sleep in the same bed. He used to come home late, and go out early – too early to be going to the faculty..." Clarisse paused and turned resting her face on my shoulder unexpectedly sobbing.

"He must have been an idiot or something bad had got a grip on him." I replied comfortingly.

"I have forgotten the last time he hugged me it is so long ago, and there was just no level I seemed to be able to reach him on. He despised my intellect, and did not seem to care when I damaged his music projects. It was not the action of a ragingly jealous woman, but someone desperate for some attention, or at least an explanation". Clarisse clung to me and I felt my hands moving over her body. All those wonderfully well-toned exciting curves.

"We are animals in part still, and we all need some contact and reassurance, but why did you stay?" It was a clichéd remark but all that I could momentarily think of.

"Because I still loved him. I still found him attractive. I have my own money, but he took care of us well enough materially, and I would do everything I could to avoid making the children victims of a broken home, but they almost may as well be. It was the way I was brought up to be by my Mother Lady Fenshaw in England. After Finishing School in Switzerland I travelled to America with my Father Viscount Erindale on one of his business trips and opted to attend Uni here. I guess that I have a rebellious streak and I was enchanted by Hanwell's gift for Poetry as well as his handsome charm. They would have had me marry an English Lord." Clarisse stopped sobbing for a moment and our eyes met. The next moment our mouths met in a passionate kiss, and now her hands were moving all over my body eagerly.

"You see how it is for me, I have let an excellent career lapse, and my marriage failed also. I was tempted to go back to England but I hated the thought of all the 'I told you so' remarks from my Mother. But, that is what I am going to do now. I have already sent the children to my Mother with a friend and a plain clothes escort for their own safety. At the moment my Father is visiting friends in Washington, but he will be visiting here soon. Hanwell liked the cool minimal décor, he hated clutter, but the Police have turned Hanwell's studio into a trash can and even looked inside the furniture. I do not really know what they are looking for – drugs, microchips, even bomb material, I have no idea." Clarisse continued, and now began to heave with sexual passion instead of sobs.

I was ready. Boy, I was certainly ready as my heat inadvertently rose. It is a cliché situation isn't it. Sexual relations following a session of comforting and I was loathe to take advantage, but my hands had already caused her dress to slide to the floor. She was unfastening my belt and I managed to step out of my pants without removing my hands from her breast as I popped the small frontal bra fastening.

I felt her hands pushing my briefs over my buttocks. Again I stepped out of them and lifted Clarisse with my hands cupping her buttocks and worked my organ gently into her. She was ready and as she gripped her legs around me her strong pelvic muscles worked me up to the hilt. I moved back slightly to brace myself against the wall. I held back before ejaculation point, and lowered her gently onto the soft rug. As her breasts flayed beneath me she held me fast with her legs and caressed my neck and head so tenderly that I felt as though I could melt.

Thrusting and thrusting and each thrust was reciprocated, until I was stretched over her, my mouth drooling beyond her shoulder. As the flow was no longer restrainable, we rolled over, and she rode me as my ejaculation burst into her, and she yelled holding her head back working me, working both our pelvic muscles until I was dry, but the blood stayed, and Clarisse continued until with a cry of complete satiation she fell upon me, and I held her tight, stroking her hair and back before we separated and we both lay on our backs in silence with our mingled sweat glistening in the afternoon light softened by the white nylon curtains.

Presently I turned towards her "Sorry--." I began and simultaneously she turned to me.

"Forgive me---." Clarisse began to say still with that perfect intonation, but now I saw a new life in her deep blue eyes. We both laughed.

"Oh! Mrs Nnagobi." I said smiling.

"Oh! Mr Martin-Schally." She responded with a sweet smile.

We did not need to say anymore, but she turned on her side and began stroking my chest gently. "I guess that is a case of The Ice Maiden melting is it not – we have not behaved too disgracefully have we?"

"Not at all disgracefully. What is the harm in two friends comforting each other?" I replied

"Hanwell never er 'comforted' me so completely even when we were first married. He would take his pleasure and leave me wanting more. I have felt that the children and I were sometimes props just there for a semblance of normality and conventionality." Clarisse moved closer and snuggled up to me with such beautiful familiarity that I knew I had desired since I first met her and I felt suspended in a time warp that I did not want to end.

"I have talked with him by the South River and discussed beauty and transcendence and the fabric of the Universe on many occasions and I never knew that is the way he was." I replied pensively.

"He probably spent more time with you than he did with me, and he would sometimes bring friends around whom I really did not like. They were not like you and other Faculty members, they would disappear into his studio and he would never introduce them properly. I realise now that his music was a cover for something else." Clarisse continued in a confidential tone.

"Yes but what? The circumstances of his death were really horrific, and I think that the Police know more than they tell you and me." I tried to stretch my brain inwardly in the hope that a flash of intuition would enlighten me, but I still drew a blank.

"The sight of him was pitiful, but after I shed my tears, I cannot honestly say that I miss him, but if I knew the perpetrators, I would do the same to them." Clarisse spoke with conviction.

"So would I, but he probably had himself to blame for his ignominious demise." I agreed genuinely.

"What does life do to us Brandon?" Clarisse suddenly asked raising herself on her right arm. Her beautiful breasts swayed and her mid carnation lips were equally fascinating. "You create beauty with pigments and Hanwell created beauty with words and sound but here you are now with doubt and uncertainty and possibly in danger by association, through no fault of your own. I have continued writing but I have not tried to publish, as I felt like just another broken hearted housewife who would set herself up just to be torn down again. Why is true and lasting happiness so elusive?"

"Well, like the Universe which we are all a part of, we evolve and take pleasure and comfort where and when we can. There is no static 'norm' as far as I can see and maybe it is unreasonable to expect permanence. Maybe it is unreasonable to try and grasp a definite and unchanging goal, and accept that what we achieve will always be just one of a number of alternatives." As I replied I marvelled again at the fact that I was lying here with such familiarity and rapport with someone that I had thought was cold and distant, and yet always secretly desired.

"You mean in fact that grasping these is the only concrete permanence I can hope for?" Clarisse playfully fondled my testicles as she spoke.

"In one sense they represent the source of life. They are full of volatile life, are they not?" I laughed as I spoke, and enjoyed the sensations.

"Do you know – I could love you, I feel so full of your life, but the Police are returning and it is probably better if they do not find you here as we do not want to arouse more speculation or they will think that I organised Hanwell's death to collect the insurance and share it with you." Clarisse kissed my mouth tenderly as she spoke and I was thankful that she was sensible, as I was loathe to drag myself away from her embrace. The Ice Maiden had certainly melted and so had something within myself and at that moment I could have stayed in the fluid conjugation forever.

Clarisse by the Window.

CHAPTER 4

Bound and Blindfolded

I did not see Clarisse again after that afternoon rendezvous, but I thought about her a lot. I called round about a week later against my better judgement, and it was kind of obvious that there was no one at home. I expect that her Father Viscount Erindale was able to put a word into the right ear, and end her tribulations and take her back to the Ancestral home in the South of England. Is it in Sussex? I think that it is. Apparently they have a tremendous collection of Modern Art, which they occasionally open to the public, and the grounds and tea rooms are open in summer. My Father Ralph, apparently is quite well acquainted with him and informed me that one of her brothers is a prominent member of the Arts Council of Great Britain, and Chairman of the London group of Contemporary Artists as he is quite a talented traditional painter in the manner of Sir William Coldstream. I have heard of Cecil Fenshaw, but I had no idea that Clarisse was related to him. He is not an imitator, but continues the ethic of Sir William who headed the Art department at a London University for many, many years. Sir William Coldstream was a co-founder of the Euston Road group in the late 1940's along with Claude Rogers. The subject matter of homely kitchens, still life and rooms with muted lighting that they favoured may seem mundane to some people, but the technical mastery is unassailable.

Hey, I hope that I am not being boring but we artists whilst capable of being very practical are always composing pictures in our minds, and seeing beauty where others may not, and so whatever I may be involved in, I am always thinking this way. It is my view that it makes life richer.

Sir William was the cousin of one of the English Prime Ministers who relinquished his peerage to take up office. I think that I would have preferred to stay on the back benches and remain a Lord. Anyway – do you see what I am trying to say here? Clarisse was connected to a privileged sector of a society who were both ethical and philanthropic. The world is really a small place and who is connected with whom, is sometimes surprising. When I do talk to my Father the extent of his knowledge and connections is always equally surprising.

I did call him as I was worried and although I am a big boy now and a successful New Yorker, I needed some kind of reassurance. I visit my Mother Vanessa, regularly and I like Brooklyn, well not all of it, but a lot of it. She still lives in the detached house where I was born, and there is a handy man friend who helps around the house. His name is Larry Meeks and the twinkle in Mother's eye makes me think that Larry does more than cut the grass and oil the gate. I am pleased for her, as I do not want her to grow into a lonely old lady. She still goes Gospel singing on Wednesday nights and Sundays and enjoys showing off to the tourists who attend the services. I have heard it said that opposites attract, and sometimes I can think of no other two people who are more opposite than my Mother and Father. I remember that my Father would be in his study writing a lecture on the influence of Lautrec and Paris on 19th century American Art and my Mother would be playing a version of My Baby Loves Only Me, like Nina Simone, in one of the front rooms followed by a Bach Fugue. She could imitate the old Rose Murphy song Busy Line, and the three of us would gather around her and join in with all the purrp-purp, and chee-chee's. She lovingly taught us all how to play the piano to a very reasonable standard. My Mother is a born entertainer. She was a classically trained pianist, and she and my Father met after he had been enchanted by her playing at a concert at the Carnegie Hall with a well-known Orchestra. My Mother would take iced tea, but my Father always wanted hot Earl Grey tea, even on the warmest of days. But what a combination. What a striking pair they would make at a function. My tall Father in a Black Evening Suit with tails and a grey waistcoat and either black or white Bow Tie, with his goatee beard, and my Mother in an African style dress wrapped tightly around her shapely figure, with a traditional matching turban, maybe in shades of green and yellow, or black and white.

As I mentioned already my younger brother Wolfgang takes after my Mother playing jazz in Chicago and teaching Musicology, whereas I take after my Father more. Did I say I was afraid of Mom becoming a lonely old lady? No way. She still has a lot of relations down in New Orleans, and some of them came to stay with her during one of the disastrous floods there, and she has so many friends. She still gives the occasional recital and also private piano lessons and she plays for Dancing Studios. Vanessa does very well financially, and some of her down home cooking is to die for. We visit once a month for dinner and believe me, it is not a duty but a real pleasure. And I mean a real pleasure. Naomi is no mean cook herself, and she agrees. My elder sister Esmeralda is a Jazz Dancer, and also teaches Dance-drama at a local school close to where she lives near Coney Island. Her kids love it there in season. She could have followed in Father's footsteps as an Historian, but chose to dance after some early success in some Broadway shows. My elder Brother, Dietrich, very uncharacteristically studied engineering and works for a consultancy in Manchester and Newcastle, England, and sometimes visits the parent company in Frankfurt. He was always a little detached and always engrossed in his computer - studying aerodynamics or engine components, or single span bridges. Maybe on second thoughts he is not so different, as the technical drawing and plans he is involved with require a certain artistry when he has to work without the aid of a computer.

New York to me is as homely as Mom's cooking and as familiar, but now I know that I am being watched by someone. If not by the Police, by someone. Inspector McArthur asked me to be available to help with further enquiries, so that means do not try and leave the country, or maybe the City. They are still holding Hanwell's body as the case is by no means closed. I have changed my jogging habits and every night I arrive home apprehensive in case I find my apartment ransacked or the children abducted, well Kurt anyway, being more mischievous, as Andrea always waits inside until Naomi collects her. Of course I fear for my beautiful Naomi too.

It happened one evening as I passed by a dark doorway obscured by scaffolding. It was on my usual route which I thought would still be safe. There was a man with his back towards me wearing a hood and a yellow waterproof jacket leaning on the safety barrier as I approached along the narrowed passageway between the hoarding and the scaffolding. I thought that he was part of the Construction personnel working late. The street was virtually devoid of pedestrians although the traffic was spasmodically still fairly heavy, and so I avoided jogging in the road. Suddenly he pushed me sideways with considerable force, and I stumbled into the dark temporary doorway, and simultaneously someone inside put a cloth sack over my head and a rope around me pinning my arms to my side.

"No!" I shouted. "I do not know anything."

"We aim to find out what you know and what you do not, or your family will never see you again alive! Now move!" A muffled voice answered me.

I was gripped firmly on either side and forced through the building, almost carried in fact, and I am not a small guy. I am not a weakling either, but I was taken completely by surprise. My feet scrunched upon rubble and I stubbed my toe on scaffold poles and maybe concrete building blocks. Then I could sense that we were outside again, and I was forced into the back of a car, with a gun barrel jabbing my ribs painfully. After a short drive of maybe only 20 minutes my assailants dragged me out roughly onto my knees, and I heard the sound of a large gate closing. Then I was dragged to my feet with a man on either side and one behind and I was forced to descend steps which by the smell and damp feel led to some kind of basement. The man behind me poked something hard into the back of my head all the time, and I could feel that it was another gun. Next I was forced to sit on what felt like a hard wooden chair, and my ankles were deftly bound to it. Another rope was put fairy tightly around my neck on the outside of the sack. All of this time, the three men had remained silent.

"What are you going to do to me? I know nothing about anyone or anything connected with Hanwell Nnagobi." I shouted trying to remain calm so as to avoid choking.

"Quiet!" the man behind me ordered and rapped me hard across the head with the gun.

"If you do not cooperate we will truss you up like a chicken with your neck stuffed up your butt, and deliver you to your front door." Another somehow more cultured voice took over at a slight distance.

"We will hang you first of course, still tied to the chair." A closer voice threatened, and I felt a choking tug on the rope around my neck.

"I do not know what you want to know." I managed to answer in between coughing fits and blows from the gun but.

"Okay. Since you know about whom we want to talk," The cultured voice answered. "Let us start at the beginning."

He began with how I first met Hanwell and asked who some of our other friends were. I told him false names to appear cooperative. Somehow I knew that if I could stall for time I might be saved. When there was nothing I could tell them of what activities Hanwell was involved with other than literature and music they began to threaten me again.

"You are an Artist are you not so you would be sorry to lose a hand, maybe your right?" the cultured voice suggested as they clamped my fingers between two wooden blocks.

"Now I will ask again what did Hanwell Nnagobi tell you about his other involvements and contacts." He continued with feigned patience.

"Nothing, I really know nothing." I responded quietly.

"Wrong." The voice remarked as someone hit the block with a force that numbed my fingers. "The next blow will break all you fingers irreparably."

I was on the verge of begging and wailing to see if that had any effect, when I heard someone else enter from another inside room.

"Stop!" What are you doing? Who is this man? I said no more until this present case has become history." He commanded, and I somehow almost recognised that voice – where –who--? But it just eluded me. There was a faint accent there - may be from another country.

"He is the Turkey who used to hang with Nnagobi." The gunman behind me informed him.

"You bloody fools to bring him here. He is a well-known international artist and recognisable as the man who discovered Nnagobi's body. McArthur could be using him as bait. This Turkey would have squawked already to the Police if he knew anything." That voice, that faint accent—who?

"Sorry boss, we just wanted to be sure." The cultured voice replied timidly.

"Imbecilic jerk-off. Get him out of here and put him back close to where you found him, but not exactly, as the Police could be swarming all over the area by now. You did make sure that you were not followed - did you?"

"Yes boss all the way." Another man answered who was probably the driver.

"Good, and YOU jerk off, never act without my direct authority again, or you will find yourself as food for the fishes."

They released my hand and partially dragged me back up the stairs. I could smell cigar smoke now, and that certain brand seemed to be in my memory cells somewhere, but I could not summon up any images. I was forced back into the car and after about twenty minutes' drive again I felt the car swerve and turn sharp left before stopping suddenly.

"You better not squawk about tonight Turkey, or we will be back for you." The gunman announced.

"Let's kill the Motherfucker" The other man said.

"Na, the boss is right. He aint got nothing on us, and the boss will kill US if we do." The driver announced, to my relief.

"Okay Turkey it must be your lucky day." The gunman announced as he dragged me out of the car. These guys were strong, and I mean really strong.

"Yeah, but even if he does Squawk to McArthur now, he does not know who we are." The second man answered.

"Just untie him and let's get out of here." The driver hissed.

They stood me up against the car and I could sense that it was a large saloon. Then I was totally winded by a blow to my stomach and another to my groin. I had not felt such excruciating and debilitating pain for a very long time. They let me drop to my knees and although I was still in darkness I momentarily blacked out. I felt the rope being removed from arms, and the sack being lifted from my head as I slumped forwards, with heavy eyes that refused to open.

I heard a movement on my right like a metallic door opening, and a voice inquiring what was going on.

"Security – I thought this place was abandoned at night." The voice I recognised as the gunman's was panicking.

"Come on, do not shoot Security for God's sake or they'll trace the bullet. Get in the car quickly." The second man was already seated as far as I could tell, and the gunman dropped the sack back over my face and I could sense that he only just made it before the car took off at speed with a squeak of burning rubber, and a highly revving engine, as I heard the rear door close.

"Hey man are you okay?" The Security Guard asked as he attempted to help me to my feet. I clutched the sack to my stomach. There would not be any Karma Sutra for a day or two I guessed, whether I eventually made it back home or not.

"I. I need a cab." I ventured hoarsely.

"Let's get you into the cabin you look like you could use a coffee or something stronger." I was still kneeling between two large portable cabins in front of another building project in a dark and deserted street. I knew where I was. Not really all that far from my favourite haunt of the South River, and I was surprised to find a Security Officer there too.

"I think I got their number and I am going to call the Police." The Guard did not wait for my negative reply and I was only just able to stand up, and my head felt as though it had been slammed by a wrecking ball, when a patrol car arrived.

I had no choice but to take a ride to the Station, and soon I was sitting in front of Inspector McArthur, who seemed completely unfazed by my dusty and bruised appearance. In fact there was a faint humour around his lips as I related my ordeal. As I expected, he wanted to keep my clothes for forensic testing, and his eyes lit up gleefully as I presented the sack which had been over my head.

"Hopefully we will be able to trace this, and there may be DNA and finger prints." If you were an undercover agent I would complement you on your good work. We are also going to test those tyre marks by the portable cabins, but I do not expect to find that car intact, and the registration that Klem gave us may be false, but at least we are moving towards the light." McArthur concluded.

I arrived back at my apartment with yet another Police escort dressed in a spare Police uniform and shoes. This was a double shock for Naomi so much so that she temporarily lapsed into her Canadian French.

"Sacre Coer, Mon amour, ce sont tous ces ecchymoses sur votre visage. Oh Mon amour qu'ont-ils fait pour vous ? Ou avez-vous été, et c'est cet uniforme ?"

"Ma chérie je ai pensé que je ne vous reverrai jamais. » I replied as I hugged her.

«Je ai été tellement inquiet, presque hors de mon esprit. » Naomi's eyes were wide with anxiety.

"Donc désolé ma chérie, mais je ne étais pas capable d'appeler. » As I apologised for not calling I almost laughed because it sounded as though I had just been delayed at the faculty.

"You can return the uniform anytime sir, and once again I am sorry for the inconvenience Ma 'me. Good night." Sargent Kinross departed smartly.

"Merci beaucoup sergent. » Naomi thanked him and smiled vaguely.

"Thanks Sargeant – I feel quite at home in these togs." I answered, but my swollen split lips would not crack into a smile.

"Venir se coucher, ne permettez-moi de vous apporter un peu de soupe – je ai fait, fait le poivron rouge et la carotte et du poisson avec du riz, vous devez etre affamés. » Naomi aimed for the bedroom, and then swerved towards the kitchen and I followed slowly as the pain in my groin reoccurred. I was starving, in spite of the feeling that every vital internal organ had been mashed, and the prospect of red pepper and carrot soup and fish with rice sounded very tempting.

"Merci chérie, je vais sortir de ces vêtements alors qu'elle se réchauffe et prendre une douche rapide. » I decided on a shower first as I caught site of my blood-stained face, in a mirror, and my hair retained small balls of fluff from the inside of the sack.

"Les enfants étaient très agite et il a fallu les âges pour les amener à dormir. »Naomi shouted from the kitchen, and I realised that it was my turn to read the story and the children had not wanted to sleep without it.

"Je suis désolé, mais je vais vous expliquer, si peux rester assez longtemps éveillé. »I apologised again and hoped that I could stay awake to eat; that is if I could pass the food between my lips, and fill in Naomi in with some of the details as the shower began to relax me, and sooth some of the pain.

I had lost track of how many times the gunman had hit me across the head and face with the gun, but my face was testament enough, as new swelling seemed to be appearing. It was bad enough, but the sack had softened the blows a little, and I was thankful that my right hand seemed to still have full flexibility. I thought of the Universe and thanked my Lucky Star wherever it is.

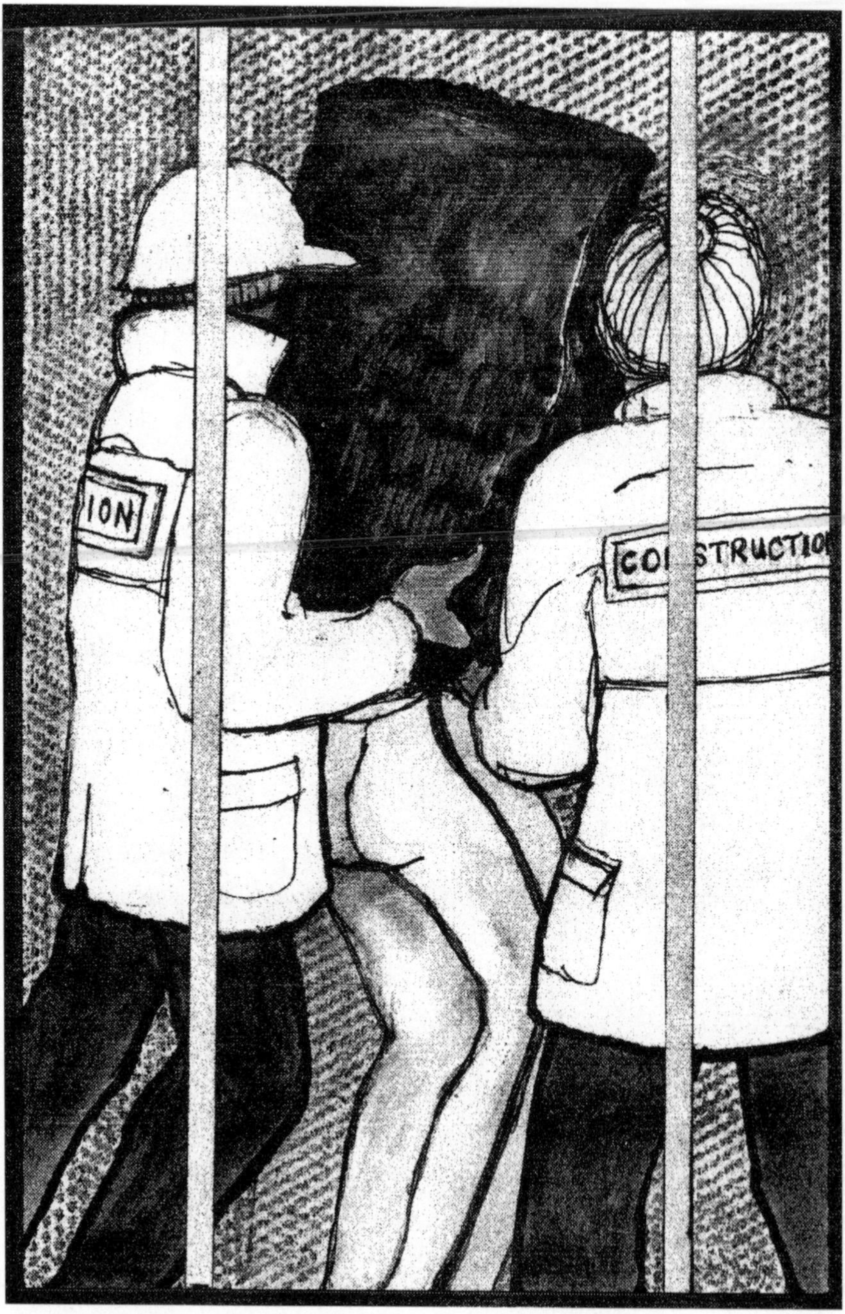

Abducted by Mobsters in Disguise.

CHAPTER 5

Smoke

Very uncharacteristically I had to call in sick. The Professor's private secretary, a very warm and charming woman expressed her concern and assured me that she would pass on my message and make the necessary arrangements for my absence to be covered. Everyone called her Maggie though she had the very impressive name of Margurita von Hessen-Bach. Like myself she had a Grandfather from Deutschland. I often spoke a little German with her. It was not over familiar, she was only forty five years old or so, but she was like everyone's Mom, including staff and students alike. She was also a singer with a rich mezzo-soprano voice performing with several classical music groups. I saw her performing in a version of Gustav Mahler's Das Lied Von Der Erde, which I thought approached greatness. The repartee which we indulged in was really approaching the theatrical.

"Danke Liebling, ich schulde dir ein." I limited my repartee today because my swollen lips resolutely pushed my mouth sideways, defying all attempts to correct it.

"Es ist mir eine Freude, erhalten gut und mach dir keine Sorgen, du bist niemals abwesend." Maggie was so efficient that I could rest easy knowing that my students would be taken care of, and I turned my attention to laying with ice packs on my face to reduce the swelling.

The body blows were so severe, I think that they used something other than a fist, as my stomach and groin were actually bruised and purple. Maggie was right I had never been absent due to sickness, or even skipped my classes due to a hangover, so I felt at ease, well as much at ease as my aches and pains would allow. I decided that a couple of days at home would be better than trying to do a Printing demonstration with a half closed black eye, and a swollen mouth.

After taking Kurt and Andrea to school Naomi picked up some extra bags of crushed ice even though we have an icemaker in the large two door refrigerator.

"What are oo doing, planning thell-e-bration?" I managed to ask, my swelling seemed to have worsened.

"No, I am taking up ice sculpture." Naomi laughed before adding. "I want you to sit in the bathtub with some ice and maybe a little cold water to reduce those bruises on your groin, and I have some frozen peas which make good icepacks for your face, and then when it is all back to normal we will celebrate."

"Are oo mith- thin' karma Thutra?" I asked partly jokingly.

"I may be." Naomi replied with a demure smile, "But come on now into the tub."

We had a low level bathtub in a primrose yellow colour, with Jacuzzi features as well as a walk–in shower, in the ensuite room, and a separate bathroom which we used for the children. Horizontal bands of ultramarine blue divided the alternate yellow and white tiles. Spotlights created a softened and atmospheric light, which created a pleasant sunny room. Naomi spread some ice for me to sit on, in a little cold water, and then stacked some between my legs and up to my stomach.

"Oh, I think that I would rather have bruith-es than the cool-d." I said.

"Now, hold this pack of peas on your mouth, and I will hold this one on your eye." Naomi sat on a wooden stool next to me, and held the back of my head as she administered the ice pack without further ado. "Are you sure you do not want Dr Berkley to have a look at you? He is a friend after all." She continued.

"No, I think that I will juth-t free-th to death." I replied, but I was actually beginning to feel better already.

When the peas began to feel warm Naomi placed them in the freezer wrapped in a plastic bag and replaced them with more, as well as replenishing the crushed ice in the bath. She gave me aspirin for its anti-inflammatory properties, and ginger tea to help with my internal circulation. I counted myself lucky to have such a tender nurse, and as I was rarely ill apart from a very occasional cold, I was surprised at her knowledge and care. When I managed to ask her what made her such a good nurse, she replied that it ran in the family, and that she had assisted her Mother with her Grandfather and her Grandmother as a girl in Canada.

"Il est juste de le connaissance commune. » Naomi replied with a slight shrug.

"Oh, je vois." I answered, as she slipped back into her Canadian French. Maybe a lot of 'common knowledge' had escaped me. I always thought that raw steak was good for black eyes, but I was not about to try this now clichéd remedy.

"Maintenant, mon amour, vous sécher au large at obtenir le lit et je vais aire de la soupe de poulet." Naomi eventually declared when she decided that my ice treatment was enough for a while, and I must say that I was ready to vacate the bath, and the idea of chicken soup was very welcome.

"Merci beaucoup, mon Cherie." I replied quietly, as I put on my black shorts and T shirt and lay on the Bauhaus inspired black and white duvet. The small cuts on my cheeks and the long graze on my forehead were quickly healing and the swelling to my mouth was greatly reduced. My eye was fully open again.

"No getting frisky, you are not better yet." Naomi declared as she returned with the soup on a tray, and some fruit and yogurt compote, and I attempted to hold her slim waist. "There is some chopped smoked sausage in the soup for extra flavour."

"Mmm, I can smell it. This looks delicious darling." I replied and then a flashback from the previous night hit me. SMOKE. I remembered smelling cigar smoke of a familiar brand. Obviously popular brands will be smoked by many people, but there was something so familiar and so special about that particular smoke. I recalled my painful repartee with Maggie that morning. I saw the medium oak wood panelled walls of her office, and the doorway to that of the Professor just behind her to the left. I heard again that voice with the slight accent. Professor Beldossa! Professor Emile Beldossa – surely not? And yet, I know that he has specially imported cigars. I am familiar with the timber of his voice – Mother's music lessons had made me attentive to sound. Could it be that he was the mysterious boss who had saved me.

"There is no smoke without fire." I heard my Irish Grandmother saying.

"Ja sehr wahr, mein Liebling." I heard my German Grandfather replying.

Beldossa how can that be? My own voice within my head was asking.

"If it is fiction you want look no further than the truth." Grandmother was repeating.

"Ja gibt nichts merkwurdig" Grandfather was agreeably reiterating.

How can I be sure before I accuse him? My own voice was inquiring.

"Charming diplomacy is a most effective weapon." I heard my Father declaring.

"Sometimes let the heart lead the head." I heard my Mother advising.

I saw my Father sitting there with his research books open comparing a historical treaty to modern politics. He raised his kindly face to me, and his narrow gold framed spectacles glinted in the light of the desk lamp. His main subject was art history as I said earlier, but often political history was reflected in the Arts of a period. I was about twelve. "Charming Diplomacy is a most effective weapon." He informed me. "Always remember that my boy." I did not often venture into the study whilst he was working, but I think that I had gone to report some grievance with my elder brother. We were a happy family, and he did make time to play games with us, to take us swimming and to the Bowl and the Yankee Stadium to watch games. Even after working in The USA for many years there remained something very English about him, due no doubt to his own excellent education.

So, how was I going to be diplomatic about finding out the truth concerning Professor Emile Beldossa? We were well acquainted through work, but not socially. I think in fact that Beldossa maintained a certain privacy which not many of his faculty colleagues shared. Yes, that certainly could be a reason – the fact that he headed some kind of gangland operation. I was still not clear about Hanwell's place in the scheme of things. Had he chanced upon some secret, or had he infiltrated the operation and maybe become an informant. Just how much did Inspector McArthur really know?

A frustration gripped me again combined with a stiffness in my torso and intermittent aching. All my functions seemed to be okay, indicating that my internal organs had not been affected. I was thankful that I had followed a fitness regime, and that I was fairly muscular so that my resilience was high. All the same I felt fit to burst with anger and resentment by the time Naomi returned with Andrea and Kurt from their school, and they nearly caught me in the process of uttering curses and swearing vengeance.

"How are you Daddy? Gosh, you look like a Boxer. I think that I want to do boxing." Kurt ran into the bedroom noisily.

"Do I, well Boxers make a lot of money to look like this, but it is the loser who looks like this very often rather than the Champ. Maybe you can have lessons sometime and learn how to defend yourself properly." I think that I answered rather sharply as he looked momentarily downcast.

"Do not bother Daddy too much, he is not very well." Naomi shouted as she switched on their favourite TV channel.

"Did you not know how to defend yourself Daddy?" he asked gravely.

"Yes I know how, but there were three or more and they took me by surprise and put a blue sack over my head and hit me with a gun handle." I thought that I would tell him straight so that he would have no romantic notions about violence.

"Why Daddy? Have you done something very bad?" Kurt was bright, and I cursed my fate inwardly again that he should be presented by this spectacle.

"No I have not done anything bad to anyone, and you must not do so either, - they thought that I was somebody else." I decided to tell a small lie and hope that his curiosity would be satisfied.

"Will someone hit them for doing that to you? I will when I am big." Kurt decided resolutely.

"No! I mean yes. The Police will punish them, the Inspector is my friend, but you must not go around hitting people. If you are a Boxer there are rules. I want you to remember what Granddad says. He says that 'Charming Diplomacy is the most effective weapon'. I felt like saying just the opposite, but I know how a wrong impression can affect the behaviour of a young brain in later years.

"What is dip diplo-ma-sassy?" Kurt asked wide eyed with genuine interest.

"It means getting what you want by being clever and not going around hitting people." I answered in a much more down to earth manner than I usually did and I hoped my lucky star would prevent my recently acquired bitterness from being apparent.

"Kurt come and have your meal now, and leave Daddy in peace this evening. I will be reading the story again tonight." Naomi called from the kitchen.

"Dip diplo- ma-sassy! Dip diplo-ma-sassy!" He ran off shouting his new found word.

I sighed with relief and closed my eyes. I must have dozed, because contrary to my intelligence I found myself in Maggie's office. As she rose in alarm I told her to sit, which she did in astonishment. I opened the door quickly and saw Professor Emile Beldossa silhouetted against the window behind his desk. He also rose in astonishment as I levelled the automatic rifle at his head.

"You low life." I snarled. "Your gang has murdered my friend and beaten me and ruined my blissful family life with your venality, and now it is your turn."

"No please Brandon it is all a mistake, - I can explain. I saved you." Beldossa shouted as he took the fat cigar out of his mouth, and blew out a cloud of smoke.

"I know, but it was only to save your corrupt operation, and you thought McArthur had set me up." I snarled again as I took aim.

"You are making a big mistake, this does not end with me – how did you know it was me?" He was stalling for time and I expected him to pull some trick.

"By your exclusive cigar smoke and the sound of your voice." I answered viciously and conclusively.

"You are a reasonable fellow, I can do a lot for you." He inhaled deeply on the fat cigar and I could see that his hand was shaking, as he blew out another cloud of smoke. The pungent aroma of it sent a flame of passion through my brain and I opened fire until there was hardly anything left of his head, and most of it was spattered on the window.

For good measure I walked over and shot his lifeless body through the heart as it slumped back in the chair. I turned and walked back to the door. Maggie stood there aghast. I told her to sit again and I smashed the telephone with the gun but. I turned and withdrew the key from the inside and locked Beldossa's door on the outside. I coolly pocketed the key and walked out of the office.

“Guten tag mein Liebling – justice has been done.” I said looking back at her.

“Brandon mon amour. Brandon –.” Naomi was standing over me with another tray of aromatic food, as I opened my eyes slowly.

“Oh Naomi Mon Cherie—.” I began in dazed surprise as I orientated back into the familiar sight of our bedroom.

“Are you feeling worse darling? You were mumbling something about SMOKE in your sleep. Did the sausage not agree with you?” Naomi looked really concerned.

“The smoked sausage was lovely darling, with the chicken soup. I think that I had a dream.” I almost laughed at Naomi’s suggestion. I remembered my dream vividly and I was relieved that she did not suspect what was on my mind.

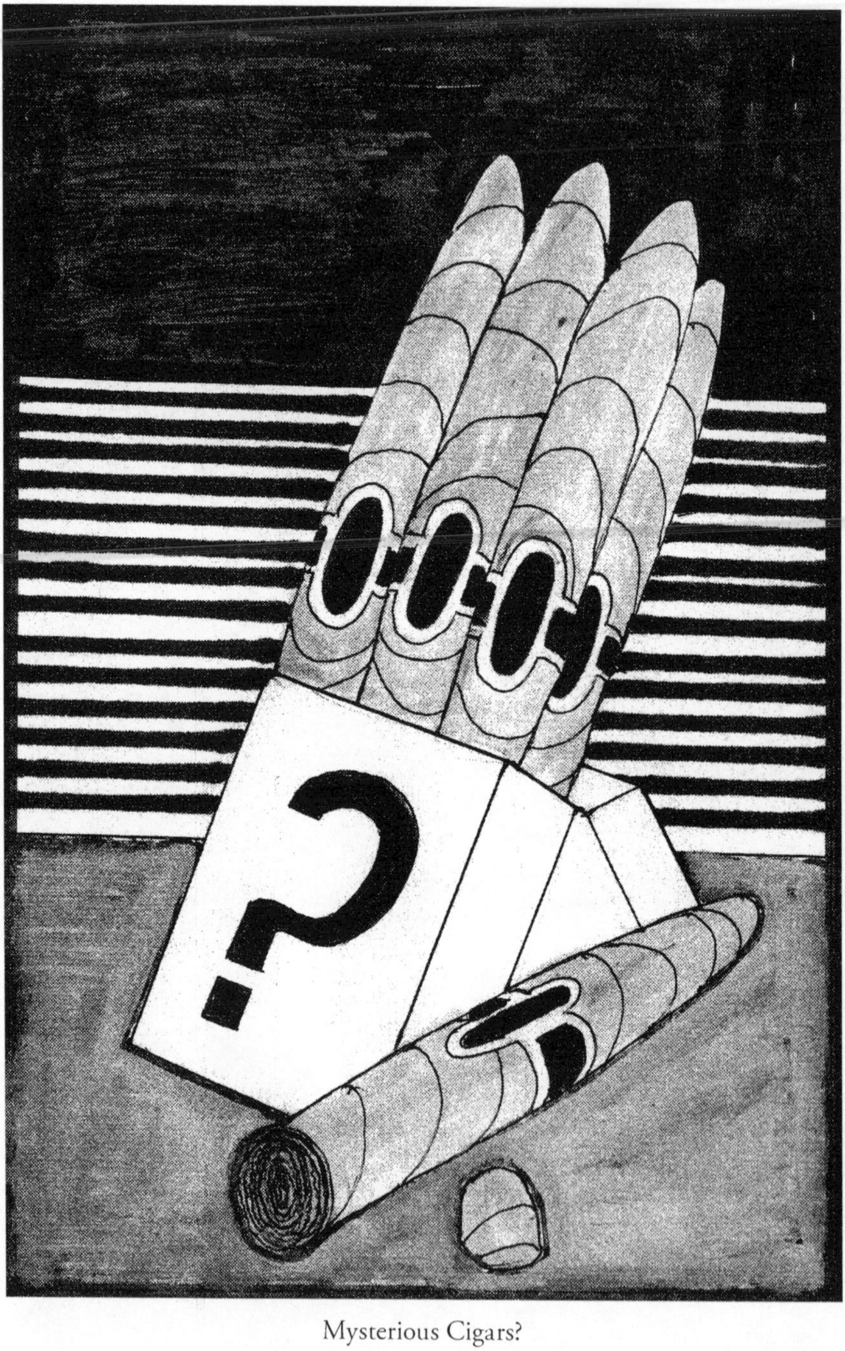

Mysterious Cigars?

CHAPTER 6

Unexpected News

Several months had passed and I was no closer to being able to denounce Professor Emile Beldossa. I had tied to ingratiate myself with him, to such an extent that Maggie had begun to suspect that our theatrical repartee was turning into serious flirting. I was a daily visitor to her office, and sometimes he was engaged, so I had to wait, or call back later. I was not an accomplished player of Golf, so I could not really accompany him on the course, which was an excellent social scene. He would have thought my efforts embarrassingly pathetic.

There were only so many suggestions I could make to him about the Printing facilities and the curriculum, and there were only a few Private viewings at Galleries where I could engage him in conversation of a more personal nature. Diplomacy was not working, and yet I could not bring myself to divulge my suspicions to Inspector McArthur. I knew what he would say, that it would be difficult to bring charges against someone based upon the smell of cigar smoke and the sound of a voice. I would need visual evidence and even photographic evidence. I had not been into contact with him, so there would not be any of his DNA on my clothes, even if they were able to approach him for initial questioning. All this time I expected to see the news of more people murdered in the same way as Hanwell Nnagobi. Then I thought that maybe his killing had given the necessary message to whomever it was intended. As you may imagine, I did not find it easy to tolerate Beldossa's company, and I often felt a subterranean force of violence and vengeance rising from deep within myself, which needed a great deal of effort to control.

I had changed. I could see it in the children's faces, and occasionally I even caught Naomi with a hint of sadness on her face, which was not there before. I wanted so much to blow the whole operation apart, not just focus upon Beldossa, for with him out of the way his henchmen would remain underground, to emerge later when he was forgotten about. I was becoming paranoid, and I could see this reflected in my paintings, which were becoming vehicles of dark expressionism, instead of constructed balanced harmony as they had formerly been. Some were almost Post Traumatic nightmarish images where figures were pursued and victimised by gigantic Birds of Prey. Beldossa was still a highly rated artist himself and had produced works for an exhibition which I begrudgingly had to admit were par excellence.

In the midst of this quandary, I received a parcel sent to the faculty office and marked strictly private. I know this makes for greater curiosity than if it was just a plainly addressed piece, anyway Maggie handed it to me with fake ceremonial respect, and I accepted it in the same manner. My feigned light heartedness quickly dispersed when I opened it at my desk before visiting the Print Studio. There was a Hardcover Book, and a letter. It was beautifully written with a neat hand –

> Dear Brandon,
>
> Your Son was born prematurely but he is ok, and is gaining weight and growing as he should. Otherwise he is perfect. I have called him Pharoe, I hope that you like the name. He is yours most definitely, but for the sake of propriety here, as I was widowed, and not yet remarried, he will have the surname of Nnagobi.
>
> You are welcome to see him anytime you wish, and I am not asking anything from you in the way of mental or material support. Benjamin and Amelia have adjusted very well to life in the UK. I am happy, and I send my love, to you and your family.
>
> Pharoe will be a great comfort to me as you were. You restored my life, and I hope that you enjoy my novel which

I had lost the heart to publish. It is dedicated to Hanwell, but in my heart I dedicated it to you.

Yours affectionately,
Clarisse.

I heard the perfect intonation of her voice as I read, and tears of sentimentality came into my eyes. In spite of our passionate and agile lovemaking, I still remembered her natural beauty as she stood half turned and framed by the large window on the first day that I met her. I had been captivated by her beauty and chilled by her coldness, which concealed the warm and passionate woman beneath that curt façade.

I was overtaken by a sudden desperate urge to see my new son and of course Clarisse. I would have to engineer a visit carefully – maybe I would pay a visit to my father in London. I did not really want to arrive at Erindale Manor in Foxglove, Sussex, unannounced. Clarisse had been very sensible to write to me at the faculty. I could show Naomi the new book, but never the letter of course, so I found two envelopes and sealed the letter in one, and sealed the book in the other. I wrote Gallery 65 on it, where my Paintings and Prints were often exhibited and held in a permanent collection so that it would appear as part of a normal communication. I placed it in my inside pocket to secret within my studio at the apartment later. This indeed was very unexpected news.

I had not exhibited in London for a while but now it occurred to me that a new exhibition there would be the perfect excuse to invite Clarisse and view my new son simultaneously. I would try and finish my expressionistic works, and call the exhibition 'Subterranean Territory'. I set to work like a man possessed, and actually Naomi was pleased to see me occupied with enthusiasm again, instead of someone working out a torment. Kurt and Andrea were both pleased that I began behaving like 'Daddy' again. I overheard him saying that to Naomi after I had read the story one night.

"I told you that Daddy would get better." She replied sweetly

I felt full of remorse. Had I been more morose and preoccupied than I realised? It seemed that I had. Naomi knew that even the most resilient can be affected by situations they are subjected too and I blessed her for her patience and insight. She had not complained to me and as the bruising in my groin cleared, she had taken the lead most gently with our lovemaking. I had not been full of fire, but it was adequate enough to keep frustration at bay. Love and sexual activity could easily be separated as far as I am concerned as well as going hand in hand. I did love her and I had been surprised by qualities that I had not really seen in her previously. I was even more surprised however when about two weeks after I received the letter from Clarisse, Naomi announced that she was pregnant again. This again was very unexpected news as we had never discussed expanding our family at this time. Obviously I was pleased as this was the final proof that the severe blows had not affected any permanent damage. After all what man does not like to feel virile even after fathering several children? It is only human animal nature after all. Knowing the unlimited boundaries of Naomi's cleverness, it occurred to me that she had allowed this as proof that everything was Ok. I had my Health Insurance yes, and I had a friend who was an MD, but I had not felt like dragging myself around for tests and electronic scanning.

Naomi surprised me again one evening when I returned home.

"I hope that you will not be upset to be reminded, but there is a new publication by Clarisse Fenshaw which is arousing quite a lot of interest." She announced.

"Clarisse Fenshaw? Er--." I began. I had really temporarily forgotten her penname.

"Yes, Clarisse – Hanwell's widow. Fenshaw is her maiden name. Her father Sir Winstanley Fenshaw became Viscount Erindale. They have a large estate in Sussex in the UK, but he is quite an international entrepreneur." Naomi continued brightly. "I am going to download an e Book copy. I believe that it includes some illustrations by her brother Cecil Fenshaw.

"Oh, I am pleased that she is doing something positive, and not sitting in mourning." I replied. I had decided not to show Naomi my complimentary copy and had left it at the Faculty in the large envelope. I had read much of it and found it quite compelling as well as very witty.

"I am delighted for her. They are an extremely wealthy family, but I know that money did not bring her happiness, and as I said, she was the most brilliant student of her year. I feel inspired. I have been secretly writing for myself as well as working, so maybe it is time for me to publish."

"I think you should darling." I said hugging her.

"What shall I call myself?" Naomi continued in very high spirits.

"The best and most beautiful wife in all the world!" I replied sincerely.

"I was thinking of something slightly more esoteric." She answered laughing brightly.

"Why not just you." I replied. Holding her warm body was wonderful without feeling an ache or twinge and for a moment I felt completely like my old self. For once in my life I had experienced what it is like to be an invalid, and I hoped that it would only be once. I looked into her deep eyes and the love that we felt for each other flowed through us. We kissed lingeringly before we were distracted by Andrea.

"Just you!" That will not do." Naomi broke away from our embrace and laughed again.

"That statement rhymed, but I meant – Naomi." I concluded.

Even more unexpected news greeted me the next day as I entered Maggie's office. She looked at me in an even more jolly way than usual.

"Guten Morgen Brandon, Liebling, dein Geheimnis Bemuhungen haben Fruchte getragen." She announced, and I was almost unnerved to be informed that my secret efforts had borne fruit.

"Ach Was? Wie? Ach Maggie Liebling Sie immer sehen, durch Mich!" I replied just managing to maintain my theatrical repartee, and admitting that she always saw through me, and hoping that she would enlighten me further. But I was bemused. How could she know what I was trying to do?

"Und die ganze Zeit dachte ich, es war meine Frisir und Parfum, das Sie nicht widertehen konnte." Maggie continued almost laughing. As it happened I did like her hairstyle and perfume – everyone did, she was the ideal PA.

"Ich bete dich Liebling." I informed her that I adored her, with a charming smile to hide my inner trepidation.

"Gut, den wir werden enger zusammen arbeiten, will Emile, etwas mit Ihnen besprechen," Maggie announced that WE would be working more closely after Emile had discussed something with me, with an underlying sincerity.

"Ich kann nicht warten." I concluded that I could not wait, as I entered Emile's office.

"Good morning Brandon, I trust that you are fully recovered by now. Are Naomi and the children well? I will cut to the chase as it were. I am taking a sabbatical for at least a year, and I wondered whether you would like to fill in for me here as head of the Faculty. Normally there is an exchange basis, but my counterpart has been taken seriously ill, so I am in fact offering you a Professorship for a year, maybe longer. Obviously this will be reflected in your salary, and not many people know the Faculty as well as you. I have discussed the matter with the governors and my colleagues, and they are all in agreement. I am afraid that I shall have to ask you for a quick answer, as it will be affective as from next Monday." Emile blew out a huge cloud of cigar smoke as he waited for my reaction. I nearly wretched as the pungent smell of it reminded me of the basement and the stifling dark sack over my head and the rope pulling tightly around my neck, but I was literally gobsmacked.

"This is a most unexpected honour." I managed to reply evenly. Was this a ploy I wondered, to sweeten me and to throw me off the scent? Did he suspect that I suspected him of heading an undercover scam?

"Well we have become very friendly recently, and I can think of no one better suited to take my place, and to run the Faculty. After all you are a highly respected international Artist also. I know that to some Artists a completely academic role is abhorrent, almost a contradiction in terms, but from your record here, I know that is not so with you." Emile smiled at me almost ingenuously, and for a moment I almost forgot my loathing and revenge for his murderous operation.

"I would be honoured to accept and I am most gratified by your confidence in me." I heard myself replying and found myself shaking his hand as though it was the thing that I desired the most in all the world.

"Good. Good. I can take up my residency in Buenos Aires with an easy mind. We will keep in touch of course. Consquela likes you and she will be delighted that you have accepted. Vasilly and Portiaetta are both in Europe. We have family in Argentina you know, as well as in Mexico, Panama and France, so she is looking forward to packing up camp and relocating as it were." Emile was in very good spirits today and his mood was infectious. He certainly was charismatic. He had already divulged more than I already knew about him and I even ventured to make a joke.

"There is just one reservation," I said with tongue in cheek seriousness. "I do not have to smoke those cigars do I, I do not even know where to buy them from."

"Oh, ha, ha, Consquela hates them too." Emile answered laughing genuinely. "I am afraid that I break all the no smoking rules everywhere, they are a special import from Panama. I started smoking these secretly when I was eleven, and I have never stopped. They are actually Dutch, but I get them before they are exported to Europe. My Father was in the business, but he did not approve of my misspent youth I fear, but that is another story"

Maggie was right, my secret plan had worked but in a way that I did not expect. In five minutes he had told me more than I had discovered during the months of working my way into his confidence, and he had offered me his coveted job into the bargain.

As I drank the vintage Brandy which he offered me to seal the deal I had a cacophony of thoughts whirling through my head. What about my new secret son and my plans to spend some time in London? How was I going to follow the leads Emile had just provided me with? Was Inspector McArthur still watching me? Why was he suddenly so eager to leave town? How well could I fill Emile's charismatic boots?

This was very unexpected and strange. I was about to take the place of an older man that I had sworn to take vengeance upon and he had brought me good fortune instead.

Post Traumatic Nightmare Image.

CHAPTER 7

A Creep!

I had forgotten to return the uniform that McArthur sent me home in on the night of my ordeal with the unknown assailants. I felt kind of comfortable in it, and it gave me the idea of carrying out some investigations in a Police Officer like manner. I know that it is an offence to impersonate a Police Officer, and I was bound to meet some on the clandestine locations I intended to check out. It was myself that was going undercover, as a Police Officer, rather than a civilian disguise hiding a Police Officer. I must be out of my tiny mind – yes? I would be running the double risk of getting myself killed without back up, or being arrested for flouting the law. I already possessed a gun and a licence. Shooting had been a hobby when I was a student, so I would not be breaking any laws on that account. But how many people were? Well I do not have the exact figures but it is quite a lot.

There had been a raid on a warehouse somewhere on the West side, but no one and nothing was apparently found there. This could have been as a result of forensic evidence found on the dark blue dyed sack which I presented to McArthur. I had tried to talk to him on one or two occasions, but although friendly, he was always too busy and evasive and would not divulge many details.

"They could have killed you and they did not, so I would guess that you are not in any danger, if you do not do anything foolish." This was all that he would say, which I suppose, is to be expected, but I managed to push him a little further one morning.

"Some of those guys were just crazy and gun happy, they would kill me or my family without a second thought." I replied agitatedly.

"From the information that you gave me I deduce that the outfit really wants to lay low for a while." McArthur continued patiently.

"Yes it is lucky that the boss seemed to be an educated intelligent kind of guy, but I still have not figured out how Hanwell Nnagobi fits in, I know now that I really did not know much about him. I always took him on face value." I still felt that I was on the edge of a chasm which would open up beneath me at any time, as I replied.

"I think that you may have reached some kind of conclusion, that Hanwell, your friend was a CREEP." McArthur actually surprised me with this remark.

"A CREEP?" I repeated inquiringly.

"Depending on the viewpoint that is." McArthur surprised me again with a short laugh. "An informer, - someone who infiltrated an unlawful organisation, and gave information to the Police, or to a rival organisation."

"I see." I replied still in disbelief. "Like one of those friendly guys who might approach one in the street and ask for directions to someplace and lead you to another guy as you speak, who flashes a Police badge and demands to know who you are and where you live or where you have travelled from and to see your passport."

"You have obviously travelled in Europe." McArthur laughed again. "Yes that is exactly what I mean, but much deeper one might say. Like a Mole, or a stool Pidgeon; Hanwell could have infiltrated the heart of an outfit and been ready to expose them, when his dual identity was discovered.

"I understand why plain clothes Police work in this way. Everywhere Police are on the alert to the dangers of terrorist factions, and illegal immigration, and illegal trafficking, but it is nevertheless very annoying to the innocent." I replied.

"You have probably gathered also that the way his body was displayed, served as a clear warning to other would be infiltrators, or ones which they have not discovered yet." McArthur continued. "He had been bludgeoned to death and his neck was broken and also his lower vertebrae before he was wrapped in black polythene, so there was no bullet in his body to match to a gun. There are unidentified finger prints on the polythene, but the bloody finger prints were left by gloved hands and a wooden mallet was used to hammer his body onto the blunt point of the breakwater. We found that in the river, but again without identifiable finger prints or DNA other than that of Hanwell. Whoever is in charge of these subversives is a very clever brutal guy."

"Hanwell was well known in literary circles and his music was popular on line, but all the while his real involvement was with something else –?" McArthur interrupted me as I replied.

"I will tell you confidentially as a friend, that his studio was a cover up, and we found sophisticated communication installations, but as yet we have not cracked the access codes." He stated in a very matter of fact manner.

"So this sounds more than just a small time racketeer, or a casual drug dealing syndicate." I added.

"Right. This is something big, but your guess is still as good as mine. His involvement probably goes way back to student days or even earlier, so I would be grateful for any information you can give me. Anything that you may remember, you can write it down and give it to me personally, or send it as an email attachment, rather than an open letter." McArthur I could tell, wanted to bring the conversation to a close now.

"I will be glad to oblige in any way that I can." I continued thoughtfully.

"And Brandon, - you are much too well known now, as the guy who discovered Hanwell's body, and as an international Artist, so for goodness sake DO NOT TRY TO BE A CREEP." McArthur emphasised this with genuine concern.

"Okay, thanks for filling me in a little, and I will try and remember something useful to you." I assured him. I felt as though he had read my mind.

"Good. Take care, and congratulations on your promotion by the way, but my son misses your classes. He thinks that the new Tutor does not have your expertise or inspiration. Bye." McArthur rang off and left me with my thoughts.

I still feared for the safety of my family. When they were at school Kurt and Andrea were vulnerable, I could not help but constantly remind myself. Hell, there were gunmen who attacked whole classrooms full of children for some vendetta which had really nothing to do with those who were mown down. What if one of the assailants who was not as clever as the others took it upon himself to send me another message as were? What of Naomi? She was vulnerable also on the school run, and when she was shopping. It would be a greater punishment for me to see my family shot dead, than if they killed me, if they decided that I was still a threat. It occurred to me also that McArthur might indeed be using me, and that the police were watching me, hoping that I might lead them to some discovery that would expose the organisation.

Now that the boss had apparently taken refuge in Argentina, had they abandoned whatever operations they were involved with, or simply relocated? Maybe Professor Emile Beldossa, whom I had inadvertently begun to like and respect – well – I always had respect for him – maybe he was not the actual boss. He could be in charge of just a small section of something much larger and international.

As Professor myself now, I had access to records and files of staff members and some of the previous activities of Beldossa, but not much of it was very illuminating, or subversive. It was strange at first to have Maggie as my PA now, but we still maintained some of our former theatrical repartee, which I appreciated as it was diverting from the constant gloomy cloud in my head. I had never understood before when I heard people wishing that they could turn the clock back, but now I did. I had been happy with my own progress in life, and looked towards the future ever optimistic. I had looked forward to watching my children grow to maturity in safety and with confidence, now it was like living on the edge of a volcano which might erupt and engulf me any moment. In spite of my elevated status, I would gladly have turned the clock back to the morning before I discovered Hanwell Nnagobi's body, and I would have taken a different route for my early morning jog. I might still have been in danger though, through my friendship with him. Maybe I should look into his background more. Although he had belonged to a different section of the University, I was able to gain access to his files. Maggie was a whizz on the Computer and when I told her that I had been asked to write a short appraisal for a publication, she assisted in accessing more information than I could ever have hoped for.

"Alles fur dich mein Schatz Chef." Maggie said, looking very pretty with her neatly set hair, and her pink frilled blouse underneath her tailored black jacket. I was happy to be her darling Boss.

"Danke, dass meinen speziellen Engel." There was a genuine affection beneath the repartee, as I called her my special Angel.

Maggie made it possible for me to access personal details from Hanwell's files inter Faculty. It was all in the strictest confidence, and the rapport which I had established over the years had resulted in mutual trust. I was amazed to find that Hanwell had been orphaned when his parents had met with an accidental shooting incident during unrest in one of the Central African states when he was six years old. An Uncle had taken care of him and travelled to Bahia in Brazil. Apparently he had left his Uncle and travelled to New York to stay with an Aunt and some cousins when he was fifteen. Always bright and thirsting for knowledge, he progressed well during his last years at high school, and qualified for entrance into University, where I made his acquaintance.

It was like researching a family tree online, and the information showed that he had travelled via Columbia and Cuba on his way to New York. His mentality was moulded by a hatred for the rival African faction that had ransacked his village and made refugees of many of the women and children whilst many of the men were shot. He had no illusions about Africa and the cruelty and strife that Africans inflicted upon each other, and this made him cynical about his relationship with other ethnic groups. He apparently could never forgive his own countrymen, as he stated in an unpublished dissertation which he had written. He asked the question as to how could he demand better treatment in a different country, wherever it was, when his own kind showed such disregard for each other. At the same time he would defend his heritage against the enlightened philanthropy of a less troubled environment, if pushed to the bottom line. I knew that he was maybe a bipolar personality, as many creative people are. Sometimes their creativity is the subconscious attempt to find unity and balance within themselves and feel at ease in the world. I was aware of this from knowing him, and from some of the poetry that he wrote.

As I discovered more I realised that probably the basis for our friendship was the fact that I am from a very mixed ethnic background. I am Black descended from African slaves on my dear Mother's side, and White from my dear Father's side, and my Father is in turn Irish and German, as you know. I have inherited a lot of those traits too. But when I reach the bottom line, I realise that people are people with a great variety of bodies, which interests me as an Artist, but each body is a temple for a soul. I have heard it said that a mixed race man or woman is never one thing or the other, whether or not there is a colour difference.

A very famous South African singer wrote a song which stated that- Often the White man is happy, sometimes the Black man is happy, but the man who is neither Black nor White is never happy. I think that Hanwell looked at me and examined me to see if there was a truth in this theory. But who made the Coloureds of South Africa, or the Creoles of America, or the Mulato's of Mexico?

A God? Well maybe, but it is a Black person and a White person, so how can either reject us. We have a right to belong to both, but it calls for intelligence not to hate one or the other when we face rebuffs, from less enlightened individuals. My Father and my Mother taught me and my Brothers and Sisters to fully embrace all of our rich cultural heritages without embarrassment.

I realise now that Hanwell felt safe with me because he could never resent me. He could never see in me what he despised about his own countrymen, and yet he could still share his heritage with me. That is why we had been firm friends at University. Obviously our personalities were compatible, and our Auras met on a different plane beyond physical appearances. I am not saying that we were gay. Far from it, but I think that a lot of friendships work in this way. As I have said he studied Literature and there must have been something of the 'Griot' in him as his poems had much of the story telling aspect in them. Sometimes they were like a saga. We were not together all the time and we had other friendships and relationships with girls, but we met our respective wives after we had graduated. Clarisse and Naomi attended a different University. We never spent a vacation together, and he did not invite me to his Aunt's home, and on the occasions when I invited him to meet my family in Brooklyn he always declined. In fact he was always very vague about his family and I had not known of the existence of his Aunt or Uncle. He always had some pressing business to attend to and now I know that it was true. He was working with subversive organisations and reaping the monetary benefits, and then exposing them. His latest involvement had proved to be his undoing. It had seemed like a coincidence that Hanwell began teaching on the same campus as myself, and revived our friendship. Prior to his appointment in New York, he had briefly held a position at a University in Columbia, and also in Buenos Aires, both in South America of course.

What I am leading to is my realisation that he was a bipolar guy with a vendetta. It was not a religious one in any sense, but he wanted to see justice done to somehow avenge the fate of his parents. At the same time, he wanted to be a part of something which may not be acceptable to the mainstream of the culture he was educated to appreciate. This is nothing new one might say and lots of people may feel this way, but I gather this is why he became a CREEP.

It became apparent that he was driven by bitterness and hate rather than by love or compassion, and that was the source of his strength. Hanwell would overturn governments if he could and it appeared that this is what he was working towards. I guessed that his allegiance was to America where he had found stability and education, but for the moment the international intrigue that had led to his death was still a mystery.

Whilst I was reading, my thoughts turned momentarily to the South River Park on those sun kissed days with the orange and yellow water taxis buzzing to and fro to the Statue of Liberty and Brooklyn Bridge. I remembered again our occasional days filled with poetic romanticism and the balanced beauty that I managed to create within my semi-abstract paintings. I remembered again some of our discussions on Art and Eternity and the Music of the Spheres. We accepted the theory that music is the expression of the Universal harmony and geometric web which we are all a part of. He had a very agile mind and our friendship allowed the creative dreamer within him to be reciprocated as a brief respite from his perilous subterfuge. The spinning, imploding, magnetic and gravitational pull of the Planets, Suns and Stars is part of a harmonic motion. What of dissonance and violence – well - dissonance is still a part of harmony like Yin and Yang, Alpha and Omega? In my beginning is also my end, someone has written that already, but that was a typical stance for Hanwell. He believed that in our Birth is also our Death. We grow and procreate and maybe achieve greatness or notoriety, or maybe we fail, but all the time moving towards our death and the slow return to the infant state as we shed our outer shell passing briefly back through our youth as our bodies prepare to be discarded. The Universal passage of Time is a constant and our auras move in and out of it maybe. Our Astral bodies, our souls as some people say, endure on a different time scale than our physical bodies.

If we strain our ears in silence or through all the noise of the city, is it possible to detect the faint echo of creation? A tumultuous explosion now just a high C. Is it to this that all composers and musicians aspire to transport themselves and their audience back into a harmony with the Universe through a gamut of emotions? To reinstate the balance of our lives as well as their own? There is a theory that a lot of humans and maybe animals have a desire to return to the womb, but Hanwell would say that it is the desire to return to a state beyond the womb to our pure atomic core.

Hanwell was strangely free from sentimentality. He lived apparently always on the edge, where every day could be his last. I unfortunately, or fortunately am not, depending upon how other people view things. I can be quite artistically emotional to the point of tears, or moved to momentary hatred, but underneath I maintain an equilibrium, rather like a sound mixing console which regulates the volume of each track. I see my canvasses and prints stretching forwards like monumental pillars to each year ad infinitum. I should correct that as I move out of this pensive state, and say that now my complacent assuredness has been shattered as I fear for the safety of my family every day. My paintings are now more akin to 'The Scream' by Edvard Munch or the disturbance of Wassily Kandinsky, rather than classical allegorical, 'The Birth of Venus'. I almost feel as though I am living in the grotesque world of Albrecht Durer as I approach my graphic work. I cannot depict my world with the smooth but disturbed dark luminosity of Mark Rothko, I am not as dark in mood as that, and neither do I find myself moving into the Graffiti style of Goldie, or Banski. I guess right now if I have to categorise myself, I would say that I am a Neo-Expressionist.

I am still working towards a new exhibition in the UK as an excuse to see my son and Clarisse, but at the moment I am pondering about Emile Beldossa and the Argentinian connection. Simultaneously as I read through more information about Hanwell Nnagobi, I am trying to be a good Professor, and maintain the high standard of my department. One might say that I was at the pinnacle of my career, as one of the youngest

Professors, but what happened I wonder to the free wheelin' Karma Sutra loving Brandon?

The question which looms the largest, however, is how the heck am I going to become A CREEP?

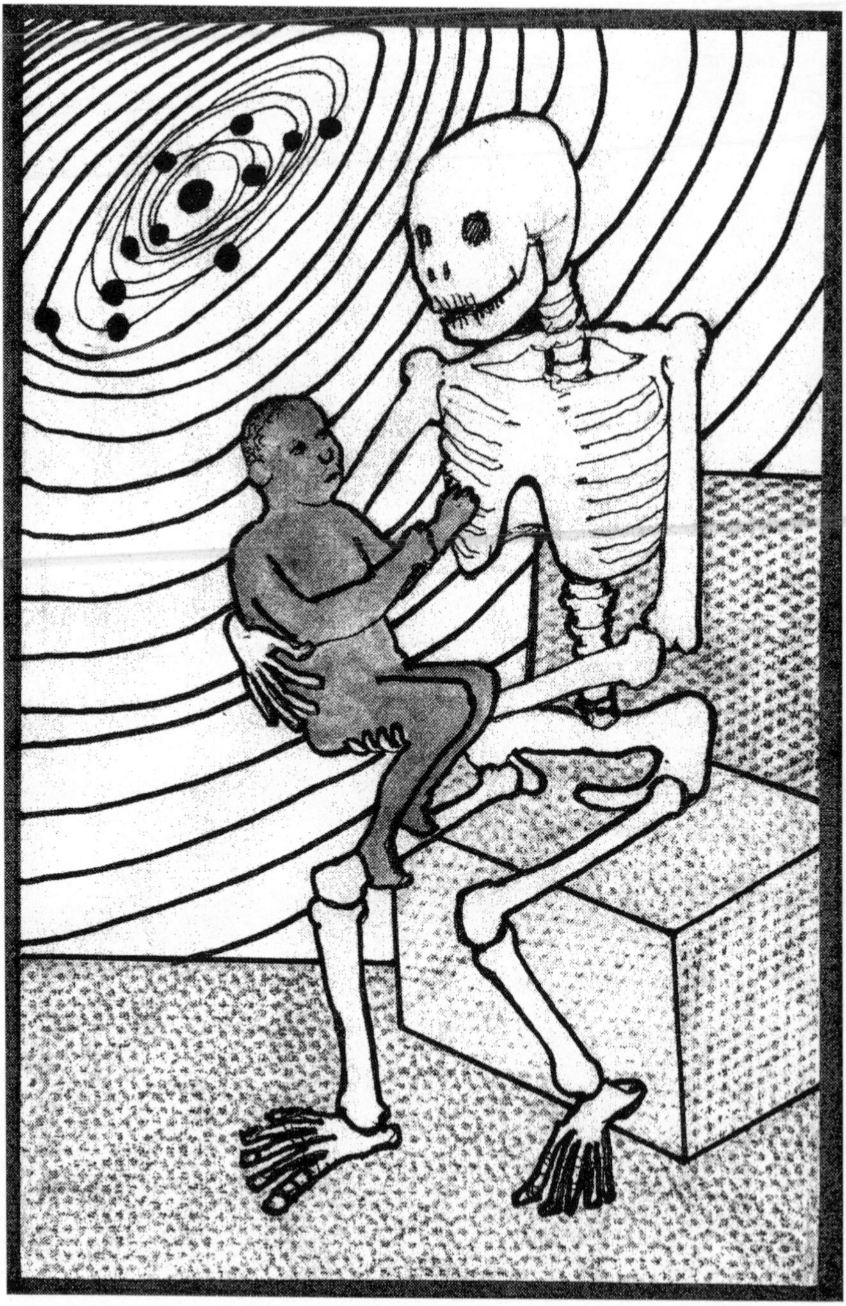

In My Beginning is My Ending.

CHAPTER 8

Masquerade

The most obvious sometimes passes one by. It was the Birthday party of one of Kurt's little friends. The theme was Masquerade – Circus, and some of the small girls were wearing white tutu's and silver and cerise leotards and carrying wands more akin to Christmas tree fairies than trapeze or sash dancers. Many of the boys had opted for a colourful clown outfit with a red nose and some were dressed like Cowboys. One or two children had chosen animal costumes. One small fellow however, had insisted on being an old style Ringmaster complete with curly moustache, goatee beard and top hat. A bubble of inspiration popped inside my head. Of course, I needed a complete disguise to conduct the undercover investigations that I intended to do. It would have to be very professional, with moustache and beard and wig.

I decided to pay a visit to an associate in the Performing Arts Department. Serena was amused and surprised at my enquiries about make up.

"Why Brandon, honey – are you taking to the stage now?" she asked.

"Well no, but there is a fancy dress party coming up, and I really want to fool everyone." I replied ingenuously.

"You have quite a charisma, you would probably be very good at performing." Serena continued, flashing me a genuine smile.

"Who knows? I may tread the boards if the right thing comes along, but I want something that is easy to put on and take off, without looking as though it comes from a joke shop." I continued. Serena laughed, and I had to laugh myself in spite of the deadly seriousness of my intentions.

"Come and sit here for a moment, I take it that you want to cover up this gorgeous blonde wiry hair." Serna directed me to a room with large mirrors, and gently cupped my head between her hands. "Bring me one of those black wigs from drawer 5b, Joanne, please." She shouted.

"That is quite a transformation already." I said almost in surprise, as Serena fitted a wig with tight black shiny curls, which covered more of my forehead.

"What about a large moustache, and a curly beard? They are easy to apply and will tolerate quite a lot of movement without falling off." Serena smoothed my chin gently with her right hand. I could have sworn that she was flirting with me and I began to feel excited.

"I had something like that in mind." I said as the heat ran through my body.

"I would love to attend this party Professor, to see the reaction." Serena said softly as she applied the moustache and leaned closer with her head next to mine as we looked into the mirror.

"I think maybe slightly thicker eyebrows, if I may say so." Joanne said entering the room again with a selection of eyebrows on a display pad.

"A very good idea." Serena said standing back a little. "Joanne is a final year student and brilliant at make up as well as being a good dancer." She added, turning back towards me elegantly. The loose fitting scarlet shirt and matching stretch pants flattered her full and well-honed figure, maintained by exercising at the bar every day with some of the dancing students. She allowed Joanne to gently apply various eyebrows until she stood back satisfied.

"Yes, perfect." Joanne exclaimed.

"Yes, perfect." Serena repeated as she leaned over me again with her breasts touching my shoulder. "Thank you Joanne, carry on with the class, and I will just make a few adjustments."

I rose from the chair and Serena was close to me. Suddenly with our lips locked in a kiss we moved swiftly and spontaneously a short distance into a changing cubicle, and I had unbuttoned and discarded her loose shirt, as she released my belt and gripped my buttocks inside my pants. She sighed as I popped her bra and fondled her breasts. I pushed her stretch pants and thong down her thighs as she removed my shirt. I raised her buttocks as she gripped her legs around me, and I could not restrain a shout as I entered her muscular pelvis. I was almost taken by surprise at the force of her motion. With her lips still fixed upon my own she answered my every thrust and double thrust.

Sweat trickled from beneath my wig and I wanted to tear it off but I could not as I burst inside her as she orgasmed, gripping and clinging to me with even greater force. Our breath was exhaled in short sharp bursts as our mouths separated.

"Mrs Madistone, I am sorry to disturb you, but Dr Foster is here, I gather that you have a meeting over luncheon this morning." A male student shouted, as he knocked on the door.

"Thank you Josh, I am just helping someone with a project, I will be with Dr Foster in five minutes, please offer him a tea or coffee." Serena managed to sound cool and impartial as we separated.

"Oh!" Serena exclaimed in surprise and we hoped that Josh did not hear, as my released penis did not retreat but sprung up rigid and flat against my stomach.

"Well, I guess that the disguise has been put to the test, everything is still in place." I said.

"It certainly is, and I have certainly seen some reaction." Serena said with a smile.

"Had you forgotten – It has been quite some time now, we always had a magic, but just not compatible for the daily long term marriage." I said.

"No, well, yes I guess that I had a little, and I am surprised that you are fortunately unchanged." Serena said laughing a little. "I guess a shower will have to wait, but do not forget to remove your disguise and dry your face on a towel."

"Wait, maybe I will leave it, and see if anybody recognises me for certain, until I return to the department of Fine Arts." I said. The idea came to me also that maybe it would be more discrete. "Have you got a plastic bag, and I will remove the disguise in a washroom."

"Good plan honey, if you wanted to change your facial structure I could have someone practise their skills on making a prosthetic mask, but that would really retain the body heat, and may be uncomfortable." Serena replied as she quickly and deftly adjusted her own make up and washed her hands before spraying a little perfume. "I had better not attend a meeting exuding the aromas of the essence of man." She giggled.

"What about Urwin? Are you happy together?" As the heat of the moment retreated I began to ask the questions which some people might ask beforehand.

"We are." Serena answered emphatically. "But he is not like you, and I guess not being in the Arts makes a difference, but I do love him and we have an adequate relationship. We are mature and a family, but maybe he lacks some of that spontaneous magic. I am still a dancer at heart, and involved with physical expression, I need someone to take me on that level like you always did, like you have done today. He looks after me, and I look after him, but sometimes regulated bedtime sex can be boring."

"I guess that could be the case." I ventured non-committaly.

"How about Naomi, and your lovely children. Three now isn't it. I have not made you feel that you have betrayed them have I?" Serena was suddenly very serious.

"I,- I love Naomi and sometimes I think that I do not deserve her, but in a sexual way I am frequently what some people may call unfaithful. We have good and still exciting relationships, but that is the way that I am. In fact, I think that it helps to keep our relationship alive. I adore the children, but they are the result of my expression of sexuality, so by expressing my sexuality I can never betray them." I was careful at this point not to indicate that the reason for disguise was to try and put an end to the desperate fear I held for their safety.

"Good, Professor Brandon, then it has been a real pleasure to assist you." Serena replied with mock formality, and then added coyly. "If you need any further assistance you know where to find me."

I exited before her, and several people looked at me as I passed on my way back to the Fine Art Department, but looked away as though they did not quite recognise me. Some exchanged a polite good morning, but by now it was almost afternoon. I must say that I loved my short MASQUERADE, and I hoped that I could reapply it as expertly when I seriously entered the undercover world. Making sure that no none saw me enter one of the washroom cubicles I stripped off my eyelashes, the moustache, and then the wig. I must say that it was a relief to feel the air on my natural hair again. With the artefacts securely stashed in the carrier bag, I washed my face well. I must not allow Naomi to know what plans I had hatched in my vengeful mind. I felt somehow as naïve as the masquerading revellers at a Venetian Carnival. I think really that the often beautiful and elaborate masks which had traditionally been worn at Balls, were really to show how clever the disguises were, rather than to really hide the identity of the participants.

I needed a drink as I suddenly felt a little dehydrated after making love to Serena. It had been a long time and it was great to revive the old magic, but then a thought struck me, I had better make sure that none of Serena's perfume was discernible upon my person. Variety is the spice of life as the saying goes, but it is often more prudent not to flaunt it, so I bought an odour neutraliser on my way to lunch at a fairly lively bar close to the Faculty, and sprayed myself fairly generously. After three Budweiser's, a large portion of fries, and an excellent burger with a salad garnish, I was ready to take on the world and its brother again and some students were surprised at my vigour and enthusiasm as I paid a visit to the Fine Art Printing department, and then inspected some of the work by the Painting students.

Several final year students who had mounted an exhibition at a recently refurbished gallery were practically crying on my shoulder, and I had to try and pacify them. A very unkind critic had been quite scathing about most of the work. He was full of praise for the refurbished gallery in part of an older building. He loved the glass panelled passageways with the reflective thin triangular columns which imaged the brickwork of the former external wall. He was enthusiastic about the addition of a mezzanine floor, part of which formed a balcony, and cleverly constructed ramps plus the addition of new lifts for disabled and impaired mobility access.

He found the work of one student who painted on stretched thin cotton bed sheets with a fluid golden and black paint, transcendent and uplifting. It was rather like a stage set depicting mountains and valleys and he claimed that the whole thing suddenly attained a three dimensional depth interacting with the facsimile of a pool on the gallery floor. White boards had been placed on the floor and part of the work was curved to add to the natural sweep of the scene, which was rather reminiscent of traditional Chinese painting. He said one almost breathes the mountain air and wavelengths of light seemed to create a tangible as well as visible alternative all enveloping window of reality. One was momentarily and all too briefly transported into a world of timeless existence. It conveys a breadth of vision and a state of being which cannot really be described, it has to be experienced.

That is where his enjoyment ended. He was of the opinion that on the whole, the building was a more enjoyable work of art, than much of what was exhibited inside it. I quote now from the rest of his critique –

Unfortunately the other young artist exhibits take one to the limits of banality. There were framed examples of old window blinds, and geometrical outlines. 30 metre long sheets of synthetic red industrial cloth from which flower shapes had been mechanically stamped out were hung on the walls and from the ceiling of one medium sized room, creating the effect of an empty tent. Surely to complete the environment there should have been a plain red carpet of the same colour. It seemed incongruous or lacking in imagination to walk upon the polished Parque flooring of the gallery, albeit more beautiful and interesting. We are by now well acquainted with the practise of scraps of litter, or artefacts salvaged from building refurbishments being framed and presented for our appreciation as though they were priceless documents unearthed from ancient temples, and I find that they do not uplift the soul or really provide any social or historic interest. Are they history in the making? I do not think so and they are not of any real interest as related to the history of an object. Will someone come along in a hundred years' time and remark on the qualities of a square of waxed cloth window blind with the darker beige damaged edging where it was joined to the wooden rod? Or will they read into it the abstract qualities of spacial landscape? I think probably not, and although artistic value may be found in what industry discards, it is generally preferable for it to remain discarded, or better still, recycled.

Likewise faint figurative etchings and blotching's on A4 sized handmade paper hung on wire lines as though still drying, failed to impress me with either the draughtsmanship, or the social commentary that they invite us to participate in. We all know the slightly kitsch appeal of work in progress as though peeking into the artist's mind at work, before a final print is presented for our appreciation. Or is it just a case of exhibiting the whole lot of preliminary proofs in the hope that volume will be a substitute and excuse for quality? As one walks

between these varied images displayed at eye level, it seems that we are invited to join the artist in a stand against racism, female exploitation, sectarian warfare, nuclear power, global warming, political corruption, poverty, destruction of the rain forests, homelessness and all manner of injustices. We were warned that there may be images which could give offence and an attendant would guide anyone of a sensitive nature through the lines, so as to avoid them, as the images were meant to shock in order to emphasise aspects of social behaviour that we should seek to eradicate. However, the only offense to my vision was the poor quality of much of the draughtsmanship, whether it was intentionally childishly bad or just lacking in skilfulness. Lines full of normal household clothing might have been a more interesting visual proposition than these incongruous proofs.

And what of rag dolls about one third of average human size situated on chairs standing upon real tins of spam? Inexpensive flesh for consumption like cheap sexual delights or a substitute - is this the lot of the homesick soldier in the trenches as suggested by the helmet? What of the doll on a black swivel chair – an artful temptress or just another routine office snack? And how about the illuminated translucent toilet pan placed on top of a small fridge/freezer - the pinnacle of banality? Yes, we know the process of sustenance is inseparably linked to the processing of waste material, and we do not need crude assemblages to remind us, or is this meant to be the ultimate nihilistic statement about everything? Well, in this case the gallery room in which these exhibits stand, certainly dwarfs their impact and the architecture is certainly of greater interest than the masturbatory and excremental fantasies of the artist.

I was acquainted with the critic, and I was usually impressed with the flow of his writing style, and his integrity. I could see very clearly where he was coming from. I also knew from my own experience that artistic styles had developed so radically during the twentieth century that everything was wide open. How did one really teach, and who was really to decide what was acceptable or not. Even during the long 14th and 15th Century Italian Renaissance, artists were constantly innovating, and slowly extended the perceptions and awareness of the public. The Twenty first century sees the rise of large graffiti works in public places, and natural talent stands alongside that which is trained, and it is also an age when sophisticated international symbolism is accepted. It is maybe a time when the unique and innovative is accepted more than traditional methods of expression.

"Often inferior art masquerades as avant-garde, and eclecticism masquerades as originality." I said to them. "Maybe expression is the only constant by which one can judge. I mean by harking back to the Ancient Greek ideal of 'Man be true to thyself' which was later revived during the Italian Renaissance, as the influence of the Church grew less, you might find your raison d'état."

"I thought that I had." Melanie Wilson suggested to me tearfully. "I think that is a very sexist critique. Just because I am a woman he thinks that I could be better occupied hanging out my washing. I varied the graphic styles deliberately to maybe indicate the mentality of the people who perpetuate the social, religious and political intolerance."

"I know, and as I say, stay true to yourself, and maintain your standpoint. A critic may only give an opinion. What he says is not 'written in stone' as the saying goes, and after all, you are dealing with controversial issues, so maybe you cannot accept a smooth reaction. If you set out to be thought provoking, you have to accept unfavourable responses, and although people may wholeheartedly accept your social conscience, they may possibly find your means of expression less satisfactory."

"I agree, with Melanie, I think there is still a certain amount of sexist ideology expounded by men. The Ancient Greek idealism which is sometimes seen as the foundation of contemporary philosophy with its roots in European culture was all centred on the freemen of Athens, and was not an American woman executed as late as the 18th century for claiming that the American Bill of Rights should specifically include women. The men in power really only applied the principals to one half of the white population." Laverne Mattheson added, with a spark of anger displacing the tearful emotion which she had displaced earlier.

"Your historical knowledge is correct, Laverne, but fortunately this is the 21st Century. It goes without saying almost that I with my mixed heritage would not be your Professor, but it amazes me that in the late 19th Century some women in the UK could not read or write. I have seen copies of the Marriage Certificates of some of my relations round about 1860, and whereas the husbands have signed their names, the women have made a cross, and there is a footnote from the clerk stating that he witnessed the mark made by the Bride. Even as late as the 1940's there were women who had gone into service in a Hotel or into the Textile Industry who could not write their name." I replied truthfully.

"Were they impaired in some way?" Victor Rossily asked.

"No. They were intelligent capable women whom society had failed." I replied. I was surprised by the way this conversation was developing.

"So are you saying that a female should then accept male chauvinism? If so it would be like a black or mixed race man accepting themselves as second class within a certain situation." Melanie interjected. I was pleased that by talking it through, the effects of the adverse criticism were turning back to positivity.

"Not at all. I am saying that fortunately society is evolving slowly and continuously. There is a whole backlog of history and misunderstanding which may still affect individuals. You know – like – is that guy or that woman really accepting me for myself, or do they really see me as inferior? Conversely, do I see them without a faint bell ringing somewhere which reminds me to see them as belonging to the perpetrators of injustice?" I continued, almost forgetting my earlier preparations for my personal masquerade.

"America is a rainbow nation. Nelson Mandela called South Africa a rainbow nation. Everyone can celebrate their individuality and still be a part of something larger together." Victor stated brightly. He had been indignant rather than emotional about the severe arts criticism.

"Exactly, and sometimes I feel that America is the best place to be in this respect." I added sincerely.

"So, what do we do about this guy, this well known, er – critic – I could name him by some less favourable epithets. Shall we write a collective reply? Melanie returned to the main subject.

"No. Let it ride. He has obviously provoked some thought and that is often what critics set out to do. Where does one go? The world of Representational and Abstract Art is wide open. There is the whole of known History to choose from, plus the realms of innovation in the future. All I can say is that whatever you choose to do, do it with conviction, and do it well. It brings back my first point really. Be true to yourself and with a professional approach. That is what will give your work credibility regardless of style and genre."

"Thank you Professor." Laverne said now with her eyes dancing with a merry smile. "I think I can say that you have made us all feel very much better, and we are going to go and have a drink now to celebrate our thought provoking success. Would you like to join us?"

"Good, it is my pleasure, after all that is what I am here for, but no thank you, I have a previous engagement. Maybe I will join you on another occasion." They exited, talking excitedly and my thoughts slowly returned to my intended MASQUERADE.

Masquerade; Birthday Circus.

CHAPTER 9

Déjà-vous

The there was a dank damp smell emanating from the grey and worn, old stonework steps. It reminded me somehow of a dilapidated men's toilet in the need of much renovation. There was an occasional drip of water from a decaying black gutter way up above, and I wondered how my instinct had brought me to such a place close to the Brooklyn side of the river. Warehouses with tall blank doorways greeted me, and the paving was uneven. Although I am still athletic, I nearly stumbled and fell into an oily puddle. I was not among the tenements or offices, though only a few streets away from where two feuding guys had managed to wound each other pretty badly with firearms, and bullets had ricocheted off the walls of the buildings and narrowly missed a group of children on the previous morning. This was not near my Mother's house, but something had brought me here.

I had driven to the Brooklyn Bridge and over it and followed directions which I seemed to sense when I was abducted by my assailants. A heavy gate had yielded groaningly to reveal a fairly large square courtyard with several closed doors and a couple of smaller ones which seemed to be open. The place seemed to be abandoned and yet had a very familiar feel. There were several dilapidated signs advertising letting and buying options. Blank black windows with no glass stared back at me anonymously and others with fragmented panes seemed to grimace as the moonlight caught them. The street light cast jagged shadows diagonally across the courtyard and I guessed that it would not be long before the developers moved in. Maybe there were legal wrangles taking place, as to ownership or price. It was eerie, and it appealed to my artistic sense of drama as though I was stepping through a surrealist dream, and Salvador Dali or Chirico would suddenly step out of the dark depths of a doorway with a sketch book in hand. Lurking above there was a crescent moon sailing in and out of the dark clouds of an even darker blue sky.

I suddenly heard a stealthy footstep behind me and felt the bony grip of a hand on my elbow.

"Hey Cop what are you nosing around here for, they have all gone." A slightly rasping voice behind me announced.

"Stay back!" I shouted and instinctively turned and whacked the shadowy head behind me with all my strength with my two handed reinforced torch. In truth, I had forgotten my disguise and I was quite startled. The man fell to his knees with a sigh, and his plastic cup and old cap filled with coins and some bills of a small denomination, hit the weeds and gathering dust before scattering their contents noisily.

"Oh man, I am sorry, but you should be careful how you approach an Officer, I am conducting a special search. I want to know what you can tell me about this place, and who was here. I guess that you are homeless and jobless, and squatting here." I was secretly pleased that my masquerade was so good, but after all, it was pretty dark. He rubbed his head, and I could see that I had made a small cut above his ear. He was obviously stunned, as he was rubbing the opposite side of his head to the wound.

"Filthy jackass lawman." He muttered groggily, and began to crawl about retrieving his money. I assisted by sweeping the area with my torch, but making sure my face stayed shaded. I decided to take advantage of my advantage, and I placed a black booted foot on his right hand, enough to hold it, but not to damage it.

"I said that I wanted to know who was here, or did you not hear too good?" I spoke to him gruffly, after all I was desperate for any clues, and this masquerade was not a game. But it was suddenly familiar. As unfamiliar as it was to have an unfortunate individual grovelling beneath my feet, it slotted into place, and I knew that I had lived this moment before, or that I certainly always knew that I would. "Them. The dealers and wheelers. I mean wheelers and dealers. I watched them. They did not bother about me an old beggar man if I was passing. If you want to know any more it will cost you. I will need my head fixing. I expect you are a bent cop if the truth were known." The late middle aged man now felt the cut on the left side of his head, which was where the abrasion was bleeding a little as he spoke.

"Do not push your luck unless you want to spend the night in a cell and be arrested for trespassing." I replied staying in character very easily to my surprise.

"Trespassing! Trespassing? No one will touch this place unless it is demolished. That is why they used it." The man continued.

"What for. Drugs trafficking? I enquired. "Here hold this on your cut." I added, handing him two tissues out of my pocket. He proceeded to have a violent coughing fit and at one point I was afraid that he would choke.

"Murders! Murders. You see the end of the street – there is access to the river, and they had a small boat. I have seen them take what looked like a body down there and I have heard yells and shouting like they tortured poor bastards out of their mind down these steps." He indicated the damp dank steps with his left hand.

"You had better not be giving me false information or you will be the next." I threatened, as I released his hand. He rubbed it for a moment and spat out a slug of phlegm into the dust.

"Now sir, if you please -." He held his hand up and cupped it before rubbing his thumb and first two fingers together.

"Ok." I said handing him a twenty dollar bill. "But tell me more and I will double it and leave you in peace."

"Haunted, they say, evil presence they say, and I have seen 'em. Lordy, have I seen them!" He fished a bottle of what looked like Vodka from his old brown overcoat pocket, but it could have been pure alcohol spirits, and took a swig of it gulping noisily and sighing. It had a faint smell of methylated spirits or even something surgical.

"It seems to me that what you see are hallucinations. Now – are you going to give me some proper information?" I answered beginning to feel less confident and hopeful within myself.

"Come down these steps and I will show you where they used to interrogate some of those poor bastards. I expect they were double-crossers themselves." He stood unsteadily, already forgetting about the abrasion on his head, which seemed to be coagulating.

"Okay, but no funny business I will have a gun aimed at your head this time." I commanded as I followed him closely down into the basement. A familiar stench invaded my nostrils and the smell of residual cigar smoke hung faintly in the air. That particular brand of cigar smoke that I would recognise anywhere. I knew now that this homeless man was not lying.

"See here." He said turning to face me with a kind of broken down triumph in the dim electric light.

I saw a hard wooden chair and a large wooden mallet lying next to it with a kind of wooden hand clamp open on the floor. I remembered how that had felt, and I was slightly surprised that my instincts had led me directly here, or rather, that this Deja-vous was unfolding.

"Tell me more about the men who came here. Do you know their names, or who the Boss was?" I asked, hoping that he would give me a description.

"Ah an evil son of a bitch. Smoked big fancy cigars like the ones you cannot buy. He had them all scared. Big men, bigger than you, and they practically licked his boots, like dogs licking a sore paw."

The man stuck out his tongue, which was coated in an unhealthy yellow film, before wiping his lips with the back of his hand and taking another swig from the bottle. I looked back at the hand clamp and recalled the feeling of helplessness which had seemed like an eternity as I awaited the second paralysing blow which would have shattered my fingers permanently.

"How did they travell?" I asked him and I could not restrain a slight wavering in my voice.

"Heh, hey" He laughed a little and swayed holding onto the table for stability, almost knocking over a spotlight which had obviously been used to aid interrogation. "That will cost a bit more- remember your deal Cop, - bent Cop."

"Okay, you done well, but I would have found this anyway." I had the sudden urge to beat him senseless, but I gave him another $20 instead.

"In small vans, and sometimes regular hatch back or saloon cars. Small Japanese and European models. The Boss though, often travelled by boat and entered through the small quayside entrance. He had a sleek little number, grey with black stripes and a quiet engine, though it looked like a hired speedboat. It could be mistaken also for a patrol boat of some kind." The man continued.

"How many were there here." I urged.

"Depends. Sometimes eleven or more. Sometimes four or five. They are not always the same guys. I often saw one guy that I recognised with some others, and one night they were pushing him about and holding him at gun point. He slipped down these stairs and they kicked him through the door. I saw from across the yard from a window, and then I heard terrible screams like a soul you would think was being tortured by demons, before they broke him, and there was sobbing and he was pleading for the safety of his family – they always do. Sound carries surprisingly well around the enclosure and I am surprised that they never aroused suspicion, but people stay away from here at night. He must have told them what they wanted to know because he was shouting and suddenly he was silent, and then I heard the Boss boat leave, and after about half an hour another boat leaving in the opposite direction. The others left in the vehicles, but I think two men took the other boat. I expect that the poor devil turned up spiked on a breakwater for all to see, or was just never seen or heard of again." He looked at me intently with narrowed eyes as he spoke with surprising eloquence.

Suddenly there was a movement in the far corner. I averted my shaded gaze from his and flashed the torch onto a small pile of heavy blue sacks, similar I thought to the one placed over my head on the night of my abduction. I instinctively reached for my pistol, but before I drew it, three large rats emerged from the pile, in quick succession and scurried across the stone paved floor into the next room. There was also a large industrial roll of black polythene sheeting. Then I saw barbed chains and other metal instruments of torture, some of them positively Medieval, in a heap alongside the back wall. I had been negligent I realised, and a trained Police Officer would probably have checked out each corner and each room immediately up on entering. Still I had learned a lot, and the description he had just given me was probably of my friend Hanwell Nnagobi.

"Heh hah, ha hah." The ageing man gave a hoarse laugh and I guessed that if I had held a match to his breath it would have burst into flames. "Just me and the rats live here to tell the tale."

"Okay." I said temporarily relieved, as I felt sweat beginning to trickle from under my wig. "Do you know what they were moving?"

"Sometimes boxes, sometimes sacks and boxes which they stacked in small white vans. Sometimes the stuff arrived by small boat, and sometimes they took stuff from the vans to the boats." The man answered thoughtfully. I was tempted to ask his name, but I sensed that it would be a false one anyway.

"Did you never see what was inside? No trace of white powder or illegal cigarettes or booze, or diamonds or firearms?" I asked, as I moved around him and into the other room which seemed to have been some kind of office. The pine wood desk and drawers were completely clear apart from a few staples and paperclips. There was surprisingly, a medium sized heavy safe which had been left wide open. There was quite a fashionable three seater black leather sofa, which Eric, as I decided to call him now used as a bed. There were a couple of creased up chequered car blankets, and two cushions on it. The white stripes of the cushions were now yellowed in patches and stained by tea and lager. There were a couple of black leather chairs and some utility chrome and ply wood chairs stacked in a corner. Covering part of the floor was a worn red and blue pattered matt. A large brown rat looked at me dolefully before deciding to vacate the green marbled top of a cabinet and leave the drying loaf and slab of cheese and salami and the unwashed plates and mugs. The smell of milk turned sour added to the damp stench, and small flies hovered around an empty Baked Bean tin now full of drying tea bags. A long legged spider ran quickly over a rotting half eaten banana, and disappeared behind an electric jug Kettle which surprisingly still retained its silver sheen. There was also a small silver microwave oven, and a black gas hob, which also exuded its noxious fumes when I turned the valve. A couple of encrusted non-stick saucepans showed evidence of tinned macaroni cheese, and beef casserole.

"Damn Jackass bent Cop, you will not find anything in there. I would have traded it already." The man wheezed as he appeared in the doorway.

"I guess so" I replied as I opened a door which led to a store room with rows of shelves on two of the walls, and a second door which gave access to a small loading bay, and several steps leading to a dark narrow quayside.

"What do they call you?" I shouted as I returned to the office room.

"The only name that I answer to is Eric." He replied hoarsely.

"I thought so." I replied with a kind of expected fatalistic inevitability. "Can you tell me what the Boss looked like?"

"Like a Boss man. Fairly tall and thin about your size, always smart in a dark suit, light shirt and dark tie, and a hat, - a Fedora or Trilby, and shades. He was somehow always in shade, and many of the guys wore cut out hoods over their faces whilst they were in the courtyard, just in case someone like me was peeping. I do not really know whether some of them were White, or Black or Asian. Maybe sometimes I could tell from their physique or the way they spoke, but they did not speak very much. That guy ran a really slick show." Again Eric surprised me with his lucidity and eloquence as he replied, and I was convinced more than ever, now, that Professor Emile Beldossa had been Boss Man of this section of the organisation.

"And what about all this nonsense about ghosts and haunting, if everybody around here is so scared, how come that you are not?" I ventured. I was really curious.

"Don't scare me – they don't - for all you know I might be one." He replied.

"Come now, ghosts do not usually bleed do they or go around begging do they!"

"Well Mr bent Cop Sir, how do you know I am not a ghost inhabiting some else's body?" He answered scornfully.

"Surely a ghost would choose a more salubrious lifestyle if it was free to inhabit living bodies." I replied almost on the point of laughing myself, in spite of my interest in all things metaphysical, and before I remembered the need for tough austerity to carry off my masquerade.

"Maybe you do not know what ghosts really are, and maybe it is for a purpose. Maybe I was meant to meet you here tonight." The man answered as he took another swig from his foul bottle, and then suddenly he was convulsed with a body racking episode of coughing.

"Heck man, I should run you in just to let a Medic take a look at you." I said sincerely, and I wished that I could, as I was genuinely moved by his condition.

"Leave me. Please leave me." He said breathlessly, as he slumped onto his knees next to the table, and I noticed that there were several cigar buts underneath it. I picked up a couple and thought that they may provide some kind of DNA link. I would get one of my scientific colleagues to test them for me, and maybe it would be evidence to present to Inspector McArthur somewhere along the line.

"No! No!" he wheezed suddenly scrabbling under the table on all fours. "Not my smokes. Jackass devil - you do not take my smokes."

"Old man you really do demean yourself smoking these discarded butts off this filthy floor. You must have an immune system made of stainless steel. They must have left in a hurry, or they would have cleaned up better, - they must know how advanced forensic science is, or else they were over confident about their anonymity." I could not help but feel compassion for the ageing squatter as I answered.

"DNA, huh, well I guess that you will have the place crawling with the Force now, but I aint movin'. I came to America in search of a better life many years ago, you would not believe that would you? I was educated but fate has not been kind to me. I will tell you why I am not scared. It is because I have already passed over onto the other side, and I have lost my soul" He stared at me vehemently with bloodshot eyes as he knelt before me almost like a penitent in a grotesque 17 th Century picture by Hieronymus Bosch. His salt and pepper hair and grey whiskers framed the creases around his eyes and his deeply lined face, almost like a halo.

"Here – take another $50." I said, suddenly feeling that it was time for me to make a timely exit. "Keep this investigation just between us for the moment. There is a lot of paperwork and departmental red tape to wade through before anything comes of this, so do not worry, we need a lot more evidence, and this place is just a tiny part of it. I will leave you in peace with your ghosts. Stay vigilant!"

"For a bent Cop you are a gentleman Sir." He said almost smiling in gratitude. Then he stood in the murky doorway as I crossed the jagged shadows of the yard to the high thick gates with fading green paintwork and shouted, or rather wailed, and laughed. "I aint scared because I have lost my soul. I have not a soul to fear for – I have Noooo soul, heh ha hah ha…….."

Like stepping through a Surréaliste Dream.

CHAPTER 10

Meine Lippen Kussen Mit dem Feuer

"Wunderbar, ach wunderbar." I whispered to myself. That encounter with the old man was very fortunate for myself. I had hit the jackpot instantly, and so had he for that matter. I had an excellent salary and so I could afford it and $90 was really a pittance to pay for all of that information. I just hoped now that my instincts would turn up trumps again as the saying goes, although I have never been a gambler.

I walked stealthily down the short street and round the corner to where I had parked my car in another cul-de-sac. It seemed to be deserted. I could her the sirens of a Police car and an Ambulance a short distance away and the noise of traffic on the main road a block or so away, but for the moment the stillness and quietness seemed to still engulf me. I eased my silver Mercedes Estate car over the cobbled street and onto the tarmac, and joined a flow of traffic which would take me back over the bridge to Manhattan. I knew a quiet dark spot where I could change out of my uniform and wig, pack them in a bag, stow them in the boot and arrive home looking casual in my red sweat shirt and grey jogging bottoms and black and white trainers. All that Naomi had to know was that I had been out running or sketching at night.

You might wonder if I had stopped thinking about Karma Sutra in the way that I used to do, or neglected to read the children their bed time stories. True – sometimes it seemed like the magic had departed from life, and I performed with a slight sense of unreality as my quest to uncover this subversive murderous gang became the focus of my attention. It sometimes seemed like I was on automatic pilot as I attended meetings with my staff and studied events and curriculum and yes executed Karma Sutra moves at home. I must admit though that increasingly our sexual relations became relegated to the missionary position. Naomi seemed to be often tired now with three children to look after and her work, but we still managed to have fun and there was not any tension between us. Some people call it gaining maturity as youthful passion begins to fade. I am not sure whether or not I would agree.

As I drove back I was preoccupied by what action I needed to take next. There was a rhythmic savagery growing deep within me that I did not think was sexual. It wanted revenge. Blind revenge. Revenge for Hanwell regardless of what he done, revenge for myself and all the others whose happy lives had become fraught with the prospect of danger at the hands of this murderous organisation. Was I afraid? No! I was willing to kill or be killed. I would commit an action of Kamikaze If I could destroy them. What I was fearful of was that I had begun to not recognise myself. Maggie had begun to detect something. Our banter was somehow not so light hearted.

"Guten Morgen, mien Liebling." I announced cheerily the next day as I entered.

"Guten Morgen mien Liebling Hier." Maggie answered, with her customary smile, and then added seriously. "I have an email from Emile, he hopes that you are enjoying your Professorship – are you or is there something troubling you Brandon?"

Every muscle in my body inadvertently tensed at the mention of his name, as I fixed my smile to try and avoid betraying any emotion.

"Nach all den Jahren, konnen Sie mir sagen, und ich werde Ihnen helfen." Maggie continued, offering to help me after all the years that we had known each other.

"Ja sehr sogar, und zweitens Nein, es gibt nichts beunruhigen mich, Danke Maggie, Sie sind immer ein Schatz." I answered without allowing my smile to waver, telling her that I was enjoying it, and secondly nothing was troubling me, and that she was a treasure.

"Well you know that I am always here for you – of course I am a treasure." She added with her customary laugh looking up at me.

I stooped, to give her cheek a friendly kiss, but I somehow misjudged my distance and kissed her on the lips, and wow, fire! I felt as though my lips were glued to flames and would never separate, but there was a knock on the door, probably a student with some query or other, and we had to separate, as Maggie turned back to her desk. The operatic song flashed into my mind, as I made my way to my office door, - Meine Lippen Kussen Mit dem Feuer!

"Enter" Maggie called, and then with a mounting flush on her cheeks she turned to me and whispered "Meine Lippen Kussen mit dem Feuer, Brandon Liebling."

So this was the culmination of all the years of light hearted bantering. MY LIPS KISS WITH FIRE. I know that she still sang, and if her lips had been any hotter I would have called the Fire Fighters. I ran my finger between my collar and my neck, and adjusted my pants and belt. There certainly was no sense of unreality about that. Hot, hot, hot – Fire. I recalled also the classic soul song by Sister Sledge, - Lordy when they met – ooo-ooo-Fire! Talking about sledge – a sledge hammer - and emotionally I felt as though I had just been hit by one. I liked Maggie a lot, but I had not really thought of having sexual relations with her – or had I subconsciously done so for all of these years?

As I said, it felt like one of those days when I had awakened in the wrong place and on the wrong day. I had no pressing engagements for the afternoon, that day, and so at lunch time I told Maggie that I would be out for the rest of the day. Maggie answered me with her customary friendly efficiency, but I detected new slightly sexual overtones in her body language. She certainly showed no embarrassment at the emotion which had passed through us, and I was thankful because it meant that nothing had really changed between us and I would not need to apologise, or for the moment make any further advances. I think that she had been widowed quite young, and I had occasionally met her son, but she had not as far as I knew, remarried. I began to wonder about what kind of relationship she had with Emile Beldossa.

I decided to take the subway to Brooklyn and to pay a visit to my Mother. Walking and riding without driving, I thought would help me to decide upon my next move in my capacity as a 'Creep'. Everything was familiar as I walked, the markets the streets, and yet it was as though I still did not recognise anywhere. What a strange day this was. Was I ill in some way I began to wonder. Everywhere seemed to have a slightly strange quietness about it and I seemed to notice that more buildings than I remembered, were closed or boarded up in the afternoon sunshine.

Suddenly something hit me hard, and I tasted blood on my lips. This time a smarting pain replaced the elating fire of Maggie's kiss. For a fraction of a second my vision jumped and blanked out as though in a cartoon strip with a speech bubble exclaiming – BLAM!

In spite of this, my reactions were quick and I grabbed the offending fist and pushed it back into the shoulder of the younger man I saw behind it. He already looked stunned at the ease with which I did this, before I followed with a severe blow to his own mouth and felt the softness of his lips split against the hardness of his teeth. He fell back momentarily against the stacked vegetables of a stall outside of a shop, grasping his mouth with both hands. A youth who was with him ran off, but a third lunged for my leg to bring me down, but I caught him also with a swift kick to the jaw and he staggered away trying to stem the blood which spurted from his lips. What was happening to me I wondered as uncontrollable rage ripped through my veins as I turned and smashed my left first into the eye of the first assailant, who appeared to be preparing to launch another attack. He too staggered backwards away from me again, repeatedly holding his right eye with his right hand and looking at it to see if there was blood upon it, and then wiping away the blood still oozing from his lips. I wanted him dead. It was not enough. I wanted him lying at my feet inert and senseless, whilst I kicked the remaining life out of him. I mapped out the punches in my head and was just about to kick his groin and administer a two handed uppercut, when I became aware of people rushing to my assistance. As the young man pushed a bystander away to run off after his compatriots, a torrent of foul mouthed expletives issued from my lips the like of which I had rarely used before. I turned and seemed to great my helpers in the same manner ignoring their surprised expressions. I adjusted my jacket and wiped my mouth on a tissue. My lip was not split, but my upper teeth had punctured my lower lip a little. I think various people had photographed me, as I ordered them to go about their own business and not to interfere with me.

"Are you ok Professor?" a concerned voice greeted me as I continued walking, and a hand on my shoulder. I turned exasperated and ready to throw another punch when I recognised Nigel McArthur, now looking so like a younger version of his father Gordon Daniel.

"Yes thank you." I managed to say quietly. "Please excuse my rather colourful language –"

"Do not apologise, I never knew that you could throw punches like that. It is I who am sorry that I was too far away when I saw them attack you. I will tell my Father, and I can be an eye witness if you want to bring charges." Nigel surprised me.

"Thank you, but I do not want to trouble the Police, and I expect that they have disappeared by now." I continued.

"Probably not, I called 911 immediately, and managed to take some photographs. Are you not aware that gangs have been terrorising Brooklyn recently? They have been named 'One Blow' gangs as they go around trying to knock out people with one blow. I think that it is all bound up with Video Game Culture. They even hit middle aged women. I do believe that there are similar occurrences in London, and other cities." Nigel spoke very agitatedly and passionately.

"Yes, I have seen news clips, but somehow today I seem to be inhabiting a rather distant planet, and I usually drive when visiting my Mother. Maybe that is what I should have done today." I replied with a faint smile."

"If you do not mind my saying so, I am surprised by your resilience and strength, Professor. You are by no means small or skinny, but you look like the kind of guy that would be taken by surprise very easily. It would be a feather in their cap if they managed to down a guy like you." Nigel continued.

"Well, I stay fit, I work out, but it saddens me that one might be at risk when just taking a pleasant walk." I replied. "By the way, how is Inspector McArthur, is he any closer to solving the Nnagobi mystery killing?"

"Dad says bodies turn up in the river all the time, but I think that the Nnagobi file is still inconclusive. He does not really discuss much of his work with me, but he does mention that case sometimes, because it involves the University. Do you know Professor, that in spite of all your excellent tuition, I am thinking of joining the Force after Graduation, and training for the special Detective Squads?" Nigel spoke with a gentle gravity and determination which I had not recognised in him before.

"You are a talented Artist and Graphic Designer, maybe you could combine that with Police work such as Identikit Research." I replied. Gratefully, I was returning to Professor Brandon mode again with a concern for the welfare of my students.

"That is something that I may consider. Thanks, I had better go now, but if they catch those guys, I will be your witness and I expect that Dad will be in touch, I gave a brief description already." Nigel smiled and departed jauntily, with his University scarf slung over his shoulder. I was struck by the thought that there are many thresholds in life and for the young it is often confusing as to which of them to enter. I hoped that his decision would be the right one, at the right time.

I dabbed my lips as I walked, and could not help smiling a little as the thought entered my head that now the lips which had burned with kisses of fire now pulsed with the taste of my blood. I bought a bottle of water from a store, and rinsed out my mouth. Very uncharacteristically I spat a mouthful out into the gutter. Very quickly the stinging abated, and there was hardly any swelling. My shirt and tie were still clean, so I could greet my Mother without causing her any alarm. Naomi and the children were all due to accompany me on the following Sunday, but this impromptu visit had been the excuse to wander a little through areas of Brooklyn that I had lost touch with somewhat since my youth, and I wanted to reassure myself that she was alright, and not just putting on a show for us during the monthly visits. There was something puzzling me. There was something that did not quite add up somewhere since my harmonious life had taken a violent turn. The nightmares, had only just stopped plaguing me, but with my fast track promotion and extra cash, I should be basking in the glow of achievement at the peak of my profession at quite a young age, but for the moment there was something just out of reach. I felt that I should speak with my Father and the idea returned to me again that I would like to visit England and also see my other son. Added to this I was still digesting all that I had learned from Eric. So deep in thought was I and trying to allow my instincts full reign, that I arrived at my Mother's house almost by instinct, and I paused at the front door, as the beautiful strains of an early Beethoven Piano Sonata reached my ears. The early compositions when Beethoven was working in Brandenburg, and very much under the influence of Bach, with almost a Baroque contrapuntal style. I smiled to myself again at the thought of Beethoven almost being beaten by his father to make him stick to his piano practise as a boy, in comparison to my own boyhood when I was eager to learn and copy my Mother. I was a reasonable player still, but certainly no Beethoven. Maybe Father should have beaten us instead of retreating to his study and his research. Still it thrilled me momentarily to hear her playing, it told me that she really was ok. I am a visual Artist, but I believe in the emotional power of music, to calm, to inspire or to arouse, and of course the very therapeutic effect of playing it.

"Hello Brandon darling." My Mother said with a smile whist she continued playing. "What brings you here on a week day afternoon, not a domestic fight I hope?"

"No, I just thought that I would make sure you are okay on this pleasant day." And I could not help adding as I thought again of Maggie, "Apparently Mein Lippen Kussen Mit dem Feuer."

Blam! One Blow Gang.

CHAPTER 11

A Perilous Profession

Hey, you must forgive me. Have I been sexist? I mean obviously I cannot help but see the world from a man's point of view, but I have neglected to relate the fact that there are female creeps out to catch unsuspecting wayfarers and lure them into Police investigation. As one may imagine this can be a PERILOUS PROFESSION. What is in it for them you may well ask? Is it just to see justice done, or does it give them a buzz? Most decent citizens want to see drug dealing for instance, along with other evils cleared from the streets, but maybe they have a secret hang up. Maybe they enjoy the possible dangers that they expose themselves to. Like myself are they trying to avenge a friend or a relative? It becomes clear that my friend Hanwell Nnagobi was no ordinary kind of creep, but when I met up with an old friend who had just returned from Berlin, he had quite a gruesome tale to tell.

Tessa, or rather Fastiotessa Murfurzec had worked as a creep. Actually to him she was always obvious and may just as well have worn a badge bearing the words 'CREEP'. He had been sauntering after dinner one early summer evening in a very popular part of the city. He actually felt the need to visit one of the city toilets surrounded with small flowering shrubs, and a grassed area. As he made his way through the temporary plastic fencing of road works he saw her with feigned puzzlement on her face, as she held one of the rather unhelpful kind of tourist maps. Tessa was fairly attractive with dark brown hair streaked with blonde, a short beige jacket over a primrose blouse, and matching pants decorated with thin black lines producing a check pattern. She was wearing brown high heeled ankle boots. He managed to ignore her as he gained the pavement and turned away from her towards his goal. There were not many other pedestrians at that moment and to his dismay she followed him. Well - who would not want to help a damsel in distress? He would normally, but not this one, but reluctantly he complied.

"Excuse me, but maybe you would know where the metro station is?" She asked, quickening her pace to walk along side of him.

"There are quite a few fairly close by." He replied as he looked at her pathetic map and began to discuss which one might be the most convenient. His name by the way is Lenward Grayson-Baden and he too as you may have guessed has African American, English and German ancestry, and he was born in Brooklyn. Obviously, she showed no real interest in where the U Bahn or the S Bahn were situated. She asked him where he was from, and then if he lived in Berlin. He thought he was going to get away lightly until she produced a bunch of notes from her purse and held them pathetically on display.

"Maybe you know where I might change some money to get a taxi or something." She said. He thought what a stupid statement that was, as the bundle contained Euro notes, as well as notes from such banks as the Bank of Singapore. Whatever other hidden agenda she might be alluding to such as money laundering, drugs, prostitution, or terrorism he had no time to ask, as they were suddenly confronted by a Policeman.

Was she really a creep? Yes she was. It was all too much of a familiar pattern and pre-arranged. The Policeman introduced himself, and of course demanded to see Lenward's passport. Naturally Lenward was enraged at being caught in this pathetic trap, by a woman with a pathetic map and a pathetic feigned plea for help. He was too full of indignation and anger to berate the woman, and what good would it do anyway. Neither she nor the policeman would openly blow her cover. Lenward would not really mind being asked to show his passport to a Police spot check, although hell, the city has a large population of minority ethnic groups and the members of which often hold good jobs in public positions. It is the usual pattern which annoys him, of feigned distress or friendliness which is difficult to escape from. He also saw her as an ethnic traitor. She had that kind of ambivalent appearance like himself as mixed race people often have, a foot on either side of the fence so to speak, if there are still fences, and therefore, often identification pivots on the tint of the skin. I know that this is not logical as the law has to be enforced and the vulnerable have to be protected; leniency is not permissible because someone appears to share a similar ethnicity from a minority group, living within a larger group. I mean, just look - I do not have to remind you of the atrocities that take place within ethnic groups. And hell again, what shmuk would really fall for it if they really were involved in some kind of illegal trafficking? As I said earlier, I am familiar with this PERILOUS PROFESSION myself during trips to Europe, as I told my friend Inspector McArthur. My money was checked for authenticity, and my Passport, and then I continued on my way and the creep quickly disappeared. A creep is a creep is a creep in any language or ethnicity. Lenward had to laugh, because after the incident during which the Policeman was quite pleasant, he found that the toilets were out of service, and there were guys with sleeping bags and blankets preparing to bed down for the night in the sheltered doorways, who looked far more suspicious than himself.

He need not have encountered Tessa, but 'Creeps' often work together, and he felt that he had been set up already by a guy who approached him as he observed tourists posing with the bronze figures of a large fountain. Lenward like myself is a trained artist and works as a photographer, so he is always on the lookout for an unusual shot or something designer, and finds it interesting watching other people doing the same thing. In a very friendly manner the guy with the same pathetic map as Tessa, asked directions to the Cathedral, which was visible through the trees. It was obvious that he understood English, but asked Lenward if he spoke Catalan. Now if I am not mistaken there are factions viewed as rebellious in Spain and something in the implications of his questions alerted Lenward to the possibility that he was being targeted as a member of an undesirable group. Still, resignedly Lenward explained the directions even though he knew that he was being set up, and the guy left him. He suspected that Tessa had been assigned to watch him further and lure him into 'the tender trap' with the Police.

The profession of 'creep' can be a perilous one as there are some desperate characters who are maybe less civilised than we, and the point of this tale is to draw a parallel with my friend Hanwell, and what I may yet encounter myself. Lenward saw Tessa several times from a distance and one day he recognised her photograph in the paper. She had been robbed, and possibly raped, and left for dead by strangulation in one of the small dark park gardens in the south of the city centre. There was an appeal for witnesses – but who is going to be involved with a creep?

Lenward had also written a poem, although he is not a Poet by profession. He is quite aware, as is the whole world, of the shameful persecution of many by a few and the loss of life caused by both the first and the second World Wars. Yet he was moved by certain edifices which still stood part ruined and restored bearing testament to a former splendour. He wrote –

Berlin may have risen up out of the ashes of the Allied Blitzkrieg,
With glass and steel, but its wounds are still open and bleeding.
The gilded agony of your disrupted existence, speaks to my heart;
Your fragmented wound is all the more poignant with gilt edged despair.
You sing still, but your chorus speaks of dust and rubble and your verse,
Is distorted by the everlasting voice of war.
I hear your unworded prayer and though your face shines,
It covers but a doleful deep resounding wail!

Are you an edifice, or a stalwart monolith?
Testifying to the betrayal of dreams.
Or, does your wound lay open,
As a deterrent to butchered folly?

The blows delivered from your magnificent splendour,
Were returned twofold with added savagery.
Oh, is the beautiful new world of glass and steel,
Just an illusionary dream too easily to be shattered?

Lenward might seem pessimistic, but he in fact likes Berlin very much with its history of division now almost seamless. I like visiting my own relatives near Munich, but I must say that I have not done so for quite a long time. His tale of Tessa both intrigued and alarmed me. I know that Eric could sense that there was something not quite right about my masquerade, but I am resolved to continue. Lenward does not have such strong connections with Deutschland as myself. He only discovered that his father had been from a German family settled in America, when his step father died in a locomotive accident when he was 20. He and his two half brothers and sister were very cut up at the time, but he added his biological father's name as a hyphenated name, rather than changing it completely, out of respect for his stepfather who always treated him as his own son. He may be described as a young man living in a kind of void. He lost the role model he knew and loved, only to be told that his biological father was a stranger, and he had roots in an area that was a mystery. After carrying out some research on line he found his biological father's family, only to discover that he too had recently died in a mountaineering accident. What bad luck, he had lost two fathers at the same time. He was still trying to find and absorb some of his roots, and maybe this accounted for his perception and sensitivity. Probably it is why we were already friends as he already sensed a kinship.

It had been quite a while since I had chatted to Lenward, and he accepted my dinner invitation very eagerly. I noticed now that he and Naomi had a great rapport. I asked her in advance not to mention any of our business with McArthur. He had never met our third Brandon – Matteus, but it was Kurt who of course caused the need for awkward explanations.

"You and Daddy are not going to fight are you?" Kurt asked looking oddly at Lenward.

"Why – no - I knew your daddy when we were kids, and we never fought then, well not seriously anyway." Lenward said laughing.

"Well daddy had a big fight and he was covered in bruises." Kurt replied gravely.

"That does not sound like your daddy, he was always too clever to get beaten up." Lenward replied.

"Well he was, and he had to stay in bed, and I am going to beat them up when I am old enough." Kurt answered with great resolve.

"I see, well, I will help daddy too, that is what friends do." Lenward looked at us unsure what to say.

"No Kurt, I told you to forget it. You do not go around beating people up except in self-defence. I have already said that." I cut in sharply but kindly.

"I will kill them I will." Kurt reasserted defiantly. Naomi and I exchanged worried glances.

"Why Kurt? Lenward asked slightly guardedly but curious to learn the cause of his passion.

"Because daddy could not speak properly and so he had to stop reading our stories at bedtime and he could not play with us because they hurt his tummy too." Kurt was obviously disturbed by the results of my ordeal with the gang and a flash of anger raced through my body at the thought of what they had done to us, to him.

"Well that does sound pretty bad, but sometimes these things happen." Lenward answered carefully and looked at Naomi and then myself wide eyed, opening his hands in an inquisitive and yet accepting gesture.

"It is a long story and maybe we can discuss it some other time." I said calmly and firmly. "Now Kurt that is enough, be quiet and leave Lenward alone. Kurt gave me a quizzical look and ran off to his bed room whispering "kill them, kill them for daddy."

"Gee, I am sorry – I do not know what to say, but seriously if there is any trouble I will help. I know a few guys who can handle themselves." Lenward spoke quietly and seriously.

"It is rather more complicated than a good rumble, but I may take you up on that offer sometime." I answered with the same quiet seriousness.

"Brandon, darling, I hope that you are not heading into gang warfare." Naomi cut in with alarm.

"No, but I still wonder who my assailants were, and if they are still watching me." I poured three glasses of Brandy and decided to relate the whole incident to Lenward, swearing him to secrecy.

"I see old buddy that you are in quite a predicament. It seems to me though, that you are safe, because if you posed a threat to the organisation, you would be dead already." Lenward swirled the brandy in the glass I had refilled. "I must say that this is more interesting than the usual after dinner conversation."

"What I hate the most is what they have done to us. This whole affair has brought a trauma into our lives and Kurt is still obsessed with some kind of revenge. We are hoping that as he grows he will understand." I replied.

"I will make fresh coffee." Naomi announced, rising elegantly and heading for the kitchen.

"Why don't you take a vacation? Naomi tries not to show what stress she is enduring." Lenward leaned forward and whispered concernedly. I was momentarily taken aback, but as I said, he is a very perceptive guy.

"It is difficult at the moment. I was thinking of visiting my father in England, but then I was appointed Professor when Emile Beldossa took a sabbatical to Argentina." I answered thoughtfully, and I was still hiding the real reason that I intended to indulge in the perilous profession of creep more deeply.

"I know, but she needs a break, and she will not tell you so." Lenward spoke confidentially as Naomi returned.

"My, that was quick." Lenward announced.

"The coffee was already heated in the maker." Naomi said with a smile as she poured. I watched her with a different eye, and I could see that there was an effort behind her beautiful efficiency, that I had not noticed before.

"I must say that you two are lucky to have each other." Lenward suddenly announced.

"Well I cannot speak for Naomi, but I know that I certainly agree." I replied, and had he not been an old friend I would have been jealous of the way that he watched her.

"How about you? Naomi asked charmingly as she swirled and sat elegantly next to him balancing her coffee cup expertly as she did so. "Is there anyone special in your life?"

"I have to admit that at the moment there is not anyone very special. I ended a relationship about six months ago, and people come and go, you know. I enjoyed hanging around the Schonberg area in Berlin. It is quite Ethnic and Gay. It is in fact a little bit of everything. Near one of the Metro Stations, there is a large Menswear shop which sells slightly risqué sporting and swim wear. Probably the Europeans would hardly give a second glance but in the USA it may be a little controversial for some people." Lenward paused for a moment to laugh. "And on the opposite corner, several er – professional working girls stick out their legs, and wave at passing cars. They are dressed in such a way that is striking and attractive, but leaves no doubt about what their profession is. Night after night they are there. It would have seemed strange to me in fact, had they not been there. So you see relationships of an ambivalent or dual nature are easy to find for anyone who has the desire, and maybe I am not looking for anything permanent at the moment."

"I see, well I expect that you will find someone meant for yourself." Naomi said, placing her right hand gently and almost absent mindedly on Lenward's left knee, before rising elegantly again to refill the coffee cups. It was obvious that she felt something for him. More than she would allow herself to feel maybe.

"Maybe, but at the moment I find that variety is the spice of life, or life is a spicy variety!" Lenward had grown into a handsome guy and his half coy smile turned into a laugh which I knew Naomi found hard to resist as he answered.

"I think I have forgotten what it is like to be young free and single." I said trying to be light hearted and I could hear that my laugh was slightly forced.

"Well, I may be single and free, but I am not so young as you know yourself." Momentarily a shadow passed over him like a dark cloud that blocks out the sun before a shower, but it approached and departed in the time it took to blink, and he was still grinning as he replied.

"I suppose not, but I can hopefully see forty years stretching ahead, and then if we make it we will realise how young we are now." I smiled and yet inwardly my spirits were sinking as I saw that there was an unhappiness about Lenward which I could not quite define. He was wearing the latest New York skinny suit which emphasised all of his fit masculinity in grey-blue, as he looked at his Rolex and suddenly rose from the couch, announcing that it was time for him to leave.

"Oh, - you are welcome to stay as long as you want to, - the night is still young as they say." Naomi said with genuine surprise and disappointment at his relatively early demise.

"Thank you." He said kissing her hand. "Thank you for the lovely dinner, and I must return the favour sometime, but it is fairly late, and I have some early shots to take in the morning.

"I would love to have you stay longer, but keep in touch now that you are back." I said warmly, shaking his hand in the doorway.

"Thanks I will, and remember, if ever you are in a tight spot give me a call." He looked seriously deep into my eyes for a moment, and then his handsome smile was back in place as he gave a brief wave and headed for the lift.

I know that mentally Naomi's hands were caressing Lenward's lean and well-built body, but I clasped her waist and made straight for the bedroom turning the lights off as we moved.

"But the dishes need washing and--." I cut off her words with a kiss, and I could tell that her hormones were whirling. I just prayed that the children would remain asleep for another hour. Her nipples were already like rocky peaks and as I entered her without much foreplay, she orgasmed almost immediately, and then we rolled over and she rode me with an avidity which had been missing recently. My Karma Sutra days came flooding back and I held on, forcing back my ejaculation with my body taut and rock hard as she caressed it like an undulating wave, flowing and flowing and then her head was flung back as ecstatic little screams escaped from her mouth. Soon my body was arched again over hers as she gripped my buttocks responding to my every thrust and it seemed that love juice was drawn from the top of my head and from the tips of my toes, until I sank on to her completely satiated and barely able to speak. We remained conjoined enjoying the touch of skin upon skin as she continued to clasp her arms around me.

"Where have you been Brandon darling?" Naomi sighed eventually.

"I have been right here. Where have you been Naomi my love?" I whispered, and then we both laughed. It was true that we had become distant and routine, and I realised that holding a marriage together is also a PERILOUS PROFESSSION.

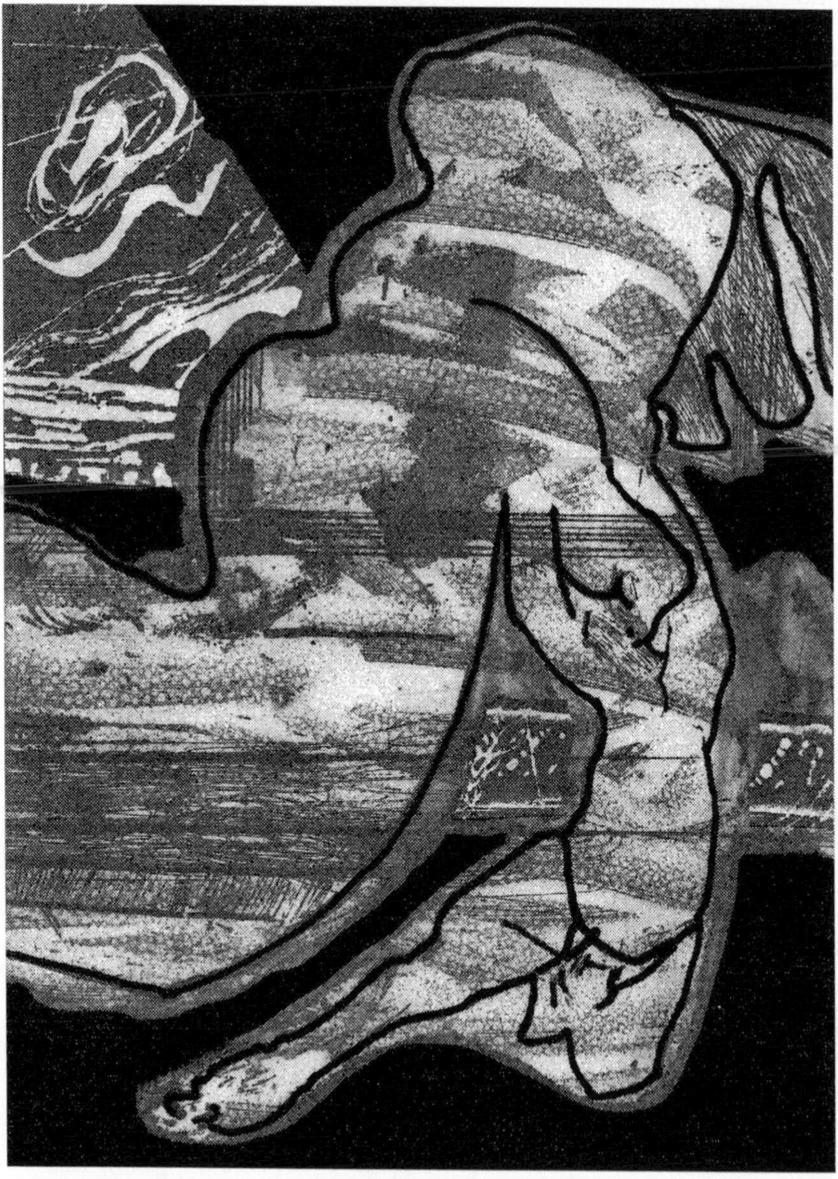

A Victim.

CHAPTER 12

Lucky Break

I was visiting my sister in Coney, and decided to take the Metro instead of driving. On the platform I hesitated for a moment taking in the metal structure again, from a dramatic artistic viewpoint, and found myself alone, strangely alone. There had been heavy showers, so very uncharacteristically, I was wearing a blue waterproof cap pulled low onto my forehead and a brown waterproof jacket with the collar turned up. I wore my black trousers, and black leather shoes as usual. As I turned towards the exit ramp, I was approached by a woman of maybe Spanish descent as her accent indicated, who was dressed in a very plain beige raincoat and black low heeled shoes. Her black hair was straight, and a little uncared for and I guessed that maybe she was five years older than myself. Crimson lipstick added a touch of sensuality to a careworn face. She moved a dark blue covered pushchair backwards and forwards, as though to comfort the inhabitant.

"Excuse me sir, but I have to meet someone at Macdonald's. Is there a Macdonald's on a corner near here?" As she spoke she showed me a piece of paper written in Capitals and lowercase, with alterations. At first I scanned it casually and told her that there was a corner Macdonald's below, and if she walked down the ramp to the exit and turned left under the railway bridge she would see it.

"Can you help me please Sir?" She looked at me intently and made no attempt to walk down the ramp, but showed me the paper again. "Do you know where this place is?"

M ~~a~~A C ~~d~~D O N A L D'S C A F E

~~o~~O P ~~P~~p O S I ~~T~~T E C O N E Y I S L A N D ~~M~~m E T R O.

O N T H E C O R N E R.

M E E T M ~~e~~E T H E R E .

I was just about to repeat myself impatiently, when the altered characters stood out, like a code. ***ADOPT ME.*** A flash of inspiration excited me, and an answering word glowed like a neon sign in my head. "***BABY***"

"Baby" I answered. "This is the right place, Baby".

"Thank you Sir" The woman replied, and passed me a small envelope very stealthily, as she folded the note, and to my surprise quickly boarded the train just about to leave for a Manhattan destination. The dark blue covered push chair was very still and silent, and I suspect that there was not an infant in there, but maybe a large doll, or something illegal. I put the envelope in my pocket and walked down the ramp as fast as I could without arousing suspicion. I wished that I was wearing my disguise, but what the heck. I know the area well, and I did not walk the direct route to my Sister's house as I wanted to make sure I was not being followed. In a quiet passageway I opened the manila envelope, and found a Flash Connector inside. I placed it in one of my inside jacket pockets, and took out my mobile.

"Oh Esme." (Short for Esmerelda), - I said as she answered the call. "Something has come up that I have to deal with at the Faculty, one of the hazards of being a Professor you know – will you all be terribly disappointed if I visit another time?"

"Yes it will be catastrophic, I can hear the horses of the Apocalypse already!" She replied, before laughing. "Of course it will be okay, but the kids will expect double ice creams the next time."

"Thanks Esme, I hear your sense of humour is still as active as ever." I said, also laughing. "I will be in touch."

I was sorry in a way that I had intercepted whatever exchange was taking place, as I liked, Ranulf, Chloe, and Jürgen, and Dorotheen, my Nephews and Nieces. Emanuel, my brother in law travelled with a company as a Constructional Surveyor and so he had less time to take them out than he would have liked, so they always looked forward to my visits. After checking again that I was not being watched, I then walked to where I could board a bus to the Kennedy Memorial Park, where I walked to the closest Metro Station. I did not know whose place I had usurped, but I could hardly wait to return to my studio, and discover what information was stored on the connector.

What had I got myself into now? I was so obsessed with discovering what Hanwell had been mixed up in, that I was now taking foolish risks that might not advance my own cause. My hands were almost shaking with excitement and anticipation as I inserted the green and black connector into my PC. There were diagrams, and data, and times which at first made no sense, and directions. After a little thought, I realised that the information was about locations maybe on the river and quantities of goods which would be delivered to them. But what was I expected to do as the recipient of this information? Was I to arrange transport and gather a team of people to deal with the distribution of the deliveries? I guessed so and I expected there was a team or a gang just waiting for someone to give them the go ahead. This was a quandary, as I made a copy of the information, I decided that I would pass the Flash Connector on to Inspector McArthur somehow, but not until after I had visited the first rendezvous. This could be a lucky break for me maybe, - this could be part of the subversive organisation that I was trying to uncover. There were a couple of days before the first delivery and so I embarked upon a reconnoitre of the designated area.

I exchanged my customary suit for blue jeans, brown work boots a black T shirt and a chunky black windcheater, and a black knitted woollen hat. I felt like quite the lumberjack, and finished my transformation with a pair of large dark spectacles, and of course I had my pistol ready in my pocket. Pistol in my pocket! My own words echoed around my head. What if I had to really use it? Was I prepared to maybe kill someone in cold blood, or maim them permanently? I looked in my driving mirror and decided that I was. Had I strayed too far from a Professor of Fine Art, or was this merely the flip side of my artistic temperament?

Again the coordinates indicated a dilapidated pier and warehouse this time near the Queens Borough Bridge. It was a fresh sunny morning as I walked stealthily but sure footedly over the metal plates to reach a large unused warehouse. There was normal noisy activity in Queens, but here, the sound of my own breath almost drowned out the lapping and wash of the river. So it was quiet and still with the rusting metal cladding now a rather sad testament to former commercial enterprise. Occasionally the floating rectangular jetty scraped upon the four steel pillars holding it in place, and I could see that it was well used. What was I intending to take delivery of? It appeared that money had already changed hands, and the delivery was the fulfilment of the deal. There were many good friends that I could call upon, but I would not involve them in something that put their lives at risk or their families, so if this was a job which required many hands, I would have to bluff my way through without getting myself killed, or arousing suspicion.

Just before night fell completely, when the moon was a faint crescent, and a film of deepening blue still shrouded the stars from view, a small sized Ferry Boat slowly approached the dark jetty on the brightly shimmering water. The dark figure of a man leapt off the deck and expertly moored the craft. He signalled briefly with two flashes of his torch, and I answered with mine, rejoicing in my own wisdom in equipping myself for every eventuality. He motioned with his left arm to another shadowy figure on deck, and then I was startled at what emerged from within the boat. A line of bedraggled and frightened women stepped unsteadily from the boat. One of them was reluctant and tried to resist and the man pushed her so that she fell on her knees with a cry, dragging two more women down with her. I could not believe my eyes as they continued to emerge tied together with ropes, with their hands behind their backs. I could not discern the exact nationality of them in the encroaching darkness, but some were wide eyed with anger as well as fear. They had already been subdued into silence. Some were sniffing and weeping quietly, giving cause for the man to prod them viciously with a stick. After the women, a few men emerged in the same pitiful state. One of them cried out for water and his reward was a vicious blow across the head with the stick.

Indignation arose in me, but I had to treat them the same way as the crew. I motioned to the door way, and pushed the first woman through. She almost fell but continued to the murky interior. They were not migrants fleeing from an inclement regime, but slaves. This was human trafficking.

"Will you adopt me?" The man on the jetty shouted as though partially joking.

"Baby, this is the right place." I shouted in reply, and he waved in acceptance as he unfastened the rope and hopped back on deck. The second man also gave a salute of acceptance, and a rifleman lowered his weapon, as the ferry boat slowly moved off across the now dark water, so gently that the jetty hardly moved with the wash.

Now you might be asking what was I to do with a group of starved, thirsty, and dishevelled slaves. Well, luckily, I had bought a second hand large van. Probably more like fourth or fifth hand. I opened the back and motioned them in. They showed reluctance, but the sight of my pistol, and a prod in the ribs with it here and there changed their reluctance to eagerness, and soon they were all seated on the floor.

"Where are you taking us" One man asked in English.

"Quiet!" I ordered, and aimed my pistol at his head. He continued to stare at me with hatred and defiance, but remained silent.

I drove steadily in the old banger of a white van and parked in a side street close to the rear gates of the Police station where my friend McArthur presided, out of sight of the security cameras. I pulled my hat well down over my ears, and quickly removed the registration plates. There were not many people in the street, so I was not disturbed. I looked like a regular guy carrying out a bit of maintenance work. After wrapping the plates in a black polythene bag, and tucking them inside my windcheater, I left the keys in the ignition, with the back still locked. From further down the street I made a call from a public phone.

"This is a serious call. Please tell Detective Inspector McArthur there is a special delivery for him at the back in Sidewinder Street. No bomb. No terrorist group, but a very special old white van, with a precious cargo. Make sure you open the back, the keys are in the ignition. There are no other white vans in the street at the moment. " I spoke through a handkerchief, but very slowly and clearly.

"Who the devil is this? Chief, Chief – some crazy guy who says he is serious says there is a van at the back---." The desk Sargeant, whom I knew, did not know what to make of my call. He trailed off as someone grabbed the telephone.

“I heard - go and check it out, immediately, check for radioactivity and explosives, take a sniffer dog – who are you?” He shouted, it was my friend McArthur. I replaced the receiver gently and exited the call box quickly before he sent someone to check it out.

I merged with the shadows and wound my way to my estate car where I changed back into my suit before returning home to a delicious supper of Salmon en croute with small potatoes and a mixed salad which Naomi had prepared. Finger prints? No, I wore thin leather gloves when I bought the van, for a pittance, and throughout the exchange of Human bondage. For the moment I placed the plates amongst the objet d'arte in my studio, and I had discarded all documentation. I call it a LUCKY BREAK for me, because I am sure that I recognised the voice of the man on the jetty, as one of my assailants when I was abducted. I am another step closer to unearthing the gang who murdered my friend.

To say the least McArthur was amazed, enraged, and dismayed, all at the same time. How do I know? Well, I bumped into Nigel McArthur, or rather he was waiting to see me without looking conspicuous when I stepped out of my office at mid morning. He was partially flushed with excitement and anxiety too.

“I am pleased to see you Professor. Do you remember when you asked me if Dad had discovered any more details about the Hanwell Nnagobi case?” He began.

“Yes, that day near the market when I was attacked.” I replied ingenuously, knowing already what he was about to divulge.”

“Last night someone left a van load human cargo who had been abducted, in Sidewinder Street. Most of them were terrified and expected to work as enforced labour. They had been forcibly abducted and treated worse than animals, bound together and beaten into a submissive state. Many were not fit for work of any kind.” Nigel paused.

“But who does such a disgusting thing?” I interpolated.

“He does not know. He thinks however, that someone somehow intercepted the delivery of them and brought them near to the Police Station. Whoever that anonymous party is could still be accused of criminal activity and be in great danger now that an underground organisation has been duped and probably forfeited a great deal of money.” Nigel stared at me intently as he spoke.

"I see, and what has become of those unfortunate people? Are they being cared for? "I asked, hoping secretly that I had done the right thing.

"Yes they were taken to the centre and allowed to shower and given a meal. Some of them had not eaten properly for days apparently, but they have no documents of course, and so they have to be treated like illegal immigrants. The guy who delivered them must be very educated as well as an experienced criminal. Dad thinks that he could be someone with a vendetta against the organisation." Nigel remained staring at me intently, and I wondered if he and Inspector McArthur had a suspicion that it was me.

"Yes, I expect too, that it would be a very risky business for someone trying to stay ahead of the Police, and a gang - one never knows who is watching. I mean to say, you could be under cover investigating crime amongst Students." For a moment his eyes strayed from mine as I replied, before he stared hopefully at me again.

"Do you think Professor that maybe some of Hanwell Nnagobi's friends would be foolish enough to become involved and by chance discover some information? If so Dad hopes that they will put the information at his disposal and allow the Police to conduct a proper investigation." Nigel now looked away from me pensively.

"I guess that it could be quite a lucky break if the guy in question could divulge more information which would help to uncover a murderous and unprincipled organisation. But for some people this is what it is all about - mind against mind, intellect pitted against intellect. All revolving around which intelligence will be victorious, besides monetary gain of course." As I replied I debated with myself as to whether or not I would send McArthur a copy of the details I had chanced upon. After all, someone would know now that plans had gone astray and the information may now be useless, or a trap would be set for anyone hoping to intercept the illegal trafficking again, even if the cargo was of a different nature.

"LUCKY BREAK!" Nigel exclaimed and he tugged on both ends of his ever present scarf anxiously. "Forgive me Professor Brandon, but my Father would not call it that. He is mortified that all of this is slipping through the network of Police Intelligence. Please, if you do know anything or anyone who may be involved in this affair, contact Dad as his friend.

He told me what some people did to you, when I said that I had witnessed your assault by a One Blow gang in Brooklyn."

"Nigel, I hold you and your Father in great esteem, and I understand where you are coming from, but although I am still deeply concerned about Hanwell's death, I really do not think that I can be of any assistance." I patted Nigel's shoulder in a Fatherly manner as I lied sincerely.

"OK Professor, I had better dash now or I will lose my time slot for the Offset Press, I hope that you do not mind my speaking to you of these matters." Nigel flung one end of his scarf over his shoulder and hurried down the passageway with his hands in his pockets and his jacket flying open.

"Of course I do not mind, thank you for your concern, and remember not to roll the ink too thickly and to operate the cylinder with a medium pace and even continuity." Maybe I should stick to what I do best, I thought to myself, before I too appear wrapped and spiked on a South River breakwater.

At Coney Island.

CHAPTER 13

Down By The Riverside

I found myself 'slugging it out' as they say, with a guy about the same size as myself with even less blonde hair, though mine was well hidden beneath my black woollen hat. There was a steely glint in his hazel eyes which suggested that he enjoyed what he was doing. There was a scar on the lower part of his left cheek and his features were broad and bony. He wore loose fitting blue jeans and a dark sweater round at the neck. His grey trainers were scuffed and stained. It was one of those old fashioned blow for blow fights, as we stayed clear of any holds and tackles. I managed to keep him at arm's length with jabs to his face and he attempted to shrug them off still doggedly counter attacking and weaving and dodging.

I could feel the blood running out of my nose, but I ignored it and concentrated on breaking bruises out, next to his eye. I was still unable to land a knockout punch, and my lips were swollen but not split. I spat out blood, and he leered at me as he suddenly pushed me backwards, and I was sprawling on the damp key side between some oil barrels which rocked and vibrated noisily. There was a momentary look of triumph in his eye, as he launched a vicious kick at my head, but I managed to roll over and dodge it. His foot sent the oil barrel spinning across the concrete, and into the water, where it bobbed and splashed, before beginning to sink slowly as water slowly entered the open top. He uttered a vicious curse which was cut short, as I jumped up and caught his mouth squarely with first a left and then a right with all the double force which I could muster. I was rewarded by the sight of blood surging from his top lip and from between his teeth. I could tell that he was momentarily disorientated, and that was the decisive turning point in the fight. I followed up by jamming my crimson fist into his left eye and I felt the impact reverberating down my arm as I made contact with the bony part of his eye socket. He took in a sharp breath and exhaled a bloody spray as he inadvertently raised his left hand to the eye in disbelief, as blood oozed from the small cut that I elicited, and then commenced dripping uncontrollably. His partially glazed expression was an admission that he was just about finished, but I had no mercy, I was inflamed. I delivered an uppercut to the point of his chin with all my strength, and the sound of his teeth snapping together was followed by a choking sigh, as he slumped finally unconsciously on to a barrel which rolled sideways and his arms flailed limply for a moment before he lay at my feet on the concrete quayside.

Normally I would have stopped as I felt a heaviness creeping over me, but I took advantage of his vulnerability and stamped on his crutch. The man made no movement or sound as I viciously kicked the prostrate spot, and I knew that the pain would certainly register as he regained consciousness. I rolled him over and though it may not be very effective, I used his belt to bind his wrists, and his shoelaces to tie his ankles. Not a very permanent solution you might say, but it would delay his attempts to raise the alarm, or to follow me. As you have probably guessed, I did not take Nigel's advice, and I had been jumped at the second esoteric rendezvous.

Foolish yes, and as I left my assailant trussed like an upside down chicken, on his stomach, I thought of the old Gospel song – Down By The Riverside. The riverside used to represent a place of peace for me, where I contemplated my tiny place within the cosmic scheme of things; a place where I did in fact lay down my sword and shield as it were. Now, it was a battle ground where I took up arms. What had happened to those days of Universal speculation and the considerations of 'Nobliesse'? I now felt like an animal fighting for survival: grubbing around covered in other people's blood as well as my own, and yet I too found a strange pleasure in my condition. The taste of blood, that vital substance of life, made me hunger for more. It seemed as though each blow increased my desire to receive another, and with each jarring blow that I delivered the desire to deliver another was increased. In fact I wanted to repeat the action again and again, until one of us was totally annihilated.

I looked around me and retrieved my dark glasses which had flown off under the impact of his first blow, and also picked up his gun. I had luckily dodged the first bullet partly because his slight movement had caused me to withdraw and stumble on the step. He was not expecting me to charge him and I wrested the gun from his grip as a second bullet ricocheted off the concrete and hit an oil barrel before hitting the murky water. He had head butted my nose, but I caught him on the side of the jaw with a left hook. I must say that much of the ensuing fight was a much reflexology as calculated blows. As he lay there now at my mercy I aimed the gun at his head and prepared to fire. Suddenly I saw Eric the squatter lying there staring at me.

"So bent Cop I recognise you, are you a psychopathic killer also? What about your cosmic soul? He said, before giving me his eerie laugh again. "I have noooo soul, eh, eh, ha-ha, ha – but I can see yours!"

I rubbed my eyes leaving a bloody streak across them, and he disappeared. The first finger of my right hand relaxed on the sensitive trigger, and I jammed the pistol into the pocket of my black wind cheater. I sensed that I would not be alone for very long. I wondered why I had encountered only one assailant instead of three, to kick my stomach back into last year, as they did previously. They probably had not expected him to bungle my demise. They did not know who I was, and maybe thought that I would be an easy and naïve target after my success with the first clandestine meeting. I hastened to my new old white van, this time bearing false registration plates, and drove out on to the highway. I pulled over at a safe distance from where I could observe the entrance to the dark deserted warehouse car park. A large black saloon passed me from the opposite direction, and turned into the dark alleyway. The tinted glass obscured my vision, but I guessed that the car would contain three gang members wondering why my assailant had not sent the OK. Message. Mission Accomplished. Maybe they had it in mind to question and torture me, to ascertain for whom I may be operating. I held the cell phone which I had found in his inside pocket in my hand waiting for them to ring. They did.

"Hey Buzz, what is happening in there, the boss said that he wanted this done simply and quickly. No fuss. No big disturbance." I was not sure about the voice, maybe I had heard it previously – it could have been the driver. I hoped that they could not trace my position at the moment, and

I listened to his breathing and footsteps as they entered the building and walked through. I had switched on the record feature also.

"Who is there? What has happened? Speak to me Buzz if you are there. "I heard the driver ask before I heard a couple of shots. "Oh no - Buzz, you blasted idiot, I said Sam should handle it!"

"Gods Gus, you have shot Buzz. Who could have tied him up that way? He must have wriggled to the step half unconscious, there is a trail of blood on the goddamn concrete." A second voice said.

"Be quiet, and roll him into the river just as he is, and do not step in the blood. The bloody incompetent fool. You know what – there will be hell to pay now and we do not know who has got inside information on us, McArthur could be watching us right now. Come on let us get out of here." The driver had forgotten that he was still running the call and I was greatly relieved to eavesdrop on that conversation before he ended the call with a curse. I likewise switched off, and prepared to head for home. Gus had probably realized that someone had operated Buzz's cell phone, hence the curse. I would have liked to follow them, but I realised that a large white van would be conspicuous. If I had been a 100% certain that the saloon was theirs as they passed I would have taken the number, but by the time I had located the saloon on my dashboard mounted camera it would be too late to give the Police another anonymous call, and probably they were clean on the surface. The clever boss would see to that. If my former boss Emile Beldossa was also a boss in this outfit, I knew that I was facing a formidable opponent.

As I sat thinking I saw the car emerge from the alley, and head in my direction. The idea hit me, that I could pull out behind them and record the number, even better, I dialled the McArthur's station on Buzz's mobile and spoke the number into it as they passed me. They did not even hesitate as they pulled out slightly to overtake. I was in just a regular old delivery van parked halfway over the sidewalk.

"I believe that I have just witnessed a murder down by the Riverside Warf, the body is in the water---." I began as I gave details of the exact location, and the perpetrators are in a black BMW saloon, New York registration--."

"Who are you? A latter day Batman or Superman trying to do our job cleaning up the city?" Jake Strood, The desk Sargeant interrupted me.

"Let him give you the bloody number. Where are they heading for now?" McArthur had grabbed the telephone and I gave him the registration, and the New Jersey location. I hoped that the handkerchief would camouflage my voice sufficiently. A corny trick yes, and I knew how astute my friend McArthur was, but I had to take the chance of being recognised, and I tried to speak with a deeper tone, and a more pronounced Brooklyn accent than I normally had.

"Ok, let us see the Closed Circuit TV information, and call the cars in that area, and trace that cell phone, this joker was on the level before, if he is the same---." I heard McArthur give the orders before the Sargeant replaced the receiver.

I caught sight of myself in the cab mirror, and not a very pretty one, unless one is the kind of person turned on by dried blood stains and rising bruises. I must admit that I felt myself turning into that kind of person. Thankfully I had some water left in a bottle, and I dampened my handkerchief to clean up my face a little. What was I going to tell Naomi? I had not thought of that. I fortunately heal very quickly and I am pretty rubbery and resilient, so I guessed that half an hour with a couple of packs of frozen peas or maybe a pack of crushed ice would suffice, and I could invent some story of being mugged by another 'One Blow' gang.

I called at a small store and bought two packs of frozen peas and stopped in a side street. With the sun visor pulled down, I lay back and placed one pack on my mouth, and the other on the bridge of my nose and partly on my cheek. As I said, I may enjoy being the battle scarred hero, but Naomi would live in anxiety for days, or maybe for weeks. I lay meditating and changing the position of the packs as they began to feel soggy and warm. l raised the sun visor and prepared to head homeward, and swap my old van for my Mercedes Estate car, as my very British Father would say. A vehicle was never a Station Wagon to him. I wondered what he would say about my changing character. Suddenly I saw Eric again outside my windscreen standing in the street, and yet I could hear him clearly.

"Tell tale signs." He said leering scornfully at me. "Tell tale signs bent Cop, think you are streetwise - but not enough. Blood on your windcheater - yours and his, and have you cleaned those boots? Alcohol is a good cleanser as well as for drinking. See that?" He pointed to a faint flickering glow between the buildings down the street. "You are a Brooklyn boy 'done good', but you were a good boy, when you see those people who have limited choices you will realise how far away you are."

"What people?" I shouted in alarm. He laughed at me again as fit of uncontrolled coughing racked his body. He spat out a slug of phlegm heavily laced with blood, and as I exited my cab to help him, Eric disappeared. I must stop all this hallucinating I whispered to myself.

As I stood in the street a faint smell of smoke was borne on the gentle fresh breeze, and the strains of some inebriated singing. I felt damp patches on my windcheater, and I looked at my boots which bore spots of dried blood. Next I noticed that there was another little store opposite me in the street full of dark shadows. As though with preordained deliberation, I bought a couple of bottles of Vodka. Out in the street again I splashed my boots with Vodka, and polished them with my sleeve. Next I took a couple of slugs, and walked down casually to the welcoming glow. As I turned a corner a patch of unused ground with a partially ruined service station came into view, where five or six guys stood and sat around a large fire singing old blues numbers. Two were playing old Diesel barrels like drums, and one guy was banging two chrome rods together in a counter rhythm. As I approached they commenced a fine rendering of - you have guessed probably ahead of me - Down by the Riverside. I picked up the harmony and slung my windcheater into the centre of the fire. This was received with great cheering and laughter, as I raised a bottle of Vodka, and handed it to the singer closest to me.

They were in fine acapella voice with call and response, which I actually enjoyed. The jollity was infectious, but I found myself watching my garment burn. At first sending up yellow sparks like stars into the night sky, and I watched the lining flare with vermillion filaments before disintegrating into the ashes. I thought how like life. How Buzz's energy had flared up and been finally subdued by my own, before Gus accidentally finalised the process. I was suddenly reminded of a Guy Fawkes Night in England, in London when I was a boy, and Grandfather was alive. The strange happiness and delight of celebrating a potential disaster averted, and I wondered again what my Father would think of my changing character. He would probably relate my behaviour to an artist or character from his voluminous pages of history, adjust his spectacles and carry on, immersed in his notes.

"Hey man, what are you so pensive about? If you have nowhere to go, you can stay with us tonight, there is plenty of room in our house." He laughed and indicated the partially boarded service station building.

"Leave him. The Brother must have had some trouble." Another of the singers said as he took another gulp of the Vodka.

"No I am ok. Thank you gentlemen for letting me share your fire, but I think that I will be moving on again." I said as I raised the second half full bottle in a kind of salute, and handed it to the lead singer.

"Thanks Bro – see you around." He said as he broke into a new song.

I feigned a slightly drunken walk, and leaned briefly on the corner of a building as I reached the sidewalk. I turned and semi waved and semi saluted as l continued with the chorus of DOWN BY THE RIVER SIDE.

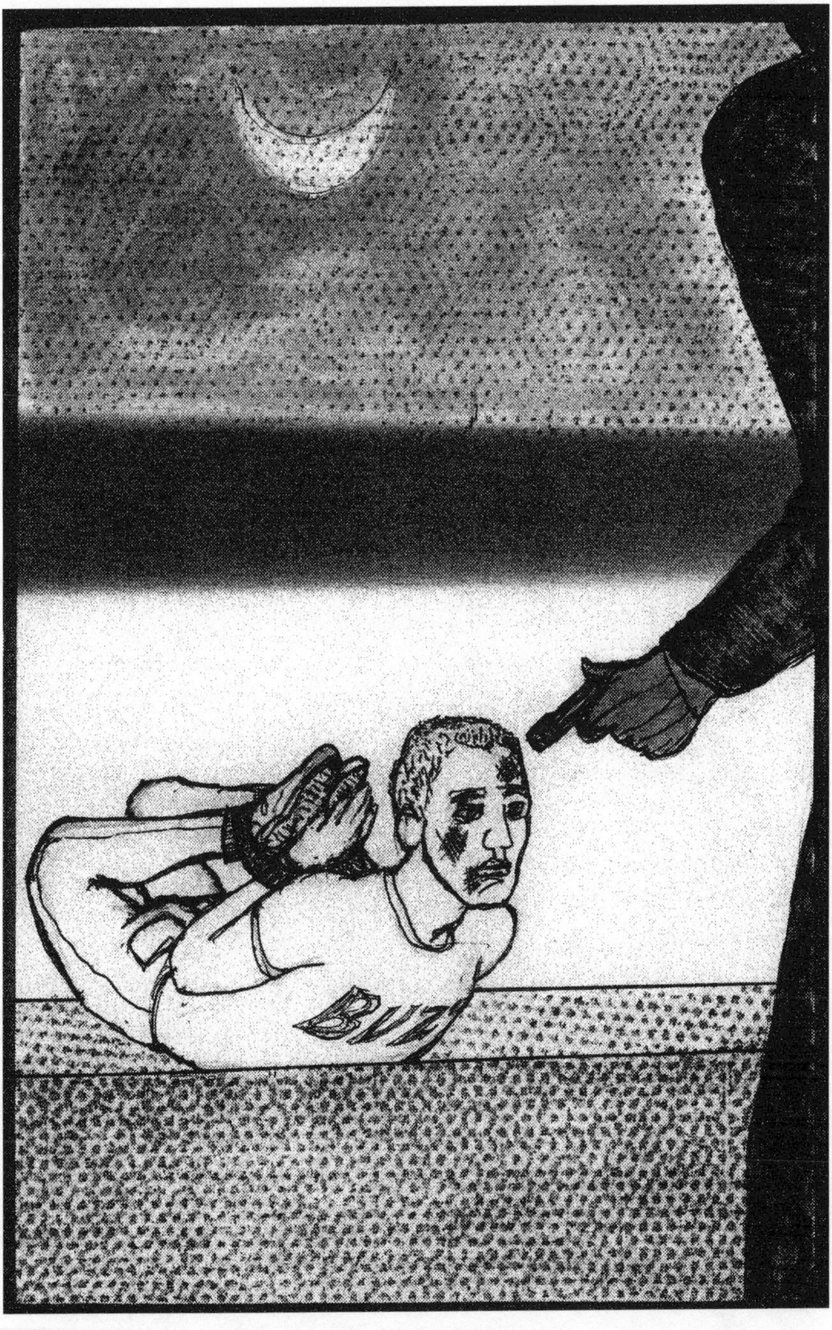

Buzz Beaten and Bound.

CHAPTER 14

Ultimatum

When you began to read this story, I will bet that you never thought that easy going, Karma Sutra loving Brandon would be presented with an ultimatum from his ever loving beautiful wife Naomi. Well as it happens neither did I in those days not so very far away.

It was fairly late when I arrived home, and of course the children were in bed and even asleep. Those days had gone also when they would stay awake for me to read a story to them. Naomi had saved my dinner as usual, and I washed my hands quickly before she served it to me in the dining room. She was not angry, and she could not complain about being a neglected wife, even if some of the fire had died in our relationships. To my mind I was looking dapper, and even sharp in my day suit, as though I had just returned from late matters at the Faculty. She sat with a cup of rosehip tea opposite me and interrogated me with her expression.

"Brandon darling, you have been fighting again. The tell-tale signs are there on that handsome face of yours, in spite of the packs of frozen peas that I expect you have used on it for about half an hour. Do not try and fool me. You know that I have medical training." She took a sip of tea, looked over her cup at me, with her large seductive eyes, but I could see the tension in them. "I do not know what is really happening during these late evenings, but I suspect that you are not dealing with University matters, and I am worried for you. I am worried about us as a family."

"Naomi, my lovely love. I am not a small boy fighting in the school yard..." Naomi interrupted me as I replied.

"No, but Kurt is. He has been more affected by what happened than we realised, and by all accounts he has become pretty vicious. His teacher had a word with me today. Kurt cannot understand the change in your behaviour, and he tries to take out his uncertainty on the other boys because you seem to be missing more frequently." Naomi placed her cup carefully on the saucer as she paused.

"I am sorry darling, but I have had important things to attend to and I did not want to worry you. I was mugged again by one of those gangs going around cities at the moment trying to knock people out with one blow. You know it is quite a cult with following on Facebook and twitter." I answered rather glibly.

"I do not believe you." Naomi stated seriously. It was not often that she spoke to me in this manner.

"You can check with Nigel McArthur if you want to, he was there one afternoon."

"And what about tonight? Was he there to vouch for you again? No! Something more is going on, and I need to be told. I need to know where we stand as a family. I have to admit that I am afraid that someone is going to abduct the children from school, and harm them. I am always looking over my shoulder for my own safety." Naomi was almost in tears.

"Come darling there is no need for you to worry, what I am doing involves making sure that we are free of danger." I said as I poured two glasses of red wine.

"Your behaviour has changed so much, and although the children are growing they miss the security and regularity of life as it used to be before all of this trouble. I am deadly serious, Brandon, I discovered today that I am pregnant again, and instead of being overjoyed as usual, I am seriously thinking of terminating it. I need some assurance that its life will not be a trauma, and I do not relish the idea of being a single mum with four children to bring up alone. Little Matteus has not somehow known the same happy stability as Andrea and Kurt. I know there are help systems in place, I know that I have family and friends, but we are your family, and it makes a big difference if you are going to be around less and less, and maybe Inspector McArthur is going to call one day to tell me that you have ended up the same way as Hanwell Nnagobi." Naomi sipped a little wine, and sighed, covering her eyes with a shaking hand.

"Darling, darling, darling, I promise that we will be a happy contented family unit again. I just ran into a little trouble. I am so pleased to hear your news." We should be celebrating, I said as I moved around and held her shoulders comfortingly.

"You know I have never tried to limit your activities, but I just know that this is not like your usual jogging or early morning visits to watch the dawn along the South River. I am worried about you, I do not want to see you get badly hurt again."

"OK. I can tell you that just by chance, I think I am close to discovering who abducted me, and why they killed Hanwell." I said as I knelt down to hug her closer.

"What?" Naomi suddenly rose from her chair, and sent it reeling backwards, as she broke free from my arms.

"Naomi ..." I began in surprise.

"You blasted fool. I knew it. Are you an imbecile or a Professor?" Naomi shouted like she never had done before with her eyes wide in a mixture of terror and surprise.

"I am certainly not an imbecile!" I retorted firmly but quietly.

"You are not cut out for the Underworld posing as a Cop or a Gangster." She shouted. "And I would not have married you if you were either. I did not want to be the wife of someone living on the edge, always in personal danger, always with the knowledge that I might be a widow at any moment."

I stood and picked up the chrome chair, and moved as if to hug her. "I may have hidden capabilities, darling, Artists are not just dreamers absorbed entirely with creating harmony and beauty, and they can often turn their hand to many things."

"Stay away from me. I seriously have to think about this new life inside me. The world can be a difficult place as it is, without being involved directly in crime and violence." Naomi backed away, and then ran to the bathroom and locked the door. I could hear her stifled sobbing, as I myself sat down in shock and tiredness at the table where I began to ask the advice of the wine bottle. We both ignored the cries of little Matteus in the nursery.

I was tired so I quickly washed my dinner plate and the glasses, turned off the light and headed for the bedroom. I decided to leave Naomi and showered in the ensuite quickly before lying down. I must say that I quickly fell asleep, and I did not awake until morning, just before my alarm was due to ring. This often happens. When I set a time, my body clock sets itself also. Since I was not resting in the warm arms of Naomi, and she was not resting in mine, I rolled over to give her a kiss, and my face encountered only the pillow. I sat up fully awake, and headed for the kitchen. Naomi was there at the breakfast bar. The blinds were half raised and the room was thrown into a dramatic chiaroscuro picture. Her hair was tussled and she looked beautiful in her multi-coloured bathrobe. It was an exclusive designer robe with squares and triangles jostling with each other for attention. It was part of a collection by a textile designer friend Martine who was just beginning to make a name for herself and also hailed from Montreal.

"Good morning my love, you have not been sitting here most of the night have you? I inquired brightly as I encountered the coffee maker.

"Bonjour, avez-vous bien dormi ? » Naomi always reverted to her natural French in times of stress or excitement.

"Oui ma Chérie, mais vous--." I answered that I slept well, but inquired of her.

"Vous savez que je ne l'ai pas ! » Naomi retorted quietly and almost vehemently.

"But why not darling? Sitting up all night does not solve anything. I am doing what I am doing so that we can be free from the threat of danger." I said placing an arm around her comfortingly.

"Vous serez – you will have to do the school run, I do not feel very well, I have not decided what to do about this baby yet." Naomi pulled the bathrobe around herself tightly. "I do not think I can live normally under these conditions. Supposing that there is a gunman attack, not only us but other children and parents could be massacred."

"But my love, that could happen anyway, without it having anything to do with us, and wherever we are, we could be targeted until this undercover organisation is fully exposed." I poured my coffee and found a quason before sitting next to her.

"Tu aimes ça. Vous êtes en train de devenir un voyou." Naomi stated tearfully.

"Non, peut-être bien que je fais, je suis peut-être-> » I toyed with the thought.

"Oui, yes you do. You are turning into someone like they are. You enjoy it." Naomi repeated.

"Mummy what is for breakfast?" Andrea wandered into the kitchen and cut our conversation short.

"I do not know honey, big thug Daddy is making it today and taking you to school before he goes off to gang warfare." I could not help but smile broadly as Naomi delivered this statement with deep felt gravity, although it was not intended to be the least bit amusing.

"What do you mean Mummy?" Andrea asked innocently.

"You had better ask Slugger Brandon, I am going to lie down, and I do not want to be disturbed." Naomi was certainly driving her point home, certainly underlining what amounted to an ULTIMATUM, but one that was impossible to meet until everything was resolved.

"Daddy ..?" Andrea began in wide eyed amazement; her Mother did not usually behave in this manner.

"You will have to be a big girl today." I said picking her up and twirling her around as I often did. "Mothers sometimes are unwell like Daddies, and need to be looked after for a change, so what shall we have – I know – microwaved egg on toast sprinkled with mixed herbs and a little black pepper.

"Are you going to have that too?" Andrea asked a little uncertainly.

"Yes, certainly." I said very enthusiastically, as I sat her down with a small bowl of muesli and milk to begin with.

"Where is Mummy? Why are you making breakfast today?" Kurt inquired as he entered already dressed, apart from his shoes and blazer.

"Mummy is not feeling very well today, so you have to be good and let her rest. Come and start on your cereal, and then I will be taking you to school after breakfast. As I quickly prepared the eggs and toast, I considered Naomi's last remark – Slugger Brandon. I must admit that I relished the idea.

Little Matteus rattling the bars of his play pen brought me out of the short reverie, and I gathered him up, realising that there was a diaper to change. Okay, so that done he started whimpering for his breakfast and also because his teeth were appearing painfully. I sat him in the high chair in the kitchen and mashed up some banana in milk with some softened flakes of cereal, and a hard wholemeal cookie to bite on. I poured fresh orange juice for the other two, but of course Matteus knocked his cup on to the floor where it bounced and spilled as the lid came off. No matter, it was only a small amount, and mopped up very quickly.

"Right, are we all ready? I inquired when all the food seemed to be consumed and lunch boxes were found in the refrigerator. I checked to see what was in them, as I realised that I did not have a clue, and I may have to prepare them in the evening. I picked up Matteus and began to move from the kitchen to be greeted by curious smiles and then laughter from Kurt as Andrea whispered to him.

"What is it now?" I enquired flatly.

"You have your bathrobe on, and no shoes, are you driving us like that? Andrea blurted out as she stifled another laugh.

I looked down at myself, I had completely forgotten that I was not dressed, and I laughed too. I put Matteus back in the high chair, which made him wail, and opened the bedroom door quietly, Naomi was actually asleep, and I quickly donned my suit, shirt and tie and socks without awakening her. I found my shoes by the door and picked up Matteus again, allowing him to continue wailing as we headed for the elevator.

We took Naomi's car as there was a baby chair attached to the back seat. It seemed as though Matteus really missed his mother, and continued to wail intermittently throughout the journey. I waited until Andrea and Kurt were safely in the compound, and then walked back to the car. Matteus was finally dozing and so I decided to call in at the Faculty.

"Ach little Liebling, may I? Und kinder facsimile of you Brandon Liebling." Maggie rose from her desk elegantly, and nursed Matteus who actually smiled for the first time since the previous day.

"Maggie, my Liebling, you certainly may - I find myself compromised today." I answered brightly, but I was really relieved.

"Ach, not a domestic fight I hope. There, there, mien kinder, how can your Mutter let you go? Maggie was genuinely enthralled, and I felt my blood heating at the sexual appraisal for me in her eyes.

"No not really, Naomi is just feeling a little nervous strain. I will just check a few things. I may have to leave everything until tomorrow." I answered trying to sound casual.

"I can look after this little darling until lunch time. There –." So saying Maggie arranged the cushions and a cover on one of the leather arm chairs and laid Matteus in it. He stood up and clung to the back of the chair smiling and happier than I had seen him look for days.

"Well Maggie Liebling, you are a treasure, where would I be without you." I said as I entered my office. "I will just cancel any afternoon appointments."

"Danke Brandon Liebling, it is my pleasure." Maggie replied, as she checked for signs of a diaper in need of a change. "I will ask Yvonne to pop to the store and buy some diapers."

"Diapers are only a precaution, he is due to attend the Early Learning Centre, Naomi has been toilet training him, and he walks quite well. He can ask for the restroom. I think we may have been taking the transition from Baby to Infant a little slowly." I hastened to explain.

"No, nonsense, they grow up so quickly these days, if you rush him he may always feel insecure. He will not be any trouble at all." Maggie replied like a doting grandmother.

I had some minor business to attend to, and then an assessment after the mid-morning break. I called at the refectory for a coffee, and literally bumped into Nigel McArthur on his way out.

"Oops sorry Professor." He said as he readjusted his scarf. "Do you have a moment please?"

"Yes, have you had coffee or—will you join me, I really need some refreshment." I replied pleasantly.

"Er yes, but yes thank you I could have a still orange juice. Dad has had a breakthrough with the Hanwell Nnagobi case you will be pleased to hear. He is delighted, at least he thinks that he has made great headway. Last night an anonymous caller gave him the location of a crime scene and the number of a car with three suspects in it. The descriptions were so accurate, that they found the location down by the Riverside again, and they saw fresh blood stains on the quayside. Dad ordered a couple of divers to search, and they found a body not long dead. The guy had been beaten up a bit, and tied up with his own belt and shoelaces, but it was a shot to the head which had killed him and his body had caught on some iron bars and debris, so the current had not carried the body away. He has been identified as a known criminal guilty of GBH and Extortion." Nigel related this quickly and excitedly before he paused.

"This is great news, I mean for the case, but how does that relate to -?" Nigel interrupted impatiently.

"They traced the car, the Squad Cars traced the car, but they followed it – er Undercover Cars did, to a private address in New Jersey. The registration plates had been subtly changed and the front and back were different from each other. They met some gunfire, but back-up surrounded the house, and the Police gave the inhabitants an ULTIMATUM."

"Come out with your hands above your head and--." I began in anticipation.

"Too right. Hands above your head and first throw all weapons down. Dad says that he even had elite marksmen on the roof in case a gunman appeared behind the others. You get the picture. The men in front suddenly fall down, and the gunman comes out blasting with the latest automatic gun." Nigel could hardly speak the words fast enough.

"Yes, but that did not happen, and guess what? They are all wanted men who have managed to slip through the net and a couple of women who have been previously convicted of minor crimes." Nigel gulped down his orange juice, and looked around furtively.

"But how does this relate to the Nnagobi case?" I asked because I wanted to secretly be certain that my hunch was correct.

"In the basement they found quite a large number of illegal immigrants who had all been forcibly abducted and treated very badly like the ones that Dad found in the van the other night. The suspects are part of a human trafficking syndicate and make a lot of money from buying and selling forced labour. The immigrants are often too frightened to tell anyone, or sometimes are not educated very well. Dad thinks that Nnagobi acted as an interpreter and operations liaison officer, and was planning to expose the whole international operation when he had enough evidence. I mean not just operations in the USA, but Africa, India, maybe South America and the UK too. Probably many more countries are involved."

"I see. This is amazingly fast work all at once, was Dad at work all night?" I asked ingenuously.

"Almost, but the great thing is that Dad let me go with the Police photographer to the house siege. Like you suggested, he is going to let me combine my artistic talents with Police work. I was wearing bullet-proofs and a helmet, I would not have recognised myself." Nigel finally came to a halt.

"I am really grateful to you for telling me all this, it helps to put my mind at rest." I said sincerely.

"Yes well I know that you are kind of involved and a victim yourself, but this is all confidential you realise." Nigel lowered his voice even more. "Whoever the present informer is must be very clever, and Dad thinks he is also very foolhardy but needless to say he is ultimately grateful. Just a few clues can lead to an extensive plot being unravelled. Dad says that even though this anonymous guy has exposed so much, he would give him an ULTIMATUM too. To quit whilst he is ahead, or run the risk of being charged as an accomplice, the moment he gets careless."

Police Raid.

CHAPTER 15

Contacts

"I am forever indebted to you, really, and I hope that I do not need to impose upon you again Maggie Liebling."

"Absolutely no trouble, I have raised babies of my own you know, and it is lovely to take care of yours. I have no grandchildren to cosset and pamper and little Matteus is adorable." Maggie was positively glowing.

"You look too young to be Grandmother, but they would be very lucky children." I actually meant this although it may sound like a terrible patronising cliché, and Maggie was obviously very pleased, as she handed Matteus to me, and I exited the office in time to pick up Andrea and Kurt from school. I had not telephoned Naomi, I thought it best to leave her, and I had not yet decided on my plan of action. Although the Police were on top of this case, there was still somethings I felt that I needed to do.

When we reached the apartment I had a feeling that something was wrong when I saw a fleeting image of Eric at the end of the passageway.

"What is wrong Daddy? What were you looking at?" Andrea picked up on my fleeting sixth sense.

"Nothing my little angel, I am just a little tired, I was working late last night." I smiled, and she jumped up and down impatiently as I with unusual nervousness fumbled with the locks.

"High Mommy, we are home." Andrea shouted as she ran into the quiet kitchen, and the small room where she worked, and then with mounting distress into our bedroom. Finally she flung open the family bathroom door, before the realisation hit her that Naomi was not there.

Now at this point you may have expected Andrea to burst into tears. No, she stood with a look of utter devastation on her face, and her mouth open, trying to formulate words and look for reasons in her head. I had been close behind her but the half closed blinds, and the fact that all the lamps were switched off told the whole story.

Kurt had been more thorough and inspected the nursery and their bedrooms and our ensuite before running back to the dining/living room area. He would have checked my studio, if it were not for the fact that I keep it locked.

"Mummy has gone!" He shouted.

"Maybe she is just out shopping," I lied.

"No! She has gone, because the little case that she always takes on vacation has gone from the top shelf of the wardrobe where her shoes are stored." Kurt looked alarmed and then added, "Will you be able to make dinner today?"

I placed Matteus in the pen with his toys, after a day with Maggie effusing over him he seemed not to mind whilst he chewed on a rubber ring and banged a rubber hammer on the large resilient keys of a small xylophone. I must say that I felt as stunned as Andrea, who now clung to me as I walked back to the kitchen.

"Have we all been too naughty, or has someone taken her away?" Andrea asked before sitting at the breakfast bar. "I want my M O M M Y she suddenly cried piercingly. Mommy where are you?" She shouted, before bursting out in hysterical tears.

"Do not cry darling I said, there is a perfectly logical explanation." All kind of emotions ran through me as I opened the refrigerator to administer orange juice or milk, and lager, and then, - there was a note from Naomi stuck to the milk carton. It was just a simple pink sticky note written in her neat handwriting.

I am very sorry Brandon, Andrea, Kurt, and Matteus, but I have gone to visit my sister in Montreal, I need a break, I need a bit of space. I will call. Love – Naomi, (Mommy).

I remembered what my friend Lenward Grayson-Baden had said to me, quite a while ago.

"I can see what a strain Naomi is under, although she tries to hide it, you should take a vacation."

I had meant to take more notice of her needs, but somehow I had had been too caught up in playing the Sleuth. I was not playing. It was very serious business indeed, but somehow for her, things had never been the same since Inspector McArthur's first visit, even though it was on a friendly basis. I nearly dropped the milk as a shock reaction, even though the warning signs had been obvious, and now with the pregnancy playing havoc with her hormones matters had been brought to a head. I banged my fist on the table, which was not the right thing to do I know, and Kurt copied me. It just made Andrea wail even louder.

"Stop crying, you are not a baby now!" I shouted, and then I hugged her tightly. "Mommy has just gone to see Aunt Dessi in Montreal, she is going to call us later. I expect that she just forgot to tell you."

Andrea did not reply, but sipped her milk slowly.

"I want to go to Montreal." Kurt announced as he took huge gulps from his glass. I could not be bothered to fiddle with the bottle opener, so I poured a glass of red wine. The Shiraz tasted good, and I drank half a large glass before answering.

"We will all go sometime. Aunt Desdomona is always inviting us to stay." I said as I took off my jacket and focussed on what dinner was going to be. I was already planning the next day. I would take Matteus to the nearby crèche, do the school run, and end my day early to pick them up in the afternoon. I could call on friends to help, but that was my immediate solution.

"Go and watch your TV programmes as usual" I said, but Kurt was already half way there, and I saw Andrea beginning to accept the situation. I suddenly heard the ringing of a mobile in the studio, and I ran to answer it, unlocking the door quickly. I knew what it was. I still had Buzz's telephone. I reached it just in time.

"Hey Buzz, buddy, why the silence, you are not holding out on me are you?" It was a deep male voice. "You better be there tonight, or Amanda may receive a surprise gift. You might say that it will cost a bomb. He rung off abruptly. Obviously the owner of the voice was not aware of Buzz's demise.

"Was that Mommy?" Andrea stood at the studio door inquisitively.

"No darling, it was just a friend" I said, placing the phone in a desk drawer.

"Why do you keep a cell phone in here?" Andrea continued.

"Oh, it is just for one or two friends that I talk to separately." I answered impatiently, before she ran off back to the TV programme, when Kurt called that she was missing some of the comedy action.

I had meant to send the phone to McArthur, but there was still some traces of my bloody fingerprints on it. The Police had already identified Buzz, and arrested Gus and his colleagues, so they did not need to hear the recorded evidence. So, anyway, I resolved to clean it with water, a degreasing agent, and alcohol, and send it to him. I would first make a list of any contacts, but wait a moment a voice inside me demanded, maybe you can still make more use of it than McArthur. How was I to save Amanda? I hit upon another bold plan that would involve the Police believing yet another anonymous call. I realised that I was really pushing things, but I sent a text to a contact number that had called, attributed to the name of Des.

"Hi Des. Sorry about the silence, things have been a bit sticky. Please meet me by the park gate in Canal Warf Street, tomorrow about 10pm."

"What is this all about, just a trick to save sweet Amanda? The answer came back faster than I had expected.

"OK. You name a new time and place." I answered.

"Bull shit! The place where we always meet is the best, down on the disused boardwalk near the end of Commercial Street. Opposite the island, you know, Staten, the Western Reach not far from Bayonne Bridge, at eleven on the dot. And Buzz buddy - any funny business, and you know where you will end up."

It worked. Des had given me the meeting place. Now all I had to do was convince McArthur to mobilise his men again.

"Daddy when is our dinner going to be ready?" Kurt stood at the door.

"In a minute big fella we are all going to have pizza." I replied.

"Wool! Pizza tonight." He ran back shouting to Andrea. "Pizza tonight".

I took a chance on not being recognised or tracked and called the Police Station, whilst rubbing a sheet of A4 paper on the back of the mobile.

"Hello." I said in the voice of my character. "This is serious - you can apprehend a terrorist, probably armed and dangerous –"

"It's the blasted 'Faceless Crusader' again." The desk Sargeant cut in.

"Get a fix on that call-." McArthur shouted. I gave them the location where Buzz was supposed to be meeting Des and ended the call quickly. I scrolled down the list of contacts and of course Amanda was near the top, I hoped that I could be convincing with her, without causing her to Panic.

"Amanda honey I am a friend of Buzz, and he cannot call right now, but you are in danger. Is there a friend or relative you can stay with tonight and maybe for a few days, and if you receive any packages do not open them. Do not panic, but this is serious." I intoned deeply, but not as deeply as Des.

"The cunning jerk off. Have you killed him or something? He deserves it sooner or later. He owes me, he owes everybody -." She suddenly faltered into heavy sobs. "Poor Buzz I know he must be dead and I will never see him again, I will never feel-."

"Sorry honey, I really am, but if things go wrong tonight and even if they don't you could be in danger because he obviously loved you." I continued emphatically.

"What did you kill him for? You bastard. Who are you?" Amanda shrieked down the line.

"I did not kill him. Someone else did accidentally, and now please take this warning seriously or you could be in line for a payback, from guys who think they have been double crossed." I switched off, and could not help feeling a moment of intense sorrow. Speaking to Amanda made me realise more fully how Naomi felt. I could empathise more accurately with her anguish and her desire not to be forced to live on the edge as the case might be.

During the fracas of the previous evening with Naomi I had neglected to deal with Buzz's cell phone, and now I was uncertain of my next step. Things were certainly moving fast. Like Nigel said, one small clue could unravel a whole chain of events. I was startled by the landline suddenly ringing, Andrea and Kurt rushed to it immediately.

"It's Mommy." Andrea shouted excitedly. She began to relate small incidents from her day, before asking when Naomi would be returning. "Why not tomorrow" She replied very sadly, before handing the handset to Kurt. Andrea then ran to her bedroom and began crying, and I realised that it was the first time she had been separated from her Mother completely,

I somehow had never really thought about that before. Whilst Kurt was also speaking excitedly, I used my own cell phone to order the pizza, before taking my turn to speak to my wife.

"Bon nuit Cherie" I answered as Naomi reverted to her natural French as she greeted me. I wanted to yell and entreat and even get down on my knees, like the old Righteous Brothers hit record of the 1960's that my Aunt Elsa-Mae used to play – 'You've lost that loving feeling' etc. But I maintained my cool. A wife who would even leave her toddler behind, still in diapers, must be seriously stressed out. This was something I had not foreseen. Naomi had always seemed so strong.

"My darling, I hope that you will make the right decision and keep our fourth child, but take some time with Dessie; we all miss you so much already but with a bit of help here and there we will try and muddle through until you return." I spoke quietly, and persuasively, but I was greeted by slightly hysterical crying.

"Brandon, this is not a good time. Don't worry I will be giving plenty of big sisterly advice, so if you can hold things together, Hubert and I will hopefully have Naomi back on track very soon." Dessie had a slight hint of French in her accent and one of those soft but reassuringly strong voices that one could listen to all day without being bored. She was not a smoker, and not asthmatic, but there was a slight break in her voice occasionally giving way to a natural hoarseness.

"Ok. Thank you Dessie, and Hubert. I am sorry that we have imposed on you. Situations arise and escalate and sometimes one is not really sure how they do. I will call tomorrow. Bon nuit."

A ringing of the doorbell, and a simultaneous wail emitting from the nursery caused a minor diversion. Kurt and Andrea ran for the door, and I ran to attend to Matteus, who was also hungry and probably very wet. The kind administrations of Maggie had obviously worn off and now he was missing Naomi too. Kurt ran back to the Nursery for money to pay for the Pizza, and to my surprise Andrea placed the box carefully on the table and began sorting out knives and forks. By the time I had changed Matteus she had arranged three plates and tumblers, and carefully placed a milk carton on the table. I thanked her and kissed her before dividing up the veritable feast complete with a coleslaw and a potato salad. I poured myself a glass of Shiraz and momentarily normality was restored, as Matteus in his high chair gurgled and splatted with his carrot and beef baby food and small cubes of Pizza. It was late in the evening by now, and Kurt and Andrea were obviously tired. I was going to comfort them with a story, but they both fell asleep after a goodnight kiss, I think that they were kind of emotionally exhausted, especially Andrea. I cleared the table as I often did and washed the dishes, as the dishwasher had not been emptied, and I decided to leave it until the morning. I think that I was maybe in a kind of automatic daze, half expecting to see Naomi in the background somewhere checking the ingredients for tomorrows dinner, or to see her emerge from her room having just completed a text for publication. I obviously had remained cool to help the children retain their stability, but I was really worried about her mental condition.

Later as I looked through a list of Naomi's contacts, with everyone showered and asleep, I wondered if the Police had apprehended Des and if they found the location in time. I hoped that Amanda would be somewhere safe. But most of all, I realised that this was the first time that I had slept alone for a very long time, and though the apartment was warm and air conditioned, and the weather outside was warm, the King sized bed felt cold and empty. The Bauhaus inspired designer cover looked cold and the Art Deco mirror and cabinets based on 1930 designs of the same period suggesting rays of sunshine, now reminded me of ice formations.

Some lines from a poem by Hanwell Nnagobi somehow infiltrated my brain as I tried to sleep.

> The fragile tendrils of stability
> Once strong break and snap so easily,
> How strange an absence brings emptiness?
> Although everything is tinged with familiarity.
> Is there a void planted also in my heart
> Where a vision of you once did rest?

The Bauhaus King Bed now looked cold.

CHAPTER 16

The Faceless Crusader

"Dad is mad" Nigel greeted me near the entrance to the faculty the next morning. "Dad is absolutely fuming, the guy that they call the Faceless Crusader has done it again. I mean Dad is also very appreciative, but he cannot work out how this guy does it. Connected criminal organisations are being exposed by him which the Police have been trying to crack for several years."

"Really?" I asked with feigned surprise. "And do they all link up with Hanwell Nnagobi?"

"Yes that is why I am telling you because I know that you still want to see your friend's death vindicated." He looked fresh and breathless as usual with his scarf slung around his neck, and his hands stuck into his light grey trouser pockets. His brown plain shoes were glossy and his maroon blazer was smart and uncreased. His short mid brown hair had a slight upturned wave at the front which added to his windswept appearance, in spite of his smartness. His white shirt was fresh and crisp which no doubt was due in no small respect to having a very caring Mother.

"I most certainly do, and I am pleased that subversive elements are being brought to justice. Does Inspector McArthur have any idea at all who this er- Crusader might me. I mean the actual Crusaders of the 12th and 13th Centuries were often more infamous, than glorious." I said maintaining my Professorly stance.

"No. They can detect a kind of Brooklyn accent which is exaggerated, but he speaks with a muffled voice, or uses some kind of static to disguise it. Last night he directed them to a guy, I am not allowed to give a name, who deals in illegal fire arms and explosives amongst other things. The police crew only just managed to find the location before he arrived, and they had him surrounded, so that not a single shot was fired. He thought that he was meeting the guy that was fished out of the river a few days ago." Nigel finished speaking excitedly.

"Did you take part again?" I asked genuinely curious.

"It is highly irregular, but Dad allowed me to travel in one of the Police helicopters. The guy obviously did not suspect anything as he approached a part of the key side that is due for redevelopment, in New Jersey. We were like a routine reconnaissance unit." Nigel continued.

"How did you know that the guy was the one that you wanted, and not someone just taking a stroll or looking for something to steal?" I was genuinely curious of course because I had no idea of what Des looked like.

"He was an older guy of heavy build quite tall and wearing a dark blue jogging suit, and a black woollen hat. He had a beard and a moustache, as he entered the disused warehouse yard through a gap in the fencing, he opened his top and produced a small hand held machine gun. A new European design with a double automatic repeating action. These are not on public sale at the moment and highly illegal, so the only way he could be carrying that was through underground contacts. He also had several prototype grenades on a belt which are not even issued to the Military as yet. He was not wired up to detonate himself, but he looked ready to make sure whoever he was meeting did not live to meet him again, or at least did not double cross him." Nigel repeated this with obvious delight.

"How did the Police surprise the guy?" I asked really keen to hear the full story.

"Well, along the side of the high yard wall there is a dark but open passageway between some former office buildings which gives way to a rotting board walk above an old floating iron landing stage. Here the office doors are missing, and the windows are broken or partially boarded. The Police snipers obviously wore black, and crouched behind the broken partitions of the offices. From the passageway there is a clear view through the building to the board walk, so he was not expecting to be jumped by anyone. A couple of riflemen crouched under the landing stage in the shadows. His actions were recorded and relayed by a cameraman through an aperture in the front wall of the office. I mean whether or not that was our man, he was certainly dangerous and illegal enough to be apprehended."

"How did you find the spot? Did this Faceless Crusader give coordinates?"

"No coordinates, but a very clear description, and of course the River Police know the dockland very well, but there was not much time. That was the area as described, close to the end of Commercial Street, from which there was a view of the Western Reach around Staten Island across the River, and Bayonne Bridge. They hoped that a literal interpretation was the right one. That spot which once serviced a small private company is almost in a crevice, in a niche amongst facilities for larger River Traffic."

"Did the intruder say anything?"

"I think that he called out – Buzz- are you there buddy? I hope that you have the money and the goods, or you will never get to kiss sweet little Amanda goodbye." Nigel in his excitement forgot the need for secrecy and mentioned names.

"What was this terrorist type of guy's name? I asked casually.

"I cannot say, I am not allowed to repeat names. I am not allowed to repeat any of this to anyone, but I know that you will not break my confidentiality." Nigel answered unaware that he had released names already.

"Of course. My lips are permanently sealed, and anything which you tell me will never be repeated. Now, however, I hope that you will not find all of this too distracting and allow your degree work to suffer." I decided to play the Professor, but I actually meant it.

"Certainly not. That is what Dad said. He wants me to graduate with top honours now as a good degree will be impressive when I formally enter a branch of the force." Nigel looked at me with convincing intensity. I enjoyed his recapping of all the action which I had secretly instigated, but I wondered if Amanda was now really safe.

There was quite a fresh wind blowing although it was summer, and as we stood on the steps outside the faculty entrance, I was beginning to wish that I had a scarf. Nigel obviously felt the chill now that his excited narrative had ended, and he pushed his scarf closer to his neck with his left hand.

"Well, I had better get to the studio and tackle that old Etching Press. I should feel tired, but these active evenings seem to invigorate me." Nigel said as he hurried through the door ahead of me.

"Good, Etching can be such a refined and precise craft, it is often abused by modern artists, and remember to have your paper damp enough, but not soaking wet." I answered as I took the steps towards my office. I always walk rather than take the elevator as a part of my ongoing fitness regime. I breezed into the outer office as usual and greeted Maggie, ever aware that her 'Lippen Kussen mit dem Feuer'.

"Guten Morgen, Maggie Liebling mein." I said as I passed her desk.

"Guten Morgen, Professor Brandon Liebling – this is my niece Amanda, do you mind if she stays with me today. She will not interfere with my work, or divulge any confidential information, well, I will not give out any." Maggie seemed very agitated and not her usual calm efficient self. I had not noticed the beautiful blond haired young woman in the corner. She had been partly obscured by the door.

"Ah-Am-anda!" I almost gasped in disbelief and surprise.

"Oh, she will not be obtrusive, but she - er, someone is, - er - there are some problems with the house that she shares today, er – refurbishments; her partner has left, and she did not feel well enough to go to work either. It is a complicated story but that is the essence of it." Maggie was very unusually faltering in her speech today. Very un-characteristically, but if that was the Amanda I thought it was, I knew the whole story exactly.

"Why of course. Forgive me for my rudeness, I did not see you in the corner there, Professor Brandon at your service, you are lucky to have an Aunt like Margurita." I managed to control my shock and retain my Professor mode, as I offered my hand. She uncrossed her long elegant legs and half rose out of the arm chair. Her white dress patterned with blue, red, green and pink flowers in small bunches sported a deep cleavage which ended with a small pink bow. Her white patent leather rounded toe shoes were fitted with a black six inch heel. To my mind she had over emphasised her eyes with black liner which conflicted with her natural beauty. I was expecting to see clear bright blue eyes, but instead I saw an indefinable shade somewhere between turquoise and emerald that danced into mine with the innocence and yet the artfulness of a cat. I was mesmerised by this well-groomed purveyor of high fashion - this lady was nothing like the

Gangster's partner which I had imagined. I noticed the lady's Rolex watch decorated with real diamonds, and then the small Platinum diamond encrusted drop earrings to match it. I almost whistled.

"I am very pleased to meet you Brandon, Professor, I hope that I will not inconvenience you in any way, it is just that I needed to get away from things rather quickly without any fuss, and Aunt Maggie is always helpful, like a Mother." Amanda spoke quietly out of pink gloss lips which matched some of the flowers on her dress and I watched their movement almost without hearing the words. Somewhere at the back of my mind I recognised the accent of her voice as being the same one which had spoken bitterly and then desperately sorrowfully on the cell phone the previous evening. How relieved I was, and yet how desperately shocked to find her in my office.

"Of course not. If you need anything just ask. Breakfast, coffee, Lunch--." I was interrupted.

"No thank you, you are also very thoughtful, I can see, but I have a migraine, and Maggie says that she will bring me something from the refectory when it is time. Please, do not worry about me at all I have work to do and I have my Android tablet and everything that I require." Amanda indicated a medium sized cream leather designer handbag, which I guessed was probably a one off original worth thousands of dollars. Her pink glossed fingernails were as immaculate as an air brushed magazine advertisement.

"Good. Well I guess that I had better carry on with my work too." I said managing to tear my eyes from her figure hugging dress and bewitching eyes as I turned to meet Maggie's full of concern and yet filled with a knowing humorous gleam.

"Phew!" What a dame as they say. The lady looks as though she could buy me lunches for a year out of her small change and not even notice it. I spoke to the window as I swivelled around in my chair, with a small shot of Brandy. I must admit that I was shaken to find Buzz's partner here in my own office. Even more shocking was the fact that Maggie was her Aunt. I guess that this must be the safest place for her. She probably thought no one would look for her in the halls of wisdom as it were. And what a looker, as they might say in London. No wonder Des was using her a lever to make sure he got what he wanted out of Buzz. I felt again deeply troubled at having played a part in his untimely demise, but his underworld activities must certainly have been lucrative.

I wondered what she would think of me, if she knew that it was me who warned her of the danger she was in. It was later that I discovered that a small explosive device had devastated the interior of their house during the night, and that she had only just made a timely secretive escape with of course a station wagon full of clothes, shoes and jewellery and money, and Credit Cards. As I sat musing on what to do about the other contacts on the cell phone, and the delivery dates which I guessed now had been re-scheduled, a light knock on the door almost startled me. I quickly swivelled around, and opened a folder of papers on my desk. "Yes?" I called.

"Here is some more mail Professor, some of it looks like junk and one is handwritten it could be a CV or someone enquiring about entry to the course." Maggie breezed in with her usual bright efficiency before changing her demeanour to one of trepidation as she continued. "Amanda is almost like a daughter to me, her Mother died when she was six years old, she was Swedish. My brother Gunter remarried a year or two later and I looked after her in the meantime, but she never really liked her stepmother. She was not mistreated, just left to her own devices as one might say, and she still spent a lot of time with me and my two boys. Somehow she seemed to have little in common with her half brother and sister, who of course were about ten years younger."

"I see, she certainly seems to have done very well. Does she work for a fashion house, or even own one?" I asked beginning to understand how a relation of Maggie's could become involved in what was after all, a very disreputable syndicate.

"She actually is a partner with Loveday & Krueger on 5th. She married Alain Loveday and she was blissfully happy on the cat walk and designing also, until Alain was drowned in a freak yachting accident off Bermuda. They had only been married about three years, and yes, she was totally devastated. Even more so, because Alain was with another woman, they were found together locked in each other's arms in one of the bunks. Some people say that it was a suicide pact." Maggie paused and I offered her a drink, which very un-characteristically, she accepted and sunk into the chair opposite me.

"Amanda exudes sophistication, I had no idea-." I began.

"She does, she is, she has packed so much in to her life already, but lasting happiness and stability seem to evade her. Really I think sometimes she is still the six year old child waiting for the warm embrace of her Mother's arms." Maggie swirled the Brandy in her glass pensively. "Oh Liebling, ich habe in eine dumme Frau Drehte sich um und zu Lange gesprochen."

"Nonsense. I know that you are deeply concerned. You are always making things right for other people, you need to share your own anxieties sometime, and I cannot imagine you ever being a foolish woman." I answered reassuringly.

"Amanda gave birth to little Kirsten just after Alain died. He was brilliant, he was clever, he was wealthy and he was a bipolar alcoholic. That is why he was able to leave her easily, as she was almost full term, promising to be back in time for the birth. I am thankful that he did. She always seems to make the wrong choices. She more or less left Kirsten to be brought up by Alain's sister Odell, who married into a farming family in Kentucky. Amanda has had several stormy relationships before she became involved with her present partner Bernard Muzzinger. I know why she liked him. I must admit that I did on the two occasions that I met him. Handsome with chiselled features as they say, like a square jawed classical sculpture, who worked out a lot, and with a physique that just begged you to lay your hands upon and grasp. Rather like yourself in some respects but differently. Excuse me Brandon darling if our long association causes me to be over familiar." Maggie took a large sip of Brandy as she paused.

"I -." I began before Maggie continued.

"Bernard Muzzinger said that he was involved with the Stock Market and the gifts he bestowed upon her took my breath away, he made Alain look like a pauper, but I know there was more to him than met the eye. I know that she loves him, and now he has up and left, and now she cannot face the world and needs a place to hide for a while. Her previous, er, associate left her almost destitute" Maggie stopped and looked down at her glass. I rose and put my arms around her shoulders. She lifted up her face to mine, and I saw there what I had never seen before, and somehow never thought that I would. Maggie's large hazel eyes were full of tears which rolled slowly down her cheeks.

"She might look like the sophisticated Fashionista, but to me she is still my sweet little Amanda. Bruno, my late husband always called her that. Maggie added, as I inadvertently brushed a tear from her cheek with my right forefinger, and then our lips met again with the same fire as previously.

The thought crossed my mind how strange that beautiful and voluptuous young Amanda sat on the other side of the wall having probably escaped great danger, and it was her lovely Aunt that I was consoling with what amounted to a lover's kiss. But what the hell? For the moment I was willing to lose myself in the fire. As it happened previously, there was a knock on the door.

"Mrs Hessen-Bach are you there? May I trouble you for a moment, your new assistant informed me that you were discussing some mail with Professor Brandon, but I need to reschedule one of the second year assessment exhibitions rather urgently and I need it to be amended in the notices."

"Ah Dr Trenton, Guilliame, just a moment I will be with you." Maggie dabbed her eyes carefully one at a time, and her lips as she regained her unflustered efficient persona and moved towards the door. "Thank you Professor, I will email a reply as soon as possible." She announced as she made a refined exit.

The Faceless Crusader huh? I repeated to myself, as I recalled the desk Sergeant's words, and I was glad that I was. I had no idea when all of this began that Maggie's life would be linked to the underworld in this way, albeit unknowingly. I felt sorry for Amanda too that she had to maintain a lie to avoid hurting Maggie but also to keep her sympathy. I hoped that she would not recognise anything about my voice or way of speaking and likewise Maggie; nor in fact anyone must know about my "Crusades".

"So bent Cop you are getting yourself deeper into something that you cannot leave unfinished!" I started, and cold shivers ran down my spine. I looked again towards the door and there was Eric, as dishevelled and unshaven as ever.

"What? You get the hell out here, you are not there really. Stop haunting me." I yelled.

"I am real enough, I always help you don't I?" Eric answered indignantly.

"Yes, I suppose that you do, but not here please." This is my day job.

"I can see you bent Cop no matter where you are day or night." Eric laughed and his body was once more racked with uncontrollable coughing.

"For goodness sake I have a job to do here." I snapped.

"Maybe, but you do not have the power to divide night and day, and time is only relative." Eric smirked showing yellowing teeth.

"What do you want? I asked desperately.

"Meet me down by the South River tonight, you know where, and you will discover something valuable." Eric said earnestly.

"I cannot – I have the children – my wife is having a breakdown." I almost pleaded.

"Meet me – you will know where." Eric said, and disappeared as I walked towards him angrily ready to strike him in the mouth in a sudden fit of anger and disbelief.

The door suddenly opened and Maggie appeared. "Did you call Professor, I thought that I heard something."

"Ah, yes" I managed to say calmly. "I have had an idea. Maybe Amanda would like to stay in the old Janitor's lodge at the other side of the Quadrangle. Stephano and his wife do not live there now and it has a private entrance onto the street. If there is any red tape to wrangle over, I will say that she is temporarily lending her professional expertise to the Department of Fashion. I will have a word with the Dean at lunch time."

"Brandon, Liebling that sounds ideal, she would probably welcome the privacy rather than staying in my apartment. You are such a dear, a real knight in shining armour, A Knight Templar, a Crusader!"

Where are you – Don't try to Double-cross Me!

CHAPTER 17

Metamorphosis

I know that it is customary for Fashionistas to change the appearance of their persona frequently and often quite radically, but Amanda managed it with such perfection that she was completely unrecognisable. Gone were the intriguing floral body hugging dresses and the natural blonde hair and the pastel lips. She wore a longer auburn wig, with a deep red lipstick and large dark framed spectacles with plain glass, which gave her almost a Retro look, and a fairly loose but very smart trouser suit with a tailored jacket. The heels were still there on smart black shoes with a small bow at the front. She had stayed for a month almost as a recluse in the janitor's lodge, and Maggie had shopped for groceries. This woman was indeed frightened for her life. I knew the bottom line of course, but to Maggie Amanda presented herself as making a brand new start after being abandoned by her partner. Maggie related to me with horror that an explosion had devastated her house but it was blamed on a gas main, and so Amanda would be recompensed by her Insurance. She eventually ventured into the establishment of Fashion which she part owned, and at first the staff were slightly uncomfortable with her radical METAMORPHOSIS. Although she still looked beautiful it was almost a case of the Butterfly transforming into the Chrysalis rather than vice-versa.

Would the undercover operatives make an attack on the establishment whether they recognised her or not? Would she be off the hook and the knowledge that Buzz was dead be wide spread by now? It was a chance that she had to take, because maybe there was nowhere to run from an international crime ring. I had barely been able to resist making advances to her on that first day in my office, and I dreamt of her at night when sometimes during a fitful sleep her face would turn into that of Naomi. I had been partly responsible for her partner's death, so what now? To the victor the prize. I had to remind myself that this was not a Greek Tragic play by Euripides or Sophocles, but entangling further with Amanda, that is if she was willing, could only jeopardise my mission, and sometimes I felt that I was now losing sight of my mission, which was to eventually expose my former boss, Professor Emile Beldossa as being one of the criminal Master minds of the organisation which killed my good friend Hanwell Nnagobi.

I found that I enjoyed the school run and the children had settled into the routine without Naomi, and one of her contacts had been willing to pick them up in the afternoon and even give them tea, for a very moderate fee. She also picked up Matteus from the Early Learning Centre. Diwani Bashier was charming and loving. Her Mother traced her ancestry to Captain Cook and Great Yarmouth in England, and her Father was a second generation Asian from New Deli. My activities as the 'Faceless Crusader' had abated somewhat as I spent my evenings with the children. I had however taken a big chance the day Eric bade me meet him by the South River, my phantom mentor and tormentor. I hurriedly employed a child minder at short notice, again from Naomi's list of contacts and headed for the meeting place after dinner with Matteus, Andrea and Kurt. They were a little perturbed about being left with a complete stranger, and so was I at leaving them, but I knew that I had to go.

Instinctively I headed for the spot, and Eric shuffled into view from out of the shadows of the shrubs as I approached. I opened my mouth in order to revile him, rather than greet him, but he motioned me to be silent and I obeyed, and waited with him in the blue black shadows. It was dark and the river traffic had abated somewhat, but a large black rubber craft approached the edge of the jetty almost without a sound. Two men were visible as the moon emerged from behind a cloud, and lights dimly shimmered on the water. They steered the craft skilfully between the points of the breakwater. I knew what they were going to do, and I was already alerting the Police and describing the location, as they hoisted a large bundle wrapped in black polythene onto one of the smaller sharper points. With some vicious blows from a large wooden mallet they pinioned the bundle and an arm and a hand became visible as the polythene accidentally ripped.

"Another Creep exposed, and punished Bent Cop, you are getting closer." Eric looked at me with bloodshot alcoholic eyes, and spat out a slug of phlegm, which even in the dim light I could see was laced with blood. "Take care now."

"I guess that I am indebted to you again-." I began, but he had disappeared with his customary laugh ringing in my ears. I could see search lights playing over the water as Police Launches approached from two directions. The rubber craft reversed too quickly, and I heard the crunch of the outboard propeller before it shattered on a submerged spike. One man dressed all in black like myself with his face covered by a balaclava raised a repeating rifle, but an accurate shot knocked it from his grasp and he sank to his knees as another shot ripped through his shoulder. The second man tried to slip into the water, but remained hung over the side of the craft gripping his thigh in agony as another Police marksman fired with well-trained accuracy. The launches closed in at a safe distance, and a small dingy was despatched with armed Police to pick up the two men and retrieve the pinioned body.

I heard squad cars approaching down the carriageway, as I crossed the road and gained the shadows of the trees, and then I jogged to where I had left my Estate Car. I removed my short dreadlock wig, and moustache and the Police uniform which McArthur had never asked to be returned, and packed them into a zipped canvas bag with Buzz's pistol and my own. I placed the mobile in a separate compartment, and closed the hatch. My own Metamorphosis completed, I was transformed into Professor Brandon again as I drove back to my apartment.

I wondered who the poor bastard was to meet his fate this time, and I remembered that it could so easily have been myself. If the two men broke and gave in to questioning, as I somehow guessed that they would, the Police would be a heck of a lot closer to the centre of the crime ring. I wondered if tonight's victim was really a 'Creep' or had been falsely accused of being a double agent. I could somehow visualise his desperate protestations and maybe his heart-breaking plea for them to believe him. How else could so many of the gang have been exposed except by him? I could imagine the anguish on his face as he tried to convince them that he had not leaked any information to the Police or any other agents. Maybe after tears and despair, he had accepted his slow torturous death with dignity and silence as the welcoming arms of oblivion gradually eased all of his pain. Maybe this was the case or not, but I guessed that it was me, 'The Faceless Crusader' who was the real thorn in their side.

Did you think that I had slipped into celibacy with the role of single parent, as Naomi's sojourn became extended? Well no. I do not know if you remember the handwritten letter which Maggie had presented me with also on that morning when I was shocked to see Amanda in my office. Well, it may not come as a surprise when I tell you that it was from Clarisse. She announced that she was visiting New York with our son whom I had never seen and would love to meet me. Long-time no see indeed, and by now she had penned a second bestselling novel. I telephoned the Hotel on the appointed day and we met for lunch. She chose a seafood platter which included Pacific Oysters and a light semi-sweet white wine. Her perfect English diction seemed to have been honed to even greater perfection, and she was amusing and charming now that she felt fulfilled, after all those years of neglect and frustration. I was eager to meet Pharoe, but her female companion had taken charge of him for the day. I remembered the first day I had seen her silhouetted against the window, and how later we had made love on the welcoming rug. All my passion for her flared up again, and I was not disappointed to be asked to escort her to her suite. Her passion was equal to mine still, and I forgot all about the incident by the South River on the previous night, as she flung her arms around my neck, and I felt the warm softness of her body pressed close to mine. As Clarisse untied my carefully knotted tie and unbuttoned my shirt, I unzipped the Chiffon Satin day dress and let it slide to the floor with an almost silent whisper of fine fabric. Her delicate hands searched my body inside my shirt, before she released my belt and our lips refused to part, even for short passionate intakes of breath. As my grey pressed pants slid to the floor Clarisse searched inside my continental briefs and I allowed them to slide over my buttocks and down to the floor also. I released the single clasp of her satin bra pushing it upwards as I cupped her lovely still firm but pliable responsive breasts. There was no fumbling as I slid easily between the open crotch thong and she wrapped her legs around me thrusting with a force which almost took my breath away. I cupped her buttocks in both hands and now our lips parted as she threw back her head and her breasts rubbed against my pecks.

"Oh, how I have missed you!" Clarisse declared.

"And I have never forgotten you." I answered as I made a gargantuan effort to retain my release so as to sustain our heavenly copulation. I shuffled to the large bed and laid her down taking a quick second to release my feet from my pants, and then we finished in earnest. Clarisse writhed beneath me scraping my back with the six inch heels, as she alternately tightened and relaxed the tension in her legs. I was free to drive home supporting myself with hands beneath her shoulders, as my teeth and tongue sought out her breasts, and then it was as though our bodies were stretched and welded together as we became a mass of multiple orgasms and uncontrollable ferocious ejaculation.

"Hold me, never let me go, caress me." Clarisse whispered, as she clasped my head in her lovely hands. Her breathing became more regular but she continued to hold me and caress me and enfold her arms around me, and I relaxed into her warm enveloping aura. This was only the first of many lunchtime rendezvous at her hotel. We joined each other in the steamy shower and the Jacuzzi tub before descending to earth and the restaurant for afternoon tea.

And it was as if I descended to earth from the windows of another realm. I knew why Hanwell had treated her the way that he did, but how could he? Clarisse was like the beautiful traditional Pink English Rose compact and fragrant, that transformed into the most exotic of Canaries Lillies. I could not help but feel that my fascination had turned into love. I felt a pang of uncertainty as I remembered Naomi. Remembered Naomi? Another voice from somewhere spoke to me. Remember Naomi? Your wife is ill, and she has been absent for only – how long? I know, I know, another part of myself answered, I can count the days, and yet it seems like years. Light years. Aeons of time and space.

"Perfect timing." Clarissa I could tell felt the same transforming emotion as her perfect intonation cut through the sound of other diners chatting, and my own reverie. I rose automatically and greeted a slightly older woman than ourselves with a very modern short spikey haircut of blond and black, as Clarisse introduced her as Trudi.

"And this is Professor Brandon Edwin Martin-Schally." Again it was unusual to hear my full name being announced outside of the most formal of occasions, and I met the intense gaze of a small boy with the most attractive red-blonde hair which decorated his head in large curls, and a Mediterranean tan. In his smart little grey suit with crisp white shirt and royal blue bow tie and brown shoes, he looked air brushed and ready for a magazine advertisement for sunshine foods and perfect health. A row of large even white teeth suddenly appeared between his lips and the large eyes which I thought were brown lit up with a deep indigo blue tinge. A small dimple in each cheek transformed his initial sombre demeanour into some recognition of familiarity.

"This is Pharoe, my youngest son. He is the lucky one who gets to travel with me. His brother and sister are still at school." Clarisse continued, and I shook his hand firmly and warmly, and I was surprised by the firmness of his small hand.

"I am very pleased to me you Pharoe," I said almost automatically. I had not imagined meeting our son this way formally. I wanted to pick him up and twirl him around, but Clarisse was sensible with the correct sense of propriety. "How do you like New York?" I asked.

"We have been to The Top of the Rock, and Trudi would not let me have anything from the cafes because we are having tea here, but I like it." Pharoe spoke with confident perfect English pronunciation also, which seemed to make me more aware of my own Brooklyn based accent.

"I must admit that I nearly had to drag him past the ice cream shops before our short taxi ride." Trudi spoke like a contralto with a rich operatic voice, and she looked demure in her fashionable grey and black striped jersey tunic with one bare shoulder revealing the wide pale blue denim strap of her underdress. I had noticed that she wore a thin black belt and black tights with cream coloured six inch heels. Somehow she represented an artistic fraternity from areas such as Camden Town.

"See, we have some excellent photographs." Pharoe narrowly missed knocking cream cakes off the stand as he waved them proudly for inspection. There was one of him sitting on an RSJ which made him look as though he was balancing above Manhattan, and one of Trudi half self-effacing, but slinky as she looked sideways at the scene behind her.

"Careful darling" Clarisse admonished softly, as she elegantly poured the Earl Grey tea from the ornate tea pot.

"Mummy may I have a trifle now?" Pharoe was reaching out as he spoke.

"No darling we will begin with a sandwich first." She replied indicating the array of varied diamonds and triangles of Wholemeal and White bread, with the silver tongues.

I must say that I had almost forgotten my own manners and almost jammed a cream split bun into my mouth without the use of cake forks, as the display was absolutely tempting and mouth-watering. I felt such a conflict of emotions again, and almost a jab of a tear behind my smile. Here I was desperately in love, in a situation which could never be, with an unresolved family issue which was not due to the lack of love, and I was secretly overjoyed that there was an instant rapport with my son. I had been worried that he would reject me, or that there would be no connectivity, and I could only guess at what his physical appearance would be. I was full to overflowing with delight and sadness simultaneously.

"Professor Brandon was a very good friend of your late Father." Clarisse remarked gently, as though interpreting and answering my thoughts.

"Was he nice like you Professor?" Pharoe asked with a contented smile.

"OH- Yes, er yes, he was very talented and we appreciated many of the same things." I said, and then began to wonder if we really did, or whether I was a part of the subterfuge too.

"Why are you a Professor?" Pharoe asked.

"Because he is clever and talented too." Clarisse cut in quickly.

"I – I must be very good at my job, but you can just call me Brandon; most people do." I added.

"Pharoe is very talented too, and so is Trudi." Clarisse continued, as she offered the cakes. "Trudi is now my illustrator and proof reader, as well as a very good friend, and she works wonders with Pharoe."

"He is so adorable." Trudi replied enthusiastically, as she toyed with her cake fork. "But I am afraid that I belong to that group of individuals who prefer to love other people's children, rather than have my own, because at the end of the day, I can always hand them back." She laughed charmingly before taking a sip of tea and I noticed that her carefully honed nails were turquoise blue, a matching colour of the denim dress.

"We always have a good time whilst Mummy is busy writing." Pharoe beamed after swallowing his large mouthful of chocolate fudge cream cake. It was obvious that he liked her, and that also he had been trained already not to speak with his mouth full. "And Grandfather sometimes takes me golfing with him." He added.

"I see and how do you fit school into all of the good times?" I asked.

"Oh, I like school too, and later when I am older I will be attending a private boarding school like Benjamin and Amelia they say that they like it.

"I see, - how is Viscount Erindale, and Lady Fenshaw?" I asked, directing the question towards Clarisse.

"Oh - wonderful as ever." Clarisse answered sincerely. "Father is often travelling on business as usual in spite of the internet and modern technology, he prefers the personal touch, and Mother is involved with her social round and charity groups and she takes a particular interest in Glyndebourne, she is a patron. Some of the staging there is now quite ingenious and avant-garde".

"Good. My Father often enjoys visits to see the Operatic productions there. I was hoping to stay with him in London, but with my sudden Professorship, and Naomi being taken ill, I had to abandon my plans to visit England, temporarily. I was working towards a new exhibition, but for the moment that is on hold too." I had not really spoken with Clarisse during our renewed encounter.

"Will Naomi be recovering soon – how are you managing?" Clarisse was suddenly full of concern.

"A professional friend of Naomi drops Matteus off at the early Learning Centre now and takes Andrea and Kurt to school, and picks them all up. She even gives them a meal and sometimes makes one for me."

"Oh, so where is Naomi?" Clarisse asked full of surprise.

"Staying temporarily with one of her sisters in Montreal." I replied reluctantly. I had not really wanted to discuss any of my pressing problems.

"Not divorced or separated I hope." Trudi cut in, also full of concern.

"No, no, just a temporary arrangement." I said with forced nonchalance, and even a touch of jollity. "Say why don't you visit the Faculty tomorrow, and I will show you around. The students are producing some very formidable stuff. It may be of particular interest to you Trudi, as an illustrator, and I can show Pharoe what a Professor does."

"Well that sounds like the best offer that I have received today. I would love to." Trudi reciprocated with her dry humour again, her mauve-to –purple lipstick gave her mouth a fascinating aspect without being gaudy.

"I would too. Can we mummy?" Pharoe stated very enthusiastically.

"Of course darling, but I have to visit someone involved with publishing, so would you mind just going with Trudi?"

"Mummy you are always busy." Pharoe replied very matter of factly.

"I know darling, but then, I know what a great fan of the theatre Trudi is – She will not tell you, but Trudi Jasper-Armitage is also a well-respected script writer for TV-." Clarisse declared, addressing the last statement to myself. "So we can all meet and have lunch at Sardies on 44th, it was once the Theatrical Producer's haven, and I insist that it is my treat."

"That will surely be a hoot." Trudi smiled delightedly.

"I must say that I have never actually eaten there, although I frequently pass by," I concluded. "So until tomorrow, when I delight again in your company, I will call for you about 9.30."

Central Park from Top of The Rock.

CHAPTER 18

Emerson

She had the appearance of well-honed ebony, and a voice as sweet as honey and silky smooth. Her hair was gelled into large glossy black curls and she was somehow cool, but warm and friendly at the same time.

All of my artistic instincts were brought into play, and I wanted to immortalise her in a painting. A painting which would be reproduced as a household feature like one produced by an artist during the 1950's, particularly in the UK. But this was no exotic fantasy or like a jewel from a far off land enveloped in a dream-scape which one might visit one day, or which might be far enough away so as not to be obtrusive. No she was here and now with a charisma which emanated from her like a rich and heavy scent intoxicating all of my senses. She was not like my Mother or my Sister, and yet she was. She was not like Naomi who still sojourned with her sister in Montreal, and unusually I felt a tightness in my throat when I tried to speak.

"Yes Professor Brandon, how may I help you?" Miss Emerson, or Emerson as she liked to be called as I later discovered, whispered her query over the desk like the rustling of an eternal wind through the russet branches of a perpetually beautiful autumn.

"I just desire to float upon the silky tones of your voice and the warmth of your breath and be enveloped within your charisma until the end of time, after time ends." That is what I wanted to say. "And I would gladly melt into the inviting heat of your body as I caress all of your charms."

"Professor Brandon?" Emerson repeated my name questioningly, and I managed to drag myself back from the solar winds and the fabric of the interwoven Universe as I locked onto her large brown eyes without any feeling of embarrassment.

"Ah – Miss Emerson," I began, as I read the name plate on the desk. "I need to speak with Professor Hardland, on a rather urgent and confidential matter if he is available."

"No, I am sorry sir, but at the moment he is giving a lecture outside of the Faculty, and he may not return until this afternoon." Emerson gave me a smile that must have been fashioned within the clouds of Heaven with the radiance of the sun.

"I see, so could I make an appointment?" I asked, as my knees felt weak on the inside, and my body seemed to steam like wet foliage when the sun shines after a rain shower.

"Of course." Emerson cooed with her natural vermillion lips and a hint of pale pink tongue between her perfect teeth. "Tomorrow morning at ten would be the earliest certain time."

"Will it – (will it be that long before I see you again?)-I only just stopped myself from uttering these words with intense seriousness.

"Yes sir, I will make an appointment for ten tomorrow." Emerson continued to smile at me rather professionally.

"Good. Our paths do not often cross, but I know that he is an expert in Criminology, and I would like to discuss a rather interesting topic with him. Something which may interest him." I replied and then I just asked outright. "And Miss Emerson if you do not have conflicting plans, I hope that you will accept my invitation to dinner tonight."

For a moment a serious look crossed her face as dramatic as a cloud rolling over a deep blue ocean, which highlighted her beauty to even greater effect. Her eyes never left mine and she answered so softly and yet so audibly, that I almost turned to see if anyone else was present or listening.

"Yes Professor Brandon, I would love to accept your invitation, but to where?"

"Do you know that charming restaurant where they mix a mean and original cocktail, and produce some Southern style food - I think maybe on 45th West?" I answered with suitable academic restraint, when I really felt like whooping and jumping with my fists punching the air.

"Do I? That is W's Cuisine, one of my favourite places." Her eyes danced suddenly with excitement. "Not that I frequent it that often," she added, on a more subdued and coy note.

Good, where will I call for you?" I mentally crossed my fingers and hoped that I could enlist another of Naomi's contacts to take care of the children for the evening, as Diwani usually left at 17.00 hours. Clarisse and Trudi had returned to England with Pharoe and I guessed that I was trying to fill a space in my life, but what a space filler Emerson turned out to be.

I was delighted that Clarisse had taken charge of the situation with Pharoe from the start and she was giving him the first class English upbringing that would benefit him greatly. I was a little sad also that I could never divulge that I was his father, and not Hanwell Nnagobi. I had introduced him to Andrea, and Kurt, and Matteus and they all seemed to like each other. I know that somewhere along the line they instinctively felt an empathy, a family connection. Let us face it anyway the last thing that I can cope with at the moment is another child. It was strange but now I felt an even closer connection to Hanwell, now that we shared Clarisse. She had accepted his demise probably rather thankfully if the truth of the bottom line were to be spoken, and unlike myself seemed to show no interest in discovering who his actual murderers are. I guess that she had grown to feel safe on the sprawling family Estate and channelled her energies into her writing. I know that she was writing a third book and basing a character in it on myself. I caught her studying me sometimes, and I did not feel worthy of the accolade she apparently bestowed upon me. Yet, at the same time she made it clear that there could never be anything more between us than an occasional liaison.

I must admit that I had become a bit of a war zone within myself. I did not want to divorce Naomi, and yet the love between us had somehow faded and it was Dessi who always telephoned or answered the phone to inform me that Naomi was suffering from depression and mental stress and was being treated by their physician, and it was probably better for me not to visit. Naomi was missing the children of course, but still felt unable to cope and so I left the situation hanging, and considered what my next move should be as the 'Faceless Crusader'. Now temporarily my thoughts were full of Emerson and I felt a little guilty for neglecting my children in the evenings, as I had begun to do.

"Daddy you never read us a story in the evenings now" Andrea admonished, as I prepared to make a quick exit to meet Emerson as soon as the child minder arrived.

"That is because you are growing up now, and you have friends visiting." I answered unconvincingly.

"Yes, but Matteus is not grown up yet." Andrea replied reproachfully.

"And I am older than Andrea!" Kurt exclaimed also reproachfully.

"I have to go to an important meeting" I lied.

"I think that you are going to meet a new Mommy, a lady friend." Andrea announced

"Is Mom staying with Aunty Dessie because you made her ill?" Kurt suddenly asked.

"No! I did not make Mommy ill. Sometimes people just need a long rest, even though they still love everyone." I answered rather sharply and it pained me to see them. This whole business I had got mixed up in was in order to ensure our family safety and security, but instead, it had forced us apart.

The timely arrival of Michelle the child minder ended the conversation thankfully, and I closed the door behind me with a heavy heart. I was just about to enter the lift at the end of the empty corridor when Eric suddenly blocked my path.

"Oh no, not now". I groaned.

"Heh – heh – ahh." Eric laughed through his yellow teeth, and spat out a slug of yellow phlegm. "So the pleasures of the flesh are the strongest factors after all". He announced with a slightly triumphant, and also disparaging leer.

"What is it now? You know that I want this gangland business settled more than anything." I replied very impatiently.

"Dating the Criminologist's Secretary or discussing things with him will make no difference to discovering how this operation works." Eric spoke seriously, as he stepped aside to allow me to enter the lift. I never knew whether he was really there in person, or an hallucination. "You will discover something tonight which will surprise you – bent Cop."

"Stop calling me 'bent Cop' I need some company; I have needs--." I trailed off as he disappeared.

"You will always be bent Cop to me – I can see you ooo – ooo- ah-hah ha--." Eric's voice faded with his usual eerie laugh.

I must say that by now I felt almost too distraught for a dinner date, but soon I was basking in the velvet tones of Emerson's soft voice, which seemed to caress my very soul and she became the focus of my attention. The conversation of other diners, the questions of the waiters, the mixing of expensive cocktails at the table, the aromas of other food besides our own, and the occasional mirth which broke out from a table satiated my senses. A feeling of warm wellbeing spread its veil over me until suddenly a voice separated itself from the rest, and I inadvertently turned in the direction from whence it emanated. A tall thin man with a shaved head, and beige suit sat at a table by the wall and the convivial tones of his cultured voice were none other than those of the man in charge of my abduction and interrogation. Although that evening as I sat with a sack over my head seemed like a very long time ago, it was still sharp in my mind. He would have had me tortured, if the real boss-man had not entered and ordered my release. I would have recognised that voice anywhere.

"Do you know that man?" Emerson had been quick to notice my distraction, and I wanted to kick myself.

"No, no – for a moment he reminded me of an old friend." I managed to lie smoothly and coolly.

"He is a partner with Patterson and Peterson Attorneys, and he too occasionally consults Professor Hardland on criminal matters." Emerson informed me confidentially. "His name is Daryl Kabell."

"You must know quite a lot of influential people." I retorted with my utmost charm, but I narrowly missed choking on my cocktail in surprise.

"Well, - I suppose that you could say that." Emerson replied modestly and thoughtfully, "But not many so charming or handsome as yourself." She added.

How quickly Eric's words had come true. Mentally I walked slowly to the table and introduced myself. As the man turned to take my proffered hand I quickly grabbed his steak knife and deftly jammed it to the hilt in his left jugular vein and sliced downwards with all of my strength to ascertain that the severance was complete. I wiped my hand on his napkin and threw it over his face before walking calmly back to my table leaving his guests open mouthed. 'Come on let us go' I whispered to Emerson and grabbed her arm as she too sat open mouthed. I informed all of the diners and staff that he was a big shot in an underground organisation, and ordered them to back off, using Emerson as a hostage as I drew Buzz's pistol, and backed towards the door.

"Sorry," I whispered to her fondly.

"Sorry what for?" Emerson was looking at me with a bemused smile. I realised that I had spoken the last word from my vengeful reverie out loud.

"That I have to confess that I am still married, and your compliment was so touching." I managed to hastily construct an appropriate sentence.

"Oh, Professor, er Brandon – I know that you are. "Emerson replied coyly, and also very matter of factly.

Luckily Emerson's charms were sufficient to distract me from further interest in the Attorney. I felt so certain that it was he whom his superior had called an imbecilic jerk off. As the sack had completely obscured my vision, it may also have distorted my hearing. I wondered for a moment if I was becoming paranoid. The Post Traumatic Nightmares had ceased, but sometimes I awoke feeling that someone had placed a sack over my head again, only to find that my head was only buried in the pillow.

Speaking of my head being buried, I found the prospect of burying my head between Emerson's appealing cleavage, ever more attractive and occasionally she returned my fascination with a coy look as she maybe toyed with her fork, or took a sip from the straw of the cocktail.

Those cocktails! I ordered two more of the ones which included red wine and were mixed into outsized glasses at the table. So satisfyingly mellow they were and surreptitiously inebriating, that Emerson's sequins on the black dress sparked like the stars on a clear night. I could easily have let myself believe that I had finally taken flight into the Universe, a Universe of sensuality, with a Primeaval temptress. I will swear that her smile grew warmer if that was possible and every word she uttered was a seductive eulogy of love. I wondered what impression I was making in the flickering glow of the table light.

"Ooh, this is so nice." Emerson cooed as she dabbed her pink-blush lips with her napkin as we finished our smooth and creamy deserts. "I do not often visit here with such a handsome and courteous man as yourself. Are you aware that you have quite a reputation as a heart throb at the University?"

"Well, again I find your flattery very encouraging, but I am not too sure that I am". I answered with a smile which I could feel broadening perhaps rather more than I intended.

"I know that sounds like a very old fashioned cliché, but you certainly set my heart throbbing Professor, - I mean Brandon honey." Emerson practically breathed honey as she softly intoned my name, which left me in no doubt at all about how the evening should continue.

"Unless you would like another drink somewhere, or to visit a late show or a club, I will drive you home. The time has passed so quickly and pleasantly here; I do not often find myself in the presence of such an enchanting lady." I replied as I took care of the cheque.

"Not even your lucky wife?" Emerson almost whispered and raised an eyebrow in a kind of mock admonishment.

"My wife is staying with her sister in Montreal at the moment and will not be returning for quite some time." I replied pleasantly and matter of factly. Nothing was going to quash my ardour.

"And the little ones, are they expecting their daddy back home tonight?" Emerson was teasing me with her ingenuous look and naïve questions. This was a side of her that only made her more endearing to me.

"They are being looked after very well." I answered in a confidential manner.

"I see. In that case we will have plenty of time to try out my new coffee machine at my apartment, filtered of course." She looked at me seriously, and then burst into a delightful laugh.

"Filtered will be excellent." I replied, and I laughed also, a happy and somehow carefree laugh, as I drove the short distance to her apartment, parked the Mercedes, and we made our way to the lift with an arm already familiar, around each other's waist.

Outsized Cocktails at W's Cuisine.

CHAPTER 19

Daryl Kabell

Our evening of passion was certainly hot. So hot in fact that we had to repeat it, but this time we had dinner at one of the excellent Smith's bars which proliferate in New York. It was a much less formal affair, but Emerson was sparkling again, this time in a little Royal Blue number with real diamonds around her neck. There was nothing fake about this girl. What you saw is what you got, and she was certainly a deluxe package.

At the back of my mind Daryl Kabell and his cultured voice haunted me, but I doubly thanked Emerson because our date had coincidentally filled in another piece of the puzzle. I did of course not suspect Professor Hardland was also an accomplice to this undercover mob, but I had cancelled my appointment with him just in case. I craftily asked Emerson to do it, with suitable excuses, by saying that I had made an appointment solely on the pretext of asking her for a date. She was dubious at first and determined not to be fooled by more honeyed words, but eventually she agreed. I wanted to bathe in her aura and bask in the heat of her body so the honey was genuine. I felt revived as in the Karma Sutra days which I enjoyed with Naomi before fate appeared to turn my life upside down. I wished that I could stay all night and share a breakfast in the morning, but Michelle was only a listed child minder, and not a live in Au pair, and then the idea formulated properly in my head. As a Professor I could easily employ an Au pair girl or student, eager to spend some time in New York. The idea had been there lurking just below the surface. How would the children react to this I wondered? They had almost got used to the idea that Mommy may not return for some length of time, and her sister Dessie had also informed me that this may be the case. Somewhere amidst my whirling thoughts I still loved her. I still missed her, and little Matteus should not have to grow up without his natural Mother, but he seemed to adapt the most easily. I made a financial arrangement with Dessie to take care of the extra expense which Naomi's stay incurred and I was relieved to hear that the baby she was carrying was growing healthily, and that the Doctors had persuaded her to go the full term of pregnancy.

Anna-Maria was a sweet British student with an Italian Mother, and Emerson insisted that she relieve her of her duties some evenings and the weekends and on her days when she was not in the office.

"Just call me Aunty Labelle." She informed the children and I made the excuse that she was my brother's wife from Manchester in the UK.

"How come you do not speak like people from Manchester England?" Andrea asked dubiously.

"Because I lived in America before, honey." Was Emerson's glib reply which was accepted unconditionally?

So, soft spoken Sussex girl Anna-Maria occupied Naomi's former office room, and it was logical that Emerson stay in Daddy's room, and on the evenings I stayed at Emerson's apartment we were with Uncle Dietrich who was too busy to visit my apartment because of his exchange work schedule. Hunky Dory – right? Well, yes if pleasures of the flesh take precedence, and I have to admit that Eric was right, and my activities as the Faceless Crusader temporarily ceased as I embarked upon this full-blown affair with Emerson.

Why did we undertake such subterfuge and lie to Andrea and Kurt? They were now aware of the facts of life I am sure, although we had never actually instructed them formally, but probably I should. Matteus was probably more innocent at this stage. It was because somewhere in the nether regions of my mind, I still hoped to be reunited with Naomi, and our formerly normal happy family life would be reinstated. I felt strongly about Emerson but I did not expect permanence and I wondered if our wonderful roller coaster infatuation would end abruptly. Emerson surprised me as she turned into supermom. She would be up and showered before me, and rustling up pancakes and eggs and ham and fresh orange juice. She did not need to enforce the children to sit at the breakfast bar before going to school, they were more often than not, eager and waiting.

Anna-Maria was actually a student of Fine Art and Art History so she was officially in my department although she was taking a form of gap-year, before possibly embarking upon a Master's Postgraduate course. She took care of Matteus and as she could drive, I allowed her to use Naomi's car for the school run, and any personal business. Like myself she was enthralled by the 14th Century Flemish tapestries depicting the rather cruel story of The Lady and the Unicorn, in the Cloisters Museum. This magical animal which had proved to be a great benefit to the town was captured and slaughtered for the properties of its horn. One may draw a kind of parallel with the illegal Ivory Hunting of the present day, but this mythical animal was renowned in some European Medieval circles for the healing properties of its horn. There was bogus 'Ground Horn of Unicorn' present in many an apothecary laboratory. Life is not always kind and ideal, and maybe children should not be brought up to expect it. They should be ready to be knocked back as well as to succeed and take life as it is in an explosive and violent Universe. Idealism can be useful, even necessary as long as one remains grounded in reality. One should remember that Giovanni Bellini's Madonna of the Meadow sits there in perfect peacefulness during a brief respite before the invading army of a rival township is again bombarding the castle walls. Much can be learnt from studying Art, I was always delighted to discover, as from written history. Nowadays the media of TV and online information brings us news instantly of how the localised wars within relatively small states can eventually disrupt the stability and freedom of a much larger collection of states who have learned to live together for their mutual benefit. Barriers which have been removed have to be reinstated to protect the rights and freedom of the citizens within from the insurgencies of others. Might I venture to say that jealousy and misunderstanding lies at the heart of much warfare and so called terrorism, although it may be conducted under the flag of morality or religion?

I may appear cynical but I think that much more base emotions and motives lie beneath those which are claimed in fighting for a so called noble causes. Every gain must be someone's loss. For every mountain peak, there is a corresponding valley. Another peak, as it were rose out of my valley of uncertainty quite unexpectedly. The Gallery 65 which often exhibits my work contacted me one morning.

"Brandon Liebling, could you put on an exhibition at very short notice?" Maggie inquired of me as she presented me with some mail to read and a curriculum amendment to approve.

"Well, maybe, but the pictures that I have are not really typical of my previous work – I had been aiming at an exhibition in London, which I have not negotiated yet." I replied thoughtfully.

"Your Gallery has had a cancellation. Apparently Anselm Wurtenberger has withdrawn all his work which was due to go on show at the end of next week, after Mabel Dexternas closes, and he has taken off to Indonesia to find new inspiration. They would like to discuss it with you when you have a moment." Maggie continued with her usual charm, and I decided not to ask her how Amanda was faring.

"I see. The new work is less of what might be interesting in an office environment, and more to that of a private collector." I had uncertainties about how I might be received now that my harmonious balance had become expressionistic.

"They are really keen to have you, and they have tried to contact you on your home number." Maggie continued enthusiastically. "I would call them immediately, as you have not exhibited for some time now."

I did call, and as they were large canvasses many of them did not need framing, and at the private view I was rewarded and startled slightly when Shirley, one of the managers, introduced me to someone.

"Hello, Brandon, I am very pleased to meet you, I must say that I find this recent work of yours very fascinating." The very cultured voice of Daryl Kabell greeted me as I shook his hand, and looked into his surprisingly mild pale brown eyes. In fact he looked smooth and cultured in every way. His expensively tailored slim-fit brown suit fitted him perfectly, - not an off the peg job for this guy. His royal blue tie had a perfect sheen, and a perfect knot without the tiniest crease or wrinkle. And the collar of his cream shirt was perfectly measured for his neck and as crisp and clean as a magazine advertisement. I was surprised at the long slender artistic fingers and the firmness of their grip. His pants had such razor edge creases that I almost asked if I could borrow them to shave with. If I had examined his dark brown shoes more closely, I am sure that I would have seen my own reflection mirrored perfectly.

"Thank you Mr Kabell." I replied as graciously as I could whilst I fought with the emotions and aggressions welling up inside of me. I noticed that a faint line of a designer moustache adorned his top lip as he pursed his mouth rather like a Frenchman would, although his accent was more derivative of Oxford English. He gestured towards a particularly stormy picture with both hands expressively and I noticed that he wore a plain wide gold band on each fourth digit. I guessed that maybe one of the attractive women I had seen him with in the restaurant was his wife, but just as likely not.

"I find this painting particularly beautiful. Rather turbulent, yes, but the interplay of deep vibrant colour really suggests the passage of space and time, and yet it is definitely here and now. It is easy to perceive the lucidity of your artistry and the assurance between hand and eye. If I may continue, I suggest that you create the pulsing arcane metaphysicality of a Mark Rothko, with the excitement of Wassily Kandinsky and the mastery of Oscar Kokoschka." He continued as he walked and gestured elegantly and articulately backwards and forwards between the work and myself.

"I am indeed very flattered." I replied sincerely, in spite of a mounting desire to split his elegant lips with my fist.

"I really mean what I say, Brandon, your art is somehow derived from the 20th Century, but it is not eclectic Abstract Expressionism, it is unique and strangely representational at the same time, and entirely grounded within the 21st Century." As he continued I found it harder to connect this cultured intelligent man in the prime of life with one of the brutal bosses of the underground gang dealing in human trafficking and grotesque murder amongst other things.

"Yes, so much of what was formerly Painting has become 3 Dimensional, and what was classed as 3 Dimensional has incorporated many elements of painting, and even graphic design can be realised in 3 Dimensional terms, but I am still very traditional in a sense, and enjoy working on a flat surface." I answered very truthfully, deciding to keep my mind entirely on the subject in hand.

"And you evoke such a strong 3 Dimensional experience. I could almost step into your paintings and yet there is no suggestion of conventional Perspective." His eulogy seemed inexhaustible, and something like a slight consternation must have registered on my face. "Forgive me, I must appear to be like a lecturer, but Art is my passion, although by profession I am a Barrister, an Attorney. I studied in the UK amongst other places." He added with a charming smile, and another flourish of his long artistic fingers.

"Your eloquence in fact causes me to be quite envious. I must admit that sometimes my enthusiasm fails me and my vocabulary becomes empty when I am addressing some of my students." I added again very sincerely; his charm was so infectious.

"Ah yes Professor, and one of the youngest I gather from the viewing brochure. You do not need me to remind you of how distinguished you are already, but tell me what prompted your change of direction? I am tempted to describe it as an awakening. Was this a conscious decision, or is it a kind of natural artistic progression – almost subconscious as it were?"

I was tempted to call him out right there in a loud voice and see the reaction that my words might cause, but this may have revealed my own identity as the Faceless Crusader and I wanted to know more now that I was moving even closer to the centre of my objective. That objective was still to expose all of this murderous gang completely and irrevocably. As if to underline my thoughts Eric appeared between us. He spat out a slug of phlegm which landed nowhere, not even on the mirrored sheen of Daryl's shoes. "Careful Brandon boy, the most fiendish plans are hidden by silky charm, and you have much to discover yet." Eric smiled briefly baring his yellowed uneven teeth, and through his face I could see Daryl still waiting for an answer before Eric disappeared again.

"I think that the best answer is that I was living through some personal family traumas, which might seem trivial, but strangely had a great impact upon my artistic sensibility. I found my focus moving from the desire to create something harmonious and beautiful, to a desire – no – a need to explore more expressive elements simultaneously." This is a part of the truth and I hoped that it would be totally convincing.

"Bravo. My admiration for you as an artist is undiminished. As much as I enjoy Art, and understand it, I just do not have the transformative temperament to translate my mundane successes and failures into another language, or another window of existence: into in fact, an alternative reality. Oh that I might be the bristles on the end of your brush so that I might experience the sensation first hand." Daryl regarded me with direct seriousness without any sign of mirth or deviousness as he placed his left hand over his heart for the final words of his poetic eulogy.

"Thank you again, I can only say that it is almost a humbling experience when someone such as yourself appreciates one's work, as well as ultimately rewarding."

"Now. I know that I can be a persuasive orator, but I am a man of my word, and I always put my money where my mouth is, as the saying goes, and I would like to buy three of these paintings which I see as a kind of triptych."

"Again, Mr Kabell, I can only humbly thank you yet again.

"There is just one favour, though, that I would like to ask in return, and that is not for a discounted price, as other businessmen might do, but that you visit my house, and decide the most effective positions from which to view them.

"It will be my pleasure." I said, and I must admit that I was almost astounded.

"Good, then we will converse again in a week or two, at the end of your exhibition, but I will reserve my paintings now and I look forward to your visit. I have considerable influence in this city as you know, and nothing is too much trouble for me when dealing with friends and those that I admire. I hope that I can count you amongst my friends Brandon." His tone seemed slightly sinister, and I wondered if his generosity was both a sweetener and a warning, but maybe I was reading too much into the situation.

"Thank you Mr Kabell, I look forward to it." I replied as again I accepted his hand. I could not help noticing his long thin fingers which were often associated with artistic ability.

"Call me Daryl please – I see you are interested in my fingers, well to cut a long story short, I trained as a classical pianist in my youth before I decided that I was better suited to Law. I had the technical ability to follow all the notations, but, as I said, I somehow lack the creative imagination to translate emotions and feelings and ideas into an artistic format." He regarded me with a kind of astute smile that was both friendly and impersonal.

"I see Mr, er Daryl, and I find that strange because you obviously understand so much." I could not help continuing the conversation, because this voice that haunted me belonged to a man that I could normally have a large measure of respect and liking for.

"Words are my forte, but I do not write fiction either, I have a very retentive memory and an analytical mind which is greatly advantageous to my chosen profession, and I may add a considerable aptitude for finance." Daryl placed both hands in his trouser pockets as if to end the discussion of them or maybe I had made him slightly self-conscious. I wondered if there was some underlying bitterness beneath the suave charm and obvious wealth that caused this well-educated man to delve into unscrupulous crime. Was it the workings of an extremely towering ego that made him uphold the law publicly, and privately exploit those same criminals with less intelligence that he condemned or defended?

"You may not know." He added as though interpreting some of my thoughts again, "That I am better known for my ability to defend rather than prosecute."

"I think now that I recall several successful cases that were reported in the New York Times. Quite controversial I think according to some minds, but then of course I did not have the honour of meeting you." I replied.

"Honour – a much maligned attribute if I may say so Brandon. What is an honour or not may be purely hypothetical. What some regard as an honour can appear as depreciating to others. It sometimes depends upon culture and the way that people within a given culture perceive that culture." He regarded me still with the same astute smile, as one who has, or thinks he has superior intelligence.

"That I would agree with, but both the innocent and those who are aware of their own guilt are entitled to a defence under mainstream American and British law and I have respect for those who are able to successfully do that. I have both British and African American parents, so I did not intend to imply anything more than that.

"I know Professor, but it is very easy to think within the box as it were." Daryl continued and drew a box expressively with his hands. "You must often be entreating your students to expand their horizons of awareness. I wonder what the Poet Wordsworth would have thought nowadays about the World Wide Web –'The world is too much with us late and soon getting and spending we lay waste our powers, little we see in Nature that is ours' – The world outside of ourselves is laid before us every day with a myriad of impressions jostling for attention, and is there anywhere on this Earth now without mobile phones? Wordsworth's sentiment may yet still be very true, but how much more expanded is the knowledge of the world each day for anyone everywhere, and the world is always with us whether we like it or not. It may be inspiring to view a peaceful lake or mountain, but surely one does it against a background of the crisis of warfare not really very far away, not to mention the conflict of religions."

"You are right of course, Daryl, and it is easy to think lazily, to think habitually and localised, even though one is always aware of the bigger picture, and to speak colloquially. Sometimes it appears that the most pertinent meditations on peace, are produced in the midst of war." I was amazed at myself still, having this frank first name conversation with a man that I had previously considered part of a low life and now being engaged by his charm. I was eager to continue, but Shirley advanced upon us determinedly with another prospective client, and Daryl mingled with the other guests, leaving me with an acquiescent wave of his eloquent right hand.

Die Expression von Victory.

CHAPTER 20

The Box – A Play without dialogue

Needless to say my encounter with Daryl Kabell left me with mixed feelings. It was interesting that he should talk about thinking outside the box, as on the following Monday I received a memo from Serena Maidstone, my friend who headed the department of Theatre Design, who was very excited about a new play by a mutual friend Aaron Beckslammer. It was entitled 'The Box' and due to be premiered on Wednesday evening of the same week. I invited Emerson of course, but also I invited Maggie who was delighted to accept. We met Serena and her husband Urwin in the Theatre bar where there was a general buzz of excitement about what we were about to witness. Very much influenced by traditional French mine and contemporary American body-popping artists, Aaron had written, Directed, and Produced a play without dialogue, apart from the musical scenes.

The curtain rises on a full size screen showing a JCB excavating a large enclosed square area. (The mound of Earth is gradually reduced to reveal the yellow JCB behind. Conditions and venues permitting, it would be real rubble and a real JCB on stage).

The camera moves to reveal a once white brick wall as the screen moves backwards and the audience is now looking inside the space, instead of outwards from it.

Four people dressed in long dirty grey coats – three men and one woman – walk in from the stage right. They have woolly hats and dirty faces and scuffed trainers. The woman wears black Doctor Martin's boots and a long skirt and carries a white cardboard shoe box. The three men carry empty fruit crates. They place them towards stage left, together. Two men sit, and then the woman, and then the other man. The woman places the white cardboard box on the ground in front of her, and they all sit and stare at it.

The sound of the JCB has now been replaced by the sound of regular traffic on a high street. The man on the end stage left scratches his beard and long unkempt hair and produces a sandwich from his pocket and begins to eat it, turning sideways to the audience. The woman with greying dirty blonde hair takes a half bottle of gin from her right pocket and takes a long greedy gulp from it. One can see that she is wearing soiled half fingerless navy blue gloves, over soiled yellow ones.

The man next to the woman at the other end of the improvised seats also turns sideways. His untidy dreadlocks catch on the collar of his coat as he fishes a chrome coloured electronic cigarette from his left pocket and drags on it deeply. He wears dirty grey woollen gloves. He passes it to the woman who wipes her lips on the back of her hand before producing a large white handkerchief and proceeds to wipe the mouth piece of the device carefully, before also drawing on it. She passes it to the next man who has sat hunched and immobile staring at the white shoe box. He does not respond but sits with his hands together pressed between his knees. The woman reaches across him, and the man on the end takes it after carefully wrapping the remains of his sandwich in the cling film. He produces a red handkerchief with white spots from his other pocket and also wipes the mouthpiece before taking a long drag upon it. The end glows brightly in the dimly lit stage. He passes it back to the woman who wipes the mouthpiece again before handing it back to the man on the other end, who draws on it deeply again before putting it back in his pocket.

The woman offers the man on her left the bottle of gin, but he remains immobile staring at the box. The wall behind them grows brighter and shadowy lights play across it, as the figures become more silhouetted against it. The white box also appears brighter in a small spotlight.

The dreadlock man yawning stretches his arms upwards, and scenes of Jamaican beaches and Mountains play across the wall, to the strains of the old Bunny Wailer song 'The dread, black, holy one, the Rasta Man is coming from Zion'. The scene shifts to a rock side café, and below floating in the clear blue water a large Catamaran with 'Skinny Dippers' emits loud rock music. The water is so clear and calm that the boat appears to almost hover on the surface. Girls on deck in yellow bikinis dance the 'Twist'. The music fades back into Reggae with the classic Bob Marley song 'Love and be Loved' and a second catamaran appears round a headland, with girls gyrating at the railings, and waving. He rests his elbows on his knees and his head in his hands after pulling his yellow, green, red and black striped woolly hat over his ears, and snoring sounds are heard. As the wall becomes blank.

Next, the man on the other end produces a bottle of lager from his pocket and as he drinks scenes of Las Vegas play across the wall with cabaret girls to the song about Las Vegas. (Elvis Presley, Viva Las Vegas). Gaming tables appear and Roulette wheels spin as the croupiers perform, and vast stacks of chips are pushed to and fro. Men insert carton after carton of tokens into the slot machines whilst pulling the levers and pressing the buttons arbitrarily as they move from one machine to another. The scene ends as a machine spews out a vast jackpot of tokens, too many for two men to gather up. He puts the bottle back in his pocket and also rests his head in his hands, after adjusting his red and white striped woolly hat. The images fade from the wall, and he too begins to snore contentedly.

The woman pushes the gin bottle back into her pocket and adjusts her grey and red check scarf and pink and orange hat. She rubs her hands together before yawning dramatically. Scenes of elegant women at tables overlooking the sea in Niece drinking from cocktail glasses play across the wall. Elegant waiters and waitresses dressed in black and white move in and out of the tables offering canapés and Champagne. Next scenes appear from an elegant 1920's ballroom with shimmering dresses, and men in smart evening suits dancing to the classic song, The Continental. A woman wearing a tiara and partially hidden by potted palms raises her white gloved hand and a man in semi military uniform with a row of medals kisses it. He bows and the woman takes his hand as they descend down three steps and begin a military two step dance. The ballroom fades and the old woman smiles and sighs, before she too rests her head in her hands and falls asleep.

The third man continues to stare at the white box immobile, until unexpectedly he removes his navy and white woolly hat to reveal neatly cut ginger hair, and a relatively youthful face. He looks up and all around at the audience, and up to the gallery, before emitting a long desperate wail which is enhanced and echoed. A large black rectangle is displayed in the centre of the wall as he twists his hat around his hands. He then sits immobile and still but with his mouth open, and then emits another long loud desperate wail, which oscillates and gradually reverberates away to complete silence, as the black rectangle fades. He then resumes staring at the white box, in a pale spotlight, after replacing his hat, as the wall and stage are dimmed.

Slowly a warm pale yellow light illuminates the wall, and the dreadlock man stirs and stretches again. He takes off his trainers and produces a pair of cerise patent stilettos from the folds of his coat, and puts them on before concealing his trainers in the voluminous coat. He stands and takes off the coat after also producing a small briefcase from it. It reveals a shapely black jacket with the ruffles of a crisp white blouse beneath. He then pulls the old ragged pants apart at the waist like a stripper, and off his legs, to reveal a short smart black skirt and shapely legs. He faces the audience directly and pulls off his beard and face and hat all together to reveal the face of a beautiful 30's something business woman with blond hair pulled neatly into a back comb. She folds the coat neatly onto the box, and struts smartly toward the front of the stage, twirls, and then struts back and out at stage right, when a door slides open in the wall.

Sounds of early morning traffic resume with some fragments of conversation as people head for work or shopping etc. The young man continues to stare at the box. The other man remains asleep; he rises as though sleep walking and walks into the wall in front of him, stage left. He turns and shuffles across to the stage front, and fakes bumping into an invisible wall, like mine artists. He rubs his nose and then feels his way across with flat hands on the imaginary wall to the stage right and bumps into that wall still sleep walking. He then shuffles to the rear wall and bumps into it, but surprisingly a sliding door opens and he falls through it. Enhanced heavy snoring sounds accompany his movements. The door closes seamlessly and strains of atonal classical string music are heard, similar to a Shostakovich violin concerto, and faintly the sound of pneumatic drilling.

The woman awakes and takes out a compact mirror and attempts to tidy her straggly hair. She produces a well-worn lipstick and smears some on her lips before smoothing it with her thumb and finger of her right hand. Suddenly the young man makes a grab for the box, and the woman chases him around the stage, he outpaces her, but falls over the boxes as he looks behind him. The woman is upon him and kicks and slaps him as he drops the box almost back in the position that it was in. She picks it up and nurses it like a baby, and lifts the lid slightly to look inside. She sits again and places the box back on the floor whilst she takes a swig of gin. The young man resumes his positon next to her, removing and replacing his hat and rubbing his left knee, but still staring at the box.

The rear wall grows a brighter yellow to indicate sunshine and maybe midday and the spotlights on the two remaining walls grow brighter. The woman fans herself with the large white handkerchief, and takes off her coat and scarf and skirt to reveal that she is wearing a formal black suit with a white shirt and black bow tie. She puts the handkerchief over her face, leans backwards and when she removes the handkerchief, she has removed her face and grey-blonde hair, to reveal the features of a very smart black man (Mixed African &White, African or similar). He rises and pulls the end of his trouser legs from the long socks so that they hang with sharp creases over the black boots, and he too walks towards the audience, and stops whilst he answers his cell phone which he produces from an inside pocket. After a jolly mimed conversation, he turns sharply and proceeds to stage right, before walking back and out at the side of stage left through another sliding door.

The lights grow cooler with an evening feel and the high street sounds change with strains of Dance Beat, and Modern Jazz Saxophone, which change to a faint high pitched oscillating note. The young man rises unsteadily and runs to each wall, but no door slides. He walks dejectedly back to the improvised seating boxes, and the folded discarded clothes, hanging his head, but before he sits he remembers the white shoe box. He looks up and points to it. He pounces on it and hugs it victoriously. He holds it above his head with both arms outstretched like a trophy. There is silence. He lifts off the lid and discards it impatiently. He looks up at the audience, and all round in disbelief before running open mouthed to the front of the stage. He emits another oscillating heart rending wail as he holds the box open in front of him turning to the left and to the right, to show that it is completely empty. He stands open mouthed emitting wail after wail growing fainter as the stage dims into complete darkness. He is standing on a lift panel, which lowers him and closes again before the empty 'BOX' stage is brightly illuminated briefly. Stage hands have also removed the coats and fruit boxes before the stage is relit.

Another moment of darkness ensues before the stage is moderately lit as the actors stand holding hands for the curtain call.

Based upon a dream Aaron presented this almost nillistic view of life in his usual esoteric way, with his usual preoccupation with dual and interchangeable identities. This is certainly not new to Theatre or Opera but there is an uncompromising and fearless seriousness in his work, which of course is not lacking in ironic twists of humour.

Serena was doubly overjoyed because the young ginger haired man was one of her most recent graduates. Liam Hardcastle was in fact a British actor and this was his big off-Broadway break. We joined a backstage gathering and Serena introduced us. He had a striking charisma, and appeared to be the direct opposite of the empty and desolate character he had just played. He was from Durham where his parents still lived, and some of that accent was still discernible in his speech and he had an uncurbed natural quality about him which was quite refreshing.

"I have actually worked amongst Paranoid and Bi-polar patients, and I was thinking of becoming a Psychologist, but the lure of the theatre proved to be greater." Liam informed me.

"Well it appears that you have made a good choice, but I was not sure about the mentally challenged aspect I thought it was more about the search for something in life and finding nothing." I replied, cautiously.

"That is what Aaron intended, but I have a whole-a lot of experience of my own to bring to the character. I am too full of myself people often tell me, but I can empathise completely with those kind of guys who-a go through life without finding interest, solace or inspiration in much of what they encounter. I mean I know-a some guys who are like that, and they would be unable to play the part on stage because they cannot externalise their problems or even see them clearly. Playing a part would be beyond their realms of understanding because for some reason they are trapped in emptiness both internally, and externally." Liam delivered this reply with a bright intensity and I realised that he was such a good actor because he had the burning desire to express and communicate.

"I understand, and for such a person who remains in a kind of void the problem could be caused by something physical or chemical appertaining to the functions of that wonderful and still mysterious organ named the brain." I was intrigued and I could see why Serena was so enthusiastic.

"Yes, but are there not those people around who have perfectly normal functions one might say, and yet find themselves in an intellectual void of nihilism. You knowa- those who consider everything and decide that ultimately life means nothing other than an ongoing biological process which at the same time is pointless and self-preserving, and not part of a greater consciousness?" Liam continued, with fragments of his Durham dialect appearing.

"Aaron is a clever old friend, and I know that if illness had not prevented him from being here tonight, he would say that there is also much fear involved, which you portrayed very well. The fear of living and still finding nothing of real interest or without even achieving what appear to be basic human goals." I was very interested to continue this line of conversation.

"Yes man and wheeras those intellectuals are content to live within their nihilistic void because they have already archived a certain status and carried out the basics of existence, our man in the play has not, and cannot understand why." Liam continued.

"And that brings us back to your point from your Psychiatric experience, or the question rather- how does one enter the private enclosed void of a mentally challenged individual in order to release them from their isolation and help them move on?" I suggested.

"Yes man, and I must admit that I have-a too much going on to ever have the patience ora level of commitment to make a good practitioner in that field." Liam concluded.

Our meeting was cut a little short by another mutual friend in the form of Emily Robertson a critic and columnist who approached Serena, Urwin, Maggie, Emerson and myself for an opinion. Serena was of course effusive, and I added my very favourable comments. Maggie was equally enthusiastic and thought what charm and charisma all the actors displayed in spite of the rather nihilistic theme. Emerson at first polite decided that it was too harrowing and unrealistic. Urwin decided that the acting was excellent, but found the playwriting flawed and just clichéd theatrical tricks under cover of the avant-garde. Needless to say Urwin received a kick behind his ankle and a steely angry glare from Serena for his unperturbed candid assessment.

Someone that I did not expect to see was Nigel McArthur, with the ever present scarf almost hiding his black bow tie, but it did not detract from the smartness of his 'skinny fit' black suit. He was as excited as Serena, because the third man was an older cousin. He came over to me in his usual agitated way and after enthusing about the play, informed me that his father had no new leads, and no new evidence had been revealed since the man they called 'The Faceless Crusader' had fallen silent, just as abruptly as he had begun.

"He was a regular pain in the arse and Dad would have charged him if he could, but at the same time he was more than grateful for his work in exposing many criminal gang members." Nigel expounded.

"Ah yes, I remember you telling me about that and I was hoping to see Hanwell Nnagobi avenged, but from what you said I have been thinking that maybe Hanwell's death has been vindicated. There could be a lot that I did not know about his character and activities, which would make more sense of the whole affair, even though his death cannot be excused." I did not feel the time was appropriate to discuss the case too fully.

"Dad is beginning to think along those lines too. Although what appears to be horrific ritual murder maybe by someone with a perverted sense of justice can never be excused, Nnagobi is viewed as less of a martyr than was otherwise apparent." Nigel continued.

"Obviously I would feel safer if the core of the rotten fruit was exposed, so to speak, but I wonder if that will be possible." I replied.

"Yes, well obviously performing such tasks is what Dad has committed his life to, and he is very optimistic now." Nigel continued before he was called away by a signal from his cousin, much to my relief as I did not want Emerson or Serena and certainly not Maggie, to have the slightest idea of what I had involved myself with. I wanted them to think that I was safely within my particular 'BOX'.

The Box.

CHAPTER 21

la Maison du Soleil

I have to admit again that I was influenced greatly by Daryl Kabell. It was not proven of course that he was one of those responsible for perpetrating violent and heinous crimes, but I know a voice when I hear one as I expect most people do, and I do also know that voices can be very similar to people sharing the same ethnic background, so in spite of my feelings I decided to reserve judgement for the moment. I know that my old friend Lenward Grayson-Baden had the same mixed race parentage as myself and often we sounded identical especially over the telephone. I attributed some of the rapport that Lenward had with Naomi to the fact that he was so much like myself. I hoped that was the case anyway and I often thought about his early warning. His advice to take a vacation to ease Naomi's mounting stress, which was something he discerned more than I did myself. I would not accuse myself of insensitivity, but he had certainly been far more perceptive than myself on his visit to us, after he returned from Germany. I still thought of her every day and the fact that the children were growing up without their Mother at an important stage in their lives.

Emerson had become indispensable and showed a greater desire to look after my family than she had done with her own, and the children adored her. There had not been any tantrums about 'wanting my real Mom' not even by Andrea and they seemed to accept the situation. Kurt loved our Au pair, Anna-Maria, but now I had to take in a new situation.

Dessie informed me both joyfully and sorrowfully, that Matild had been born successfully, and did I agree with the name – but Naomi had been admitted into care and what had seemed like emotional stress was an early form of Dementia.

"Already Naomi does not recognise me on some days, and never seems to really know where she is. Sometimes when I mention the children she does not recall who they are and only once recently has she asked about you. Now we know what the problem is, you can visit, it would not cause further problems and see your new daughter, and she is a pretty little baby. Dementia does not run in our family as far as I know, particularly in one so young as Naomi, and so we are all a little dismayed and shocked to say the least."

"You and Hubert have been wonderful Dessie, and I cannot thank you enough,-." I began.

"We will look after little Matild for the time being." Dessie interrupted and continued. "We know that you have commitments and your three to look after. It really is no trouble for us, and we will take her to see Naomi so that she will have contact with her natural Mother. What happens in the long term will be your decision of course and we can discuss any financial arrangements later. As you are aware, Naomi is still a Canadian citizen and has been resident again for more than three months, so Health Care has not been a problem financially. Philippe our physician has been more than happy to treat her as his patient, and the money you send has been more than adequate for her other needs."

"I will visit as soon as possible, probably on my own." I answered sadly, "Maybe it is a blessing that the children do not have to witness the trauma of their Mother not recognising them, it is hard enough for adults to cope with, but for children it must be really disturbing. My beautiful clever Naomi – I can hardly believe it myself."

It seemed as though all my beautiful sunny days had ended. In fact all the happy peaceful warm sunny days had ended in the world everywhere. No longer did I contemplate in my mind's eye the tranquil reflections of the South River. All those images of early morning sunrises and evening sunsets were like faded and crumpled parchments mildewed with mocking irony. I thought of the black night sky filled with dots of light from stars which were already dead, like the legacy of a person may live on after their death. Is that what we strive for? Is that what I strive for – to leave a legacy, to create something for posterity so that my brief existence will not vanish unnoticed? I often wondered - where does all that noise and energy go to for instance, as one watches a person who is resigned to death; and all those vital activities become merely empty actions. Like one going through the motions of living: but whose core of existence and awareness is somewhere else. Yes I live, - maybe you live also in between a kind of spiritual reality and actual concrete everyday reality, and often wonder which is the most real. Had I passed through a veil of darkness into a deeper state of existence like a parallel universe? I seriously began to wonder especially since my involvement with Eric. Did one have the right to expect to live a simple pleasant uncomplicated life, or was this just a fantasy suggested by people who never did, and always thought that the grass was greener on the other side as the saying goes. When we learn about history, it is not the ordinary people, but the unusual ones who have lived extraordinary lives or attained wealth and authority, that we learn about. I hate the term 'ordinary people' because everyone is unique whether or not they achieve something remarkable.

And so, it was as though moving under a personal heavy black cloud that I accompanied the delivery of my paintings to the residence of Daryl Kabell in due course. After being checked by security at the gates, I was astonished when I arrived at the simplistic, yet opulent la Maison du Soleil. In the morning sun the house seemed to radiate its own light from within like a large Art Deco sun, and yet it was also a triangular and rectangular steel and glass construction built by Daryl to be functionally ecological. The House of the Sun was no mean claim with clever and decorative Solar panels providing all of the energy for lighting, hot water and air conditioning. I learned later that under floor heating was provided by tapping into the surface heat of the Earth and fed through ducts. This is a method already established, but it surprised me to find it here. I was amazed at the knowledge and resourcefulness of this man whom judging by his voice alone I had dismissed as little more than a hired killer.

Water was recycled and filtered for the decorative fountains in the garden, playing over the rouge, black and green marbled bodies of modern figurative representations of Apollo, Venus, Mars, Mercury and Ceres. Water cascading almost silently down the glass panels on either side of the wide front doorway gave the feeling of entering a waterfall, or maybe a sanctuary of prayer and meditation. It seemed that wherever my vision was focussed, dazzling light was reflected back to me echoing the motion of the swishing and rhythmical truckling of the clear water.

Added to this sensation of light was a strong sweet smell of late summer blooms. So pungent was this that I felt almost intoxicated as though it were incense infused with some subtle hallucinatory herbs. As I entered the fresh smelling large entrance hall, Daryl came forward to meet me. His soft cream coloured shoes were hardly audible as he strode over the immaculately polished 'terrazzo' floor. As if to emphasise the aspect of sunlight, today he wore a white suit, and a yellow shirt open at the collar. This was the most casually dressed that I had seen him.

"Good morning Brandon. It is a beautiful morning is it not? I am so pleased that you could come. Do you like my garden sculptures? I commissioned them from Artur Bradlee, he is a friend of mine." Daryl took my hand into both of his and shook it warmly. "I hope that I can count you as a friend also." He added again, with an ingenuous smile.

"Of course you can-Daryl-and yes, I know Artur, and his reputation is certainly justified, the sculptures are magnificent." I answered openly in spite of the reservations I still held about him.

"Good. Now where do you think your paintings would look equally magnificent?" He looked at me as though it was a foregone conclusion, almost a rhetorical question.

"Well, I have not seen the rest of the house, but right here in the entrance hall. The natural but slightly indirect light on the back walls would suit them very well." I answered truthfully.

"Excellent. You are a man after my own heart. I thought so too. Those dark greens and reds and deep vibrant blues will have a life of their own and command the full attention which they deserve from everyone who enters la Maison du Soleil." Daryl engaged me fully with his unflinching pale brown eyes which at the same time were both friendly and distant, but I could see again that his praise was genuine.

"That will be very gratifying." I replied and also smiled charmingly.

"And believe me, there are many influential people who pass through the portals of my humble abode." Daryl added almost absent-mindedly. "I would not be surprised if several commissions came your way."

"I am already indebted to you, and may I say that your humble abode is also magnificent." I added.

"Thank you. I designed it with Piere Brun-Aire. My Sun sign is Aquarius you know, Fixed Air and also traditionally represented by a symbol of the Water Pourer, in Western Astrology, with the polarity of Leo. It is literally representational of myself. The Sun shines on me so to speak - I have a Jupiter and Sun conjunction at Mid Heaven and the Moon in conjunction with Uranus in Libra. I could be purely academic in my approach to life, but Gemini and Pisces have swapped rulers as it were. Saturn rules my Pisces from Gemini, but Mercury rules my Gemini from Pisces, so my scholarly mentality is modified by spiritual and intuitive elements. Not conflicting in direction, but complimenting each other. I rejoice that I have been given penetrating philosophical insight by Neptune the co-ruler of Pisces from its position within Sagittarius. I probably chose a profession in Law because the ruler of my Sun sign, Uranus is in Libra represented by the scales. Never underestimate the power of the fast moving Moon, as daily I consider the balance of everything. The case for, and the case against. Piere is very clever and has designed for Hollywood Stars, and is also sought after in Europe. As you know, I have the ideas, but not the practical talents, so I rather explained what I would like, and Piere produced the goods." Daryl paced a little whilst gesturing with his eloquent hands as he spoke.

"That is very interesting. My wife and I planned our family, so that we would all be of different but compatible signs." I replied, almost swept away by Daryl's knowledge and enthusiasm, before I remembered again that I suspected he was part of the events which interrupted our happy family life. I reminded myself again that everyone was innocent until proven guilty, and I had no visible or concrete proof but only the sound of a voice. I knew now that Naomi would still have fallen ill, even without the stress which had been placed on her through myself, or the subversive elements I had been thrown into conflict with. I managed to maintain a bright expression and he continued.

"I knew you would be a compatible associate, Professor. Some people would be completely negatively unresponsive to my interest in Astrology, or dismiss it as pure conjecture without seeing into the ramifications beyond the graphic mythology." Daryl was still for a moment as though looking into me afresh with the intensity of a laser beam.

"There is the vast Universe which we humans can see and feel and are a part of, but there is also a parallel Universe to consider, and we can often sense more than we can see or explain easily in words or pictures." I replied as though he had extracted the thoughts from me with his magnetism.

"Quite. It is not just a coffee table indulgence or the banal blanket predictions of the day in a magazine column. In my chart the Trine of air signs is paramount, but my Mars in Taurus in first House gives me weight and tenacity, and maybe even stubbornness. I always get what I want, and I always complete what I set out to achieve." Daryl returned to his charming effusive gesticular manner of speech as he delivered this sagacious proviso.

"I am certainly fortunate to be amongst your friends rather than your enemies. You are indeed blessed." I answered lightly, for I knew that there was probably much more which lay hidden, than what he chose to divulge.

Daryl laughed and placed his hand on my shoulder briefly. "It is I who am honoured to have you as my guest and your friendship. Now let us further enhance my beautiful house with the addition of your paintings, if you will direct the hanging, and then I hope you will stay for some refreshment and meet my wife."

My spirits began to rise and rays of sunlight trembled tentatively upon the edge of full brilliance, in my mind, as my large paintings were unloaded and I decided the right height for them to be hung, and I seemed to absorb the light and magic of la Maison du Soleil. I felt more optimistic than I had for several weeks and Daryl's enthusiasm was infectious. He was more meticulous than myself down to the last millimetre, as he studied each painting from a distance and then closer and so on almost like an ethereal figure in his white suit gesturing and waving whilst moving almost in sequence like a ballroom dancer.

Presently all was completed to Daryl's satisfaction and the two Gallery men departed, thanking him for the generous gratuity which he gave them along with profuse appreciations of their efforts and patience. He then opened a frosted glass door at the right side of the entrance hall and called-

"Salenaola" A beautiful young African American woman appeared, and I recognised her as one of his companions that I had seen him with at W's Cuisine. I was just about to greet her as Mrs Kabell, when Daryl continued. "Tell Mazolina that the pictures are hung, please, my darling." With a slight movement of obedience in her tight orange fitted pencil dress with round neckline, Salenaola pirouetted in her white stiletto's and disappeared down a glass corridor and then turned sharply left. The frosted door swung slowly shut casting fragments of prismatic colours as it did so.

Mazolina Mitchell Kabell was more dazzling than I had anticipated. As the door re-opened a woman as tall as Daryl strode elegantly through and her golden seven inch heels in fact gave her a slight edge over his height. With greater poise and elegance than a catwalk model, each golden clad trouser leg was placed perfectly in front of the other and appeared to be almost endless before they joined a lightly swinging hip above which a loose and open broidery-Ingles white blouse tentatively clung to the nipples of well-formed and firm breasts. A sparkling diamond cluster nestled in the cleavage rising and falling with each breath and the thick gold chain disappeared behind an elegant neck which supported an oval face with sublimely prominent slanted cheekbones. This was framed by a shock of tightly curled blonde hair speckled with ginger, and then the most bewitching deep blue eyes gazed intelligently from the green and orange eye shadow and liner. The light tint of her complexion was silky and sun-kissed and as smooth as an airbrushed magazine photograph. Golden bangles shimmered on each wrist and her crimson lips revealed perfect white medium sized teeth as the beginnings of a demure smile parted them.

"Good morning Professor Brandon, It is a pleasure to meet you." The finger nails of the hand which she offered were the same crimson as her lips, and her voice was soft and yet strong with an accent that was somehow indefinable. "I am Mazolina Mitchell Kabell."

I was almost too absorbed feasting upon her attributes to speak, and I was aware that Daryl had become uncharacteristically static, as he also watched her with admiration, and also watched my own reaction." Good morning Mrs Kabell the pleasure is all mine." I managed to sound professional, as I took her surprisingly soft and warm hand. I turned to Daryl saying "You did not mention that your wife was so beautiful."

"Maz is the Sun in my Heaven." Daryl said as he put an arm around her waist and hugged her close to himself. "She is a Capricorn - my Venus in Capricorn and my counterpart. Whatever forces there are in the Universe, I constantly thank them for drawing us together."

The face of Mazolina radiated a full smile as he kissed her on the cheek, and indeed I felt as though the sun had burst forth after a long period of cloudiness. "The name seems familiar." I ventured as something in my memory began to revive. "Mitchell -."

"That is absolutely correct Brandon." Maz interrupted with less formality. "Mitchell Real Estate, and Construction."

"And were you not a Tennis Star, forgive my presumptuousness –." I continued.

"Bull's Eye again. But that was several years ago and I do not play professionally now, though I still love to beat Daryl on our court." She laughed and it was sweet and lilting.

"I always let her win." Daryl said as he too laughed. I had not seen this lightly bantering side of him before which was quite disarming.

"Don't you believe it Professor – Daryl hates to be beaten at anything." Maz smiled and exquisite dimples formed on her cheeks giving her an almost Oriental appearance. She leaned into him as he held her more tightly, and the left side of her blouse finally gave up its precarious hold and slipped away to reveal a perfect breast. I had to severely restrain myself from stepping forward to cup it in my right hand and fondle its perfect shape.

"Do you think my Maz would make a good model?" Daryl asked with a sly smile. He had read my impulse, and Mazolina made no attempt to hide her perfection.

"Without the slightest doubt." I replied, trying to stay cool.

"I mean an Artist's model. You must be familiar with painting from life at least during your training, even though you do not produce those kind of paintings now. I would love to have your artist's impression of her. She does not tread the Catwalk now – she never needed to except for the fun of it – others walk the Catwalk for her approval."

"It is quite a few years since I actually painted from a live model, and as a student we rarely, if ever had the privilege of studying one so beautiful as your wife." I answered truthfully.

"Would you find it embarrassing now?" Daryl asked with absolute charm, as he deftly slid his hand behind her and removed the blouse completely. She twirled and finished in an inviting stance with one arm raised and the other by her side showing an open palm.

A surge of desire and defiance swept through me, and I inadvertently gulped. I was being drawn into something here that I had not anticipated. "Not at all. I would not be embarrassed at all. I am sure that I can revive my skills, but I would like to take photographs so that the actual sittings are not too long."

"Excellent, Brandon. I think that you are one of the most brilliant contemporary Artists and I am sure that you can do justice to the beauty of Mazolina. I want you to immortalise her. Believe me, I will pay you well, you will not regret it." Daryl was visibly pleased and I knew that he meant what he said and also that he was very discerning.

"Good. I want to be painted near the pool so that it is a modern take on of a Nymph. Come - I will show you, and we can have lunch at the same time." Mazolina replaced the open short sleeved blouse casually and led the way bewitchingly down the corridor and out into a gorgeous high walled garden of variegated blooms and hanging baskets, to where the pool was situated with a glass roof and sliding walls of glass, which today were all open.

"This is utterly beautiful like an exotic oasis." I remarked, genuinely breath taken.

"Yes I had a hand in designing this part of la Maison du Soleil." Maz remarked softly but her voice carried like the whisper of a balmy summer breeze. Without any embarrassment or coyness she sat on a carved stone bench and removed her shoes, before peeling off the slim line gold trousers to reveal a tiny golden thong which she also removed, before sliding elegantly into the inviting turquoise water. Like many women she glided easily through the water with a breast stroke managing to keep her face and hair above the surface.

"Fancy a swim before lunch Brandon?" Daryl asked from behind me and I turned to see that he was now naked also and showing off a trim well-formed body.

"I do not have a costume." I said feeling that as a new guest I should still show some propriety, and not because I was embarrassed to show off my own well-toned body.

"You do not need one." Came the gentle reply from Maz at the poolside.

"Come on take a dip." Daryl shouted as he shallow dived into the water.

"Okay. Thank you. Why not." I replied quickly undressing, and soon I was swimming the length of the pool feeling totally at home and relaxed. It seemed strangely predicable that we were joined by Salenaola who also graced the pool with an elegant breast stroke.

"You have a very fine physique if I may say so Professor Brandon, you look as though you can lift more than a paintbrush, and probably handle yourself well." Salenaola did surprise me with this comment as she looked at me appreciatively.

"I manage to maintain my fitness routine and of course weights are included." I answered, remembering my life or death fight with Buzz, and I wondered how much Salenaola knew of Daryl's business, or indeed of gangland business, she was obviously more than just a secretary. I knew that they were checking me out just as much as I was checking them out.

"That is another thing I am delighted to see that we have in common, I have my own private Gym here too." Daryl added as he swam over to us.

"What do you think of our pretty fishes Brandon?" Mazolina inquired with a smile as she too swam over.

To my surprise again, beneath the glass floor of the pool was another illuminated and oxygenated pool filled with tropical fish and coral, so that it was like snorkelling or diving in the Caribbean. The lower pool extended beyond the swimming pool at one end so that the glass covers could be removed for easy access to facilitate cleaning and feeding. This was part of a viewing terrace where I could now see that a cold luncheon was already laid with Salads, Caviar, Chicken and Lobster.

"I am absolutely breath-taken, and I will try to include them in my portrait of you, but I feel that my talents pall with the splendour of this amazing Maison du Solei." I answered sincerely.

"Nonsense, but that will be easy, I will sit on the lower viewing terrace." Mazola answered with an almost seductive giggle, whilst Daryl looked approvingly.

"Well I sure could use some luncheon, I expect that you could Professor Brandon, - allow me to direct you to the showers." Salenaola stated, as she exited the pool elegantly and wrapped a large towel around her firm body.

After a refreshing shower and a slow walk through the drying chamber and donning yellow bathrobes, we were chatting convivially around the Luncheon Buffet. A young man whom Daryl introduced as Garreth, a wine waiter, wearing a white coat, shirt, and orange pants, appeared with chilled Champagne and sweet Red and White wine. Daryl also informed me quite matter of factly that it was from his own vineyards in California. What ever happened in the future I decided that this first visit to la Maison du Soleil and its dazzling brilliance would be one that I would never forget.

la Maison du Soleil.

CHAPTER 22

Canadian Capers

It was cold with a promise of snow for Christmas. I prefer to see snow in Vermont, rather than on the streets of New York, but I know there are many who might not agree. It was even colder in Canada over the border, and I wondered how Dessie and Hubert were content to live there. Whenever I asked, they replied that it was crisp and healthy, with snow lingering for maybe four months, and then the summer could be hot and humid. They are in the city of course, of monumental Montreal, so I guess that they are not snowbound as people further north. Am I a Skier? Well no, I guess that you must have guessed already. I must admit that this sport has never really attracted me very much, but as an Artist I know that there is great beauty in hillsides covered in snow and dark green pines protruding defiantly, maybe speckled with white from the last flurry of snowflakes. Craggy mountain tops with blue shadows catch passing clouds and frozen lakes glisten when rays of sunlight break through. Montreal once the Capital city of trading and commerce, is a composite city still in flux and shares the honour with Buenos Aires and Berlin of being declared a UNESCO Heritage Centre.

When I think of Canada I know that there is always at the back of my mind an image of Niagara. The classic Films with Marilyn Monroe and contemporary Travel media have planted it there, although I know that one side of it borders the USA, like Argentina and Brazil border Iguassu Falls. Here the tremendous force that water can command is paramount. The same could be said about Victoria Falls in Zimbabwe. I am always reminded too of how fragile our life support systems are. I can sweat at the Equator, and freeze at the Poles. We cling to the surface of what is still a hostile and indifferent Planet - simultaneously cooling and warming - pursuing our emotional entanglements and fighting each other for something that humans will never really own, even though we lay claim to it, trying to establish a permanence in our overall temporary habitation. I wonder if there is a primal yearning to be elemental and reinstated within the natural forces of the Earth, which makes thousands of people brave the narrow decking and covered in fine spray almost dare the tumults of water to grip them and wash them away. These waterfalls really are awe inspiring as tons of water surge above us, and pound the rocks below. I wonder if it is the stuff that dreams are made of to leap and ride the tumult, without being battered on the rocks, or suffocated with foaming spray, as the Indian legends indicate.

I did not travell by night and wake up starry eyed across the border like one of the tourist options proposes. No- I travelled by day and as much as I found it uplifting to observe the tranquillity of the atmosphere above the clouds, inwardly I sank into a deep dark abys at the thought of seeing Naomi. Would she recognise me? Would she speak? Would the sight of me arouse some adverse delirium? In spite of Dessie's optimism, I feared the worst.

I made my way by taxi to their house in Ville-Marie, one of the older areas of the city where the French colonists had established a settlement on the plains leading to the central mountains of what is basically an Island. It seems that the Italian name for this, rather than the French or native Indian, is the one that has been adopted. Hence Mon-tre-al, is descriptive of the three peaked mountain around which the city areas cluster, and although Canada was surrendered to the British and remains part of the Commonwealth, it is the city with the largest French speaking population outside of Paris. Like Desdemona and Hubert and my dear Naomi, a majority of citizens speak both French and English. A fact which surprised me from a purely architectural point of view is that St Joseph's Oratory, has the largest copper dome of any church in the world apart from St Peter's in Rome. It is also the largest Church in Canada. Naomi's Mother frequents it quite often, and I am sure that she prays for her daughter's recovery. I do not often contact her parents, as I know that they do not condone our behaviour. They think that Naomi should have stayed in New York, and that I should have been more insistent about her return. However, in Montreal like many cities during this Century, the past is preserved and the present soars to the sky.

Maybe you know that the sound of a voice can be more attractive than the features from which it emerges, which may disappoint. Well, it seemed like centuries since I had met Dessie, but her appearance was not a disappointment, in fact it was a delight. She was like Naomi, but slightly older of course and with lighter hair which framed her face like a large halo glowing at the edges as she stood with her back to the light in the hallway. The sadness in her features was dismissed by a sassy smile as she hugged me and kissed both of my cheeks.

"Bienvenue, Brandon, belle de vous voir, mais vous êtes toujours si beau, s'il vous plait venez dans. » Dessie exclaimed. I was surprised that she called me handsome, as she invited me to enter.

"Merci beaucoup, Dessie, vous me flattez, mais vous cherchez belle!" I replied hugging her in return, and I really did think that she looked lovely.

"Bonjour Hubert, je l'espère que vous êtes bien." I stepped forward and shook hands with Hubert in a rather British way like my father would do, whilst wishing him well.

"Merci Brandon très bien, il est bon de vous voir, en dépit de ces circonstances difficiles.

"Oui » I answered before reverting back to English. "It must have been a harrowing time for you and it is sad that we have to meet again after such a long time in these difficult circumstances."

"Come – I know there is someone you must be longing to see." Dessie took my hand and led me down the hallway and to a small room just before the kitchen, on the right.

"I most certainly do." I answered enthusiastically. I was glad that they were presenting me with the good news before we discussed the bad.

"Ah Matild mon petit trésor, la est ton papa!" Dessie stooped and picked up the small bundle from the blue painted cot, and handed it to me gently.

"Merci à vous deux mon elle est exquise." I thanked them both, remarking on how exquisite she was.

"Sorry that the cot is blue, but it was one that we bought for Elmer. It is lucky that we kept it although we thought that we would never use it again, well maybe for Grandchildren I suppose. Genevever and Elmer have both fled the nest but are not married yet, unlike Dessie and myself who married young. We were childhood sweethearts you know." Hubert suddenly burst into very eloquent English which was a surprise, because I recalled him as being rather quiet. It is touching how new life can suddenly arouse unexpected sentiment.

"Now Hubert, give Brandon a chance, he does not want to know about our romantic past at the moment." Dessie clasped Hubert's arm as she spoke with a twinkle in her eye, and I could see that they were still very much in love.

"Naomi must have remembered that we often spoke of naming a daughter after my Great Grandmother in Munich. Did she suggest another name also?" I said as the little face in my arms began to crinkle into a cry, as she began to awake fully.

"No just Matild, but you will be able to add a name if you want." Dessie replied.

"I think that I would like to call her Naomi as well." I declared, as I tied to contain the mixture of emotions running through me.

"An excellent choice." Hubert announced very supportively.

"Yes, Naomi would appreciate that if she were well enough to know." Dessie added with a warm understated approval.

"You will be as beautiful as your Mommy was." I said gently rocking Matild and letting her grip my right forefinger. Her crinkle turned into a smile and gurgle and she looked at me with already intelligent eyes.

"She likes you." Dessie said with a kind of relief. I think babies have very definite ideas about whom they like and dislike and who likes themselves. "More so than people are often willing to admit."

"I think that you are right." Hubert agreed gravely.

"Better go and check on your wife, bent Cop, Matild will be okay!" I almost jumped in surprise and let her slip from my arm as Eric appeared by the window opposite me. He spat out a slug of yellow phlegm as usual that landed nowhere, and gave me his customary laugh, before his image faded.

"Here, let me take her, I will put her back in the cot, you probably could use a cup of coffee or something stronger, Hubert has some good Cognac." Dessie noticed my slight reaction and fortunately mistook it for tiredness after my journey.

"Ah – thank you Dessie, I am used to snow in New York, but I think I not acclimatised to Montreal temperatures yet. That is not to say that your house is not lovely and warm." I actually did need a drink before visiting Naomi, and I wondered what Eric was preparing me for. I momentarily wished that Emerson was with me, but she had decided in her wisdom, to stay and help Anna-Maria with the children at the apartment.

I had bought a snack on the plane, but I was feeling like something more substantial and somehow seeing Eric here in Montreal had knocked the pit of my stomach into my shoes. I felt empty and yet full of nervous ripples. He reminded me that whilst I had languished in the luxury of la Maison du Soleil during the late summer weekends the work of The Faceless Crusader was not finished. I had become friends with Daryl and Mazolina and Salenaola without discovering anything really sinister about them. Daryl had occasionally watched me work without making any comment and Gareth had provided me with healthy snacks and drinks. He even insisted on helping me to clear up at the end of a session by wiping my brushes and disposing of soiled tissues and rolling up the plastic sheet protecting the patio terrazzo. Mazolina had walked casually about holding a cocktail as if unaware of her fabulous nakedness. Sometimes she would lean on my shoulder and I would feel the softness of her breast. She would look at me sideways with a pouting smile which sometimes ended with a slight giggle without making any comment, before returning to her seat, but I could sense that she was pleased. The canvas was large so that her image was almost life size, and I worked with a sexual fervour as well as analytically, and quite quickly, revising my work until I was satisfied, and the Mazolina on the flat surface appeared to breathe in a vibrant three dimensional space. The exotic multi-coloured fishes swam behind her, and she really did take on the appearance of a fabled marine Goddess. You might expect that I ended each session with rapturous intercourse, but no, this lady was strictly off limits and for Daryl's pleasure only, or so it seemed. Sometimes I would stay to dinner. They were very persuasive and Daryl sent his chauffeur to pick up Emerson when I eventually intimated that I was separated from my wife, but had a partner. Occasionally we visited W's Cuisine, and Emerson could hardly contain her delight at actually being entertained by Daryl Kabell. I felt like an Italian Renaissance artist at the court of Lorenzo de Medici, the Merchant Banker who presided over Firenze in the age of City States. I knew that they only really let me see the surface of their life, and there was more staff and visitors whom I never got to meet, but I thoroughly enjoyed myself. It is so easy to become caught up in administration and status and forget that I am a Professor because I had creative talents and experience to pass on to others, and to neglect those talents. I know also that I am a selfish sensual animal who can be manipulated, and I could not help but feel invigorated. Luxury, Beauty, Money, and Respect all contributed to the feeling that instead of condemning Daryl, I would gladly defend him in a court of law. Little did I realise that one day I might be almost in a position where a defence was necessary.

"I hope that you can manage a bowl of this. I remember that Naomi said it was one of your favourites." Dessie brought me out of the reverie Eric had instigated, "You do look a little bit like you have seen a ghost."

"Oh – no, I may have been overworking recently, but yes please, Soupe de poissons is one of my favourites." We sat at the comfortably sized table with a homely green and red check table cloth on it in the shining and spotless kitchen with pine wood cabinets contrasting with stainless steel-effect work surfaces. A stainless steel canopy carried condensation away above the Aga where a large stockpot still simmered with the assorted fish and vegetables in white wine. An induction hob was next to it and beyond that an eye level oven and grill. Along the next wall, two stainless steel microwaves stood side by side before the work surface terminated at a very contemporary chic deep porcelain sink with a double draining area and waste disposal unit. Above this a long narrow window with white blinds still open, and red and green check curtains, showed fluffy snowflakes silhouetted against the encroaching darkness of evening. Somehow in spite of the homeliness of the room, the dark window made me feel inexplicably cold and desolate, in spite of the delectable hot and spicy fish soup that I was savouring.

"How is the soup?" Hubert asked. He seemed determined to keep the atmosphere light.

"Absolutely perfect, in my humble opinion." I replied.

"I will wager that you did not know I am famous in Montreal." He continued whilst smiling broadly like one impatient to add the punch line to a joke. Dessie also smiled.

"Really? I did not know – in what way?" I replied in anticipation.

"There is a road named after me - St Hubert Street, off route 320. I must be a Saint to endure Dessie's cooking all my life." He laughed hugely and it was very infectious.

"No more soup for you in that case, Brandon and I will finish it." Dessie laughed also, more out of relief than because she found it really amusing.

"Another interesting fact that you may not know which fits with your Irish ancestry, Brandon, is that Ville-Marie was originally known as Kelly Bay, named after the first settler James Kelly who lived as a Hermit on the banks of Lake Tamiscanning." Hubert continued in fine form as he occasionally stroked his goatee beard.

"You amaze me." I replied managing to rise to the 'banteresque' repartee. "I always thought that the Amerindians were the first settlers."

"Yes there were several sites, and particularly a Wyandot, at the junction of the St Lawrence River, and the Riviere St Pierre, before Samuel de Champlain built a Fort in 1611 on an area he named Place Royal, and the French and Amerindians began trading furs." Hubert's deep brown eyes took on an intensity as he was obviously very interested in the history.

"I see, so how come this area is now Ville-Marie?" I looked at him in half amusement but I was also interested.

"Beware Brandon! Hubert is very proud of the part of his ancestry that is Algonquian." Dessie said with a twinkle in her eye and kissed him briefly on the forehead as she collected the empty bowls.

"The Algonquians were also trading with the French before 1670 before a store was built a century later about 1785 which became incorporated into the Hudson's Bay Company as late as 1821. Then in 1874 Joseph Moffet, of the Oblates of Mary Immaculate, moved to Kelly Bay, and it became temporarily known as Baie-des-Peres, or Bay of Fathers." Hubert continued.

"I see. Again it is amazing that so much is relatively recent history." I answered.

"Moffet was only 22, what faith for someone so young, but about nine years later he was joined by settlers from Nicolet in 1883, and by 1886 they had established the Parish of Notre-Dame-du-Saint-Rosaire-de-Ville-Marie."

Hubert paused and again I really was surprised at his eloquence. I think that I had only heard him say bon jour previously.

"What a CAPER. I mean it is sometimes incredible to think that people who were enterprising enough could just take off from one continent and settle in the middle of another." I answered.

"Or to be dissatisfied enough with their homeland to want to do that." Hubert retorted thoughtfully.

"To me it is quite a caper. I mean move over inhabitants, there is room for us as well, and we mean to inundate you with religious fervour too." I answered almost with a laugh as Dessie offered some tempting French chocolate tartlets and crème whirls.

"And – if we cannot force you to submit to religious fervour, we will use force." Hubert added as he wolfed a tartlet in one bite.

"Can you really truly imagine a world today without extensive security, and creeps pretending to befriend you or to be in need of help so that they can lead you into a Police interrogation?" I asked truthfully.

"Well no, I certainly cannot, and I wonder whether I would have been an adventurer in those days. I am not sure whether one should thank our ancestors or curse them." Hubert was beginning to sound quite fervent.

"Anyway, I take it that the 'CANADIAN CAPERS' of the Nicolet settlers finally gave James Kelly's bay the name of Ville-Marie." I continued between a mouthful of chocolate and crème.

"Yes a Post Office Baie-des-Pere was opened in 1891, and the Village Municipality of Ville-Marie became Incorporated in 1897 a year or so before the Hudson Bay Post closed, and was renamed, but it was not until 22 of December 1962, that the Village Municipality of Ville-Marie became the Town of Ville-Marie." Hubert concluded decisively, as he took a sip of steaming coffee from a small elegant cup.

"Now as one of the principal areas of Quebec within the composite City of Montreal, Ville-Marie is the seat of the judicial district of Temiscamingue." Dessie added.

"Wow, and I always thought Canada was simple, it is quite a caper, - history still in the making." I concluded.

Matild began to cry at that point and Dessie rushed to attend to her, and now I had to face the question that hung over us, of what to do about Naomi.

St Joseph's Oratory, Montreal.

CHAPTER 23

Where Are You?

It was decided that as it was already evening, I should visit Naomi in the morning, rather than possibly disturbing her with a visit and making it difficult for her to sleep. Montreal General Hospital was part of the McGill University Health Centre where medical research was developed in conjunction with the usual Hospital facilities. I must say that I was already warming to this City with its mixture of French, English, Amerindian, and Irish. At the moment I was surprised not to find more of a German element too. The Hospital is situated on Cedar Avenue on Mount Royal at the junction with Cote-des-Neiges-Road. How is that for a meltdown of multinational locations I thought to myself? Apparently, Hubert also informed me, the Spanish had checked out the North of the country in the 16th Century and were unable to find silver or gold. They decided not to try and colonise it after naming it el Cabo de nada – Cape Nothing! On their maps they wrote 'aca nado, aqui nada, or ca nada'- nothing here.

I often wondered, and I must say that I had never bothered to check, how Canada became known as Canada. Some historians accredit the Spanish with naming the country in that negative way, but most at the moment agree that the name Canada has been used since the 16th Century based on a St Lawrence Iroquoian name 'Kanata', meaning settlement, village or land. The Laurentian language spoken by the inhabitants of the St Lawrence Valley, Hubert also informed me as we drove to the Hospital, has become extinct, but at one point the British considered renaming the whole country 'Hochelaga' which was the Iroquoian name for Montreal. Dessie was right, and Hubert was fearsomely proud of his ancestral roots stressing that they were a distinctly separate people from the Mohawk Indians. Again I was slightly surprised to learn that the country was not unified until 1841, and the colonies became officially known as 'The Dominion of Canada' in 1867. Queen Victoria chose a new capital city of Ottawa to be built in 1857 which became the national Capital.

"It is strange." Hubert turned to me and laughed. It was the only bit of mirth which surfaced on our short but grim journey. "The complications of political expediency. I mean the term Dominion was chosen based on Psalm 72:8 in the King James Bible, by the Premier of the Province of New Brunswick. *'He shall have dominion also from sea to sea, and from the river unto the ends of the Earth'.* The word Dominion, although it can mean the same, was thought to be less provocative or offensive than the word Kingdom to the USA, which had recently emerged from the civil war."

"Ah, I see." I said speaking at last after listening to Hubert's well informed narrative. "That explains the Canadian Latin motto – *A Mari Usque Ad Mare* – From sea to sea."

"Spot on Professor" Hubert answered with a smile. And it is strange in a way that although Canada has moved towards Political autonomy from the United Kingdom since the 1950's, and Dominion Day was renamed Canada Day in 1982, The Canadian government registered *the Maple Leaf Tartan,* with the Scottish Tartans Authority, under the name *'Dominion of Canada'* in 2008."

"Yes I see there is this desire for autonomy, and at the same time a desire to belong to what might be named the establishment. Rather like a child which longs to be free of parental control, and yet longs to be safe in Mutter's arms at the same time." I answered.

"Mmm, I detect a reversion to your own German ancestry there, you said Mutter instead of Mother."

"Astutely detected, Hubert." I replied with a slight smile. "For a moment the final song from Mahler's Kindertotenlieder passed through my mind, kind of ominous maybe."

"Songs on the Death of Children?" Hubert enquired.

"Yes, 'oft I think I see them all returning, safe in, safe in their Mother's arms'. Maggie, my PA is a wonderful Contralto, and she sang the complete cycle in a concert recently. Not at Carnegie, or The Met, I afraid, but a well-respected local venue.

"You do not think anything is going to happen to little Matild do you?" Hubert asked full of concern.

"No, probably it would be more in relation to Naomi, Heaven forbid as one might say. I am sorry, but I obviously cannot help fearing for her." I replied tentatively.

"Of course not, there would probably be something wrong if you did not show any concern." Hubert answered, and he too fell silent and pensive again.

The snowfall was light and so transport was no problem, but it felt like minus 5 degrees. Hubert was driving me there in his Saab four wheel drive Estate car. I still use the British and European name otherwise I would describe it as a dark blue Station Wagon. He was already on vacation like myself, as he now worked at the University Research Laboratories dispensing the expertise that he had acquired in the Pharmaceutical Industry. Dessie had worked in the customer service department for the same company, but she had discovered the secret of earning very acceptable pay checks by working on line from home. She found looking after Matild no problem at all. I had planned to book into a hotel, but they both insisted that I stay with them.

Naomi was being cared for in one of a series of small rooms that formed part of a larger ward. Before I go any further I must pay humble tribute to those who choose to spend their lives caring for others. I know that by nature I am not suited to this kind of essential service and I think I would be clinically depressed dealing day after day with death and terminal illness. I know that Doctors and Nurses are expected to be stoical and immune to the traumas and face relatives with calmness and reassurance. I know that they are expected to be professional at all times and unfalteringly efficient hiding their human frailties and emotions, and I take my proverbial hat off to them.

"Is that Naomi Bethesda Martin-Schally?" I asked inadvertently, of the nurse who directed me to the door.

"Yes, sir, I will leave you for a moment; as you can see she is very ill so do not expect too much of her." The young nurse replied and left me by the door.

"Naomi my darling I am so pleased to see you." I said quietly. In fact I felt just the opposite. Her face was already lined and drawn thin, so that her skin stretched like tissue paper over the bones, and somehow her lovely full mouth, the purveyor of so many passionate kisses was stretched and pale and contorted. Greyness replaced half of the blackness of her hair. Her wide eyes met mine and I was chilled and momentarily horrified. Instead of gazing into their warm intelligent depths I beheld blank pupils half covered in a glossy white cataract. I knew then that the Dementia was irreversible, as the malfunctions of her brain were already causing heavy calcium deposits to hide those once lovely eyes.

"Naomi my love can you still see me?" I asked as she looked straight ahead without any sign of recognition.

"Where are you" Naomi asked faintly before she lapsed into a kind of gargling soliloquy of completely unintelligible language.

"I am here, where are you my darling, can you still see me?"

"OU ES TU?" Naomi repeated emphatically whilst gazing straight ahead. "Ou es tu? Ou es tu? Ou es tu? Ou es-tu? Ou es tu?"

"Ici, je suis, mon amour. » I clasped her hand which had become cold and bony and whispered close to her ear that 'I am here my love'.

"Will you not bring them in, they look so lovely, oui?" Naomi responded slightly but her blank gaze was focussed on the white wall beyond the bed, as her speech slipped in and out of French and English.

"What my love. Tell me what to bring in for you." I answered soothingly.

"The flowers – they will die without water." Naomi insisted.

"There are no flowers and visitors are not encouraged to bring any to these wards. They can be a source of allergy and infection as you know." I realised that it was no use trying to hold a normal conversation, even though I tried. I attempted to address the once intelligent Naomi that must be inside her distorted shell somewhere.

"Stupid – I can see them on the front step – look - outside of the door!" Naomi continued.

"There is no door there darling. Where are you?" I asked gently and hoped that she would show a bit of real recognition for me. Was it only nine months or so since the night we had discussed the life or death of Matild? So much seemed to have happened that it felt like a century ago.

"Where are YOU? Naomi retorted emphatically. "Where are you – where are you – where are you-"

"Who? Do you want your child? Do you want Matild? I am going to call her Naomi also." I answered as though she herself was a child.

"What is Mmmm – maaa-? What is Mat-til.? Naomi suddenly pulled her hand free and garbled some indiscernible words before attempting to raise herself on the already raised pillows. "Out – out- out of here – I have to go-wo-wo-oooo…"

"Relax darling you cannot go anywhere at the moment." I answered as she lay back gasping with the effort and her voice trailed off into faint blankness. Her breath rasped through her distorted mouth, and I wondered did she remember somewhere our insatiable days of Karma Sutra.

"Will he come?" Naomi briefly returned to lucidity and looked at me fully with her baleful expression whilst gripping my wrist surprisingly tightly.

"Who darling? I am here- your husband Brandon." Naomi turned away from me again and to my surprise she smiled slightly. The life momentarily returned to her features fleetingly like a fast moving cloud reflected in a tiny pool of water.

"You are mistaken, you do not fool me" Naomi answered surprisingly clearly, and looked away from me whilst releasing my wrist and resignedly smoothing the creases in the sheets with both hands.

"I am Brandon." I love you." I stated insistently but this time she did not respond at all, just lay with closed eyes. I realised that this was about as much as she could take for the time being. I did not know what private world she was inhabiting and I know that we are all alone in a sense, even if surrounded by a crowd of well-wishers. I knew that she was somehow resigned to her fate and that death was closely stalking her.

Was this the same Naomi who had nursed me after my abduction and beating? It flashed through my mind that she may have loved someone else secretly like Lenward Grayson-Baden maybe. The question turned around and around in my head like a revolving neon sign. How could Fate have plucked my precious flower in the bloom of life and taken her from me? How could it be that she appeared to have aged sixty years prematurely?

"Doctor Francis Melancourt would like a word with you if it is convenient, Mr Martin-Schally." The nurse appeared in the doorway. "Come this way please."

I followed, and shook hands with a Doctor wearing a smart grey suit and a white shirt with light blue tie in a small bright consulting room. "It is good to meet you at last er – Mr – Professor Brandon." He said glancing at the open file on the desk for confirmation.

"Thank you. I can see that my wife has been well cared for. Was the birth of my daughter easy or traumatic?" This is something that I had been longing to know, but Dessie and Hubert had been reluctant to discuss Naomi in detail until I had the chance to visit her.

"I am afraid that I was not present in the Maternity Ward, the notes do not indicate any trauma, and instinctively she remembered her previous experience. As she was becoming weak, however, forceps had to be used, and that in no way affected the infant, but since giving birth the Dementia affecting your wife has accelerated rather quickly. Often we are able to treat the conditions with medication and patients are able to live relatively normally with a little help, for many years. We have been researching your wife's condition, and there are other complications. Her body is not responding to treatment because of an accompanying degenerative disease related to what is generally named Cancer. I am sure you are aware that cell malfunction, growth and distortion takes many forms, and often it is not immediately recognisable." Francis Melancourt obviously was one of the 4% of the Montreal population who spoke both English and French as a first language. There was only the occasional accent which indicated that he was familiar with the Gallic.

"And of course some of the treatment might have affected baby Matild." I said, pre-empting his next comment.

"Exactly, and as your wife was very close to the full term of pregnancy before the diagnosis was complete we took the decision to preserve the life of the child as the principal course of action. No one is at fault here, but I understand that Naomi was treated for Stress and Clinical Depression as far as possible by a family Doctor before she was admitted to Hospital." Francis continued gravely, consulting the file and looking at myself alternately.

"That is so, I believe that he has a very good reputation, and my sister-in-law cared for Naomi also, as she works from home. In fact Dessie was hoping to persuade her to return to New York and thought that it was better if I left it to her, as Naomi was too emotional to even speak to me over the telephone." I replied confidentially.

"These maladies can often be so surreptitious. The symptoms can emulate less serious conditions, until it is too late and they have established themselves within an organism. That organism is of course your wife, and we are dealing with cunning life forms which in their own quest for life inevitably cause death. I am sure that you understand what I am saying. You can take consolation in the fact that we have learned a considerable amount from your wife's condition which may help others." Doctor Francis concluded with a faint smile of hope.

"I understand perfectly, Doctor, but I must ask if Matild will have contracted any diseases which will manifest themselves in the near future."

"We did take blood and plasma samples and we see no reason why your child should not live a normal life over a normal life span. However, sometimes these things are genetic and in order to further our research we would need to take DNA samples from your wife's parents and her siblings if they are agreeable, and of course yourself and your parents, to aid with the process of elimination. The accelerated deterioration of your wife's condition is comparatively unusual and makes her a vital case for our research."

"Of course. I have no objections, and I think I can vouch for the rest of the family."

"Good, thank you for your understanding Professor Brandon, and I will arrange the details for the collection of DNA samples. Where is the best place to contact you in the next few days?"

"I will be staying with Desdemona and Hubert Delacroix, at the same address you have for Naomi. Thank you very much for your time" We shook hands briefly and Francis returned to perusing his notes.

I left the consultation room and called in briefly on Naomi again. "Goodbye my darling, I will call again tomorrow." I said quietly and kissed her pallid cheek. As much as I wanted to, I could see that there was no point in sitting by her bedside. In fact to do so might cause anxiety.

"Goodbye" She repeated. "Who are you? Goodbye, where are you? OU es tu?

I met Hubert in the Café reading the news on his lap top. He declined to visit her, but expected that Dessie would visit in the afternoon whilst I spent time with Matild.

The next time I gazed at my darling Naomi she had slipped into a coma, from which she never emerged in the early hours of the next morning. Dessie sat and gazed with me. How very empty a body can appear to be without the spirit and energy which dwelled within it. As we sat Eric appeared at the bed head. He gave a discomforting laugh, before convulsing into fits of coughing. I half rose in anger as he spat out his customary yellow phlegm which looked as though it would land on the pillow, but in fact disappeared. I stroked Naomi's hair to vindicate my inadvertent movement. Eric looked at me slightly sardonically as he spoke.

"You were only just in time bent Cop. Trust me I will never give you bad advice." His image faded and I was left staring at the electrical equipment in a state of anger suffused with sorrow.

After the usual formalities and the issuing of certificates I registered her death and contacted a Funeral Director who was actually a cousin of Hubert. They had a tasteful and pleasant Chapel of Rest, where last respects could be paid discreetly, but even then I feared the Eric would be there reminding me that my work as the Faceless Crusader was still unfinished.

As I admired the embalmer's work and the pink satin robe, a poem by Hanwell Nnagobi came to mind-

If death were but for the duration of an hour,
I would gladly join my precious flower,
Plucked in full bloom to fade and whither,
Whilst I am left in despair to lament and dither.
If death were but for the duration of an hour,
I would quickly be with you again to hold you dear,
But I must await my time without fear,
Be it a century, to me, you are always here!

Separation.

CHAPTER 24

Theodoric Marsden

There was still a chill wind blowing when I returned to the faculty after the Christmas vacation, and again I felt the need for a scarf like Nigel McArthur, as I walked up the steps with him. His neck was wrapped up tightly, but he was not wearing an overcoat, though uncustomarily his blazer was fully buttoned. I realised that I would miss him when he completed his course in the next six months. We exchanged the usual formalities and pleasantries, and I wondered whether to divulge my sadness over the death of Naomi. As part of my mind pondered on this, he adopted his familiar confidential manner.

"Dad is worried, Professor, as there have been two more ritualistic murders discovered in South River this Christmas. He thought that he was so close to cracking the underground organisation responsible for these when he was able to make many arrests with help of the Faceless Crusader.

"I see. Was he not able to obtain any information from the men he took alive?" I answered in genuine surprise.

"Apparently one of them said that he knew Hanwell Nnagobi and that – I quote – he was a vicious bastard who got what he deserved." Nigel continued.

"Well of course those whom we think we know the best may have a hidden agenda." I replied thoughtfully.

"Maybe he did. The prisoner also gave Dad another name, Theodoric Marsden, in return for earlier parole." Nigel continued enthusiastically as we stopped momentarily in the foyer.

"Mmm – sounds Dutch, or Gothic." I suggested maybe a little lightly.

"He may have connections with the Netherlands, but he is a wealthy entrepreneur and guess what – he is an associate of Daryl Kabell." Nigel looked at me inquisitively.

"Daryl Kabell bought three of my paintings for a very satisfactory sum and I would consider him a friend." I replied a little defensively.

"I know, I was at your private view, and Dad knows that you painted a portrait of Mazolina, his wife. Well everybody in New York knows, as he is very proud of it, and had it featured in the New York Times." Nigel continued in his serious confidential impartial manner.

"Really?" I exclaimed in genuine surprise. "I have been rather preoccupied with family matters in Canada this Christmas."

"Dad says that you should be careful who you become identified with, so I thought I would tell you. Apparently Theodoric Marsden is planning a gala opening of a new Hotel, well the building is not new, but it is a franchise he has bought and refurbished. He has an international chain, not quite as big as Sheraton, or Radisson, or Hilton; but does Doric Mars - Luxury Amongst the Stars, ring any bells?" Nigel was full of concern.

"I do believe that I know that slogan, although I am not quite sure." I replied, a little defensively as I could see the image of Eric fading in and out of vision behind Nigel, and I wondered what he wanted to tell me. "Now that you mention it, yes, I am very familiar with that slogan, although I have never had the pleasure or not, of staying in one." I answered more positively, and I must admit that I felt slightly shaken, although I tried not to show it.

"Confidentially Professor, as you are a friend of my father, I can tell you that Theodoric Marsden will be covertly investigated." Nigel leaned closer to me and then turned as he said this and rushed off to one of the graphics studios. I entered my office and greeted Maggie brightly as usual. She was looking even prettier than usual and radiant.

"Liebling, du strahlender aussehande." I remarked.

"Danke, Liebling, ich habe die moisten wunderschonen Urlaub hatten." I knew that she was bursting to tell me, and I wished that my own vacation had been wonderful.

"Good. You can tell me your secret recipe for happiness." I replied.

"Simple darling. I met the most wonderful man. I had a solo part in a Christmas concert at St John's and he congratulated me at the end. He normally resides in Amsterdam, but he is here in New York on business, well he owns hotels and to cut a long story short I have been wined and dined in luxury in what used to be the Dutch Antilles. In Saint Eustatius to be exact near the Capital town of Oranjestad. The currency there is the US Dollar, which may have something to do with it. Anyway, I do not expect that you know him, but his name is Theodoric Marsden." Maggie answered with as much excitement as her position and reserve would allow.

"Ye--. Er no, I am not acquainted. Er –well Maggie you leave me speechless with happiness for you." I was genuinely pleased for her but I could not believe another coincidence. First Amanda, and now Theodoric as though a net was cast about me and all that I was associated with. A net cast by the evil undercover agents of corruption, murder and human trafficking.

"I may have to leave at lunchtime, if that will be okay. Your schedule is fairly simple today, with just the vacation work of year one to evaluate this afternoon, and the new curriculum to authorise for year two this morning, and one of your friends Ansell Milo wants to liaise about his hours as visiting Tutor." Maggie was still radiant, and I was really pleased for her.

"Of course, and I guess that the reason is – you are meeting the mysterious Theodoric Marsden." I answered with a light humour. I was hoping that she was not going to get hurt.

"You want to tease me Liebling, but I know what I am doing - ach, I am almost an old lady and my heart is not on my sleeve." Maggie answered with a dismissive smile and a slight wave.

"No Maggie, we have to enjoy what happiness comes our way regardless of age and experience, and you deserve to be happy you do so much for others." I decided to leave the matter and entered my office. As I closed the door and turned to face my desk I saw Eric sitting there.

"Time to take more bribes. EH? Bent Cop. Do you know what will be happening in the basements and sellers of Doric Mars 39 whilst the opening ceremony is taking place this evening? Daryl Kabell is not your worry – he really likes you and he knows that you will not be tangling in his shaved head." Eric delivered his speech without his customary cough and looked at me.

"Listen you hapless apparition. I did not take bribes from Daryl, and anyway I am not really a Cop." I remembered to speak quietly although I really want to bellow in rage.

"Mmm – well why do you think this guy is courting Maggie?"

"Because she is talented and still very desirable." I replied.

"AH-ah – wrong! Somebody has a hunch and he wants to get close to you. Somebody thinks that they should have killed you when they had you and the gang would still be intact." Eric pulled his old coat around himself and shivered.

"And who might that be? Would it be this Theodoric Marsden that the Police are going to be watching anyway?"

"That is for me to know and you to find out." Eric laughed and vanished as I attempted to grab his arm and force a more explicit explanation from him.

At this point you might well think that I am crazy accepting so easily the presence of an apparent apparition and taking his advice. Well maybe I am, but I guess that it is because of sheer persistence on his behalf that I treat the situation with such normality. How many people witness such a phenomenon? I think that many do, and there are more who never divulge their experience for fear of being thought of as abnormal. It might be a case of – you know my friend the freak, he claims that he talks to a ghost very often which advises him on what course of action to take.

Still, as the case maybe or not, I remembered that I still possessed the cell phone which belonged to Buzz. It was bound to have my own finger prints on it and although I did not have a criminal record, Inspector McArthur had taken my prints as a matter of course, primarily at the time, as a process of elimination. I wondered if any new calls had been made to it, which might lead me to exposing more of the organisation. I thought of Beldossa and the trade mark cigar smoke. I was beginning to have grave doubts about my own senses and intuition. As though Emile Beldossa had been intercepting my mind–wavelengths, the first letter on my pile of mail was from him. He had written to me rather than send an email to inform me that he would not be returning from his extended sabbatical, as he had been offered a position in Buenos Aires, and so he had recommended that the Governors make my own appointment permanent. He informed that he had received excellent reports from various sources and could think of no one better qualified to retain the position and direct the faculty.

I must say I felt greatly flattered, and greatly relieved financially, as although I was paid handsomely for my Painting, I had a lot of expenses with the children growing, an au pair, and of course assisting Dessie to take care of Matild for the moment. I buzzed Maggie to draught a reply. We had just finished when there was a polite knock on the door.

"Enter please." I called.

"Thank you, I am so sorry – I hope that I am not interrupting, but I was directed to this office. I was hoping to find Mrs Margurita von Hessen-Bach." A tall, quite well made man in a dark brown and beige pin striped suit with flattened steel grey hair pushed the door open tentatively as he spoke. His dark ultramarine eyes however had a metallic glint behind the spectacles with thin black frames, which betrayed a more menacing and certainly less tentative personality.

"Theodoric." Maggie exclaimed delightedly as she turned elegantly in her chair.

"Margurita, my Tulip, I am a little early, but I was hoping that we could have luncheon before the Gala Opening." Theodoric came forward and kissed her hand.

"Brandon Liebling, this is Theodoric Marsden." Maggie flushed in excitement as she spoke and turned to me. I rose and offered my own hand, not to be kissed of course, but to receive a very firm and steely handshake, one that somehow made me feel cold and defensive.

"I am Professor Brandon, and I am pleased to meet you Mr Marsden." I said decisively.

"How do you do? It is my absolute pleasure to meet you sir." His thin lips parted in a thin smile to reveal what looked like natural even white teeth that almost sparkled, but the smile did not reach the steady gaze of his eyes, or permeate his features. If his clothes had been Flemish 15th Century, with a Burger Master hat, he could have stepped straight out of a Jan van Eyck Painting. As a court painter to Philip the Good, Van Eyck had been extremely well paid, and produced many portraits of wealthy and powerful men such as Baudouin de Lannoy about 1435. Theodoric seemed to have an aura of Northern European precision and light about him such as the Dutch Artists portrayed during that era and somehow the words fastidious ruthlessness came to mind.

"Oh I am so glad that you two have met. Brandon has always been my little Liebling, Theodoric, you must forgive my familiarity without being jealous. He has a lovely family, but he is just recovering from the loss of his wife." Maggie continued in her motherly way.

"Oh, I see. I offer my condolences, but I do not want to share my precious flower. Margurita is the name of a bloom as I expect that you know already." Theodoric kissed Maggie's hand again and I wondered if Eric's warning was actually true.

"Thank you. I will always hold Margurita in my deep affection, and I am delighted to see someone bring her the happiness which she deserves." I replied, or rather almost hissed in spite of my attempt at charm.

Theodoric gave me a cold steely look for only a fraction of a second, which I know inadvertently spoke volumes, before it was replaced by his thin smile. "Whilst I am here Professor let me compliment you on the excellent portrait of Mazolina Kabell, it is exceptionally fine. I would like to commission you sometime to paint one of me to hang in my headquarters in Amsterdam in the Dutch tradition. I need to replace an earlier one I hope that you will be able to find the time, but we will discuss that in the near future if you are agreeable. Daryl is only a business associate of mine, we are not really close friends, but I often visit the Maison du Soleil."

"Thank you for the compliment. I would be honoured." I replied smiling a little myself for the first time during this meeting. I expected Theodoric to speak some words with a typical Dutch accent, but his voice although sharp edged, was very cultured in an English way rather than American. I began to wonder if his was the voice that I had heard in the basement that evening, which although very vivid had begun to seem a long time ago.

"Good, then may I take my Tulip to luncheon and relieve her of her duties for the rest of the day?" Theodoric continued with politeness, as he offered Maggie his arm.

"I was going to change." Maggie protested mildly, but I knew that she had taken a great deal of effort already.

"Nonsense, mauve and white suits you perfectly. You are more beautiful than a whole field of spring Tulips, but if you insist there is a boutique within the hotel, completely at your disposal before the afternoon event." Theodoric appeared to speak with sincerity.

"You spoil me too much my darling. "Maggie said as she rose elegantly and took his arm. I had in fact never seen her look more beautiful and radiant throughout all the years I had known her. The dress hugged her trim but curvaceous figure without being too tight, and ended in a slight flair just below her knee. A wide collar upstand ended in several small ruffled triangles on her left breast, a narrow fitted belt encased her waistline. The modest V neck was perfect and somehow complemented the tight three quarter sleeves. Her white patent six heeled shoes were immaculate. I walked around my desk and opened the door for them and I recalled how she had whispered earlier 'mien Lippen Kussen mit dem Feuer', when our long term flirting had taken a more serious turn. I felt a small pang of envy as I watched her pick up her matching designer handbag designed by a friend of mine for Lawrence Victor a leading Fashion House, and Theodoric placed his arm around her waist.

"Oh Brandon Liebling, Katlyn will be arriving shortly to take over my duties, as you know she is very efficient." Maggie said giving me a sideways glance. I had rarely seen her look so happy. I prayed to all the power in the Universes that this was not all going to end in tears.

"Thank you Maggie Liebling – miss you already." I answered with an attempt at joviality which obviously worked, as they both departed with a laugh and a final quick wave from Maggie.

I was pleased that Katlyn was filling in, as she would not be obtrusive or find my own actions odd, if I left early when the important assessment was over in the afternoon. I knew also that she would be able to handle any unexpected business or queries. I knew that somehow I would have to resume my masquerade and investigate the Hotel premises. Luckily the spring days had not yet returned to New York, and darkness descended in the afternoons still relatively early. Of course everywhere would be brightly illuminated by artificial light, but somehow that still created shadows and distortions which might cover my disguise. There was also the question of the cell phone. I resolved to check through the list of contacts again before wiping it with an alcoholic cleanser and posting it to my friend Inspector McArthur.

I take my position seriously, and I found the assessment very engrossing with much original work and ideas. In fact, I gave it a 101% of my attention and almost forgot the arduous task ahead of me. There were discussions with other Tutors, so that finally I only left about half an hour earlier than normal.

"Oh Brandon honey I am so pleased that you are early, we will be in good time for Andrea's concert." Emerson greeted me with a smile and I saw that she was already prepared in a shimmering emerald green dress with matching emerald droplet earrings. Her nails were already painted a lighter shade of green and her full lips were peach and honey in contrast. There was a hint of silver sheen on the dark green eye shadow above her eye lids and her skin glowed with a myriad of subtle tones of amber and ebony. I opened my mouth in surprise, she may as well have hit me with the heavy based frying pan.

"Now do not tell me that you had forgotten. The children have been rehearsing for weeks." Emerson continued.

"No honey, wow, you certainly look beautiful, I just wanted to gaze at you for a while." I answered honestly, well almost, as I had completely forgotten, but the sight of Emerson would make any man run home early just to look, let alone indulge in for what was to follow.

"Do not fool me honey, you had forgotten, but hey I love you and here is a kiss to prove it." Emerson hugged me and quickly I held her enveloping warmth in my arms and I wondered if I could hold on to my resolve to go out again after the school concert. I had still to find an excellent excuse, and that was going to be the really hard part.

Lower Town Beach, Oranjestad, Sint Eustatius.

CHAPTER 25

Caged Rats

Andrea was showing great promise as an actress and singer, obviously taking after my Mother, and we ate dinner in a restaurant of her choice as promised after the concert. We all returned home happily and still headed for bed at a reasonable hour. Excuses failed me as my brain whirled ineffectively between several possibilities. In the end I decided to accept the promise which Emerson presented between the sheets of hot romance and defer my criminal investigations.

"Yeah, bent Cop, as ever, - succumbed to the pleasures of the flesh and money. You will never make a good creep." Eric's voice whispered in my ear about one AM. I felt like I had barely begun to sleep. I blearily opened my eyes, but my body refused to awake. I felt warm and comfortably heavy. Eric was standing over me at the edge of the bed.

"What---?" I whispered faintly before realisation kicked in, and I recalled the image of Theodoric Marsden.

"If you go now there is something for you to do, do not post Buzz's cell phone – I hope it is charged."

"Eric--." I began,

"Always in a conflict between what you want and what needs to be done eh?" Eric laughed and spat out a slug of yellow phlegm which landed nowhere and a fit of coughing racked his body.

"Wait." I said trying to grab his arm as he began to fade. "Tell me more."

"Yoooo'l seeeee, ha, he ha, ha, ha-a." He hollered faintly and disappeared with his customary laugh.

Cautiously I slid out of bed and crept around the room dressing hurriedly, careful also not to awaken Anna-Maria our wonderful au pair, who would soon be leaving us. Incidentally Emerson had taken it upon herself to select a replacement from several applications. She had certainly become the 'New Mommy' and marriage crossed my mind, but I thought that maybe she was too much of a free independent spirit. She had travelled to Montreal with the children and Anna-Maria and my Mother, for Naomi's funeral. I think that for the children it had been a slightly unrealistic situation and Andrea had cried, but in the life of a child the years appear longer than they do to an adult and Emerson's kindness and Anna-Maria's sweetness had certainly eased the pain of separation.

They understood that Mommy had gone because she was ill, and the excitement of staying in a 5-star Hotel, and meeting Dessie, Hubert, and their Canadian Grandmother and Grandfather again, as well as their cousins, and other Aunts and Uncles, had diverted much of their sorrow. I would have been in favour of a simple service at a Crematorium, but I bowed to her Mother's wishes and we held a service at St Joseph's. Melisent Lacramonte was very devout and she chose to be thankful for the relatively short life that her daughter had lived, rather than to bemoan the fact that one of her youngest children had died before her. Dieudonne Lacramonte supported his wife admirably during their time of sorrow, even though he too was ageing and combatting ill health. Naomi is often in my thoughts, and strangely so now. I am sure that in time she would have understood the importance and necessity of doing what I do as a self-appointed creep.

I pulled the Mercedes Station Waggon over into the usual dark spot in a small street, and donned my Policeman's disguise. I took both my own gun and Buzz's gun as usual. When I reached Doric Mars 39 there was still a party in progress. Lots of activity. Limo's arriving and departing. Some celebrities from the Film and Music world posing for photographs on the wide steps, but the Police presence seemed to be fairly low key. I realised of course that Theodoric had his own security system and officers which might be quite hard to beat. I decided to investigate around the back near the kitchen area where several small vans bore the names of suppliers of food stuffs.

Bus boys hurried in and out of swinging doors with refuse bags for the recycling bins and one or two Chefs in uniform took a smoke break, leaning against the wall in the cool night air as a respite from the heat of the kitchen. I patrolled casually at a distance, but what really caught my attention was a recently bricked enclosure at the end of the service yard where there were two large builder's skips. still full of debris from the refurbishments in front of it. The large gate was closed, but I could see the top of a larger possibly 7.5-ton Van and it appeared to be at the top of a ramp. Under the welcome shadow of the skip I approached the solid metal gate, when I heard two men speaking as they approached from the other side.

"They are in there like a bunch of CAGED RATS." One gravelly voice announced softly.

"Good, you had better inform the Man." A second voice spoke with a European accent which I could not quite determine.

"And the SHIT is all secure, no one noticed a thing with the charade in progress out front." The first voice answered.

"Excellent." The second man replied. "There is nothing less suspicious than hiding things right under the noses of people."

"Too right." The first voice answered and laughed.

"Damn, I am losing the key to the gate. I must go to my car." The second voice exclaimed as the gate opened slowly and they stepped into the shadows of the skip. "Stay here I will not be very long."

I knew instinctively what I must do. I prayed to my Universal Muse that I would not fluff it. As the first man fumbled for a cigarette with his back to me I rushed him and whacked the side of his forehead with all my strength with my baton as he turned in complete surprise. He reeled backwards slightly and I followed with another blow. I jabbed him in the stomach, and as he bent over I caught him a blow on the point of the chin. I leapt backwards slightly as he made a grab for me before he slumped unconsciously on the pavement. I quickly tied his arms behind his back, and to his ankles as I had done with Buzz, but this time I used a piece of sturdy blue rope from out if the skip. I dragged him behind the van and found that the doors were unlocked. I managed to push him in, and close the doors again. I ran back to the skip and gathered a handful of mortar which was still slightly pliable, and stuffed it hurriedly into the lock sockets to prevent the gate from being locked, but I almost closed it, and ran down the ramp. There was a card operated lock on a small side door next to a large shutter door. I ran back to the van and opened the rear doors, and felt in the pockets of the man and to my relief I found a card and van keys. Almost breathlessly I ran back to the side door and swiped the card. With a click and an electronic humming, it opened and I entered a large basement area.

Muffled sounds emanated from a corridor to my left, which grew louder as I approached, and then in the dimness of safety lights as my eyes adjusted to the gloom, I could see hands protruding through barred gates, on either side like old fashioned prison cells, and I could hear mumbling and pleading. Sometimes it was English, sometimes languages I was not too sure about, but always beseeching and there were women wailing, and even children crying, and men cursing. A corridor to my right led to store rooms housing pallet upon pallet of sealed bags, and one or two opened clear polythene bags containing white powder and other substances. I took Buzz's cell phone out of the packet and dialled Inspector McArthur's office. Ah yes, there was a good signal.

"Ye fated Gods – it is that Faceless Crusader voice and number again, the desk Sargeant hollered, and I heard McArthur cursing also as he grabbed the desk phone.

"Doric Mars 39. Hotel. Get here now. Prisoners of illegal Slave Trade and tons of Crack. This is not a hoax. Basement." I stated.

"I thought we had that covered that is why I am still here at this ungodly hour. McArthur snapped at the Sargeant, and then." Who the devil are you anyway that discovers what we are unable to find?"

"You will never know, but please get here. Service yard. Basement. New enclosure." I switched off and ran to the door from where I could see the gate was still as I had left it. Opening it cautiously, I saw that the second man had not returned, so I started up the van, and parked it closer to the gateway, so that the gates could not be closed. Next I ran back to the electronic door, and risked the sound of a muffled gunshot echoing through the night air, but I thought that it would still be absorbed by the hullabaloo taking place upstairs and in the street. The bullet rendered the lock completely ineffective. I heard a car approaching through the side street and ran back up the ramp, just managing to take cover behind the skip before the second man arrived in a black Lexus saloon. He stopped the car hurriedly and jumped out.

"What is happening? Are you trying to double cross us? This will not be good for you!" He shouted and pulled out a gun as he approached the van. I had locked the van of course and I casually dropped the keys into a recycling bin as I patrolled the outer perimeter of the service yard. I heard more cars approaching and then the siren and flashing lights as the police roared in and ordered him to drop his weapon. I heard women screaming and men shouting as the police presence at the front of the Hotel also became more aggressive, and they prevented anyone from leaving or entering.

I melted away down a small passage between more bins and skips and shadows, just before I entered a main sidewalk Eric appeared. "Well done bent Cop!" Was all he said as he disappeared again?

Back in the security of my bedroom and successful back in bed without awakening Emerson, I suddenly thought of Maggie. How I hoped that she had not got caught up in all of that, for Theodoric Marsden would surely be questioned. I entered the reception door of my office timidly with bated breath, but there she was. Looking slightly tired but still radiant.

"Why Brandon Liebling, do you have a hangover, or dyspepsia, let me get you an aspirin." She rose from her desk today looking relaxed in a misty blue woollen dress with a high boat neck.

"No, no," I smiled in relief. "I am good; in fact, I am on top of the world. School concerts can sometimes be an ordeal with treats afterwards and over excited bedtimes. How was your event?

"Ach, - wunderbar. But I feel a little bit like Cinderella as they say, - ya? Maggie was still all smiles.

"Cinderella why? Did Mr Theodoric turn into a pumpkin?" I was glad that I could joke with her.

"No, and Liebling I tell you this in confidence. He entertained me splendidly in an executive suit after the lavish opening dinner. I think champagne will ooze from every pore in my body, but he insisted on his chauffeur taking me home before twelve mid

night." Maggie twirled as she spoke, which I had never seen her do before, and laughed.

"Well maybe he needs his beauty sleep." I suggested light heartedly.

Maggie sat down again and laughed. "Oh my little Liebling, I think I am still tipsy."

"Do you want to take the day off?" I asked still laughing myself with relief that Maggie was here unscathed.

"What- and miss the chance to show off, at break times, no, I will be doing my duties with twice the alacrity." Maggie returned to her computer screen with a pleasant satisfied radiant smile on her face. "Doric Mars, Luxury Amongst the Stars."

"It is these things which make life that extra bit worthwhile." I concluded and retreated to the sanctuary of my inner office. I wondered how she would feel if there was news that her new found love had been arrested on serious criminal charges on the National TV. In fact, I knew it was inevitable, but how could I divulge any information? It was better to let her continue to enjoy the moment.

As I sat at my desk for a moment, I was overcome by a sense of futility. I happened to open a copy of a collection of Poems by Hanwell Nnagobi, which I still kept on the desk. I suppose a part of me was sentimental. I began to read –

Let death take me,
For I have no fear of it,
Some call it a sting but how can that be?
When surely it is a relief from pain.
Some might call it a blessed relief,
An end to trial and stress and strain.
I cannot complain if I have lived life;
Those I leave behind surely suffer still,
If I have not lived with goals, child and wife,
Surely nothing is lost to fulfil,
But the promise, potential maybe,
When Death is the death of hoping,
In the absence of fulfilment attained,
Death is, apart from existence, taking away nothing.
To die in the midst of many creative activities,
A greater tragedy it may seem, but why?
For within the joy of creation there is pain,
So let Death take me,
I have no fear of it.

The cessation of experiences maybe,
Of consciousness imprisoned in a body, a brain,
Will let my Spirit rise, not constrained but free,
Of bone, and skin and cartilage –
The temple of my soul will be defunct and ashes,
I may grow into a new one after a brief passage,
But I have no need of it.

I thought of the remark that one of the men had made at Doric Mars 39 - CAGED RATS, and I thought how unkind it is to cage an intelligent creature and I recalled the smell of fear emanating from those imprisoned humans in the basement. They were desperately trying to cling to life, waiting for their freedom regained, but I wondered if we do not make cages for ourselves. Maybe we imprison ourselves in certain circumstances for security, without realising it, and blame other people for what we perceive as a lack of freedom.

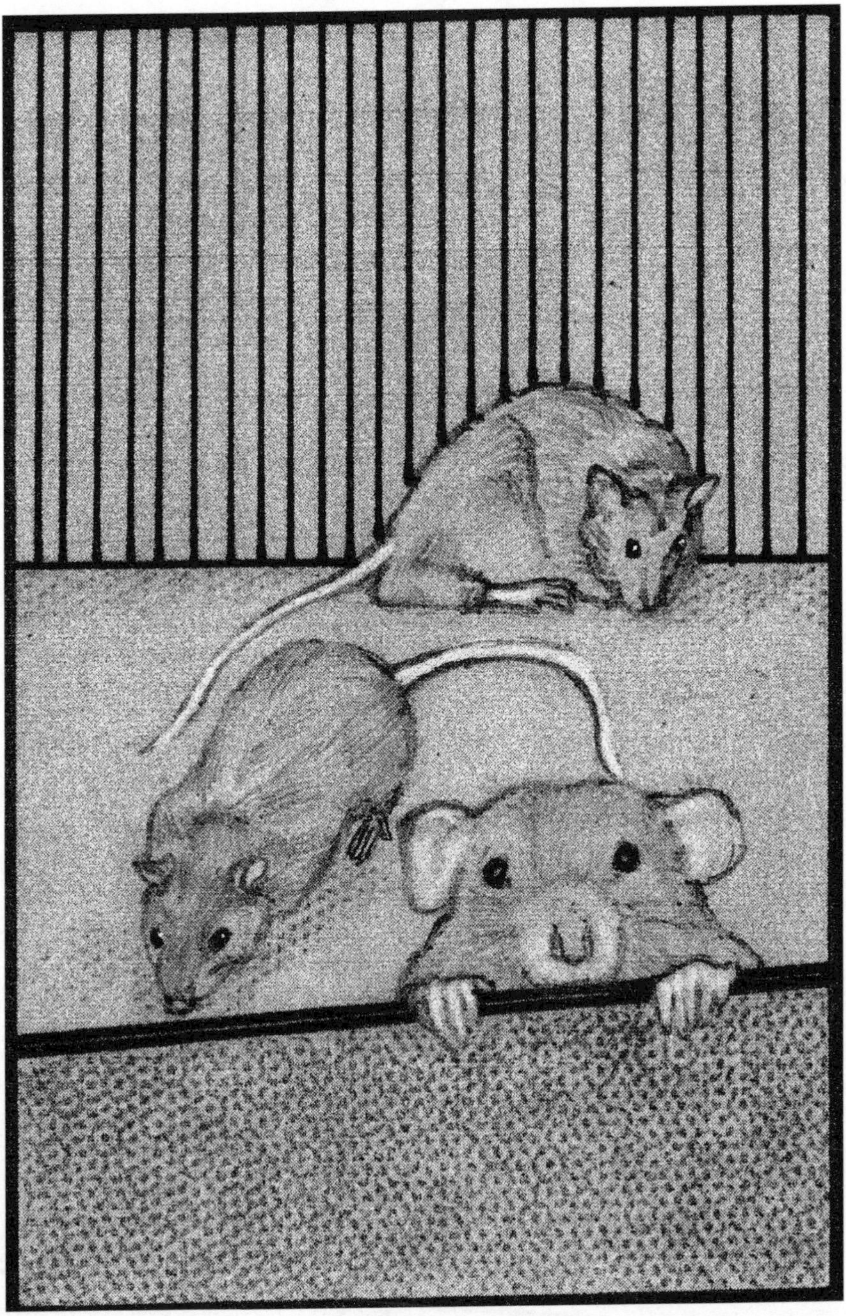

Norway Rats (Brown-Grey)

CHAPTER 26

A Faceless Fake

"Dad is really delighted. So many surprising names have been revealed by one of the guys that they caught red handed at Doric Mars 39." Nigel McArthur could hardly contain his excitement, as he greeted me the following day as I encountered him on my way to the refectory for a mid morning coffee. I could have it in my office but I liked to be about and socialise a little.

"Really? I read some of the newspaper stories, maybe the real killers of my friend Hanwell will be revealed." I answered.

"Oh, do not be too starry eyed or defensive of him, with all respect to you; but evidence is beginning to show that he was at least a treble agent, and not just an undercover guy trying to expose an evil network." Nigel looked apprehensive for a moment.

"I understand. As time goes by I realise just how little I really knew of him. I can understand that the bonne amitie which I thought was there, was not really there maybe." I replied honestly with a touch of sadness.

"Dad is still furious though, that this anonymous Faceless Crusader keeps turning up with calls from a dead man's phone with shattering evidence that they have been trying to piece together for years. I am telling you this in confidence Professor, because I know that you are still sad about your friend and worried in case you might still be in danger." Nigel lowered his voice as we reached the refectory door.

"I know, and your confidence will not be betrayed, I really appreciate everything that you are able to tell me." I put a reassuring hand on his shoulder and he smiled with relief. His trademark scarf was slung around his neck and his blazer open and his hands thrust deep into his grey pants pockets. I hoped that life would treat him kindly once his student days were over.

"One of the guys described the Crusader as a Policeman in regular uniform, and he seemed to have a lot of hair, but he could not really say whether he was Black or White or even Asian as his face was in shadow, but he is quite an athletic guy and quite large. I can tell you the guy is actually terrified. He is too terrified to give any information about anything because he says that even in prison there are ways and means for the network to punish or kill you, and he is terrified because he was jumped by the Crusader who is a mystery and even some kind of demon." Nigel obviously relished this information.

"Could this Crusader be a disgruntled gang member, for want of better words?" I asked because I would now have to be extra careful about my tactics.

"Dad does not think so. He thinks he is a clever outsider seeking some kind of moral vengeance, rather than directly personal."

"I see, and would Inspector treat him like a criminal, or reward him for his assistance?" I asked with a touch of humour.

"He breaks the law. He could be a danger to the society he is trying to purge of defects. It would depend upon the circumstances which led to his discovery. At the least he could face a suspended sentence, and at the worst a short custodial sentence, but until all of this is finally cleared up, the revelation of his identity could put him in great danger from other subversive forces." Nigel was obviously well versed in the practise of justice, and I thought what a good attorney he would make.

"Well let us hope that the network is utterly cracked and exposed and then maybe the Faceless Crusader could stop being a thorn in your father's side, and just disappear." I said again with a touch of humour.

"Between you and I Professor, I think that is what dad really hopes will happen. Sometimes what he has to say publicly does not always correspond to his own feelings." Nigel concluded and then left me to join some of his friends at a far table. How close was I to the real core of corruption I wondered? Surely I could not be far away now.

It was Easter by now, and I found myself up in Harlem. Mother was playing piano for a Gospel group, a friend of hers who normally played was suddenly taken ill, and Mother was asked to step in. She persuaded me to take the family, after complaining that I never attended any of her concerts now. It was pleasant and sunny and of course many tourists had booked for the service. Mom was looking resplendent in a pale blue satin dress and matching hat, and she was delighted that the piano was a Baby Grand. The Pastor Reverend Kane Dexter began to deliver his singing sermon after the choir had presented two or three rousing renditions of old favourites. Suddenly there was a disturbance on the outside and the doors burst open and a person dressed in black with a completely blank white mask and a black cloak and white gloves, broke away from security and pulled out a pistol with a silencer. He aimed at the Pastor.

"Yes my brother what can I do for you?" Pastor Kane asked.

"I am the Faceless Crusader and I aim to rid this city of hypocrisy." The man shouted.

"This is not a house of hypocrisy, we are true believers here." The Pastor replied.

"It is a sham, this is just a commercial spectacle for the ungodly." The man replied.

"Throw down your weapon before God and ask his forgiveness for threatening the life of another." The Pastor put his hands together in a prayer position. "We will pray for your Forgiveness and Salvation.

"Forgiveness and Salvation indeed. You are just a showman who profits from the superstitions and weakness of others." The man continued.

"Fall on your knees and beg forgiveness from all of these fine people here, we will not be intimidated by agents of the Devil." The Pastor continued.

"Stay back." The man shouted as two security men approached from behind. "If you want to see your Pastor walk out of here alive."

"May the Lord grant you peace my brother, lay down your weapon and leave this holy place." The Pastor repeated.

"Holy place-what makes it a Holy place? Not you with your clever intimidating chants." The man replied.

"He whom I serve makes this place Holy." Pastor Kane continued calmly.

"And who is that – what do you do with all the money you receive?" The man inquired vehemently.

"We maintain this fine church for the congregation." Pastor Kane replied and I could tell that he was desperately trying to think of a way of ending this. I saw the results of media exposure. Here was some disturbed character masquerading as myself, or was it someone who had guessed my identity, another gang member maybe.

"You mean that you make easy pickings and present a charade twice a week. You are nothing more than a burlesque showman." The man continued.

"Be gone you Devil's spawn and leave the Godly in peace." Pastor Kane shouted.

"I can kill you now, and I promise you that you will not see your Lord." The man continued waving the gun.

"My faith is strong within these walls, or outside." Pastor Kane continued. "Reveal yourself you are not THE Faceless Crusader that we read about but a sad impostor."

"I am he who will rid the city and even the world of corruption, and you are a part of that corruption. Religions are for the feeble minded who like a lame beggar need a crutch to walk with." The man continued almost in a delirium.

"I feel sorry for you who will never know the blessings of faith." Pastor Kane continued.

"And I feel sorry for you, and all of these people who listen to you, for you are a purveyor of false hope and dreams." The masked man continued.

Pastor Kane was beginning to sweat, but most of the congregation sat motionless. The two security men stood ready to overpower him from behind, but they knew if they suddenly seized him he could kill the Pastor with a reflex action. I was too far away to tackle him from the side, and again a sudden movement could cause the gun to fire. Mother had remained hidden from his view behind the lid of the Baby Grand on the left side of the raised podium. Now to my surprise she took the situation in hand. She hit the keys with a rolling version of 'Down by the Riverside'. The chords echoed with full resonance, which took the gunman by surprise.

"Stop." He shouted as he wavered and aimed at the piano. The security men took their chance and seized his arms whilst kicking his feet to unbalance him. The gun fired as a nervous reaction and a bullet splintered the edge of the piano lid and ricocheted harmlessly into the corner of the room. Several men seated along the central aisle assisted the security men, and in spite of his strength the Fake Crusader was flattened on the floor with several large men seated on top of him. A security man picked up the gun and removed the cartridge. Pastor Kane bent down and wrested the mask from his face. He stepped back in horror.

"Cousin Anselm Dexter. Is it really you? I thought you were in Cape Town." Pastor Kane exclaimed.

"I hate you. I hate you still. You hide behind your Godliness like a courtesan behind a fan. I took the blame for your misdemeanours when we were younger so you could be blameless and enter the ministry and you repaid me by stealing the love of my life. I have been back for few months watching you and now I hate you more ..." Anselm's verbal onslaught was cut short by the arrival of the Police who handcuffed him and lifted him to his feet before bundling him into a patrol car.

I had rushed over to Mom to see if she was ok.

"Of course I am okay. I do not let any damn fool clown frighten me. Faceless Crusader indeed - more like Phantom of the Opera." Mother was incensed and elated. I always knew that she was strong, but she surprised me today.

"Thank you everyone for your courage and calmness in the face of adversity---." Pastor Kane began as many people seemed to be on the verge of leaving – myself included and I wanted to take Mother home, but she had other ideas.

"Excuse me Pastor Kane with due respect, but I thought we were here to raise the roof with a few Gospel songs, so let us continue. I have itchy fingers that need to tickle some ivories." Mom shouted from the piano, as she launched into an up tempo and joyful rendering of 'One Two Three, Bless My Soul.'

It reminded me of when I was kid again, and with my brothers and sisters I would stand around the old upright piano and sing. She treated the congregation the same way as just a family gathering making music for the joy of it. Most people joined in, and the Police began taking statements at the back of the hall from various people. They asked Mother for one as a reliable eye witness, and the choir took over a-cappella style. Pastor Dexter Cane was asked to accompany a Policeman to the local Station and make a full formal statement. Max Bebinbroke the assistant Pastor eventually took over as proceedings drew to a close and thanked everyone for coming and staying calm, as he stood at the door shaking hands. Many of the tourists were quite elated to have witnessed a real live standoff with a gunman. They were all full of praise for Mom and her quick thinking and bravery. She accepted the compliments with dismissive grace.

I wanted to have done with the Faceless Crusader, and just live my life as a happy family man again, but that would never be the same. I knew however that since the last decouvre of the undercover operations, there was someone gunning for me as it were. Someone I had to expose who still remained at the heart of operations. Someone somehow that I knew. Was it Emile Beldossa? Was there another above him? Theodoric Marsden was clever, he was awaiting trial. He had prominent attorneys but investigations into other of his Hotels revealed similar evidence, and yet he still appeared to be a middle man, a scapegoat for operations planned and directed by others. You get the picture? Like a self-storage company who rent out space, but are not necessarily responsible for what is stored there. Detailed examination of his accounts and transactions did not reveal any evidence of shipments or dubious couriers. Everything was related to transactions with regular building companies and Hotel supply companies. Obviously the auditors did not expect to find receipts for shipments of cocaine from New York Port Authorities or a delivery of 200 illegal immigrants, but there was nothing relating to any other cargo with a false description which might indicate that he accepted delivery. It became an academic question as to how strictly the word 'possession' could be applied. Nigel kept me very well informed.

As far as I know there were no other Fake Faceless Crusaders taking my name in vain around New York. After all, I was 'faceless' because I was completely anonymous, and I did not go around like a comic strip hero in a theatrical costume.

A Fake Faceless Crusader.

CHAPTER 27

A Silent Ending

The weeks after Easter were always a dichotomy to my mind. On one hand there were the final assessments and students graduating which was a serious business and quite demanding work for the staff; and on the other hand there was also the freedom of the summer vacation to look forward to. I planned to visit Montreal again to spend some time with Little Matild, my daughter. Dessie kept me informed with weekly reports and I still found her voice fascinating.

I had begun painting again and saw a return to a more balanced harmonious style. I even ventured down to my favourite South River and found that the day I discovered Hanwell was fading and being absorbed by newer memories. Maggie did not mention her brief liaison with Theodoric Marsden. She had enjoyed the brief ride as it were, and focussed upon pastures new. I felt a mellowness returning like a symphonic deja-vu with a lilting and rocking spiral of repeated themes and inverted cadences. I had come to rely upon Emerson considerably, and Rosemary Sutcliffe, another Au-pair from England.

I knew that Emerson had let her own children be cared for by her sister and that she had split from her stockbroker husband who had left her wealthy. I did not press her to make a commitment to me, but I had begun to think that she might always be there for me, for us. And oh yes, you can see where I am going before I go there – I was wrong.

Emerson announced that she was taking a short break from domestic life with a friend. It was as in- consequential as that. Just an announcement over breakfast that she would be leaving the faculty early and taking a trip to Rio, and staying at the famous Copacabana Hotel. Her friend turned out to be a wealthy Impresario, older than myself, and older than she was. Needless to say I was gobsmacked for want of a better word. It was a word that my Brother Dietrich in Manchester England had picked up and used a lot whenever I spoke to him on the telephone. Literally I was stunned as though I had been hit hard by a baseball bat.

"It is not because I do not love you honey, I do. It is not because I do not adore all the kids, because I do. It is not because I am tired of our relationship, it is just that somehow I need a break. I know that you are very well off, and I want for nothing, but I need to be 'champagned' and pampered again before I am too old. We are sailing down to Rio on his large yatch with his own crew. He is an old associate of Professor Hardman and he has been staying in New York for a while. He has called quite often at the faculty." Emerson delivered her explanation sympathetically and once more the bottom fell out of my world.

"I guess that we all need to be adult about this. No one has made a commitment. Maybe no one has the right to ask for permanency in a world full of changes. I could beg you to stay but that would be selfish. It is better to part; remembering the good times we have shared together. I could be despicable and weep with my head on your knee and make you pity me, but no, - I will thank you for all the love and care that you have given to me, to us, and we will smile when we remember Emerson and her smile will remain as a bright light for all of our days." In spite of my words my eyes filled with tears as I spoke, and I had to retire to the bathroom and regain my composure.

"You are going away like Mommy and leaving us. You will never come back. Are you ill too?" Andrea seemed to be the most visibly devastated. Kurt blinked and looked at her wide eyed in disbelief and Matteus asked if Rosemary would stay and look after them.

"Honey I am so sorry, but I am not your Mom, I have only been taking care of you for a while. You are a big girl now, and you can help your Daddy, and Rosemary, to look after your brothers. I am not ill. At least I hope that I am not ill, but hey, I bet your daddy will find someone new. I think that if I stay I will be ill and no use to anybody." Emerson was all tenderness as she spoke.

"Daddy why does everyone get ill and leave? Do you do something wrong, or have we been too naughty?" Andrea turned sulky, but I could see she was close to broken hearted.

"Honey, honey, do not blame your Daddy, he is a lovely man, handsome and thoughtful and loving, it is just the way things are. You will understand later, however good things seem, people need to change or they just wind up unhappy and sad." Emerson tried to comfort her, but I know that by suddenly leaving she had done the worst thing possible for Andrea's stability.

"Will nobody ever stay with us? Will I never have a proper Mommy like my friends? Andrea threw her arms around my waist and clung to me sobbing on my chest. Emerson herself could hardly bear it. She kissed my cheek, as she passed and collected her suit cases and placed them in the hall. A few moments later the cab driver called and Emerson walked silently out of our lives.

Rosemary was giving the boys their packed lunch and preparing them for school. "See you later Dad. See you Andrea." they said as Rosemary ushered them out.

"Okay. Have a good day both of you." I replied and then when the door closed I whispered to Andrea. "We are going to have a good day full of treats, what would you like to first?"

The image of Emerson wearing a suit of cream and pink silk de chine fabric and pink and brown seven inch heels stayed with me for the rest of the day. Mixed emotions ran through me and ended in a blazing anger. An anger not so much for myself, as for my children and their mental happiness. The morning of ice cream and fun fair did not really cheer up Andrea for long at Coney Island, which was her choice, so after a lunch of Sausages and Pizza, I decided to visit my sister Esmerelda. It was a long overdue visit and I was not sure whether she would be at home or working. Emmanuel had been made redundant when the Civil Engineering Company that he surveyed for collapsed suddenly and went into receivership, just at Thanks Giving time. To most of the employees it was a complete shock and office staff and field operatives alike had been informed that they need not return to work after the holiday, and there had been no severance pay. Obviously claims and negotiations would follow but they would be lengthy. My Mother told me in confidence that he was finding it hard to find a position of equal status, and that he was temporarily employed as a delivery driver and working as many hours as he could. Emmanuel I guessed would be working as hard as ever for the large delivery company, so I did not expect to see him – no difference in that respect. My visit reminded me of the day I had intercepted the secret message from the woman (or man in disguise) which first opened the door on the undercover operation I was managing to expose.

"Hello stranger, and who is this fine looking young lady?" Esmerelda greeted us very pleasantly, although I thought that she was looking tired. At least she brought a smile to Andrea's glum demeanour.

"Oh it is good to see you sis, how are the kids?" I answered jovially.

"Missing you. You do not call as often now to give those treats, and Emmanuel rarely has time. He always works overtime if it is available. I sometimes wonder what we do it all for. Have kids, get a house, and then spend every hour trying to keep it all together." Esmerelda was in the middle of cleaning and almost tripped over the mop and bucket in the kitchen. She was wearing an old pair of black stretch pants, soft black flat shoes and a long black and white striped T shirt. She wore a green bib apron with red edging and straps which she took off and hung behind the door leading to the rear yard. She hurriedly stuffed her yellow plastic gloves into the pocket. Her brown wavy hair was pulled back loosely and fastened with a black and white elasticated ribbon.

"Is there anything I can do to help?" I asked.

"No. I mean that is sweet of you to offer, but I work part time at a Nail Boutique. I actually quite enjoy it. I still teach Dance and Drama, but I am getting too old to audition for parts in shows. You are lucky to catch me in actually. My class was cancelled today because there was a fire in the kitchens, and the school is closed for safety checks." Esmerelda continued.

"I see. Andrea was feeling a little low today so I thought a day off school would cheer her up."

"How she has grown. Well I mean, it must be like forever since I last saw her. Would you like tea, coffee, or a coke, dear?" To my surprise Andrea chose hot tea.

"I think that it must be the influence of our English Au-pairs, and like Dad, but I will have one too, it can be quite refreshing and fortifying." I added.

"Oh yes, I heard about Naomi. I am so sorry. Here I am complaining and your troubles seem to be greater than ours." Esmerelda said sympathetically. "How are you coping?"

"He is not. We are all sad because Emerson left today. I hate her!" Andrea stated vehemently and large tears rolled down her cheeks.

"Do not cry dear, these things always seem worse than they are. I am sure it will all work out." Esmerelda put a comforting arm around Andrea, and patted her cheeks with a tissue.

"Andrea honey, we do not want to worry your Aunt Esmerelda with our troubles." I said hastily.

"Who the heck is Emerson anyway? I do not think Mom has mentioned such a person, is it a man or a woman?" Esmerelda asked with a smile just about to burst open.

"Labella Emerson, she was a PA to one of the other Professors at the Faculty. She is quite wealthy, and bit of a socialite. She has actually been a godsend as they say, this last year or so, but now she has moved on to a guy with a yatch sailing down to Rio." I answered succinctly, and matter of factly.

"My word, I always forget the heady social circles that you move in now. I saw the New York Sunday feature by the way, - painting portraits of the wealthiest heiress, and rubbing shoulders with Manhattan's most respected Attorney." Esmerelda continued lightly.

"I kind of knew that it would only be a relatively temporary fling, but I wish that she had not ended it so suddenly. She has two or three children of her own whom she left with her sister to look after when she split from her last husband who was a successful Stockbroker. After the explanations she just walked out silently. I let her. It was such a SILENT ENDING." I added a little sadly.

"Sounds to me like you are better off without her, even if her attractions are wonderful." Esmerelda spoke with conviction.

"He is. I am never going to get married and have children because I do not want to make everyone unhappy." Andrea said in a loud voice.

"Come dear, people like each other for a little while and it is all swings and roundabouts and fun, and then they find that they need something more. Adults are only older children really, and it is better to have had the fun, than not at all. Some people like Uncle Emmanuel and myself stay together and look after each other and our children because we want to, but some people are just not made that way, and it is best to let them go and do something else." Esmerelda hugged Andrea, until she stopped crying.

"Oh I wish that Mommy Naomi had never been taken ill." She confided.

"We all do, but if medicines or faith do not make people better then there is nothing we can do." Esmerelda stated. "And now I want you to promise me that you will help Daddy, because I know that he will make everything alright, and one day you will be a Mommy too, and know that it can be a wonderful thing. And remember – the pains of life make the joys even greater."

"Ok, Aunty Esme, I will try. I will remember." Andrea replied seriously, and I knew that she really meant it.

"Gee, thanks sis, you have made us both feel better, but now, I think we had better make tracks. Kurt and Matteus do not know about today's trip and I want to be home at the same time as them. I guess that I forgot to tell Rosemary too, I had better call her on the way." I genuinely did feel better and I know that Andrea did after being able to externalise some of her emotions. I left some notes on the kitchen table as we left. "Treat the kids for me," I added quietly, "I think I have forgotten Birthdays as well as Christmas."

"Thanks Brandon, and do not leave it so long before your next visit." Esmerelda stood for a moment and waved as we walked down the street and headed for the Metro.

"I like Aunty Esmerelda." Andrea stated emphatically. "That was the best part of the day." Then she added thoughtfully. "I like Coney too of course."

Emerson silently Leaving.

CHAPTER 28

Back in the old Routine

Our journey on the Metro from Coney was uneventful and quite fast. At that time in the afternoon heading towards City Hall the train was not too crowded. We sat on either side of the window, and Andrea began to doze a little. I was feeling a little sleepy myself until Eric appeared next to Andrea. He smiled at me almost sardonically.

"So bent Cop, you have had a good day huh?" he asked as he spat out his usual slug of yellow phlegm. I pulled out my mobile so that I could speak to him without it appearing odd, and found that it was the one that had belonged to Buzz. There was a new text message on it.

"That's right. It is a message for you." He said. "Someone else has had a good day too. They think that they have discovered the gang member who is the creep. The Faceless Crusader. Read it."

"How? Why? Are they trying to trick me and trace me?" The questions ran through my head and although I did not speak Eric answered.

"No. Not all the gang members have a full set of intelligent brain cells, and Bernard Muzzinger is still on their contact list." He laughed and disappeared.

"Did you see something Daddy?" Andrea asked.

"No darling, I was just trying to remember something that I had forgotten to do." I had been looking at Eric so intently, that I had not noticed Andrea had awoken, and was watching me.

"Is that a text to remind you?" She asked.

"Yes darling, it is ok, I can deal with it tomorrow. It was only in connection with a meeting that I skipped today. You see, I miss something important if I take days off too. I will give you a letter to take to school tomorrow saying that you were ill today. But it is fun to be spontaneous occasionally." I smiled reassuringly, and Andrea seemed to accept the explanation.

'The old basement tomorrow – meeting with THE BOSS – 22.30. Blood and Guts.' The text was clear.

I knew what I had to do: get 'Back in the Old Routine' masquerading at the place where my search began. I thought that a gas explosion had partly devastated the place and killed Eric, but maybe it had not been as serious as the media had made it sound. Come to think of it – a body had not been found, I just assumed that he would have died in the blast.

Back at home at the apartment, the boys seemed to have settled in spite of Emerson's departure, and Andrea went to bed quite happily. The evening was peaceful, Rosemary was studying, and it suddenly hit me. What if my customary cleverness failed and I was seriously injured or murdered? That would be a devastating blow for the family and apart from insurance and my savings they would be left without financial support and orphaned. Who would look after them? I know my relations would rally round, but it would never be the same for my children. Still I knew that the time was drawing close for maybe a final showdown, and I had to play my part. The forces were gathering I could feel it. My skin almost crackled with static electricity and in spite of everything I looked forward to tomorrow's operations.

I was there. I was there early. The empty warehouses were even more eerie than I had originally thought.

The doorway down to the cellar was still there, but I could see that rubble had been cleared from the steps. Part of the roof above seemed to have caved in although it was a three storey building adjoining the other buildings which occupied three sides of the old cobbled yard. There were even one or two coins stuck in the cracks, which Eric must have dropped. I noticed now that there was building machinery in the shadows of the wall next to the gates which now refused to close properly, and a piece if wire mesh had been tied across them. There were yellow air pipes stretched across the yard entering some of the doorways for the use of Pneumatic Breakers and other tools. A large compressor stood silently next to a caterpillar tractor with a massive breaking drill attached to the hydraulic arm. There were signs that a Security Company was patrolling, but there was no evidence of onsite security. I expected that they would patrol at certain times, and the meeting had been arranged to fit in between them. It maybe that the Security Company was in league with 'The Boss' and thus reducing suspicion.

If Eric was correct, then 'Blood & Guts' meant that they were all going to relish the torture of some poor guy whom they thought was me. I had a plan. Maybe a bit of a wild plan, but if it worked it would be better than nothing, and it would save a ritual murder before the police could get there. Why did I not just notify the Police and save placing myself in danger. Well I must admit that I was curious, and I wanted to play a part in the final dispersal of such a cruel body of Criminals. Also I did not want to risk calling the police to a scene void of action, because then, if I had to call them they might hesitate, and anyway the credibility of the Faceless Crusader would be broken.

So I connected a large pneumatic Breaker which I found stashed in an alcove in the warehouse next to the old basement, to the air line. Next I checked that there was diesel in the generator. I found some small lengths of wire that Electricians had discarded, and wired the trigger of the breaker open. I jammed the breaker point into a large crack in the concrete floor and checked that it was pretty firm. It would probably fall over, but still continue vibrating as long as the wire held. I prayed that the generator would start first time when required. Fortunately the controls were in the shadow and not on the side facing the gateway. I hoped to create enough of a diversion to break up the meeting and make my escape through the connecting warehouses to a rusty but serviceable fire escape at the back of the central warehouse in the next street. If I made it that far I had only to sprint he length of another block before I reached a main road, and round a corner to access to the Metro. If it worked I could be at Canal Street across the river whilst they were still looking for me at the warehouse, and the Police were on their way. I would collect my car later parked just off the main thoroughfare in a place that would not be searched.

I heard one or two vehicles approaching, and four men entered the yard. I could see from my vantage point from an upstairs room where Eric had told me he could hear and see everything. Next three men entered holding another man at gunpoint with his hands tied behind his back.

He was protesting, and pleading but they pushed him forward and down the steps. Next I heard the engine of a powerful small craft heading down the river. I crept over stealthily and looked out of a waterfront window. I could see that there was debris, and part of the loading bay had been demolished and there was a pile of rubble on part of the landing stage. Obviously parts of the back rooms had been damaged by the small gas blast from the kitchen. The office and main chamber must be still intact I guessed. Although the water was kind of bright I could not make out the faces of the men clearly, but one was smoking a cigar beneath a large black hat. The man behind him toted a large automatic rifle, and the driver was equipped with one, slung across his chest. They moored the boat and entered the back of the building.

I heard the men greet the boss and then I heard the familiar accent. I was sure that it was Emile Beldossa. The pungent smell of the cigar wafted upwards and probably through cracks in the ceiling and walls.

"So at last we have discovered your true identity, Mr Faceless Crusader. Look how you have decimated the members of my operation. My wonderful undercover operatives have been seized by the Police, or killed. My top people have been arrested and as we speak properties and assets are being investigated by Interpol in France and Switzerland, in Columbia, in Mexico and the Dutch Caribbean Islands, as well as the USA. And why? Because you have taken it upon yourself to destroy my enterprises and report my activities to the Police." Beldossa spoke vehemently.

"Please Boss, it was not me, I also have too much to lose…" The man began in a wavering voice, and from the way that chains rattled I guess he was chained to a post.

"Silence. Before I kill you I want to know why, but most of all I want to know how. How did you do it? You were never in full possession of any details of rendezvous or shipments. And yet here we are and Billions of dollars' worth of my goods have been confiscated and assets frozen, and thousands of illegal slaves have been rescued by the Government authorities." Beldossa continued.

"Please have mercy I am not the one that the Police call The Faceless Crusader. I know that you never show mercy, but I beg you to believe that I am not he. I am more than sorry for your losses but I did not cause them." The man continued desperately, and I wanted to go down there and shout 'I am he' but there was no point in getting myself killed without the remaining gang being brought to justice. I heard the crack of wood against bone and I know that someone must have whacked him with a baton or baseball bat.

"Good! Silence the snivelling wretch, but do not kill him. Do you see this? Beldossa shouted.

"Ye-ye-yes" The man answered like one semi-conscious.

"What do you see? Tell me! What do you see?" Beldossa demanded.

"I-I-s-s-see a c-cut throat r-r-razor." The man replied in broken resignation.

"Good, and you will see how I mutilate you, like you have mutilated my organisation. I created the greatest Criminal Organisation that the world has seen. Well I do not call it criminal, I call it 'Expedient Business' and you have slowly hacked it to pieces."

"No, no, I am innocent, please--." The man spoke quietly and I could hear that he was straining to break free of the chains with his last ounce of consciousness.

"First I am going to cut off one ear, and then the other ear, and then – "I heard the man give a stifled agonized groan as the chains rattled, and I somehow knew that Beldossa had twisted his crutch. "And then I shall cut off something else, and ah yes two more things that I will cut off separately."

"If it w-was me I-I would gladly pay, but I am not the F- Face -l-less C-Crusa-ader." The man stated diffidently.

I knew that the ritual execution would take place, and an alternative daring plan entered my head, I leaned out of the window, and I could see that the riflemen were not standing guard on the landing stage. If I could somehow stop Beldossa escaping I would have a 'grand coup'. I climbed out of the window space and sliding down, I just managed to place my toes on the top edge of a wall beneath, close to the warehouse wall. I balanced along it and slid down onto the rubble and stopped. There was no sound outside, as they were all too busy watching the show. I crept to the boat and untied it, and I thanked all the Angels in the whole expanding Universe and beyond that the keys were still in it. I drew a smiley face with the letters FC beneath it on my notepad and secured it with a brick at the base of the capstan. I pushed the boat backwards along the jetty posts next to it, and then started it when I was clear, and prepared to head across the river with the tall jetty serving as cover. At the same time I rang McArthur and gave the location. I used Buzz's gun to fire a shot at the large shutter door which was only partially secured to the frame. It ricocheted loudly and one of the riflemen ran out. I shouted 'Hey Beldossa are you looking for me'. The second rifleman ran out followed by Beldossa still holding the razor. I saw him pick up the note page which the riflemen had ignored, and even at my distance his roar of rage reached me loudly as it echoed across the water.

The riflemen were now shouting and firing on the landing stage. I was still covered by the jetty and zig zagging just in case. I hoped that I did not encounter the River Guard, as I turned and headed for a little private area on Staten Island that I knew of where I could run the boat up onto a ramp and moor it. I made it. I took off my uniform and wig, and rolled them up. It was a medium distance walk to the train across to New Jersey and back to Manhattan. I hoped that the Police had arrived in time. My actions would certainly prove to Beldossa that he was about to torture the wrong guy.

Once I was in the relative safety of the Metro Station with the uniform packed in a store bag where I bought some water and a wrapped sandwich, I called McArthur's office again.

"Hey you friggin' freak, that last call had better not be a hoax, the River Police have headed across to that derelict warehouse and McArthur has ordered a road block all around that area. There would be Patrol cars there within five minutes. I am waiting for the first reports. It is obvious something is taking place, but if we find you, you will need a darn good attorney." The desk Sargeant Jack Strood, was not a happy chappy as usual.

"Listen, there is a small grey and black Ocean-Kraft 500hp motor boat with added spotlight, used by 'The Boss' moored at Staten Island. I took the keys to stop it being moved by anyone--." I trailed off as I heard another Officer.

"Have you got a fix on that yet? Keep him talking." He said. I gave Strood the exact location, as part of it was unchanged since I used to visit some boyhood friends near there. I then switched off the phone completely. Buzz old buddy, I will not need to use your phone anymore if tonight proves successful, I thought to myself.

"BACK in the OLD ROUTINE, he, he, he-ha –ha." Eric appeared as I parked the Station Wagon at my apartment.

"I guess so." I answered.

"Good. I taught you well didn't I bent Cop, but it may not be all over yet. You do not know for absolute certainty the identity of The Boss do you?

"Well I have not seen a clear view of his face, but--." Eric interrupted me.

"But you are identifying him with his voice and brand of cigars." Eric stated sympathetically.

"Yes, but I am 100% sure." I replied.

"100% nothing. Until you have actually seen his full face and heard him state his name, as intelligent as you are, I know there is an obvious possibility that you have not yet considered." Eric's eloquence ended as usual with fit of coughing, and he disappeared.

"Wait. Tell me. I want this to be over." I entreated, but I was left staring at the blank wall of the underground garage. I headed wearily for the lift and my apartment. The excitement and assurance of the evening had suddenly faded, and I felt drained and apprehensive, rather than satisfied with my endeavours.

"Oh good evening Mr Martin-Schally, you are later than I expected, but there is a sandwich in the refrigerator, and would you like me to make a cup of tea." Rosemary greeted me pleasantly, she really was good, going over and above her duties.

"Thank you Rosemary, yes that would be very nice, but you must call me Brandon, everyone does." I replied as I headed for the Brandy bottle.

"And by the way, there was a rather strange call not all that long ago, maybe two and a half hours ago, er, probably three hours. I was in my room studying, and did not reach the phone in time, but there is a message." Rosemary continued politely.

"Thank you so much again, I was inadvertently delayed." I lied, as I headed for the answer phone.

"I know who you are you little Brooklyn Punk." A voice that I thought was Beldossa's enunciated the message clearly and menacingly when I pressed the play button. Rosemary looked slightly perturbed.

"Oh it will be an actor friend of mine." I lied spontaneously and glibly and I am not too sure that she believed me. "We go back a long way. We used to joke a lot and when he is in town he likes to get Back in the Old Routine."

Are you Looking for Me?

CHAPTER 29

Heartbreak

There is a saying which states that there are more Mysteries in Heaven and on Earth than you or I ever dream of. Without debating whether there is such a place as Heaven or what form it may take, I am ready to accept the generalised truth of that.

For example, there is Sandy Island somewhere between Australia and New Caledonia that appears on navigational systems but appears not to exist as a land mass, even after extensive searching. Then there is our old friend The Bermuda Triangle. Bermuda exists alright as a British territory with maybe in excess of 70,000 inhabitants, but nearby is the area where on the ocean and in the sky, aeroplanes, ships and people have disappeared mysteriously. It seems that the Impresario Miles Norcoat ordered his yatch to divert to Bermuda instead of sailing closer to the American coast. He probably had some business there to attend to. It is possible he aimed to take a direct route from there straight down to Guyana the haven of Caribbean Weddings and showman ship.

The Yatch built to his specifications in the UK had both Diesel and Gas Turbine engines that could reach speeds of 70 knots which equates to approximately 84 mph land or statute speed, which for a vessel in excess of 160 metres long, is pretty fast. It was propelled with either triple screw, or triple waterjet according to what kind of sailing Miles required. However, in spite of the 39.600 horse power, luxury rather than speed was his aim, and he and his twenty guests could be looked after by a crew of sixty. At considerably slower speeds the fuel had a range of at least 6000 Nautical miles. A Nautical Mile is in the region of 1.1508 Statute Miles, and based upon the earth's circumference, so that it is equal to 1 Minute of Latitude. There were two swimming pools on board, and a Helipad with a small resident Helicopter, named 'Cupid'. We are talking here of a Billionaire's large ocean going ship built to encounter heavy seas with all the latest technology, including missile detection, and not a flimsy coracle with a sail.

The First Mate had contacted harbour authorities for permission to moor offshore. The seas were calm and the weather report was favourable, so from position and speed an accurate time of arrival was established. Somehow though, the Yatch was never sighted and contact was lost at the harbour office on the Northwest of the Island. A Helicopter was sent out to reconnoitre as Miles Norcoat was a pretty important man. The Helicopter crew apparently hit some kind of turbulence, a cloud of strange light which obscured their vision of the ocean, but when they ventured flying lower the cloud seemed to follow them. They returned to base without having sighted the yatch. They claimed that they had spent half an hour searching, but they returned one and a half hours later, and their watches and instruments were all an hour behind, and the fuel consumption verified one and a half hours of travel. They had to refuel at the base. So - had time somehow slowed down, or had they been caught in some kind of time warp, some kind of magnetic window?

No distress signals had been intercepted, and a Coast Guard Patrol boat had not sighted the yatch either. Darkness fell and radio and radar contact was attempted throughout the night but there was no response. The night stayed calm, almost too calm with hardly a breaking wave on the shores and not a breeze to fill the sails of a group of small sail boats becalmed just off shore. They reported that the sea was heavy like oil, but there was no oil and no oil Tanker within the vicinity at that time. It was warm, too warm for the seasonal average, and the fishermen who tended their night catch reported that the fish and shell fish alike appeared to be sluggish.

The dawn radiated a little uncertainly across the water, with wisps of black cloud whipped up as though a squall was approaching. Red rays spread fiery tentacles across the calm surface and the yellow sun seemed to ooze a pallid gleam as though setting at the end of a day instead of rising. It was as though the Earth waited with bated breath to see some apocalypse unfold. There should have been a rough wind, but there was not, as the black clouds scurried across the heavens. Inhabitants began to look towards the Quayside anxiously to see what the elements were going to throw at them, until suddenly the sun burst forth with an almost blinding glare, and a heat haze shimmered on the calm blue sea. Ripples of waves began to gently lap the harbour shores again and the morning appeared beautiful and resplendent.

Suddenly someone spotted what looked like the red and golden yatch on the near horizon.

"Look" a Fisherman shouted. "Ship ahoy, she is sailing too fast, she will be grounded."

"She seemed to rise up from out of the ocean." Shouted another, in amazement.

"She will be dashed to pieces." Shouted another in reply.

"She will explode like bomb. There will be debris for months." Another man Shouted.

"All those poor people! It will be a heartbreak." A woman on vacation from London shouted.

The Harbour Master attempted radio contact but reached only silence. From his vantage point and as recorded by the radar and electronic tracking devices, he said the yatch was travelling at an impossible 200 knots towards the harbour and he alerted the rescue teams and coastal patrol. The yatch loomed large but strangely stopped and drifted gently just within the safe depth. There was an eerie silence as spectators waited to see what would happen. But there was nothing. No sounds, no movement on board, though the radar mast turned silently.

Boarding parties scaled the sides of the massive yatch, and managed to drop anchor from the deserted control cabin. They ran in military fashion all along the decks above, below and checking each luxurious suit. There were cocktails on tables, clothes draped or folded neatly on beds. There were open lap tops but all the TV screens seemed to indicate some static interference. There were towels spread on loungers around the pool areas, and sunglasses and books on the small tables. Trays of drinks were ready for the waiters to distribute in the bar. Glasses were intact in stainless steel sinks of soapy water, still warm. In the immaculate Galley a lavish dinner had been prepared and many of the covered dishes were still hot. Someone, or something had the presence of mind to switch off the electric ovens and hobs. The refrigerators were still working.

In the opulent Dining Room, the Captain's table was laid immaculately for dinner with antique crystal glasses and genuine silver service cutlery. Plates were of fine pottery bearing the name and crest of the yatch 'Ariadne'. Miles Norcoat was British born and although international in his line of business, he had been granted the right to officially bear arms, and his shield decorated the spoon, knife and fork handles. A coat of arms was set above the marbled doorframe, but opposite, an antique Grandfather Clock displayed 5 pm the time when the First Mate had contacted the Harbour Master, and it was still ticking!

Cards were stacked and cut at the gaming tables, and the roulette wheels had all come to rest on 5 Red. Stacks of chips were still in front of chairs, some were scattered, but there was no sign of any panic. There was no sign of a panic anywhere. In Miles Norcoat's suite his evening suit was laid out neatly on the king sized bed ready for him to change into, and in an interconnecting suite, a long square necked black evening dress was laid out ready with a necklace of a double row of diamonds, and a pair of matching drop earrings. Black suede seven inch shoes with diamanté bows were placed neatly on the floor.

Wherever they had gone, or whatever had taken them had given no cause for alarm, but it had been sudden. The life boats were all intact, and no attempt had been made to launch any of them. The Helicopter was still secured to the Helipad. All the records were undamaged and the passenger list was intact. It did not appear that anyone had jumped overboard as there were no excessive markings on the deck, or missing guard rails. The Harbour Master was heard to say strictly off the record, that he thought they had lined up quietly and levitated, like people under hypnosis, or been drawn up somehow into the cloud which the Helicopter patrol encountered. And - the goodness knows what - a UFO, or something even more sinister.

Forgive me. I have been relating this incident as though I was there, or watching it. What I have done is repeat it, as it was related to me by Elmer, Emerson's son, and Genna, her daughter. It was agonising to witness their HEARTBREAK.

Elmer was more composed, but Genna frequently broke down as she related the strange tale to me. They were doubly upset because Emerson had not told them of her intentions to join Miles Norcoat on his fun trip to Rio. They had been contacted by the authorities and telephoned me to ask if they could visit as something strange had happened to their Mother, and I was the last person she had told them she was associated with. They wanted to know if anything odd had taken place, or if we had quarrelled. They were as surprised as I had been when they discovered that she was not with me, as she had told them how happy she was with our relationship. Although her sister Fayette, their Aunt and Uncle Zadieb had brought them up as their own with their cousins, Emerson had apologised and regretted not being a good Mother.

"It was seeing how your children missed their Mother that brought it home to her, and she even suggested starting over again and making up for lost time." Elmer explained to me.

"Can you dig that – it was only at the beginning of last week that she said that." Genna stated through her beseeching tears.

"Our Sinclair could see through her even though he is the youngest. He would not come. He says that she is no Mother of mine." Elmer continued.

"She was all fancy clothes and jewels and promises which she never kept." Genna continued.

"But we still wanted her, and when she stayed with you so long we began to believe that she would really want us again." Elmer managed to keep his wavering lips and countenance under control, but Genna just sat and wailed trying to stem the flow of tears with a sodden handkerchief. I wondered if my own heart was going to break in the face of all their heartbreak. I had lost Naomi, I had lost Emerson, and now I had exposed a criminal circle but I still felt threatened and fearful for my family's safety.

"Let it all out. WE are all in this together, and I will help you through it". I said as I sat next to Genna and hugged her. Rosemary brought out a box of tissues and I helped her dry her eyes.

"I have only been here a short while, but if I may say something." Rosemary spoke politely in her perfect English accent. "I could not believe how Mrs Emerson suddenly announced that she was leaving after breakfast last Tuesday. There had been no indication that she intended to take a trip with someone else whatever, and no domestic fights."

"Thanks. We do believe you, and we realise that Professor Brandon must be as devastated as we are. Somehow, even if she was not with us, she was somehow always there." Emerson replied.

"I am really pleased that you have both come to see me. At the moment she has left a large hole in my life, but as I am not a next of kin, and there is nothing official between us, I may not have known the full story if you had not both come to see me." I spoke sincerely.

"If I may interrupt again, I am very well read in Psychic and Paranormal activity, one of my Aunts is a Medium, a genuine one, and so I am wondering whether there was not some force which for reasons unknown at the moment called all those people together. As there is no evidence of violence, maybe one should consider it to be for good purposes." Rosemary surprised us all.

"I know that there are things right in front of our eyes which we may not even be equipped to see and life that can maybe exist in a Parallel Universe, and even visits from life forms which differ from our own. The Universe is so vast that there is room for everything and everybody. I know that on Earth we run around squabbling over the Planet forgetting that we are the tiniest of fragments in a vast panorama of phenomena." I added.

"Quite, and even though we realise it we are still not equipped to get outside of ourselves and into the larger sphere of existence, but then that is our human condition." Rosemary had dared to raise the bar as it were on the issue, and I was pleased.

"We are not quite University students yet, and we have a lot to learn, but I can see that we have to maybe accept that there is some truth in that strain of thought, as disturbing as it might be." Elmer replied.

It was natural that they should experience heartbreak, but I knew that by working through it they would be stronger, and they both displayed a maturity which was reassuring.

"Divers have found nothing in the coordinates where the Yatch was, when the Harbour Master was contacted." Genna ventured now that she had worked through her tears.

"Nor in the surrounding areas. Miles's son and his wife are very upset. They were to meet the Yatch party in Rio. They have flown to Bermuda, but do not really want to take possession of the Ariadne." Elmer added.

"From what you have told me, I might venture to think that they will scrap it, or put it in a berth in Bermuda for a short time. Maybe the port authorities will need to hold it for a while if further investigations are to take place." It certainly caught the more unconventional side of my imagination, and I considered seriously the possibility that Emerson received some kind of 'calling'.

"I know that this is a time of deep sorrow for you all, and I am very sad too" Rosemary spoke again after we had all fallen silent each with our own memories. "I wondered if somehow there was an unknown reason why Mrs Emerson took it upon herself to interview prospective Au pairs, and why she chose me. I have studied Mythology from an early age, and as I already mentioned, my Aunt is a genuine medium, with a what she calls a Spirit Guide."

"I suppose that somehow maybe subconsciously Emerson may have been guided by some force of energy, but why in particular." I answered.

"Well, I gather that the Yatch is named the Ariadne. In Greek Mythology Ariadne is considered to be a Goddess, and sometimes only a partial Deity, as the daughter of a Goddess, and scholars follow conflicting theories, but the most popular is that she was a Goddess, who fell in love with and married Bacchus. Bacchus may be more familiar to you as the God Dionysus, associated with wine and revelry, but also infidelity." Rosemary continued, as she produced a pocket sized well-worn book of poems and notations.

"You might be suggesting that this incident is some kind of deja-vous connected with Mythology, or what some people call Fate." I said, beginning to see where she was leading in an attempt to alleviate our sorrow.

"Yes. Ariadne was separated from Bacchus, who went to live on an Island, and eventually, she sought to be reunited with him." Rosemary continued knowledgably.

"I have seen the painting by Poussin in Paris in the Louvre of Bacchus and Ariadne, where Bacchus is depicted as leaping from a chariot to meet Ariadne." I had a sudden recall of memory.

"I am not too sure whether the meeting is described as so joyous, but if I may I would like to read a poetic version after a classical style by a modern Spiritualist Poet, Ris Kered.

I heard a tale such as the Ancient mariners tell,
About a ship a sight so wondrous that did seem,
To rise up from the sea only as the eye can tell,
There had been signs upon that day of an Apocalypse,
Such as an Armageddon from a traumatic dream;
The sky transformed to black and purple,
In the blinking of an eye, whilst water wind flurries,
Whipped sand to a frenzied blast that scathed
The cold hail battered beach; and tremendous waves,
Although the tide was low driven by an icy wind slashed,
The hitherto tranquil reaches as though to end all days,
With the Sun completely obscured from view,
Day to night time turned stinging the faces of me and you.
We gazed in partial wonder and partly in fear,
Before headlong running pell mell for shelter.
But upon the next day bright a clear calmness lays,
Tranquillity upon the sea when the storm did clear.
People were in awe of a sight so wondrous they says,
As a Golden Ship rose like an island far, but near.
Upon the bow the image of Ariadne was mounted
Staunch and firm by a Masters hand proudly carved;
Which seemed to writhe full of life and call out for Bacchus,
And thus the Goddess spread wings like a gigantic bird,
Guiding the ship to the shore it seemed miraculous,
But sad she was to be forsaken by the Gods,
And longed to see Bacchus on the shore with greetings.
But stranger still the Mariners say the ship did gleam,
A sublime radiance from within though not a soul was seen,
Above, below or on the empty deck bright and clean,
And somehow the vessel rested held by an invisible anchor,
As Ariadne searched the shores and the harbour.
Many tears in sorrow she shed which formed an inland lake,

She searched in vain leaving sadness and sorrow in her wake,
But there within a hidden valley where crystal water flowed,
With sweet Red Wine upon demand, gushing from a mountain spring,
Where with enraptured music ethereal Sprites did entertain and sing;
Dwelt Bacchus with his merry band and once more took her hand.

"I know that this is Mythology, but the symbolism often contains some truth, and I think that what is often seen as a tragedy, can sometimes reveal something good. My Aunt has proof that in a sense what people call the soul does indeed remain forever young, only our bodies grow old and die." Rosemary looked at us rather shyly now. I hope that I have been of some comfort she said. "Would anyone like another cup of tea?"

"But is it not possible that the soul also dies." Elmer asked sceptically.

"Not according to my Aunt." Rosemary stated emphatically.

"Do you believe that we will be reunited in our spiritual form?" Genna looked dubious.

"I would not say that is definitely the case, but you do not necessarily need to do. My Aunt says that it is altogether a different kind of melting pot, and emotions and such, connected with our human bodies may not necessarily apply." Rosemary spoke with such gentle assuredness that it was almost impossible to argue with her.

"It seems that you are saying that we in fact – transcend." I added.

"Thank you Professor Brandon, I think that is a very succinct summary." Rosemary stated very respectfully.

"Thank YOU Rosemary for sharing your knowledge with us." I concluded. "Whether one accepts it fully or not, you have certainly eased the pain of our HEARTBREAK.

Hertzschmerz wie ein Raubvogel.

CHAPTER 30

Inspector McArthur Calls Again

I was hoping that Nigel could fill me in with all the details, but as it a weekend, I would not see him until Monday. The arrival of Elmer and Genna had diverted me somewhat on the Saturday, but I did worry about Beldossa's cryptic message. I guessed that it was my own fault for my over confident behaviour. I knew that even if he might be in captivity, someone working for him could harm my family, Rosemary and myself.

I was racking my brains to think of ways to check up on the situation without incriminating myself at the Police Station. It was to my great surprise however, that I received a visit from Inspector McArthur. It reminded me of that Sunday which seemed a very long time ago now after I had discovered the body of Hanwell Nnagobi. Rosemary answered the door about mid-morning. I was making a coffee. We had finished breakfast earlier as usual and I had been for my customary jog avoiding the South River though. Andrea was chatting to one of her friends, and Kurt and Matteus were playing video games.

"Inspector McArthur to see you Professor Brandon." Rosemary announced in her polite unphased manner.

"Hello Brandon, long time no see. I hope that I am not disturbing you, but this is in the nature of an off duty call."

"Hello Gordon, in that case, how may I help you? Would you like a coffee or something stronger?" I asked quickly

"A coffee would be good, although I say I am off duty I am driving, and a Policeman is always on duty really."

I led him into the lounge, and we sat down with our coffee. He sipped it thoughtfully as he chose his words carefully.

"I have something of a dilemma which I am hoping you can solve for me." He began.

"Fire away. I hope that I can."

"You see, I have an important prisoner. A very important prisoner in deed, and one that has eluded us for many years, not just here in New York, not just in the USA, but internationally he has always slipped through Interpol's net." McArthur looked at me in a confidential manner.

"I see, is this connected with the Hanwell Nnagobi murder?" I asked greatly relieved.

"It most certainly is." He said emphatically and then leaned back into the leather arm chair, before he asked the next question.

"Have you heard of The Faceless Crusader?"

"Er, well yes, through the media of course, and there was an incident at Easter when my Mother was playing piano for a Gospel Church. A very theatrical guy with a white blank mask threatened the Pastor at gun point. He turned out to be a cousin of the pastor just returned from Cape Town."

"Yes, a family affair. The Faceless Crusader however has caught the imagination of many people, and he has annoyed my staff greatly. At the same time we have to respect him somehow, and we are indebted to him as he has almost single handedly exposed and international crime ring that we have been unable to crack, way before your friend was murdered." McArthur eyed me kindly whilst scrutinising me.

"Well that is quite a feat. He must be some kinda guy." I replied with alacrity.

"Oh he is, although technically, he is also a law breaker, even though he is our informant." McArthur rocked to and fro a little almost pouting and regarding me steadily.

"So what has this got to do with me Inspector, I mean Gordon?" I asked with feigned surprise.

"This important prisoner who shall be nameless insists on speaking to you before he will speak to us. We rounded up the remnants of his gang on Friday after a tip off from the Faceless Crusader. He cleverly stole the boat so that they could not escape on the river, and we arrived in time to block off all the roads. They were just about to torture one of their members because they thought he was the Crusader. They had made a cut across his chest, but we arrived just in time to save him, but I am afraid that he will be going to prison for quite a while judging by his criminal record."

"Well lucky for him that he did not end up like Hanwell, but unlucky in another way." I stated resignedly

"I have to treat this delicately because by virtue of this Prisoner knowing you, you are also incriminated. I have to know why he needs to see you so desperately." McArthur was genuinely sympathetic.

"If I knew who it was I could tell you maybe." I stated ingenuously.

"We have rounded up many of the people on his contact list, and it appears that he made a short call to you may be about 23.00 hours on Friday." McArthur looked at his coffee cup as he spoke.

"I see, I am not too sure whether I received a call or not." I lied again ingenuously.

"Can you account for your whereabouts on Friday evening? I have to ask you this unofficially or someone else may have to include you in the official investigations." McArthur looked directly at me but kind of unfocussed.

"I think that was the night I went to visit my Mother in Brooklyn, and I got back fairly late. Rosemary had made me a very good sandwich." I did not want to include Rosemary as an alibi, but I knew that my Mother would be quick thinking enough to verify my story at least until she could find out what was going on, if she was approached.

"Are you familiar with Staten Island by the way? As I said, this Faceless Crusader moored the boat at a fairly private spot that probably a local might know. A handy little craft it is too. It could probably outrun a Police patrol boat, we found a considerable amount of Heroin stored in the bow. We know that it must have been used for small transactions. Our prisoner is cleverer than the smugglers around Panama that have been caught, but a cargo worth $400 million is chicken feed to this guy. It is lucky for the Crusader that he left it where he did, or he would have been in deep shit, as they say." McArthur was somehow enjoying this friendly part of the interrogation and throughout he looked at me with a benign complacency that made the creases at the side of his eyes appear that he was smiling.

"I must admit that I had friends there when I was younger, some are still there, but I do not visit Staten Island very much nowadays. I think my last visit was some time ago when I took the children to the Botanical Gardens. Friends of my Mother's were one of the families who had to rebuild their homes after the hurricane two or three years ago." I waffled on a little, and hoped that I had not been caught on CCTV at the Metro station.

"Okay, Brandon, as someone I still regard as a friend I am glad that you are willing to cooperate without me having to hold you on suspicion; but now I must ask you to accompany me to the Station to speak to this important prisoner, to once again help with our enquiries. You would not believe some of the names that have been revealed in the upper echelons of society worldwide. Hitherto respected Businessmen and Politicians." McArthur spoke with a tone of resignation and I think that he really was sorry to have to ask me, to virtually run me in.

He was silent during the short drive until he suddenly asked if I thought Nigel would be better suited to Identikit and Forensic work than as a Field Operative.

"I think that Nigel is a very talented Artist and he would benefit from using those talents, but I know that he is interested in Detective work. I think also that he has a natural diplomacy and perception which would make a very good Attorney." I answered truthfully.

"Yes. I know that he has great respect for you, and he is rather sad that Graduation will take place very soon, even though he is looking forward to it." McArthur had become very serious and slightly pensive.

"He will definitely Graduate with First Class Honours, and maybe working in the Force whilst gaining more experience would be more beneficial to him than pursuing a Post Graduate course in the Arts." I continued.

"Yes deciding upon the future is a problem, a major decision." McArthur replied.

"Why not give him a gap year working as an Identikit Artist, or even as an Artist in court combined with some experience of forensic work at crime scenes as well as in the office?" If he finds that is not what he wants, he will still be able to take advantage of other options." That was the best of my advice.

"You are a darn good Professor and an inspiration to your students, I just hope that we can resolve this business today without recourse to further action." McArthur looked grim as he spoke, and we entered the station at a side door.

"Professor Brandon Edwin Martin-Schally to see the prisoner in cell one. I will use interview room two and I would like Officer Sheldon to accompany me." McArthur announced to a Sargeant.

I was seated at a small table behind open bars with McArthur stood behind me, and Officer Sheldon who was a large African American woman, operated the recording device at the side. Beldossa was ushered in through a door on the other side of the bars. He did not look so impressive now. His white shirt was creased and showed evidence of a struggle. He was minus shoes and belt and tie of course, and his hair was dishevelled and greyer than I remembered. He certainly was not broken. He stood straight and his dark eyes flashed with such a hatred that I almost winced, when he saw me.

The escorting officer stood at the back of the room and Beldossa walked forward to the bars. I could still smell the aroma of those special cigars emanating from him. He stood and stared at me in silent hatred, I looked at McArthur, and then at Sheldon. I decided to break the silence.

"Emile Beldossa. I thought that you were in Argentina, why Emile--?" I began before he interrupted.

"Emile. EMILE. Why EMILE." He imitated me and then he rushed forward and grasped the bars trying to shake them. His eyes bulged like a Heroin addict, and he spat at me, and the spittle landed on the desk in front of me. I began to push back my chair to stand, but McArthur put his right hand gently but firmly on my left shoulder to keep me seated.

"I would tear the tongue from the mouth of the lips that uttered his name in front of me." He bellowed in demented rage.

"I am not sure that I understand." I replied evenly.

"I am not my mincey wincey younger TWIN BROTHER BY 30 MINUTES whom everyone thought was so wonderful and talented with his Art and Culture. They did not take any notice of me. Yes we worked in our Father's illegal shipping franchise, and smoked the pure cigars from Panama together when we were only 11 years old, that he supplied to the Netherlands before they were branded. WE still do."

"I recognise the aroma of those Cigars of Emile's, but I never smoke." I replied and I felt a little stupid at the banality of my remark. He laughed and shook at the bars like a wild animal.

"You, a little Brooklyn Punk have destroyed my life's work little by little, and as God is my witness I will hack you limb from limb whilst you watch me and force them down your throat. I claim descent from Spanish Royal blood and I was born in Panama. I built the greatest undercover business organisation that the world has ever known, Drugs, Slaves, Diamonds, and Weapons and you have destroyed it little by little. One piece at a time. You could not imagine my wealth." He stood shaking with rage, his face red and his natural teeth almost like fangs as saliva dribbled from the corners of his mouth.

"How have I done this, why do you accuse me?" I asked deciding to try and perpetrate my innocence.

He threw his head back and uttered the most guttural and almost terrifying roar that I have ever heard a man make and his knuckles turned white as he clenched the bars.

"Because you are the one they call The Faceless Crusader, you meddling bastardo. I will crack your skull and spill out your brains and fry them like an egg and then feed them to the dogs. I will stake you out in the desert and let the Vultures eat you alive. Oh, what curses shall I bring to bear on you? They will never be enough." He began to sob hot bitter tears and sank to the ground, still holding the bars.

"Emile was Professor of Fine Art at the University before me, and he recommended me for the position when he left for Argentina." I decided to reiterate the fact that I did not know him.

"I AM EDWARDO. I AM EDWARDO. I AM EDWARDO BELDOSSA." He yelled and his voice reverberated all around the walls of the small rooms and I swear that the steel bars began to oscillate.

"I do not know you, I only know Emile." I repeated.

"I should have let them kill you, when the bunglers brought you to my basement by mistake. Yes I saved you. Your head was covered by a sack but I knew who you were. I knew where you lived. I knew who your family were. You did not see me of course but your senses are sharp. You probably thought that I was Emile. Emile who would not even kill the mosquito that stung him. Emile with his pretty wife and family who is greeted like a hero by our relations in Argentina. How I hate him. They still did not see me and my power and my wealth. I was still Edwardo who was nothing more than a market trader." Edwardo stood again and the hollowness of his eyes and the way he seemed to contract his cheeks gave him the appearance of a rabid dog that begs for its misery to be ended.

"I have never forgotten the night that I was abducted and beaten, just because Hanwell Nnagobi was a colleague." I hoped that I could withdraw more information from him.

He spat at me again. "Emile is my blood, but you are nothing. Nnagobi was nothing. I spit upon his corpse. He was not as clever as he thought. Not many people can outwit Edwardo. Hanwell Nnagobi informed what he thought were FBI agents of some of my activities, but they were MY agents and at the same time he was working for two other foreign powers, and appropriating my business for himself. He fooled you. He used you because you were already a well-known Artist and you gave his fake poetry credibility. He was no body's friend, not even when you were students. He was merciless and ruthless and a cold little bastardo. I crush him like the louse that crawls along the garden path and make his death a warning to others who would seek to double cross me."

"He had literary talent." I replied mildly.

"HA, HA – HA, HA. HE HAD GREED! NO ONE OUTWITS EDWARDO UNTIL YOU. I let the means of my own destruction live, for the first time in my life. It must be because I am growing old and I thought that your death would provoke enquiries which I wanted to avoid. I thought that the Police would be watching you already. Oh, the bungling fools I had to work with."

"I do not know why you say I am the Faceless Crusader, the point is that he is faceless –anonymous." I replied hoping somehow to find out who else was there that night. Eric briefly appeared next to Sheldon, and gave me a silent thumbs up before he disappeared again. That may have been the last time that I saw him.

"Gerrrrous- grrrrrr. Gerrrrrrrrr. Bastardo son of a scorpion. I know it is you. I know it is you who have destroyed me. Me EDWARDO BELDOSSA the GREATEST COVERT BOSS IN THE WORLD." He shook the bars in a fury snarling like a caged and wounded animal his head thrown to and fro hitting the bars until McArthur signalled the Officer to restrain him. Another officer entered, and another, and it took all three of them to prize his hands off the bars and escort him back to his cell.

"I think that we have all that we need to put him away forever." McArthur remarked after signalling to Sheldon to end the interview recording. "I think he is close to insanity, but I do not think that a plea of insanity will be accepted at his trial."

"I had no idea—"I began, and McArthur interrupted.

"You handled that very well as I hoped you would, and once again I thank you for your cooperation. We probably could not have extracted a confession like that without you. It is always remarkable to witness the extremes that jealousy can drive people to. I also expect that the work of The Faceless Crusader will be ended now – whoever he is." McArthur looked at me quizzically and pointedly as he made his last remark and showed me the way out.

"Now I really feel that I can live without the fear of being abducted, or my family threatened." I remarked as McArthur drove me home.

"Yes, I think we can all rest easy for a little while anyway. I almost envy you, as you can return to your Painting and your Faculty doing the things you love, but for me the fight will continue, and I guess that is what I love. The supply of criminals is inexhaustible." McArthur smiled as he spoke.

"Thank you, Gordon, I am pleased to be of assistance" I said as I exited the car back at the apartment block.

"Thank YOU Brandon, see you at the Graduation Ceremony." McArthur shook hands firmly and departed.

"Now." A voice whispered inside my head. "How about finding a 'proper Mom' for Andrea?"

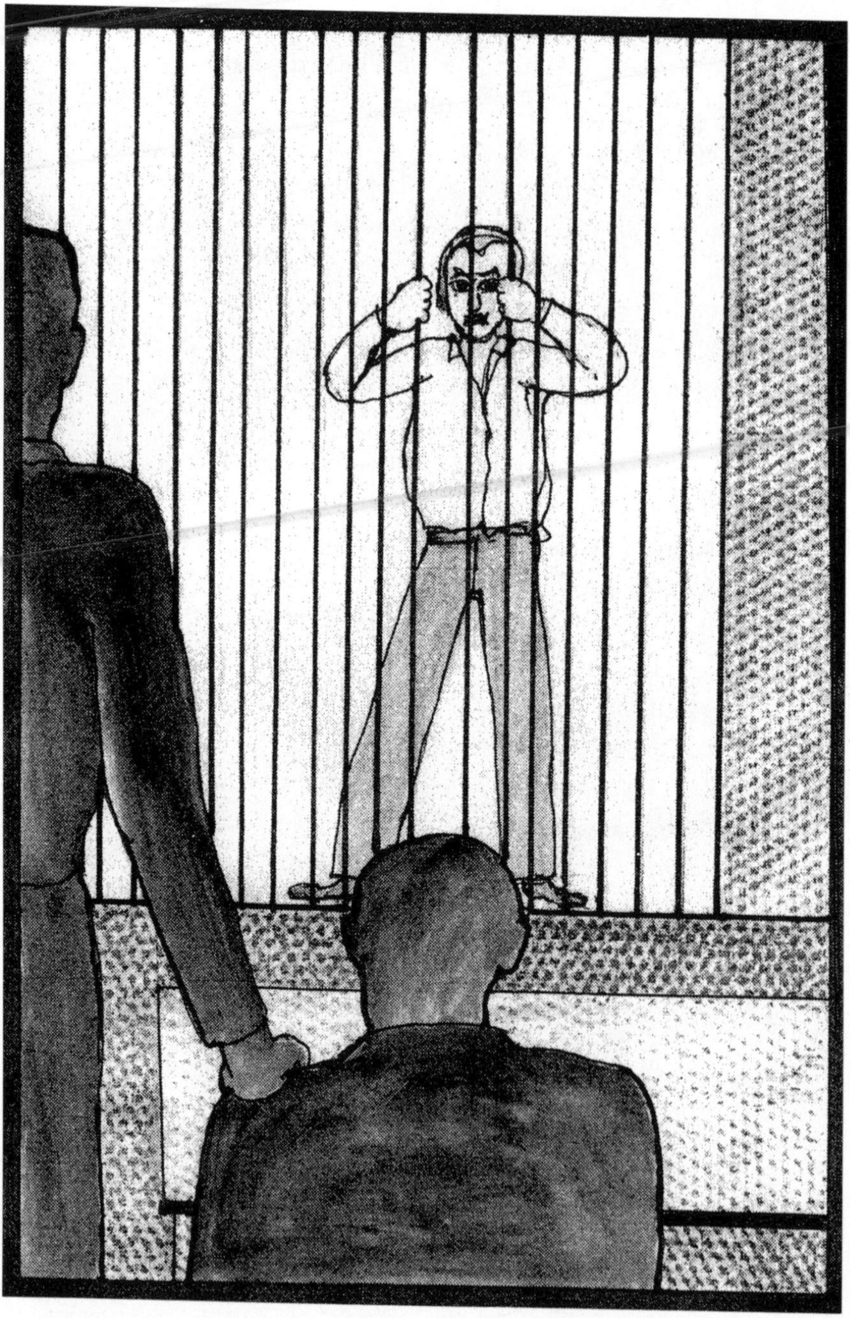

The Covert Mastermind in Captivity.

THE AUTHOR

Lee J Morrison

Dr. Lee J Morrison was born in the UK, in Lancashire, with an Afro Caribbean Father and ancestors from Kenya. His White English Mother was from Derbyshire, with French ancestors, and Viking ancestors from South Yorkshire.

Lee qualified for a BA Honours Degree in London, and Graduated from the University of Reading, Berkshire (affiliated to Oxford), with a Master of Fine Arts Degree. Studying also in Paris, Lee taught at the University College London. He is now a PhD.

Lee was also a Tutor with the University of Sussex, at Brighton, and at Hastings. Whilst married for 25 years, and living in Brighton, with a Son and Daughter, Lee extended his 'life experiences' in other professions. These included Construction, and a very enjoyable time as a Head Chef at a popular Restaurant next door to the Opera House. For several years he operated a successful Landscape Gardening business, and sold and exhibited his own Graphic Art and Paintings on a regular basis.

Working also in London Theatres, and behind the scenes at the Royal Ballet, Lee counts actors and dancers amongst his friends. His musical tastes are diverse and he enjoys Jazz, Opera, Latin and Caribbean genres. He was a semi-professional singer and dancer himself with several Musical Theatre Groups, a Stand-up Comedian, a Street Performer in St Tropez, and appeared on stage in Tunisia and Brazil.

Writing has always been close to his heart, and he has penned Poems, Songs and short Comedy scripts throughout his life. BRANDON, developed along the lines of a Detective Story. Again it is based upon elements of reality, but it is definitely a Fictional story. Although written in the first person, the book is NOT autobiographical to the Author.

BRANDON is a young Graphic Artist and Painter teaching at the University in New York. He finds himself endangered after he discovers one of his close friends, Hanwell Nnagobi, murdered in mysterious and gruesome circumstances in the South River. He becomes entangled with a subversive mob carrying out heinous crimes against humanity in his attempt to track down his friend's killers, who are a threat to his own and his family's safety. He is befriended by Chief Detective Inspector McArthur whose son Nigel is one of his students and who is also trying to crack the ring. Brandon's relationship with his wife Naomi deteriorates and there is much heartache to face with his children before he meets the Master Mind of the ring face to face.

As usual Lee J Morrison presents his characters poetically with humour as well as with traumatic sadness, but here he moves away again from the Passionate Romance genre of his previous novels in the Chrystabell Trilogy, and the happy ending of the Romantic Detective story, 'The Many Faces of April Jade'. He is acutely aware of social issues in the World, and has travelled fairly extensively, but he nevertheless aims is to be entertaining and to present a gamut of emotions which encompass Brandon. The original hand drawn Black & White illustrations by Derek Vernon-Morris highlight the Author's vision of the drama – BRANDON.

Previous Publications include:

Chrystabell's Secrets. 20th December 2011.

Theo: A Nephew of Chrystabell. 5th June 2012.

Christina: A Sister to Chrystabell. 28th June. 2013.

The Many Faces of April Jade. 24th January 2014.

Xerses Franklin: The Saga of Gabriel & Melona. 30th January 2015

Printed in the United States
By Bookmasters